D0429084

THE
SEVENTH
SUN

THE
SEVENTH
SUN

KENT LESTER

A Tom Doherty Associates Book

NEW YORK

This is a work of fiction. All of the characters, organizations, and events portrayed in this novel are either products of the author's imagination or are used fictitiously.

THE SEVENTH SUN

Copyright © 2017 by Kent Lester

All rights reserved.

A Forge Book
Published by Tom Doherty Associates
175 Fifth Avenue
New York, NY 10010

www.tor-forge.com

Forge® is a registered trademark of Macmillan Publishing Group, LLC.

The Library of Congress Cataloging-in-Publication Data is available upon request.

ISBN 978-0-7653-8222-1 (hardcover)
ISBN 978-1-4668-8657-5 (e-book)

Our books may be purchased in bulk for promotional, educational, or business use. Please contact your local bookseller or the Macmillan Corporate and Premium Sales Department at 1-800-221-7945, extension 5442, or by e-mail at MacmillanSpecialMarkets@macmillan.com.

First Edition: April 2017

Printed in the United States of America

0 9 8 7 6 5 4 3 2 1

This book is dedicated to my mother for giving me her unbridled imagination, to my father for his inspiration and sense of adventure, and to my wife, Penny, whose undying love, patience, and dedication truly made this story possible.

Acknowledgments

Introducing a debut novel is always an extremely challenging endeavor. It truly "takes a team." I would like to thank my wonderful agent, Russ Galen, for his support and acumen in bringing this dream to fruition, and to James Rollins for his boundless enthusiasm and support.

A special thank-you goes out to Tom Doherty for believing in me and endorsing the "Dan Clifford/Rachel Sullivan" story series. I can't believe my good fortune in becoming a member of the Tor/Forge family.

Thanks goes out to my executive editor, Bob Gleason, and junior associate editor, Elayne Becker, for supporting, cajoling, and pushing me to make the story as good as it could be. Kudos to Michael Graziolo for the fantastic cover art. I'd also like to thank Linda Quinton, publisher, Jessica Katz, production editor, and Emily Mullen, senior publicist, for their fantastic help and support. There are many other members of the Tor/Forge team, too numerous to mention, who have worked tirelessly behind the scenes to make this project a success, so I extend my heartfelt appreciation to them as well.

Long before publication, there was the grueling journey of creation, research, writing, and editing . . . and more editing. I couldn't have done it without the help and support of friends and family. Sincere thanks to Ellen, Pat, and my wife, Penny, for their editing advice and feedback. A special shout-out to Jim for his advice, loyalty, and support. Thanks to Gary for goading me into writing this tale in the first place.

Author's Note

I hope you find this novel, *The Seventh Sun,* to be informative as well as entertaining. The premise behind the plot is closer to the truth than we can imagine, or fear.

While all the characters and events in this novel are completely fictional, the science behind the story is real.

—*Kent Lester*

THE
SEVENTH
SUN

1

CARL JAMESON'S GEOLOGY career took a sudden turn when the unimaginable knocked at his door: an event as unlikely as a snowflake in summer.

It seemed an apt analogy for the moment, Carl thought, as he sat sweltering in the languid heat of his cubicle, stuffed into a dusty corner of the Central American Core Repository. He had arrived at the sleepy fishing village of La Ceiba, Honduras, two months earlier to complete research on his doctoral thesis. The slow pace of Latin American life and the friendliness of the locals provided him a respite from the hectic inner-city life of Columbia University. But one thing he could never get used to was the *heat,* the oppressive heat that sucked the energy from his bones. Carl leaned forward to harvest a meager stream of air flowing from an old oscillating fan he'd purchased at the local market. It provided scant relief for his racing heart.

When he first arrived at the core repository, Carl could have scarcely imagined the bizarre twist that would upend all of his research into mass extinction events. His meticulous studies of ocean sediments would need to be updated, along with his thesis title: "Mass Extinction: Sedimentary Evidence of Comet Impact at the Cretaceous/ Tertiary Boundary."

It was a huge adjustment, but Carl didn't mind. His implausible discovery offered him an opportunity of a lifetime. That's what made science so compelling, he decided: the occasional surprise that turned scientific convention on its head.

Carl checked his antique pocket watch. *Time to get moving.* Exiting the cubicle, Carl entered the building's long central hallway, his footsteps reverberating in the cavernous enclosure. The structure was old, constructed in the late fifties, and large, over a football field in length, having been expanded numerous times. Dust motes danced in shafts of light streaming from windows set high on the crumbling brick walls. Their beams illuminated row upon row of metal tubes stacked on tall shelves, like the scrolls of a primordial library.

The Central American Core Repository contained the largest collection of sedimentary drilling cores in Latin America, an archive of geological history created and maintained by several mining conglomerates. For the most part, the cores languished in obscurity, their secrets mute and unappreciated. In fact, during the entire two-month span of his research grant, Carl Jameson had not seen a single other visiting scientist or surveyor.

He knew the reason for the lack of interest: to a mining company, these archived cores were symbols of failure. The drilling of an exploratory sediment core was the mining equivalent of a stab in the dark, a pinprick through the skin of Mother Earth, made in hopes of finding a vein of mineral wealth. Any promising core samples would never make their way into the repository. They would be far too valuable and would be whisked away to another location . . . like the shiny new laboratory next door, for instance.

Someone had found something of extreme value, Carl concluded, judging from the frenzied activity taking place just a few steps away from his current location. He wanted to learn more, but . . . first things first.

As he ambled along, Carl extended his hand, letting it hover inches above one shelf, like a ship floating through time. It sailed past the geological periods—Quaternary, Neogene, Paleogene . . .

By row's end, he'd journeyed back sixty million years into the past, an eyeblink in geological time. Carl turned right and headed toward the age of the dinosaurs, the focus of his research.

The scientific debate on mass extinctions had raged for years. During the Earth's four-billion-year history, five mass extinction events had ravaged the planet's species, none more famous than the last: the extinction of the dinosaurs. Every scientific discipline had its own pet theory for the cause.

The biologists focused on pandemics and evolutionary pressure. The meteorologists believed in climate change. The astrophysicists proposed an invisible sister-star to the sun called "Nemesis" that supposedly disrupted the solar system every 26 million years or so. Paleogeologists preferred volcanism at the Deccan Traps in India. There was even an extinction theory based on dark matter.

Carl had always believed in the most obvious and simple theory: meteor impacts.

Occam's razor.

His research had seemed to bear that out . . . until a week ago. That's when extinction "theory" became something else entirely.

Carl stopped suddenly at a familiar berth.

For two months, he had been studying the sediment cores surrounding the "KT boundary" between the Cretaceous and Tertiary periods, where the last evidence of the dinosaurs could be found. Each core was like a chapter of geological history, its individual sediment layers like pages from the book of life. They had always told a familiar story, until . . .

That.

Carl's eyes locked on a microscope slide tray that had been placed on a narrow clearing on one of the shelves. He needed one last look. His hand trembling slightly, Carl removed a gossamer-thin slice of stone from its holder and placed it into the microscope.

The chance of spotting such a miniscule detail was one in a trillion, he thought, staring at the tiny smattering of colors. Fossilized minerals that had long since replaced the original material sparkled like jewels from an age long departed.

The sight sent a shiver down his spine. It felt as if he had torn the veil from a sacred act, entombed in a wash of sediment, like two mating flies trapped in amber. This tiny discovery, as big as the Earth itself, would rewrite the history books on mass extinctions and surely earn him a Nobel Prize.

After getting his fill, Carl placed the slide back into its plastic sleeve and slipped it into his pocket, patting it gently. *Keep the Nobel close.* No one here would miss it, or understand its significance.

Carl checked his watch again. It was time to get into position for his second task of the day. For weeks, he'd been watching the heightened security, the strange equipment, the jealously guarded core samples ushered into a lab constructed on a new wing of the decrepit old warehouse. One day, during a core delivery, Carl had noticed the

GPS coordinates scribbled on the side of one of the drilling tubes. Their origin piqued his curiosity, drilled only a few hundred miles from the location of his discovery.

In a few days, he'd be meeting up with Rachel Sullivan in La Ceiba for their reunion. Sharing his Nobel-worthy discovery with her would be *epic*. In all likelihood, she would be shocked, but pleased. Carl felt a tinge of pride at the prospect of showing off his latest achievement.

But, if he could find out the secret to the new *mystery cores* delivered next door, he could sweeten the pot even more at their reunion.

Two for the price of one.

His next move would be particularly bold, or foolish, depending on how you looked at it. He would be trespassing in a secured area. The slight risk seemed worth it. Besides, what could they do about it now? His residency was almost over. This was his last chance to satisfy his curiosity. Just a quick glance for a minute or two—*easy peasy*.

Carl knew the guards' routine and delivery schedule. Toiling under the weight of the cores, they had formed the habit of propping the security door open with an old trash can. With proper timing, Carl could slip inside, take a quick look around, and be out before anyone noticed. He moved to position himself behind a nearby shelf and waited.

Within minutes, the guards arrived, lugging their first load of drill tubes. The lead guard swiped his security card and the team entered the high-security area. A few minutes later, they reappeared and headed for another load, leaving the door ajar in predictable fashion. At the sound of the far exit door slamming shut, Carl made his move.

Slipping through the unsecured door, he found himself standing in the center of an inner foyer. Straight ahead, a vinyl-strip curtain door formed a rudimentary air lock between the foyer and the main lab. To his right, a circular staircase spiraled up into darkness. Treading softly, he eased up the metal stairs to a small observation room that overlooked the lab below.

This was going to be easier than he thought.

Carl backed into the shadows and studied the room below. At first, it looked like any other assay lab: microscopes along one wall; a large table half-filled with exposed cores, pushed out of their containers like Popsicles from their wrappers. The lab had even been equipped with a gas chromatograph and spectroscope. No expense had been spared.

But the far wall perplexed him: it was housing a row of stainless steel fermenting tanks like those found in any microbrewery. Titration racks, a vented hood, incubation chamber, genetic sequencing machine, and stacks of agar plates—items more at home in a biology classroom than a geological assay lab. *What is going on here?*

Biology was not Carl's strong suit, but Rachel could probably explain what he was seeing. He reached for his cell phone to take a picture, and cursed. He'd left it back in his cubicle. He'd just have to note every detail so he could share the information later.

The security team reappeared with their second delivery. Carl watched as two lab technicians, dressed in rubber aprons and full-face visors, joined the guards, helping to extract the new cores, which contained a mixture of crystalline rock and mud.

Their job done, the security team said their goodbyes. The two lab techs moved deliberately, one switching off the bright overhead lights and the other activating a bank of UV black lights.

Bathed in the lamp's purple glow, the sample cores suddenly lit up like a Christmas tree, their crystalline minerals fluorescing under the energy of ultraviolet radiation. Using the glowing minerals as a guide, the technicians extracted a collection of slices, placing them into assaying trays. When they were done, the overheads were flipped back on, illuminating a ruin of mud and rock littered across the table.

One lab tech carried the assay trays to the microscopes. The other technician moved to the nearest fermentation tank and opened the hatch, releasing a cloud of steam. Then, he dumped the core remnants from the table into the fermenter and shut the lid.

The unfamiliar procedure left Carl completely baffled. Core samples were like divining rods. Their mineral values would be tested, quantified, and charted on a map. By following the gradients of higher mineral concentrations, mining operations could zero in on the most promising claims. Core samples were always archived for further testing. They were never destroyed.

Now, more curious than ever, he scrutinized the lab techs as they turned their attention to the assay trays: making microslices, collecting small quantities of material for spectrographic analysis, studying the slices under the microscope.

He stood there watching for an hour, mesmerized, until another unimaginable event caught his attention.

The hatch on the nearest fermenter began to change color—to an unnaturally *bright* color. A deep Prussian-blue foam began to ooze out around the hatch's seal. It grew into a great steaming mound that advanced down the front side of the fermentation tank with a bubbling ferocity that could be heard from his perch in the observation room.

The lab workers turned and stared, frozen. One worker finally leapt up and rushed toward the fermenter's controls. His forward motion carried him past his destination as the slick foam betrayed his purchase. He landed on his backside with a loud *splat*.

A guttural gasp exploded from his mouth as he seemed to launch himself up from the floor. He writhed and contorted as the blue ooze sloughed off his back, along with large patches of lab coat and skin. A mist of white smoke streamed from the raw flesh as his cries morphed into a gurgling whimper.

The second worker slammed his hand onto a large red button, shattering the silence with a chorus of sirens. Seconds later, both men were contorting in agony. White foam spewed from their mouths, mixing with the cerulean mass that inched its way across the room.

Frozen in place, Carl Jameson was unsure what to do next, until the faint aroma of burnt almonds reached his nostrils and shocked him into action.

Hydrogen cyanide.

He bounded down the stairs three steps at a time, falling the last four feet onto the floor. Underneath the vinyl curtain, he could see blue foam advancing toward him. He jumped up and punched through the security door into the stillness of the warehouse.

The distant clamor of footsteps prompted him to turn down the left hallway toward the exit. He shot around the corner at the far end and collided with a wall of flesh, stinking of sweat and booze. A large, dark object descended from above, landing with a brilliant burst of pain.

CARL PRESSED HIS hands against the iron deck and felt the shudder of a ship's engine.

His mind was still swimming as he fingered a large welt behind his ear. A wave of dizziness flowed over him as he struggled to his feet, hands probing the darkness. His fingers found a dangling chain and pulled. The world turned white as a swinging bulb threw shadows across a cramped room containing a door, porthole, and stained toilet.

The stench of rust and urine assaulted his nostrils, churned his stomach. He leaned over the toilet and tore open the porthole, thrusting his face into the narrow opening to drink in gulps of humid night air.

Far in the distance, the lights of La Ceiba flickered on a long, dark jut of Honduran coastline. Above, the moon hung low and oval, firing the crests of ocean swells. It was a scene he had experienced a thousand times before as a geology undergraduate, from the decks of arctic cruisers and sloops whispering through Caribbean foam. The sea had always been as reassuring to him as a familiar mural, its nuances fresh with each viewing.

But now, the waters grew dark and malevolent. With each passing moment, the shoreline receded, and with it, his chance for survival. They had imprisoned him on this puke-stained ship for a reason. He had seen too much.

Carl strained to reassemble the past few hours. How long had he been out? Dim visions of bright-colored foam, smoking flesh, horrific screams, and dark shapes played across his mind. With sudden desperation, he groped in his pocket for the precious slide, the ticket to his Nobel Prize.

Pulling the plastic holder from his pocket, Carl stared down at . . . *sand*. The thin shard of stone had returned to the dust of the Earth.

Self-revulsion shuddered through his frame as he slumped to the toilet. This should have been a day to celebrate, but instead he'd destroyed his Nobel with a foolish act of bravado. He felt sick, the nausea worsening as he relived the horrific tragedy in the lab.

Two for the price of one.

Carl sat there, hump shouldered, for several minutes, thinking. Both tragedies seemed to converge into a single thread of thought. Slowly, deliberately, the divergent threads began to weave a tapestry in his mind, connecting the past to the present. He thought about the location of the closely guarded core samples and his shattered Nobel. A coincidence? Surely, it couldn't still be there, could it? After seventy million years?

Revulsion gave way to an elemental fear.

The tapestry in his mind's eye held the vision of a monstrous certainty. His own well-being seemed to fade into insignificance. He had to warn someone . . . *everyone.*

Reaching inside his other pocket, Carl pulled out his antique pocket watch and popped open the ornate cover. 9:13 P.M. Judging from the cargo crowding the ship's deck, they were headed to deep water. He didn't have much time.

He scrutinized the room. Behind the toilet, a plunger rested in a pool of fetid water. Above it, a rickety bookshelf held a stack of pornographic magazines and a tattered Bible. He jerked at the locked door repeatedly, to no avail. The porthole was far too small to wriggle through, the walls, solid steel.

No way out, nothing to write with, no way to leave a message.

The finality of his plight began to sink in. Carl dropped his head and stared down at the image on his T-shirt. He experienced a flash of inspiration and began ripping at the shirt's fibers, trying to tear away a vital portion of the shirt's image. Initially, the tear followed the weave of the cotton. He cursed through several attempts and finally raised the shirt to his mouth to gnaw out the requisite shape.

Then he pulled the old Bible from the room's shelf and flipped through the pages. The text was in Spanish, making it difficult to find the correct passage. After several minutes of searching, he tore out the bottom half of one page and folded it neatly several times. Opening a secret compartment in his watch, Carl removed the portrait inside and replaced it with the packet, pausing to stare at the woman in the photograph. She stared back with a radiant smile, as if to comfort him. His eyes filled as he said softly, "Looks like you won the bet."

Voices.

The first two were conciliatory, the third deeper and more commanding. Snapping the watch shut, Carl ripped it from the chain and stuffed it under the tongue of his sneaker.

Keys rattled.

He tore the handle from the plunger, stood, and braced himself. There would only be one chance. If he could force them away from the door, make a mad dash . . . the feral sea would swallow him up. A long swim to shore, certainly, but he could make it.

The door swung open and his heart sank. A familiar hulk of a man filled the opening. Leaning over to fit his enormous bulk inside, the man grabbed Carl's shirt and jerked him through the doorway.

"Hold him down!" he barked to the other men.

"*Sí, Capitán!*"

An instant later, Carl found himself sprawled facedown across the deck, his arms drawn painfully behind his back. A pair of hands rifled through his pockets as bindings tightened around both wrists. He squirmed frantically and twisted his face toward the huge figure. "Listen, for God's sake, don't do this! You don't know what you're doing!"

The captain leaned in, his breath thick with tequila. Dark eyes studied him from deep recesses. "You should have kept your nose out of our business, gringo."

"I won't tell anyone, I swear!"

The captain flashed a row of grimy teeth. "*Sí,* you won't."

Carl racked his brain for something to say, something that could describe the gravity of the situation. But how could he explain the history of the Earth in a few sentences? Straining closer, he hissed into the captain's ear.

"If you kill me—you kill us all."

The finality of the words caught the large man by surprise and the captain backed away nervously, a hint of doubt clouding his face. Carl felt a stab of hope as the captain wavered at the edge of indecision.

Finally, he straightened. "Finish him."

Something hard and cylindrical jammed against Carl's back. The men lashed it tightly and dragged him across the deck like a sack. He was hoisted to the gunwale. One heave, a cooling breeze, then a hard slap. The chaos at the water's surface soon dissolved into a dark stillness.

Carl jerked against the bindings, shreds of skin peeling away from the jute ropes. Neither hand budged. Water raced past. With two loud pops, both eardrums ruptured in an explosion of pain and dizziness. A faint metallic flavor washed over his tongue. His heart heaved against a chest cavity collapsing from the pressure. The urge to breathe welled up from his gut with a sudden vengeance. Carl struggled again, more feebly this time, but the knots were tied with a sailor's skill and only grew tighter.

Suddenly, a wall of cool water enveloped him. Unable to hold out any longer, Carl Jameson relaxed and let the salty liquid rush in. . . .

There was a loud ringing, and then—*nothing.*

A curious barracuda swam by, paused momentarily, then darted off into the void.

2

Dan Clifford straddled the edge of the past and the present—the Paleozoic era to be exact—an age when the weight of the North American crust transformed an ancient beach into sandstone. Soon after, the Appalachian Mountains rose and folded upon themselves, crushing the sandstone into quartzite. Time and rushing water would eventually carve the quartzite into the thousand-foot-deep Tallulah Gorge, located in northern Georgia near the beginning of the Appalachian Trail.

Halfway up the gorge's sheer southern wall, Dan balanced on a narrow ledge, studying an intimate view of nature's geological handiwork. His eyes traced the intricate patterns as he rubbed the throbbing from his forearms. Too many years away from serious climbing had robbed his stamina. Dan sat down on the rock and dangled his feet over the edge, thankful for a chance to catch his breath.

He always felt light and free up here, with nothing to hold him back. Five hundred feet below, twin waterfalls continued to reshape the gorge. The morning sun was beginning to peek over the northeast rim, casting a long shadow from Karl Wallenda's high-wire tower to the cliff climbed by Jon Voight in the movie *Deliverance*.

Dan took in a deep breath, relishing the scent of stone and humus. The *earthy* pleasures, he liked to call them. He'd needed this trip for a long time, a chance to escape the pressures at work, to reflect. The biggest prize of his career was coming due, and its outcome would determine his future and perhaps the future of the entire West Coast. The burden of that responsibility weighed heavily on him.

He'd been spending too much time in Atlanta, huddled in darkened rooms, staring at computer screens, yearning for wide-open spaces. His work at NeuroSys had consumed him to the point that he felt like a shell of his former self. By now, he should be settled, confident. But a strange sense of discomfort had grown in recent weeks, just when things were coming together.

"A storm is coming," came a gravelly voice from below.

Dan peered over the ledge at Ben Proudfoot, his gnarled hands grasping the rock fifty feet below. Ben was right: a winter cold front *was* approaching. It would arrive in seven hours, although the morning skies showed no hint of it.

"How did you know that?" Dan shouted back.

"My bones told me," Ben replied. "And the eagle. See him circling above? He is eager for one last flight before retiring to the nest."

Dan glanced up at the eagle and laughed. Age and arthritis may have relegated Ben to bottom rope, but it had done nothing to dull his wit or tongue. The translation was clear enough: *hurry up.*

Ben Proudfoot was an impatient man.

It was an uncharacteristic trait for a man of Cherokee heritage; he was influenced by the pace of modern life perhaps. But like his ancestors, Ben Proudfoot loved to speak in a peculiar indirect manner. Getting a straight answer from Ben was like shadowboxing.

But the stories! Ben always had plenty of stories.

Whenever Ben's students would press him for a specific answer to some complex question, he would stare into the distance with a stoic expression for what would seem an eternity. Then, he would speak in measured tones: *"There are no direct answers. The Earth speaks to us in riddles, lest it utter half-truths."*

The memory brought a smile to Dan's face. He suspected that much of Ben's "shtick" was directed against the stereotypical views of the white man, who always associated the indigenous people of North America with flowery fables, wampum, and feathers. It was Ben's inside joke, but it always shut his students up. Dan never knew quite when to take his mentor seriously, but when it came to climbing, or the complex ways of the world, Ben knew his stuff.

"Don't worry, old man," Dan shouted back. "We've got plenty of time to finish our climb." He clipped his rope into three carabiners anchored to the rock. "Ready to belay!" he shouted, and snugged the rope's tension a bit more than usual as a courtesy to Ben.

"Climbing!" Ben shouted back.

With Dan's aid, Ben slithered up the cliff with a confidence that would humble men half his age. Ben Proudfoot had been climbing the Georgia mountains for over thirty years. Within minutes, he reached the belay point, flopped down on the ledge, and cast an expectant glance Dan's way.

"Impatient already? Jeez, you just got here."

"And if the storm comes sooner?"

Dan shot Ben an incredulous look. "It won't."

Ben grinned. "I watch the weather reports, too. They're never right."

Dan ignored the feigned insult and stood up to study the cliff ahead. Climbers loved to christen their favorite routes with colorful names like Punk Wave, Flying Frog, Primitive Paradox, Cracker State, Mescaline Daydream.

His current climb was no different—a particularly gnarly pitch of twisted rock aptly named "Creatures Void of Form." It was a zigzag route, thirty feet up to an arête, then a horizontal traverse leftward for another fifty feet that ended at two slabs of rock angled like the pages of an open book. From there, the route went vertical again, dead-ending at an overhang.

It was a route he'd never climbed, even in his heyday, an advanced-level climb. Now, rusty and out of shape . . .

Ben must have sensed his mood. "Not as tough as it looks," he said reassuringly. "I climbed it in my sleep once, on a full moon, guided by the *Nunnehi*."

"Yeah, yeah, the *Nunnehi*," Dan said. "The little people who live in caves and guide widows and orphans to the happy hunting ground. I don't fit that profile. Let's dispense with the old legends for once, shall we?"

Ben cackled like a crow. "Be the mouse. Keep your nose down; focus on the next hold; do not think, just climb. You were once my best student."

"*Once* is the key word."

Ben laughed again. "I'm still here, aren't I? You never lose the skills."

"Give me a minute." Dan warily traced the rock with his eyes, imagining every foot and handhold, every opportunity to place protection in the cracks. He *did* have an instinct for stone, with its fractal patterns and randomness, but he never climbed unprepared. Anticipation and meticulous planning was his style: *calculated* risks.

Comfortable with his projected path, Dan took a deep breath and started up. The muscles in his forearms burned and he felt clumsy at first, but Ben was right. Within minutes, he relaxed and let the old climbing engrams kick in. He rallied and started humming the old Bob Dylan tune to himself:

'Twas in another lifetime, one of toil and blood
When blackness was a virtue and the road was full of mud
I came in from the wilderness, a creature void of form.
"Come in," she said,
"I'll give you shelter from the storm."

Dan reached the shallow arête and stopped long enough to place two cams in a crack; then he worked his way left, crabbing along with a series of technical back steps, drop knees, and laybacks. The route grew more difficult. Despite his planning, the traverse ended poorly at the open-book corner, with his stance off balance and stretched, shoes barely finding grip. He needed to place another cam immediately or risk a pendulum swing back to the belay ledge, but the crack was just out of reach and his strained legs and arms were starting a death wobble. He hugged the wall for relief and closed his eyes.

The image of a young boy appeared, scrambling up clay hills near home, laughing, grabbing at roots, slipping back, Father shouting encouragement from below, there to claim him if he fell. Dan had a naive confidence back then. He felt blindly for a better hold and edged closer to the crack. But then, a dark shadow swallowed the memory. The young boy disappeared, overtaken by adulthood.

'Twas in another lifetime, one of toil and blood.

A sudden ringing jolted him from the wall.

Dan's heart fluttered. He teetered at the edge of balance, found new purchase. Another ring, screaming at him with the harshness of a Klaxon. He cursed himself, locked his knees, and hooked a cam into his harness with a long leader. The crack was high and left, at the limit of his reach, a deadpoint move. If he missed, he'd be hamburger on the belay ledge. The ringing protested again. Stiffening, he lunged. The cam slid into the crack like a sword and snapped into place with a satisfying "clump." Dan gave it a good jerk, released his grip, and let the full weight of his harness fall back against the thin piece of metal.

Swinging to and fro, he let out a sigh of relief and fished the smartphone from his hip pack.

Ben yelled encouragement from below, but Dan barely heard it. His attention was riveted to the phone's display. It was the wrong person at the wrong time, calling on his day off. That could mean only one thing. . . .

Sonny Swyft never called with good news.

BEN PROUDFOOT WATCHED the climb with a mixture of delight and amazement. After years of inactivity, his student had managed a nearly impossible deadpoint maneuver. Now, Dan Clifford was nonchalantly dangling from the cliff, chatting it up on the phone like some adolescent.

Before long, Dan's movements became exaggerated. His face reddened and his voice grew louder, though Ben could not make out the precise words. It required no great insight to understand the meaning.

With a sigh, Ben sat down on the ledge and tried to soak in the moment. It would probably be his last chance to fly free on this ledge. He needed a partner like Dan to get here and those opportunities lessened every day. Ben had never fully understood the demons that haunted his young friend. They had never really talked about them. But as time passed, Dan Clifford had grown more distant, consumed by a passion for the future.

A future Ben felt had become more unclear than ever.

The clank of climbing gear signaled the end of the call. Ben watched as Dan retraced his steps back to the belay ledge. He arrived out of breath, face etched with concern and regret.

"I'm so sorry, but—"

"Say no more," Ben said, raising a finger. "I knew the climb was over before you did."

"I have no choice."

Ben forced a grim smile. "You *always* have a choice."

3

DEEP BENEATH THE *Pacific Ocean under two miles of seawater, ancient crustal plates ground and thrashed against one another. The Cascadia subduction zone, a seven-hundred-mile scar on the Earth, paralleled the western coastline of America. Tectonic forces were squeezing the crust in a vise, forcing the Juan de Fuca Plate under the North American crust and into the mantle below.*

The two crustal plates had been locked together for three hundred years, the enormous pressure building like the winding of a great watchmaker's spring. The coasts of Washington and Oregon bowed up under the pressure until the force could no longer be contained.

It ruptured in a giant 9.2 megathrust earthquake.

The compressional wave raced through the Earth's mantle at fifteen thousand miles per hour and reached downtown Seattle seconds later, fracturing a web of underground fault lines. The Alaskan Way Viaduct, a double-decked highway, pancaked along its length, burying rush hour commuters under tons of concrete.

The destruction spread eastward, rippling and folding highways like a snapped bedsheet. Tourists in the Space Needle viewed the destruction with detached horror, unsure if their tottering perch would survive.

Back at the fault line, the great watchmaker's spring continued to unwind. The North American Plate thrust up forty feet, lifting the ocean and sending a two-foot-high wave in all directions at five hundred miles an hour. In twenty minutes, it reached the West Coast and rose into a wall of water one hundred feet tall as it slowed in the shallows.

Engorged with tons of rock and sand, the tsunami crashed into the coast with the power of sixty hurricanes, demolishing everything in its path.

Time ticked backward as the death toll climbed:

50,000 . . .

150,000 . . .

Two minutes later, the tsunami reached the Strait of Juan de Fuca, gaining speed in the narrow channel. It roared into Puget Sound, carrying cruise ships and their terrified passengers along on its crest like a battering ram, razing what was left of the shattered city.

250,000 . . .

500,000 . . .

The initial wave lasted less than ten minutes, but additional waves arrived in pulses, each with greater power. They pushed farther inland, drowning survivors before they could dig themselves out of the wreckage. The destruction pummeled the Pacific Northwest for two horrifying hours before the earthquake's energy was finally dissipated.

The death count continued to rise inexorably:

Two million . . .

Three million . . .

Finally, the countdown clock stopped at 00:00:00.

SITTING AT THE head of the NeuroSys conference room, Dan Clifford swiveled his chair to face the audience, feeling distinctly unsettled. He'd run this simulation hundreds of times already, but it still gave him the creeps.

Sonny Swyft's unexpected rescheduling, combined with a lack of sleep, had made Dan particularly grumpy. After months of negotiations, this presentation should have been a slam dunk, but Sonny had pulled a typical "Swyft-kick-in-the-butt," saddling Dan with forty-eight hours to throw together a sales pitch for the most important government contract of his career.

Worse, Dan was pitching to his least favorite brand of clientele.

His disdain for politicians had started early, at age ten, with a letter-writing campaign that lasted into his teenage years. Dan's parents had always taught him that elected officials were public servants, but the politicians he knew seemed more interested in themselves than the public. No letter he had ever sent received a satisfying reply. By the time Dan was a teenager, his entreaties had degraded into a series of thinly disguised insults.

Now, what a grand irony: presenting his dog and pony show to the ultimate politician.

Dan scanned the small audience, starting with the three scientists from NOAA, the National Oceanic and Atmospheric Administration, their faces aglow in the projector's light. They seemed duly impressed by the simulation—eyes wide, smiles all around—but then, they knew enough to be impressed.

That left Senator Nolan Becker, chairman of the Senate Appropriations Committee. Dan studied Becker's cryptic expression and cursed under his breath, wondering if Becker knew of his early letter-writing history.

Senator Nolan Becker was a ruggedly handsome man, with the same chiseled features and silver hair that had propelled him into office a decade earlier. Only his wrinkles betrayed his age, etched by sun and too many smiles. The "senate smile," as it was called, was an art form designed to avoid confrontation, yet reveal nothing.

At this moment, Becker's patented smile seemed impenetrable.

The senator turned his attention toward the Atlanta skyline, pale beneath an autumn rain. Beyond the glass and steel of the NeuroSys building, a fine mist danced in the sodden air. Becker cast a finger in the direction of the window and returned Dan's gaze. "Quite the presentation, Mr. Clifford, but I thought we were here to see your company's weather forecasting program."

"And you *have*," Dan said in his most earnest tone. "But the Global Assimilation and Prediction System, or GAPS for short, does far more than predict weather. The GAPS software specializes in identifying black swan events, like the Cascadia subduction earthquake we just witnessed. This simulation was based on extensive prediction analytics."

"'Black swan'? I thought that was a ballet." Becker's senate smile twisted. "What does that have to do with your, uh . . . GAPS program?"

"You're thinking of *Swan Lake*," Dan said with a dose of indignation in his voice. It irked him that a man holding the nation's purse strings could be so scientifically illiterate. *Time to dumb things down,* he thought.

"A 'black swan' is the common name for an unexpected disaster event," Dan said. "Back in the sixteenth century, the term 'black swan' referred to something that didn't exist, because no one had ever seen an actual black swan—that is, until Dutch explorers brought a few genuine black swans back from Australia to Europe. After that, the term evolved into its current meaning: 'blindness to the unexpected.'"

Becker's brow wrinkled. "I'm still not following you."

Dan forced a smile. "Look at the defining tragedies of our time—9/11, the Asian tsunami, the Great Recession, Katrina, the Gulf oil spill, the Chilean earthquake, the Ebola outbreak, Fukushima—they're all black swan events, totally unexpected at the time, yet highly destructive. It's not the dangers we *know about* that should worry us the most, but the ones lurking in the periphery, poised to turn our world upside down. The GAPS software can broaden our focus, alert us to unexpected possibilities, *free* us from the tyranny of the unknown."

Becker grinned. "Nice speech, I'll give you that." He leaned back in his chair and crossed his arms. "But we have human experts and government think tanks for that kind of thing."

"That's the problem," Dan said. "Humans are terrible at predicting black swans. We're biased and emotional. We see the world through the distorted lens of our own clichéd expectations. Experts tend to focus on the ordinary, not the extraordinary, the outliers. The GAPS software can see the world with childlike naiveté, free from human presumption. GAPS spotted a pattern recently in seismic data that increases the likelihood of a Cascadia earthquake to more than thirty percent in the next ten years."

"Pretty imprecise odds for a prediction system," Becker said with a smirk. "Besides, don't we already have enough to worry about without your GAPS software cooking up theoretical scenarios?"

"The Cascadia subduction event is not theoretical," Dan said. "It's real. The last one occurred on January 27, 1700. These earthquakes occur on average every 240 years, so we're already overdue. We've got to upgrade warning systems, build berms, install evacuation towers—"

"With what?" Becker said, shrugging. "This is the first time I've heard of this earthquake. Besides, we can't go spending money on every far-fetched disaster scenario that comes along. The government's got limits, you know."

"Tell that to the victims' families," Dan blurted. Becker's flippant attitude pissed him off. It was always the same. Removing a politician's head from the sand was like pulling a tooth: it hurt like hell and left an empty void. "Do you want to be the next politician caught flat-footed after a natural disaster? Look at Katrina. Authorities ignored the odds of a Category 5 hurricane simply because one hadn't oc-curred in recent memory. They failed to upgrade berms, rebuild wetlands, install larger pumps. The destruction cost *billions,* not to mention the precious lives lost."

Becker's expression hardened and he stared at Dan quietly for sev-eral minutes.

Dan felt a patina of sweat accumulating under his collar.

Finally, the senate smile crept back and Becker chuckled. "Good thing I'm in a light mood today. Next, you'll tell me I can predict my election with this thing."

The comment drew a chorus of nervous laughs from the NOAA entourage.

"Frankly? Yes," Dan said with a straight face. "Weather, earth-quakes, elections—they're all complex systems. GAPS can find patterns in huge data sets."

Becker waved his hands dismissively. "All this conjecture is well and good, but my flight's in an hour. Can we just stick to weather fore-casting?"

Dan glanced at Sonny Swyft, who was glaring at him from across the room. The young president of NeuroSys was twisting a tuft of red hair around his finger, a thinning remnant on his otherwise bald pate. Sonny barely fit the image of a corporate executive—his diminutive frame lost in an Italian suit, chartreuse tie canted rudely to one side. He released his tuft of hair and waggled his finger at Dan disapprov-ingly.

Dan winced at Sonny's admonition and reminded himself that this was a *sale,* after all. He was pushing too hard, letting his own per-sonal bias cloud his judgment. The GAPS contract was too important. It didn't matter how he made the sale, just that he *made* it. He took a deep breath and counted silently from ten to one, determined to keep his cool. "How about weather forecasts two weeks in advance with ninety percent accuracy?"

Becker's eyes widened. "Your GAPS computer can do that? I thought weather was impossible to predict past a few days."

"Impossible until now," Dan said, starting to feel more relaxed. He knew Becker's hot button: the National Weather Service, NOAA's flagship. It touched the public on a daily basis, helped garner the all-important votes. "Just like its ability with black swans, GAPS can spot unique weather patterns that human analysts miss. It uses big data, massive sensor arrays, self-learning software, and neural net processing to spot patterns hidden in chaos."

"Whoa!" Becker waved his hands again. "You're losing me with all these complex swans and neural nets. English, please."

"Neural net software works like the interconnected neurons in our brain," Dan said and paused, thinking. "Let me use a political analogy. Neural nets are like voters. When a decision is needed, each node in the network casts a ballot. The votes are added up and the idea with the most votes wins. In other words, a neural net has *collective* wisdom."

Becker guffawed. "You had me with that analogy until the last line. Don't try and convince me voters have any collective wisdom!"

Dan flashed a warm smile and turned his palms upward. "They elected *you*, didn't they?"

"*Humph*, point taken."

The NOAA scientists stifled grins.

Dan moved on before Becker digested his quip. "Neural nets, or *collective networks,* need a lot of data to make decisions. Until recently, weather forecasts were made using land-based weather stations, even though the ocean covers seventy percent of our planet. It's like solving a jigsaw puzzle with only thirty percent of the pieces. That's where our autonomous underwater vehicles, or AUVs, help out. They're self-piloted robotic sensors that swim the oceans, collecting temperature, salinity, and current data. When combined with land-based measurements, GAPS can achieve a huge leap in prediction accuracy."

"Two weeks, huh?" Becker's senate smile seemed to inch upward.

Dan couldn't resist adding one last point: "Our AUVs also contain seismic sensors. They can map the deep oceanic crust and perhaps achieve something unprecedented: the ability to predict earthquakes, days or *weeks* in advance. It might save millions of lives on the West Coast and make NOAA, and *you*, the toast of Washington."

Becker smiled broadly, his fingers tapping the table. "Mr. Clifford, I think you finally won me over. I'm happy to announce that the Appropriations Committee has approved your proposal."

The suddenness of Becker's remark hung in the air like a lingering melody. Dan managed a sputtering "wonderful," and shook Becker's hand. "The entire network?"

"Yes."

"Robotics, too?"

"Of course."

Dan nodded, unable to keep a silly grin from his face. Still, it all seemed too easy and that made him suspicious. His sales pitch had been a disaster and he knew it.

"This is, of course, contingent on a six-month rollout," Becker added.

Dan swallowed. There it was: the *gotcha*. "Six months? The contract clearly states three years—"

"No worries, Senator," Sonny Swyft said, stepping forward. "Mr. Clifford isn't privy to our production advances. We can easily meet that timetable."

"Six months? That's six times our current—"

"As I was saying," Sonny said, shooting Dan a withering glare, "our Honduras plant has ramped up in record time."

Becker's attention vacillated between the two men. "Well, which is it? No way I'm having the committee cut a check—"

Sonny held up a hand. "You have my word."

Becker relaxed. "That's what I thought."

4

Dan waited until a few more pleasantries had been exchanged and the senator left for the airport, then spun around. "What the hell was that about? Six months?"

"You know the public offering is coming up," Sonny said. "We needed a dramatic rollout for the IPO, something to titillate the media."

"And if we can't deliver? We might lose the whole contract—"

"By that time, the IPO will be in the bag. Don't worry about it."

"It's my *job* to worry. What production advances?"

Sonny pointed a finger at Dan's sternum. "Let me worry about production. Just upgrade the contract."

"It'll take a while . . . there are the software changes."

"Changes? Why haven't I heard—"

"Typical last-minute tweaks. Rudi should be done by the time I'm back from vacation."

Sonny's eyes narrowed. "Vacation?"

Dan shrugged. "I left the memo with your secretary two weeks ago."

"Poor timing, don't you think?"

"I wasn't expecting the presentation to be moved up."

"Don't screw this up, Clifford." Sonny jabbed at his chest this time.

Dan slowly, but firmly, brushed Sonny's finger aside. "I started the GAPS project long before you came along. I have no intention of letting *anyone* screw it up." He left before Sonny could react and headed for the basement, taking the stairs three steps at a time.

Weaving his way through the catacombs of the NeuroSys basement, Dan stopped at a door marked NEURAL SOFTWARE DEVELOPMENT.

After a facial recognition scan, the mechanized voice intoned, "Welcome, Mr. Clifford, entry authorized." The electric dead bolt buzzed open.

Inside the dim interior, Dan could see Rudi Plimpton's gaunt frame hovering over a keyboard, pounding the keys like a bearded Beethoven, his long black hair swaying to the beat of a Grateful Dead tune.

Rudi was Dan's secret weapon on the GAPS project, hired away from NOAA years ago. Unlike the twentysomething "script kiddies" who currently dominated the programming world, Rudi Plimpton was old school. As a kid in the eighties, Rudi had learned assembly language, one level above the "ones and zeros" of a computer's binary language. Rudi had programmed in assembly for so long that Dan imagined his neural pathways evolving to "think" like a computer.

That digital wiring must have stunted his emotional growth, because Rudi was a middle-aged man-child. Dan scanned the room with its piles of empty donut boxes, computer carcasses, and haystacks of wire scattered about, and smiled. He had learned long ago to ignore Rudi's eccentricities, because the man-child could *code*.

Rudi looked up from his terminal. "So, what did *No-sense Becker* have to say? Do we have a contract?"

Dan pondered the question for a moment. "Yes and no."

Rudi thrust out his hand. "Congrats! You earned it. I know how much this contract means to you—" He jerked the hand back. "What's the *no* part?"

"Sonny promised Becker a six-month delivery schedule."

"What?" Rudi rolled his eyes. "Everything?"

"Yep."

"Then you were right, as usual. That dickhead Sonny is all show and no blow. I haven't heard squat from the Honduras plant lately, but I can't imagine them making that deadline."

"I agree," Dan said, slinging an old donut box across the room like a Frisbee. "There's something fishy going on. I just wish I'd made it to the Honduras plant before the presentation. Can you keep Sonny at bay until I get back?"

"You kiddin'? That guy hates my guts. He won't be poking around down here."

"Just keep him out of the GAPS contract until I get back."

"No problemo," Rudi said. "So, you takin' Jen along on your little scuba diving adventure?"

"No way." Dan said. "That would be like letting the fox loose in the henhouse."

"Yeah, but what a fox!" Rudi said, striking a pinup pose. "You seriously need a love life, my friend."

"With Jenifer?" Dan shook his head, grinned. "Made that mistake once."

A BLAST OF chill air cut through Dan's suit as he trotted across the parking garage. The rain had turned rush hour into a funeral procession. Dan slipped into his car and thought back to Rudi's last comment as he eased out into a line of snarled traffic. Getting social advice from Rudi Plimpton bordered on the absurd, but his friend had a point. Dan had kept to himself lately, consumed by the GAPS project. The unique geography of downtown Atlanta didn't help matters. Devoid of the ethnic neighborhoods of Chicago or New York, the metro area emptied into the suburbs at night, leaving behind a ghost town ruled by tiny squads of youthful urbanites.

Not his type.

Not that he *had* a type. Casual relationships came easily enough, but work had been his jealous consort for several years now.

His thoughts returned to Sonny Swyft. The man's meddling often resulted in missed deadlines, false promises, and dissatisfied customers, something Dan couldn't afford with the GAPS project. It was too important. Time was running out for the California coast. If something terrible occurred before the rollout of GAPS . . .

A silver Lexus lurched into the narrow gap directly ahead. Dan hit the horn long enough to register his annoyance, and seeing an opportunity, slipped across two lanes of traffic and turned right onto North Avenue.

Two blocks later, he pulled in to Club Towers Condominiums and parked. He headed for the Bullet, the Tower's glass-walled elevator that hung from the side of the building. It usually afforded a spectacular view of the skyline, but today, the buildings jutted from the mist like insidious trees. As the elevator ascended toward the top floor, Dan relaxed, allowing himself to dream of sand and surf for a brief moment. The scuba vacation would be a welcome respite and partial consolation for his spoiled weekend at Tallulah Gorge. The doors slid open and he headed to the first condo, unlocked the door, and almost ran into Rover.

"Good evening, boss."

"Good evening, Rover. One Sweetwater Ale, please."

"Yes, boss."

Rover turned his rectangular frame and rumbled toward the kitchen. The robot had been recharging in the foyer and was dragging his power cord behind like a limp tail.

Dan had grown quite fond of his electronic pet. An early NeuroSys prototype, Rover began life as a medical delivery robot. About the size and shape of a minifridge on wheels, Rover sported two mechanical arms mounted on his torso. Above them, twin cameras swiveled nervously on a gimbal, analyzing everything. Once linked to the Internet with voice and facial recognition, Rover had grown more perceptive, able to recognize Dan's friends at dinner parties. But it was Rover's sophisticated autonomous logic that gave him true independence and personality. Rover may have lacked the warmth of a dog, but at least he didn't shed hair or piss on the carpet.

Dan's smartphone chirped as he headed toward the bedroom. He heard Jenifer Coleman's perky voice on the other end.

"So, is your big contract a done deal?"

"Maybe."

"Congrats! Tell me the gory details."

"I'm not quite ready to claim victory."

"Dan, I swear, you're such a downer. You should be celebrating, with *me*. Let's go out on the town!"

"No thanks," Dan said, and realized his tone sounded callous, so he added: "I have to pack."

"Bull! I know you," Jenifer said. "Packed two days ago, I bet. Still taking that side tour to the Honduras plant, aren't you?"

Dan winced. He should have never mentioned it to her. "Just want to check things out."

"On your vacation? Something's going on, isn't it?"

"I'm just dropping by to visit Harry."

Jenifer's voice wilted. "Damn it, Dan. Give me a morsel or something. If you can't trust *me*—"

"That's the point, isn't it?" He laughed. "Still looking for the big news story?"

"Why not? A good investigative reporter uses her channels."

"Why this obsession with hard news? You're already more famous than the anchors."

She groaned. "I'm sick of the weather bimbo role. Reporting gets *respect.*"

He'd heard the same complaint for years. Jenifer Coleman's wiry frame, jet black hair, and bone-white features made her look more like a porcelain doll than a news anchor. Apparently, CNN thought so too, having refused her repeated requests for reporting assignments.

"I'm on a fact-finding mission, that's all. Sonny's been keeping a lid on things in Honduras—"

"Him again? Seems like Sonny Swyft has been eating at you ever since . . . that's funny, since the day he became your boss."

"I don't trust him farther than I can spit in the wind."

"If you find anything, do I get the scoop?"

It was a tantalizing thought. Dan would like nothing better than to pin Sonny's ass to the wall. "We'll see."

"Come on Dan. Let me nail the guy for you. I know you want me to."

She's relentless, he thought. "Listen, I gotta go."

He hung up, marveling at how Jenifer still managed to attach herself to his life. She was a friend of the accidental sort, one whom fate chooses for you, rather than the other way around. The two of them had a brief fling in college. They met in meteorology class, dated for a while, but Jenifer's personality was too strident, too demanding for his tastes. Outside of meteorology, they had little in common, so he broke it off.

She'd been trying to rekindle the flame ever since. Over the years, they kept intersecting. She was hired at CNN a few months before he'd sold them an early prototype of the GAPS system for their on-air forecasts. He'd often wondered if she had influenced the decision. Perhaps he'd been too harsh on the phone. He considered calling her back. . . .

Rover reappeared in the doorway. "Don't forget your appointment at . . . Hartsfield-Jackson International Airport . . . nine o'clock . . . A.M. . . . tomorrow."

"Acknowledged. Rover, clear appointment." Dan grabbed the beer from Rover's serving tray and stripped down. He stared in the mirror, struck by the faintly unfamiliar form staring back. His abs had lost a little definition. His eyes sagged with exhaustion, yet he wasn't sleepy. A few silvery strands had invaded his thick auburn hair. Life seemed to be racing past and he hadn't allowed himself a single moment to celebrate his accomplishments.

Or share them.

Jen was right. He *should* be out celebrating. This was the culmination of years of effort, a chance to make a real difference in the world. Yet, at the moment he felt strangely uncomfortable. He was a prediction scientist, after all. Something about Becker's sudden enthusiasm nagged at him. An old familiar churning in his stomach made itself known. Stoked by adrenaline, his anger and paranoia gnawed its way back to the surface. He needed to keep his temper under control. It had almost cost him the GAPS contract.

Not bothering with clothes, Dan moved to the great room and stood before the bay window, hoping for a clear view of the Atlanta skyline, but the scene was shrouded in gray. He closed his eyes, took in several slow, deep breaths, and began working through the thirty-seven postures of the tai chi chuan short form.

5

RACHEL SULLIVAN PLUNGED her sampling pole deep into the waters of Emerald Lagoon, nestled at the foot of Mt. Erebus, Antarctica's only active volcano. The lagoon was a steaming river that began at the base of Erebus and meandered through the ice shelf to join the Ross Sea. The combination of warm water and mineral nutrients formed an unusually fertile oasis that afforded her plenty of sampling opportunities.

With her hands stiff and tired from the cold, Rachel struggled to grip the rod. She glanced at her watch: four hours had passed without a break, and morning was gone. Morning was a dubious term in Antarctica this time of year, when the landscape was bathed in an eerie blue sunlight twenty hours a day. Without solar cues, it was easy to lose track of time. She wiggled the pole gently. The sampling bottle had snagged on a ledge and she worked patiently to dislodge it, concentrating all the while on her footing. She refocused on the task at hand, eager to finish.

The entire bay was thawing rapidly as the Southern Hemisphere's spring season advanced, spreading cracks through the floes like black fingers. A sudden shift of wind or current could break off a section of ice and carry her out to sea. Soon the continent would shrink to its smallest size in over a century as summer tightened its grasp. *If anyone has doubts about warming oceans, they should visit this place,* Rachel thought. One huge piece of the Ross Ice Shelf the size of Rhode Island had recently broken off.

Rachel Sullivan had ignored repeated warnings from her cohorts, choosing to venture out alone on the ice with nothing but a portable radio. She loved the solitude and stark desolation and welcomed the extra shot of adrenaline the risk afforded her. A little healthy fear made everything more invigorating, more *real.*

Rachel scanned the windswept horizon, barely visible through blowing ice particles. Despite the warming temperatures, Antarctica remained a desert of ice. Yet even in such a stark and wretched landscape, life still managed to gain a foothold and flourish. The heat from Mt. Erebus obviously helped things along.

She retracted the telescoping pole, removed the last sample bottle from the end, and slid it inside her insulated knapsack. Her work done, Rachel wrapped the strap of her ice ax around her wrist and began the cautious trudge back to more solid ground.

She mulled over the confusing results from her samples. This was the last of five yearly trips she had made with the *Sea Berth* expedition to test the effects of ultraviolet light on plankton populations. Every spring for the past decade, a hole had formed in the ozone layer above Antarctica. This year had been particularly bad, allowing lethal UV rays to bathe the fragile ecosystem.

The marine life in this area was unusually productive, a result of the nutrient supply from Mt. Erebus. Red algae grew in labyrinthine channels in the ice, providing sustenance for krill and other plankton in the water below. The krill, in turn, fed the whales, seals, and penguins.

For five years, she had tracked the algae as increasing UV had devastated the population—but not this year. For some inexplicable reason, the ecosystem had rebounded. The western coast was in the midst of a phytoplankton bloom. The algae had evolved, perhaps by growing an extra cellular layer or by moving into deeper water; how, she wasn't sure. But she hoped these samples would prove her theory of punctuated equilibrium: sudden leaps of evolution in response to changes in the environment.

A gust of wind slipped under the fur-lined collar of her expedition hood and cut through her skin. The merciless Antarctic winds could push the windchill to a body-numbing twenty degrees below zero. Any exposed skin would freeze in less than a minute. She cinched the hood tight, bowed her head against the wind, and headed toward an escarpment of boulders.

She wanted to make one final visit to a colony of emperor penguins, to watch the large birds during their mating rituals. The colony had found its own luxury accommodations alongside the warm springs of Erebus, its steamy pools of tepid water providing spa-like conditions for the large flightless birds.

Rachel trod through the floes to solid ground, betrayed by the scattering of rocks on the surface. They were the remnants of lava bombs—blobs of molten rock burped from the belly of Erebus. The bombs could travel for miles, and had littered the surrounding foothills like sentinels, naked against the wind that scoured the loose snow from around them. Directly beyond the lava field, a cluster of ghostly columns loomed over the wretched landscape. Nicknamed Sherwood Forest, the ice columns were hollow and as tall as lighthouses, formed from the condensing steam exiting the base of Erebus. At their tops, clouds of puffy steam continued to pour from their maws like the smoke from a great furnace. She had her own name for the bizarre formations: Devil's Smokestacks.

The emperor penguins had established a breeding colony on the frozen lake. She stopped for a moment to catch her breath and cut a diagonal path through the edge of the forest. The colony was small, about six hundred birds. The females had settled in; the males were still arriving, having completed a two-hundred-mile journey across the ice. Despite their exhaustion, the males were already crooning. Emperors performed a strange and beautiful mating dance and Rachel wanted to watch the action up close this time, so she moved in boldly. As expected, the males were distracted by the eligible females and ignored her. She fixed her attention on one amorous couple near the center of the colony and crept steadily toward them, taking care to avoid making any sudden movements.

The male raised his beak high in the air, presenting his brilliant yellow neck-band to the female. He crooned a soulful tune, dropping his head to his belly, his beak almost touching the ground. The female clapped her wings together, chirping approval. Their antics seemed to excite the other males, and soon, the entire field was alive with lustful preening. Once two penguins bonded, they stayed together for life, unlike most humans, Rachel reflected.

She eased forward, into the crowd of penguins in heat. Then she knelt carefully and rested her arm on her ice ax. The larger males were over four feet tall. She began to wonder if they would actually attack a human who had infiltrated so deeply into their domain. Her concern seemed warranted when the milling and socializing suddenly ceased.

The males grew agitated, waddling nervously in circles. Maybe she looked like a leopard seal as she knelt on the ice. She stood up cautiously. The agitation increased. *This is strange,* she thought; she had visited the colony twice before and the penguins had ignored her. But she had never moved in this close. Rachel decided to work her way back toward the edge of the colony, but several of the large adults cut off her escape, scurrying back and forth, flapping their stubby wings.

Abruptly, the colony scattered outward in a stampede of black and yellow, waddling faster than Rachel thought possible. They were falling all over one another in a mad rush. Two frantic birds collided head-on with her, knocking her to the ice. Several more birds fell over her in a mass of flailing bird and human.

When she managed to sit back up, the penguins were gone. The colony had re-formed into a large circle at the edge of the lake bed— now empty but for piles of penguin guano. A sudden silence blew over the lake. Whatever had scared the penguins should scare her too, she reasoned. Rachel suddenly felt vulnerable and exposed, like a Christian laid out for slaughter in the center of a tuxedoed audience.

Then she heard it—a faint whistling sound, like the whine from the old war movies her granddad loved to watch.

Lava bombs!

She stared in horror as a screaming projectile plummeted into the ice just yards away, sending a blast of scalding spray in all directions. Before she could react, a rolling wave of ice and water rocketed out from the impact zone, lifting her high into the air, and then down into the freezing water. She hit hard and gasped spasmodically, as the unbearable cold assailed her flesh like a thousand needles. The initial wave reached the edge of the frozen pond and rebounded. She caught a breath and went under again.

Struggling to the surface, she clawed at the broken ice that was now shattered into a thousand pieces. Solid ground was a hundred feet away. Something heavy dragged her downward and she remembered the ice ax hanging from her arm. She slung it on top of the sludge and struggled toward the edge. A sudden heaviness made every movement seem like a swim through molasses.

Paddling furiously, she moved to within three feet of the edge. With desperate energy she slung the ax forward and felt the tip drive into solid ice, but the waterlogged expedition suit was like an iron weight, and her legs were virtually useless. The ice continued to disintegrate as she struggled. With one last frenzied effort, pulling hand over hand, she dragged herself out of the water, rolling several times to put distance between herself and the edge.

Time was now critical.

The *Sea Berth* was a mile away. She would have to run for her life. Propping herself against the ax, Rachel staggered to her feet and tried to run. All sensation below her knees was gone; her legs felt like stilts. The waterlogged fur of her mukluk boots had frozen solid in less than a minute, followed by the outside of her suit. The synthetic insulation, even wet, would provide a few precious moments of warmth, but she would have to move or die.

The dry air seared the sensitive mucus lining of her lungs. She thought of the morning jogs she took almost every day. Her best time in the mile was six minutes. Six! And that was without ten pounds of ice layered on a suit of armor. She had to reach the *Sea Berth*—that was the only thing that mattered now. Remembering her radio, she groped in the side pocket, praying that it still worked. "*Sea Berth*, this is Rachel. Mayday! Do you copy?"

Nothing.

She shook it. "This is Rachel. Mayday, mayday. Do you copy?"

The voice of French Culver, the ship's engineer, crackled faintly over the radio. "French here."

She screeched hoarsely. "Had an accident, Frenchie. Took a swim. Run me a bath in the captain's quarters."

"You *what*? Are you serious?"

"Roger that."

"Where are you?"

"Half a mile away. Hurry." She stumbled and almost dropped the radio.

"Damn it, Sullivan! I warned you!"

"Save the sermon."

Her sole chance for survival lay in the body heat she was generating, but she was tiring rapidly. Where was the damn ship? Had she headed in the right direction? The ice was a blank canvas. A faint reflection caught her eye, danced around, and she ran toward it, picking up the pace with her last stores of energy. The speck of black grew larger, the profile of the *Sea Berth*.

Two hundred yards out French met her, running in his long johns and down jacket. She handed him the knapsack without stopping.

"Get these samples into the incubator," she said, gasping.

French stared at her ice-covered body. "Screw the samples."

"Just do it!" she screamed.

Several crew members met her at the boarding ramp, picked her up, and carried her to the captain's quarters, the only room on board with a tub. Justin, the ship's medical officer, had already run a bath. They lowered her in without bothering to remove her clothes, and waited for the water to penetrate and melt the frozen garments. Mary Koch, Rachel's graduate assistant, stayed to help pull off the mukluks and clothes while the others retreated outside.

Soon, Rachel was naked. At first, she could feel nothing and tried to moderate her breathing, preparing for the coming onslaught. It started slowly at first, then picked up speed—a sweeping fire that tore through her flesh as the tepid water warmed frozen skin and tender nerves. She gritted her teeth and let out a low moan.

"Omigod," Mary muttered as she paced around the tub, pulling absently at her fingers. "Omigod."

"Calm down!" Rachel barked, then spewed a stream of curse words that would shame a sailor. She squirmed and twisted against the fiery pain. After a few minutes, the worst of it had passed. With a sigh of relief, she lifted her legs from the water to assess the damage. Blood blisters were popping up at the freeze points between flesh and cloth. Both limbs were as red as a cooked lobster, but it was a deep, *beautiful* red, the sign of healthy circulation. She slumped back in the tub and relaxed for the first time, grateful she could feel pain at all.

"Damn," she said, "my legs were my best assets." She turned excitedly toward Mary. "You wouldn't believe that lava bomb. It was incredible, the size of a truck. The volcano spit it out like a watermelon seed. Strange . . . the penguins sensed it somehow."

"I don't care about some stupid rock," Mary said, whimpering. "You could have died out there!"

"But it would have been a *smashing* adventure."

Mary failed to see the humor. "Rachel, you're crazy!"

"Lighten up, kid," Rachel said, realizing that the poor girl was only twenty. "You'll grow a thicker skin after a few more expeditions."

Justin stepped in to examine her wounds. "Consider yourself lucky, Rachel. A few more minutes—"

"Luck of the Irish, doc. Are my gams going to survive?"

Justin gingerly pressed the raw skin to gauge the rebound. "The frostbite is superficial, only the outer layers of skin. Your constant movement protected the underlying dermis. There shouldn't be any permanent damage."

"Woohoo!" She struck a Vargas pose for Justin, unconcerned with her nakedness.

He frowned. "Quit the clowning and grow up. That was a foolish and reckless stunt. You knew the volcano was off-limits."

After Justin left, Rachel pondered the dullness of an adult life. It didn't sound appealing at all. Her adrenaline high was beginning to fade, replaced by a wave of exhaustion. She sent Mary away, rewarmed the water, leaned her head against the tub, and drifted into a deep sleep.

An hour later, she awoke with a start, shivering. She felt strangely invigorated, as if her brush with death had recharged her batteries. After pulling on some sweats, Rachel gingerly slipped a pair of down booties over her swollen feet. They were incredibly sore, but considering the circumstances, not too bad. She'd done worse before, much worse.

She hobbled toward the lab, shrugging off the crew's offers of assistance. A small crowd had gathered inside, and as she entered, they broke out in scattered applause. She grinned and flashed two fingers in victory.

Someone yelled out, "How many of your nine lives are left?"

"That one didn't count." Rachel giggled. "I'm just running a little hot and cold today."

"Looks like your samples fared better than you did," French remarked, noticing her distinct limp. He pointed toward the incubator. "I hope you're satisfied."

"Thanks, Frenchie. I knew I could count on you." She leaned over the tank and examined the shimmering vials of green and red phytoplankton. The algae seemed to be thriving. She felt a surge of triumph. "You doubters are gonna owe me several rounds of beer soon. Wait and see."

"Rachel, can I speak with you a moment?" Mary Koch had appeared at the doorway, grasping a printout. She motioned Rachel toward her, a look of concern spreading across her face.

Rachel wondered if the poor girl was still upset about her little adventure, but Mary soon grabbed her arm and shuffled her into the radio room.

"You're not still freaking about—"

Mary raised her finger. "It's about Carl."

"About time he answered my e-mails," she said. "Is he making our rendezvous or not?"

"I don't know what to say . . ." Mary wiped her nose on her sleeve. "After what just happened, now this—"

"Spit it out, love. What'd he say?"

She handed Rachel the printout. "It's an e-mail from Carl's department head."

Rachel stared at the sheet, scarcely comprehending. "What does this mean, Carl's *missing*?"

"Five days without a report or e-mail." Mary choked back a sob. "Carl's usually so punctual."

Rachel could feel a new surge of adrenaline. Carl's trip to Honduras had been routine research, almost boring. Geological assays. He'd been e-mailing his research back to NOAA on a daily basis. She thought back to their last conversation a week ago. He seemed ebullient, eager to share some mysterious revelation. Then the e-mails stopped. Consumed with her own research, she hadn't thought much about it at the time . . . but the department head?

If anything, Carl Jameson was meticulous. Rachel suddenly felt a heavy weight pressing her down for a second time. *Not again,* she thought.

"Well then," she finally mustered. "We'll just have to go find him, won't we?"

6

THE LA CEIBA airport was a small, sun-bleached strip of concrete that belied the promising travel brochures: faintly misleading images of khaki-dressed Latins with broad smiles and parasol drinks in hand. A world away from tourist glitz, this facility was spare, utilitarian, and hopelessly impoverished. Honduras was, in fact, one of the poorest countries in Central America.

It was also one of the hottest. As Dan Clifford exited the plane, the notorious heat sucked the oxygen from his lungs. He waited at the rear of the plane's fuselage for the luggage to be unloaded, breathing in an amalgam of torrid air and kerosene fumes as he looked around. In the general aviation area, he spotted several Lears, Gulfstreams, and Mooneys scattered among the older airplanes. Thanks to the Central American Free Trade Agreement, or CAFTA, hints of prosperity had started to edge into the area.

After finding his bags, Dan dragged them toward the customs office, stumbling over grass growing through cracks in the concrete. By the time he reached the cinder-block building, he was drenched in sweat. He showed his passport and entered a long, low pavilion crowded with weary passengers. Ceiling fans turned lackadaisically in the musky air.

It took an hour to advance past the single customs window and into a second room, where attendants stacked his luggage on a long table. A burly soldier with slick black hair worked his way down the line. He stopped at Dan's position, unzipped the bags, and rifled through the items with abandon, leaving behind a mass of clothing and toiletries. After a few cursory passes through the dive bag, the man grunted and waved him toward the exit.

At the curb, Dan knelt to repack his things. A small gang of prepubescent children swarmed around, laughing and grabbing, offering to carry the luggage for a meager tip. He flipped them a few coins and waved them off with a *gracias*. They backed away giggling, as a dented Toyota screeched to a stop next to the curb. A wiry little man jumped out and chased the children farther down the street. *"Buenos días, señor!* You need cab?"

"Sí. Muchas gracias," he answered in halting Spanish, relieved to hear the man speaking English.

The cab driver pitched the luggage into a crumpled trunk, tied the lid down with a piece of rope, and opened the rear door. With a flourish, he beckoned Dan inside the Toyota as if it were a stretch limousine. *"Amigo,* my name is Tito, your *número uno.* I show you the city, no? Go to market? *Beezinose* district? I know good places to buy things. I am your translator, no? I get you the very *best* deals!"

"Gracias, Tito, but no tours today." Dan showed him a NeuroSys business card. Tito nodded and spun the car into traffic, eliciting a chorus of honks and curses. He threaded the cab through a mélange of traffic, mottled with twenty-year-old cars and the occasional mule-drawn cart.

The drive through La Ceiba was like a journey back in time.

Dan had always wondered what became of the old machinery, the factories and assembly lines of outdated products. Here they were, re-incarnated as new Frigidaires and Hoovers, Singer sewing machines, washers with rollers for wringing out clothes, Capri pants and silk scarves, all displayed in drab storefronts with modern price tags. Honduras was living on the hand-me-downs of America's past—a past Dan had worked long and hard to forget.

Tito continued down a dusty street toward the public market area. Vendors' stalls lined the streets, selling all manner of goods, from homemade souvenirs to personal possessions. Marimba bands competed for the attention of tourists. The pungent aroma of roasted corn and *carnitas* transported him back to thrill rides, corn dogs, and side-shows at the Santa Clara county fair in San Jose, and the grip of his father's hand, firm and warm. It was one of his last fond memories of his father.

Before everything turned upside down.

Dan squirmed in his seat as a miasma of horrific images flashed through his mind, as clear and vivid as the day they had occurred: shards of light quivering on a pale surface, desperate screams, choking clouds of dust, smothering blackness. A malignant bolus of panic crept its way up Dan's spine, threatening to overwhelm him with its intensity.

Not now!

Dan drove his fist angrily into the lumpy depths of the Toyota's bench seat. He needed strength, not fear, for the next phase of his trip.

"*Señor,* you okay?" Tito cast a worried glance over his shoulder.

"*Si,* Tito." Dan struggled to regain his voice. "It's nothing. Keep moving."

Dan settled back into the seat and worked through his deep breathing exercises. These attacks had a tendency to show up at the most inopportune times. The loss of his parents at such an early age had burned the memories deep. The images were bad enough, but the emotions that accompanied them were always worse. Of all the emotions, there was one he despised above all others: a desperate sense of helplessness.

The term "post-traumatic stress" was virtually unheard of back in those days, especially when applied to an eight-year-old child. Most doctors wrote off the panic attacks and nightmares as a transient phase, but they were wrong. Even so, the experience had forced Dan to grow up quickly and he soon found solace in anger, where he felt a measure of control.

It had never made him very popular in school or easy to handle.

His aunt had coped as best she could. She even tried taking him back to the fair once, but that youthful phase had passed, pushed out by premature adulthood. There had always been an edgy tension between the two of them, a smoldering resentment—by her, for forced indenture as a surrogate parent—and by him, for the constant reminder of everything he had lost. On his eighteenth birthday, Dan Clifford left California and never returned. He'd spoken to his aunt only a handful of times since, a fact he wasn't proud of. Perhaps on returning home, he would call his aunt and share his news. He owed her as much.

In Georgia, Dan found a measure of peace, pushing the anger under the surface through meditation. He decided that emotions of any sort were vastly overrated. That's when he found another calling: prediction science.

He vowed never again to allow himself to become a victim of fate.

A bump in the road bottomed the car's suspension with a loud squeak. Dan forced his attention back to the current surroundings. Traffic thinned and the pavement gave way to a rutted dirt road that meandered past fallow farmland and rickety shacks, their porches occupied by the old and infirm, rocking listlessly in swings or chairs. Most able-bodied workers were missing, perhaps employed in the nearby factories or on the docks. An occasional new house punctuated the monotony, freshly painted with garish red billboards for Coca-Cola or Pepsi. It seemed that a furious battle was being waged for the hearts and minds of the populace between the old and the new. The effects of CAFTA were evident everywhere.

A few minutes later, the washboard road turned into shiny black asphalt and the Toyota became noticeably quieter. Tito turned right, down a corridor of chain-link fences. The fallow farmland beyond the fences had reverted to a wild state, cheap acreage owned by American conglomerates, destined for future development.

Dan leaned forward. "How much further, Tito?"

"Very soon."

Relieved to be back in control, Dan reviewed his strategy. The visit to the assembly plant had been a calculated risk. It had to appear spontaneous and unplanned. The only vacation spot he could find nearby was a small diving resort off the coast. The premise was a bit contrived, but everyone at work knew of his penchant for scuba diving.

Dan was pissed at the need for contrivance at all. As director of the GAPS project, he should have been informed of the plant's progress. The reason for all the secrecy had been gnawing at him.

He thought back to the early days of NeuroSys, when he'd been a young meteorologist working at NOAA. He took training in predictive analytics and complexity science at the Santa Fe Institute. That's when he first envisioned the GAPS program. It began as one simple question: Could natural disasters be predicted? If so, then no family would ever have to endure the agony he had experienced, just for the want of a little advance knowledge.

Dan knew then that GAPS would become his life's work. He garnered the help of NOAA's programming prodigy Rudi Plimpton, and together they developed the first GAPS prototype. It didn't really predict black swan events. Not exactly. Nothing could. Life was just too complex. But GAPS could *imagine* them and calculate the odds of their occurrence, which had the effect of alerting humans to the dangers of the unforeseen.

Unfortunately, the GAPS program required a level of processing power that didn't exist at the time. Dan hunted down a scientist at DARPA, Neal Johnston, who had invented the first scalable 3-D computer chip. Stacked eight layers thick, the chip's logic and memory layers alternated like ham and cheese on a sandwich. The 3-D architecture vastly increased processing power by eliminating the bottlenecks caused by data pipelines.

Dan immediately saw the chip's potential to emulate the neurons of a human brain. He shared this insight with Neal, and a few months later, the world's first "NeuroChip" was born. Neal founded NeuroSys, hiring Dan and Rudi Plimpton to develop and sell its products.

Those early days were filled with promise. A team of young NeuroSys prodigies toiled long hours in an old warehouse on the south side of Atlanta. That melting pot of talent refined GAPS and created several innovative robotics projects based on Neal's NeuroChip.

Everyone wore several hats. Dan inked research contracts with several government agencies. But sales quickly exceeded production of the complex 3-D chip, which had to be outsourced to existing semiconductor firms for fabrication. Needing investment capital, Neal reached out to angel investors.

That's when hell began.

The investors felt the company needed a younger, more dynamic president, suggesting Sonny Swyft. Neal Johnston reluctantly agreed, retiring to a position on the board in anticipation of the NeuroSys IPO.

It didn't take long for Sonny to fill NeuroSys with a cadre of petulant wannabes with big hat sizes and little real-world experience. The creative prodigies began to quit or were laid off. In months, product quality dropped, technical support waned, and deadlines were missed.

Dan complained to the board and was "rewarded" with a demotion to "Director of the GAPS program." Not long after, Sonny outsourced fabrication to this new facility in Honduras. It had taken less than a year to transform NeuroSys from a vibrant pool of talent to a den of profit-seeking bandits.

Dan would likely find the new assembly plant in disarray. Perhaps he could turn things around, confront the board. It seemed the only way to save the GAPS contract and perhaps rid the company of Sonny Swyft.

If he had spent more time in the boardroom, Dan might be the president instead of Sonny. If he'd been more political, befriended the board members . . . but then, that would have taken him away from GAPS.

Old Ben Proudfoot was right: You *always* have a choice . . . but making the right one?

THE TOYOTA TOPPED a slight rise. Three hundred yards ahead the road ended at a guardhouse. Beyond it, a white domed structure loomed over the surrounding forest. The dome's base was ringed with a necklace of small round windows that gave it the appearance of a UFO. It was a surreal sight, especially from a distance. The structure was at least the size of a football stadium.

Far too large to be the NeuroSys plant.

"Is this it?" Dan murmured. "This can't be . . ."

"*Sí, sí.* Is the *nooroseez* plant," Tito said proudly. "My daughter, she work there."

A couple of guards approached, waving their arms. "No entrance! Go back!" Tito smiled at them innocently. "I have a *veezitore.* Big honcho from America."

Dan held out his NeuroSys ID. The guard studied the picture suspiciously. "We weren't expecting anyone today. You're from the Atlanta office?"

"Yeah," Dan replied nonchalantly. "Sorry for the surprise. It was spur of the moment."

"Hold on." The man disappeared into the guardhouse, returned a few minutes later, and handed Dan back his ID. "Welcome to NeuroSys South," he said, smiling. "Sorry for the excess security, Mr. Clifford. Company policy. Mr. Adler will meet you in the lobby."

"No problem, just doing your job."

The gate opened and Tito drove through. *"Es muy grande, eh, señor?"* Tito grinned over his shoulder, displaying a mouthful of jagged teeth. "Tito's daughter make *mucho dinero!*"

As they approached the front entrance, the domed structure

loomed ever larger. Dan spotted the manager of the NeuroSys Robotics Lab, Harry Adler, standing just outside the front door. He was tall
and muscular, with an old-fashioned handlebar mustache kept perfectly waxed. The mustache contrasted with his head, which was as
bald as a cue ball. Harry was once part of the NeuroSys core, back
before the "fall."

"Dan Clifford!" Harry's eyes sparkled with recognition. "You
know how to catch a guy off guard. How's Rover?"

"Humming like Rin Tin Tin, thanks to you."

"Nice pun," Harry said, laughing. "You're the last person I expected to see here."

"Sorry about the surprise. I'm heading to the Bay Islands for scuba
diving and thought I'd drop by."

Harry grinned. "Well, you missed Tomás. He's in western Honduras negotiating with a supplier."

What incredible luck, Dan thought. Tomás Martin was the plant
manager hired by the angel investors. The man's background was
a mystery, but Harry, on the other hand, was an old friend. If there
were production problems, Dan knew Harry would be incapable of
hiding the truth.

"I came to see you anyway." Dan's attention returned to the building. "What *is* this place? I've got to see the inside."

"Well, I usually hide in robotics, but I can give you the nickel tour."

After cursory introductions, Harry ushered him past the recep-
tionist and up a long flight of stairs to a suspended gangway. Clad in
glass, it encircled the entire open interior of the dome. Dan was dumbfounded by the sheer scale of the place. Beneath them, a maze of
hallways, cubicles, assembly lines, and fabrication rooms crowded the
enclosure like a miniature city.

"Impressive, huh?" Harry beamed. "It's state of the art. The entire
floor below is a class 10 ultraclean environment. The administrative
offices are up on this level, sealed with negative air pressure, so the execs
don't have to work in bunny suits. Tomás sits up here and watches the
action from his skybox like a mythical god."

Harry pointed toward a steel-trussed frame at the near end of the
dome, looking like a miniature Eiffel Tower. Suspended from long
steel cables, an access ramp connected the tower's apex to an air lock
door near their current location. "That's the circuit camera," Harry

said. "See the open area directly underneath? We're plotting a new rendering of the NeuroChip. It's as big as a basketball court with more circuits than the streets of New York City. The camera at the top shrinks the image down to the size of a postage stamp." Harry started strolling along the gangway, pointing things out as they walked. "Those are the oven rooms, where we cook the silicon rods. What comes out is 99.9999 percent pure semiconductor."

Dan could see six-foot rods of silicon dangling from chains like a row of giant salamis, their grayish metal gleaming in the bright lights.

"And those are the photoresist rooms where we etch the circuitry." Harry stopped and noted a ring of showers and eye washers. "In case of chemical spills—we use nasty stuff here—hydrofluoric acid, phosphene, arsine. If it gets on you, it'll eat you through from the inside out. After the chips are etched, they're doped with copper and gold alloys. Then we stack 'em eight layers thick, over there." He pointed toward an arched tunnel resembling a greenhouse. Inside, a line of workers covered head to toe in white bunny suits worked both sides of a long assembly line, their hands undulating in rhythm like the legs of a giant centipede.

Harry continued around the gangway to a miniature dome-within-the-dome, flanked by several guards in yellow bunny suits. "We call that the mothership's progeny," he said, laughing. "Baby dome. That's where all the experimental stuff gets birthed. Tomás keeps that place bottled up tighter than a hundred-year-old Bordeaux. Even I can't get in there."

By the time they had encircled the dome and returned to their starting point, Dan was ready to burst. This went far beyond the humble plant that was supposed to assemble components from outside suppliers. He felt a sense of awe tinged with anger.

Sonny Swyft had been keeping a very big secret.

He moved into Harry's comfort zone. "What the hell is going on here? I thought we were still *assembling* chips, not manufacturing them."

Harry held up his hands defensively. "Whoa! I don't understand. Haven't you—"

"Have you heard about the NOAA deal?"

Harry's face broke into a grin. "Yeah, we're in the big time. They told us last week."

"Last *week*?" Dan was stupefied. The sales presentation had been a charade. "Simple question. Can we handle the output?"

"Definitely! We're running three eight-hour shifts a day. Robotics came online faster than we anticipated, thanks to the influx of raw materials. We're using dual NeuroChips in the newer robots. They make Rover look like a dimwit. We're testing some new chips that will blow your mind." He patted Dan on the back. "Relax, my friend. We'll make the NOAA delivery. No problem."

"Where did Sonny get the capital for this operation?"

"You don't know?" Harry's eyebrows shot up. "I guess I let the cat out of the bag, then." He leaned closer. "Look, Tomás keeps a tight lid on security, but I had no idea you were out of the loop. So, you didn't hear this from me, okay? Sonny and Tomás negotiated some sweetheart CAFTA deal with the Honduran government and some bigwig angel investor. This place is worth about two billion, to be paid off after the IPO."

"But that's *fraud,* Harry," Dan said. "Enron stuff. Off-balance-sheet accounting. I've looked at the prospectus. There's nothing about a manufacturing plant, or a CAFTA deal, or anything! The SEC will be all over this."

Harry's exuberant mood deflated. "Hey, I don't know the details. Maybe the SEC knows already. It's CAFTA, man. They've programmed in all kinds of political loopholes. The bigwigs sure don't act worried." Harry's smile returned as he laid a hand on Dan's shoulder. "Look, I know you're not crazy about Sonny, but I think he pulled it off this time. Our production is way ahead of schedule. Soon, we'll be toasting the IPO. Hey, did you know you can buy islands off the coast here, cheap?"

Dan smiled weakly. "I'm glad to hear it."

7

Squeak . . squeak . . . *squeak.*

The Toyota's springs grated like fingernails on a blackboard at every bump in the road. Dan was buzzing with anger, confusion, and a grudging respect. How had Sonny done it? Microchip plants required a year for construction, which meant this deal had been in place since Sonny arrived at NeuroSys. Dan didn't buy Harry's explanation of a sweetheart investor, or the crap about CAFTA and the Honduran government.

What would prompt an investor to risk two billion dollars on a small, struggling company? A meteoric rise in NeuroSys stock would do it, perhaps. But it would be risky, unless you could be assured of a deal the size of the NOAA contract. That explained Senator Becker's behavior. Becker's involvement might also explain why the Securities and Exchange Commission wasn't poking around.

However done, it was a brilliant piece of backroom diplomacy. Dan's jaw clenched. He wanted to head home and confront Sonny, but he couldn't. He had to finish the ruse. That meant flying to the resort for a week's vacation.

Squeak . . . squeak . . . *squeak.*

The NOAA contract seemed safe. No broken promises, no failed delivery, a first for Sonny. GAPS would happen. The board would be happy; the *world* would be better for it.

Everything should be wonderful. *So why am I so pissed?*

Dan knew why. He'd been blindsided, so focused on GAPS that Sonny's scheme had slipped by unnoticed for a year. Now, he had become an unwitting partner in this whole nasty business, forced into Sonny's conspiracy of deceit. The thought made him sick. Still, the GAPS deal was more important than his pride. The prudent plan was to move forward and hope that the IPO made it through without excess media exposure.

A sudden laugh burst from his lips. What if he had invited Jenifer Coleman along? At least some of his instincts were intact . . .

Squeak . . . squeak . . . *squeak!*

Tito turned the Toyota south, away from the main airport and toward La Ceiba's general aviation area. They stopped alongside an ancient prop-driven taildragger stripped of its paint, the aluminum fuselage gleaming in the afternoon sun. Dan recognized it as an old Douglas DC-3, granddaddy of commercial transports built in the thirties. The possibility of flying in such an antique airplane piqued his curiosity and helped push the chip factory out of his mind. In its heyday, the DC-3 had a reputation as the safest plane in the world, although he wasn't so sure about this particular one. Two fat radial engines dripped oil all over the pavement.

He helped Tito unload the bags and paid his fare with a generous tip. Two young Honduran pilots barely out of puberty grabbed the luggage and stuffed it into a compartment near the tail, then signaled for passengers to board.

Dan clambered through a small door at the rear and balked at the sight of the cramped enclosure. He slid into a window seat near the tail and tried to think of anything but NeuroSys. Most of the other passengers looked like locals, with a smattering of fair-skinned tourists, all overflowing the seats with carry-on bags, boat parts, groceries, and dive equipment. One man carried a leg of some unidentifiable animal wrapped in old newspapers.

A sweaty businessman in a white suit squeezed into the seat next to him, his fleshy arm pressing against Dan's torso. Pinned in the corner, he could feel the familiar press of walls closing in around him. The hot snake of panic slithered up his spine. It spread quickly to his chest and tightened. Fresh beads of sweat erupted on his brow.

Cursing silently, he focused on the large propellers outside the plane. *Slow, rhythmic breathing, count from ten to one, think of a cool breeze, a light and airy place.* He rested his head against the window, squeezed his eyes shut, and waited for the plane to move.

Almost on cue, the hatches slammed shut and the two Pratt & Whitney engines sprang to life, throbbing through the airframe. The old DC-3 quickly gained speed, taxied toward the end of the runway, turned, and roared down the concrete. "That was quick," he muttered aloud, relieved by the sudden gust of fresh air flowing through the ventilators.

"That's because we have to make Guanaja before dark," came a voice from the seat ahead.

A spindly woman with short gray hair popped up over the seat back. "No runway lights on the island," she said. "In fact, no runway *at all*. They use the beach, it's *loads* of fun." She grinned devilishly and extended her hand. "Hi. Iris Silverstein, and this is my husband, Benjamin." Benjamin peered over the seat and nodded.

Dan wiped his hand on his pants and returned the handshake. "Did you say . . . land on the beach?"

"Oh, don't worry, honey. We've made this trip oodles of times and we haven't crashed yet." She giggled. "We're both retired dentists, sick of old teeth. We've been escaping here for years. You'll *love* it."

"It's my first trip," he said. "I hope it lives up to its reputation."

"Oh yes, you won't be disappointed. It's very exclusive, *gorgeous*. We've been coming here for . . . oh, I've said that already, haven't I? But I *do* ramble on, I must be boring you."

He managed a smile. "Not at all. It's nice to meet some veterans."

"Oh, and did I mention the owner? Such a gentleman!" Benjamin tugged at her arm. She flashed him an annoyed look. "You'll see soon enough."

THEY REACHED THE island of Guanaja just as the sun dipped below the horizon. The DC-3 banked left and made a quick pass over the beach checking for debris, then lined up for final approach. Just as Iris had predicted, there were no runway lights, only faint puddles of orange light spilling from the windows of nearby buildings. The engines revved back and the flaps rumbled into position. A river of sand flowed beneath them and the balloon tires hit the beach with a satisfying thump.

Dan was out the door practically before the plane had rolled to a stop.

Once outside, he was struck by the contrast between Guanaja and the barren mainland. It was a verdant paradise. He took in the island's symphony of sights, sounds, and smells. An assortment of fruity aromas drifted from a group of banana trees to his left, where a chorus of parrots squawked gaily among the rustling leaves. Fishing boats slapped lazily against a wooden dock as the locals scurried into their transportation for the commute home. The air blew moist and cool here, melting away his frustration. He suddenly felt glad to have kept his appointment with the island. It would be a grand escape from computers, cell phones, cars, and the general chaos of modern life.

Just what he needed.

The pilots rushed to unload the baggage and depart while a hint of sunlight remained. In what seemed like a matter of minutes, the docks emptied. Iris tugged at his arm and gestured toward the one remaining cruiser tied at the pier. "That's our ride."

Upon their approach, the shadow of a tall, athletic-looking man appeared at the bow. As he ambled toward them, hands in pockets, Dan got a better look. The man appeared to be in his late sixties with a distinctive European air, sporting a neatly trimmed salt and pepper goatee. But what caught Dan's eye was the man's peculiar dress: woolen driving hat canted smartly to one side of a receding hairline, brightly colored tropical shirt, khaki shorts, and a pair of sandals over white socks. It was strangely comical. Dan liked him immediately.

"A wonderful evening to you all!" the gentleman exclaimed with a deep and melodic Irish brogue. "Welcome to Palacio del Sol, the jewel of the Honduran coast. I'm Duff McAlister, your host." He hugged Iris gently. "Welcome back, dearie. You too, Ben."

"My, my," Iris said, patting his cheek. "Don't you look dapper tonight, Mr. McAlister. Isn't that so, Ben?"

Ben nodded.

Duff turned to Dan. "And you are?"

"Dan Clifford."

"Ah, yes." Duff studied him with a paternal air. "You're here alone?"

Dan shrugged and grinned. "I like to travel light."

"A dapper young man with no lassie?"

"I was hoping to find an island beauty. The chief's daughter perhaps."

Duff's eyes lit up. "Ah, unfortunately the chief's daughter is an ugly wench. No matter. We'll find you a fetching young mermaid perhaps." Duff grinned as he headed back toward the dock. "We have a short boat ride to the south side of the island. So, let's hurry! We shan't want to miss the spectacular sunset." Duff helped them load their luggage on board the cruiser, aptly named *Little Diver,* then cranked up the engine and maneuvered out into the bay.

"Ladies and gents, Guanaja is a twin volcanic island forged from the fertile breasts of Mother Earth," Duff exclaimed with a wave of his arm. "Christopher Columbus visited here in 1502 and discovered the Payan Indians, a noble and industrious people. They welcomed their new visitors with open arms. Their descendants still do the same today, even for miserable wretches like myself."

Duff McAlister had a certain way with words that reminded Dan of Ben Proudfoot. He listened with amusement as they motored along the edge of shadowed slopes. Duff steered the craft around a tall point of rock, revealing a magnificent bay that stretched across the horizon, twinkling with lights from a hundred windows that seemed to hover over the water. As they passed, Dan realized that the huts were built on stilts.

"Bonacca Town," Duff continued. "We call it the Venice of the Caribbean. And beyond . . ." Duff made a theatrical wave across a brilliant vermilion sunset that framed the town like a postcard. Tracking the eyes of his guests, Duff twitched his eyebrows. "Lads and lassies, if you think this is beautiful, wait till you see the wonders awaiting you tomorrow beneath the sea."

AFTER REACHING THE resort, Dan checked in at the front desk and headed to his bungalow. The room was spacious and light, appointed with teak and mahogany furnishings and white tile floors. Large slats covering the windows were angled to shade the afternoon sun. Two ceiling fans pushed cooling breezes through the room. It was no Hilton, but it managed a simple elegance. He took a quick shower, slipped into a tropical shirt, shorts, and sandals, and headed out for the evening.

The dining hall was a frenzy of culinary activity. Dan realized he was one of the last guests to arrive, because a throng of vacationers crowded a buffet line brimming with island fare. He was starving, both for food and companionship. Iris, Ben, and Duff waved from the far corner. After passing down the buffet, he joined Duff at his table, where he was introduced to another couple, Gary and Camille Anderson, newlyweds from New York.

After wolfing down a generous portion of pescada a la plancha, Dan turned to Duff. "You've got a wonderful place here. How did you happen to find it? You don't exactly sound like you're from around here."

Duff cracked open a crab claw with the dexterity of a surgeon. "I stumbled onto this paradise ten years ago while on vacation. I was a commercial diver for twenty-five years in the Alaskan oil fields. When you work in a canvas suit for hours, in water colder than a well digger's ass . . . well, you daydream a lot about sunny beaches and white sand." He pulled the claw apart, extracted a lump of succulent white flesh, and dipped it into melted garlic butter. "Bought it from the original landowner. Did you know we're sitting on the second largest barrier reef in the world?"

"And is there a Mrs. McAlister?"

"Heavens, no! My heart belongs to Mother Nature. I owe the ole gal for all the havoc I caused her on the oil platforms. I spend my days sharing old stories with beautiful lassies like Camille and Iris here."

"Oh, don't believe a word he says," Iris said with a wink, "unless Mother Nature is a blonde with a generous bust line." She laid her hand on Dan's arm in a motherly gesture. "And what's a strapping young man like yourself doing here all alone?"

This was going to be a stubborn topic, he decided. "I'm visiting on business. I work for a computer firm called NeuroSys."

Duff's left eyebrow shot up. "You work for that flying saucer over in La Ceiba?"

"No, the corporate headquarters in Atlanta."

His expression hardened. "Pardon me for saying so, but that's the kind of exploitation the Hondurans can do without."

Duff's abrupt comment caught Dan by surprise. "I would think any new industry would be welcome here. The standard of living seems to be improving."

"*Humph.* Pollution has skyrocketed since you and your CAFTA buddies showed up. After dinner I'll show you some pictures of the effects, if you're interested."

"By all means," Dan replied.

By late evening, the festivities had moved across the hall to the bar, a cozy room large enough for twenty people if they were close friends. Hundreds of pictures lined the walls, some of inebriated guests, but mostly of marine animals and fish. Duff led Dan around the room, stopping at each photo to describe the location and sea life. He paused next to one pair of prints. "See these? They were taken by Iris two years apart." He pointed to the first one, filled with vividly colored fan corals, anemones, and barrel sponges. Then he traced the identical outline on the second photograph, its colors faded to a ghostly white.

"Coral bleaching," Duff said. "New industries are sprouting like weeds. There's a textile mill, some other high-tech companies, a mining operation."

Dan smiled politely, not wanting to come across as argumentative. "Actually, most coral bleaching is caused by warmer water temperatures and ocean acidification."

"I don't think so. The changes have come on so quickly—"

"Are you guys going to talk tech all night?" Iris Silverstein grabbed Duff and Dan by the arms and guided them toward the bar. "What about one of those special brews of yours?"

"And indeed, the woman's right." Duff laughed, his mood changing. "I'm being a poor host." He shouted to the bartender: "Port Royal for our guests." He leaned in, as if sharing a valued secret. "After World War Two, this area became a haven for the Bavarian brewing art, if you know what I mean." He winked. "These old Germans know how to brew a fine stein of Mother's Ruin." Duff hoisted his mug toward the group. "Another week, another group of wonderful guests. To you all, I offer an old Irish toast. *May ye have a wet mouth, long life, and die in Paradise.*"

Everyone raised their drinks and roared in approval.

After several more rounds and numerous Irish toasts, the crowd began to thin. A little after midnight, Iris and Ben ran out of steam and headed for their bungalow, leaving Duff and Dan alone to entertain the bartender.

". . . and you think these companies are the root of all evil?" Dan said, lisping slightly.

"I think they're polluting the environment *and* the wholesome nature of these people."

Dan laughed. "You make the locals sound like house pets. You keep saying we're victimizing them, but when I look around, I see prosperity inching in."

Duff slugged another brew. "There's more to life than money and possessions."

"Yeah, unless you don't have any."

Duff's expression grew solemn, his voice dropping to a whisper. "When I worked the oil fields, I saw enough corruption to give me nightmares for life. Oil-soaked otters and gulls rotting in rancid cesspools; payoffs to local politicians. The Gulf oil spill was the last straw. An entire way of life snuffed out for a few extra miles in a Hummer. We're lucky the spill didn't make its way down to this neck of the woods. I owe a lot of restitution to ole Mother Earth. Give the human race a tool and they'll always build a coffin."

"So man's the enemy, right?"

"That's right," Duff slurred. "With brains and a conscience. That makes us cul-a-pul-a-ble, ah *crap*, guilty!"

"But we can use our brains to fix things too. That's *my* job."

Duff slapped Dan hard on the back, almost causing him to chip a tooth on his mug. "Know what? I like you, Clifford! You got spunk. But you're naive if you think your bosses wouldn't sell their souls for a buck."

He wasn't that naive. Sonny Swyft would sell his *mother's* soul for a buck. A horrible thought occurred to him. What if Duff was right? Harry Adler had pointed out that the chip factory used some of the most toxic chemicals imaginable. Where did they end up afterward? It was a question he'd have to check into back in Atlanta.

8

BERTO ENRIQUE FLICKED the butt of his cigarette over the gunwale.
The sun still lingered below the horizon, drenching the fog with a
greenish glow. It was dangerous to be speeding across the bay at such
an early hour, but he had every reason to think it a necessity. His
young lieutenant knew better than to call so early, waking the *niños*
and worrying the wife, unless there was a true emergency.

This incident didn't seem to qualify. As chief of Harbor Patrol for
the city of La Ceiba, Berto was accustomed to finding abandoned
boats left over from hijackings, drug runs, or revenge killings. Drug
lords usually had the common sense to scuttle them, destroying any
trace of evidence, but occasionally a vessel refused to sink, drifting for
days or weeks. Fishermen would have nothing to do with such ships.
They were considered bad luck of the worst kind.

Hector was Berto's most able lieutenant, and his rookie behavior
bothered the old man. This had better be good. A sudden lurch
prompted Berto to grab at the gunwale. At twenty knots, the cigar boat
bucked like a bull. It ran smoother at seventy, but that kind of speed
would be suicide in the fog. He loved this boat, one of the few fringe
benefits of drug seizures. The drug runners definitely had good taste:
twin eight-hundred-horsepower Mercruisers, turbocharged, thirty-
eight feet of unadulterated speed. Even with the fog, he should be back
by lunch, perhaps for a tryst with the wife before the *niños* returned
from school. Berto slid farther into the seat and turned his collar to
the wind. Even in Honduras, the early-morning temperatures and humidity could chill one to the bone.

He cranked up the volume of his personal stereo in a vain attempt
to drown out the whine of the Mercruisers. The marvelous vibrato of
Luciano Pavarotti filled his ears. "The Flower Song" from *Carmen*.
Absolute perfection. In the world of Honduran thieves, murderers,

whores, drugs, and hopelessness, the operatic splendor of his beloved tenors lifted him far above the filth of day-to-day affairs. The opera represented a world of flawless melody and lyric ruled by love, passion, and heartache. Someday he would travel to the United States and visit the famous Metropolitan Opera.

Thirty minutes later, the pilot slowed the engines and Berto roused himself from his reverie to check the GPS. They were eighty miles offshore, too far out for fishing vessels. He squinted through the mist at a shadowy derelict bobbing in the chop. It appeared to be a shrimp junker—the kind of old trawler passed down from family to family and rerigged endlessly. Even from a distance, Berto could tell it was in disastrous shape, a floating miracle. A dragline ran from the junker to Hector's patrol boat. Berto stared for a moment, but saw no movement on either vessel.

"Where the hell is everyone?" Berto shouted into the radio. "Come back."

Slowly, a silhouette peeked over the patrol boat's bow.

"I repeat . . . Hector, anybody, answer me, damn it!"

A voice, not Hector's, trembled through the radio. "There's no one on board the shrimper alive, sir. Our men . . . they refuse to board her. The crew's gone. It's like . . . we should just leave now."

"Leave? I just got here, you idiot!"

The cigar boat's momentum carried it alongside the shrimper and two of Berto's men scurried about, hanging fenders over the side, careful to avoid scratching the expensive fiberglass hull. The two boats bumped gently and the crewmen lashed them together with spring lines. When the engines shut down, an eerie silence fell over the gloom. The only sounds came from the water lapping against the hulls, the creaks and groaning of wood, the clang of rigging. Berto aimed a high-powered spotlight across the shrimper's beam.

Doncella Hermosa.

He knew that name. She belonged to the Ortega family. They all crewed it—brothers, uncles, nephews—anyone old enough to handle a net. A large red eye had been painted on the bow alongside her name, a symbol meant to stand eternal vigil against the demons of the deep. The makeshift bowsprit carried a figurehead carved in the likeness of *Nuestra Señora de Guadalupe,* lashed there to bless the waters before her wake.

Berto chuckled nervously. The Ortegas sure weren't taking any chances, spiritually at least. Panning the light slowly across the deck, he saw no evidence of activity. It seemed as if Hector had done little more than wait for him to arrive. They were all behaving like old women. Perhaps the fog had spooked them, or maybe they'd been drinking.

"Put Hector on," Berto commanded into the radio.

"Hector's sick, sir."

"Sick?"

"He's dizzy and has a headache."

"Dizzy? What kind of excuse is that? Maybe I should come over and tuck him into bed, sing him a lullaby, no?" Berto threw the mike down, jumped to the shrimper's deck, and signaled for his men to follow. "Follow me, *ladies*," he shouted. Reluctantly, the two officers followed.

The Ortegas had rigged the trawler with winches and a crane for hauling in the nets. The aft hold was empty, but the hull listed toward the bow. Berto stepped gingerly through the slime and aimed for the foredeck. A quick check revealed a full load of shrimp rotting in the forward hold.

Methodically working his way back toward the stern, Berto panned his light in wide arcs. No bodies, no bullet holes, no signs of robbery or looting. It seemed as if the crew had abandoned their catch and just disappeared into thin air.

"*¿Jefe?*" a nervous voice came from behind him. He turned as one of his men nodded slightly, directing a flashlight along the seam between deck and hull. Berto leaned down close, and trained his own light at the spot. Three fingers, severed just above the knuckle, lay white and bloodless in the crack.

Berto swallowed hard and ran the light under the railing. There were several smears of blood and what looked like a handprint. He turned back to the fingers. A hijacking perhaps, but why? This vessel contained nothing of value except shrimp, and here they still were, rotting away.

He stepped into the wheelhouse, careful to avoid disturbing potential evidence. A nice lighted compass and shiny new fishing sonar lay undisturbed on a makeshift shelf under the dash. Directly behind him, the door to the mess creaked open. Berto stiffened as he caught the unmistakable smell of death, familiar to any policeman, an odor that easily overwhelmed the rotting shrimp. And there was another aroma, faint—one distinctly out of context—that Berto strained to place.

A subtle fragrance of roses.

He transferred the light to his other hand and groped for his .38 revolver. His fingers closed around the handle and caressed the knurled surface. His attention was heightened, yet he felt strangely dissociated from the moment, more like a spectator than a participant. Slowly, he nudged the door open with his foot and panned the light across the shadows.

The putrid stench left him gasping for air, forcing him to breathe through his mouth. Plates of food were scattered on the floor around a crude table. Sprawled across the table was the body of a man he recognized as Mauricio Ortega. Knife wounds covered the torso and a long slit ran from groin to throat, like the deveining of a shrimp. Hesitantly, Berto moved farther into the room for a better look. He was hyperventilating and had to coax himself to stay calm. He had seen worse before . . . maybe.

In the right corner beyond the table, the light's beam edged up another body.

It was Paulo, Mauricio's son, or so he thought. The body lay slumped and lifeless, drenched in blood, a knife resting in the lap. The face was mutilated, shreds of flesh torn away. Paulo's distorted expression was frozen in mock surprise, his hands cupped around his cheeks, his fingers digging into the skin.

The sickly sweet stench poured over him like a fog. To Berto's horror, his feet seemed anchored to the deck, his arms rigid. A loud squeal burst from the center of the room, a sound he realized had come from within his throat. Then he heard other voices, a thousand lost souls chanting a dirge, a death choir. He could hear his own breathing, coarse and hollow, echoing against the walls. The *walls* were breathing, heaving in and out, sucking the air from his lungs. Berto dropped the light and covered his ears. Trails of blood seemed to stream from every crack and crevice in endless spirals, swirling downward into a turbulent eddy, dragging him down toward a bottomless pit.

Get out, get out, get out!

He threw himself backward into the wheelhouse, his head slamming against the boat's wheel as he groped frantically to haul himself up. Bursting from the doorway, he fell into the arms of his startled men.

"God help me!" he cried. "Pull me out!"

They stared in astonishment. "What do you mean, sir?"

Don't they see the pit?

Berto tore away, stumbled madly across the deck, and thrust his head over the side. Vomit spewed from his mouth, choking him as it came up. A white-hot pain shot through his head and he tried to hold still, but his trembling hands could barely grasp the rail.

After a few minutes, the spinning ebbed and Berto began to feel the deck steady beneath his feet. He strained to make sense of the horrific visions that still swirled inside his head. He'd always approached even the most bloody scenes of violence with professional detachment, but now . . . he felt befuddled, confused. Only one absolute surety stood clear above all others.

In the pit, he was certain that he had felt the lick of Satan upon his face.

He whipped around. "Burn it!" he cried.

His men stood transfixed, too frightened to move. "Sir?"

"Burn it! Burn the whole cursed boat . . . *now!*"

9

MORNING BROUGHT DAN a hangover and dim memories of the night before. He rubbed the sleep from his eyes, got out of bed, and peeked out the bungalow door. He stepped into the morning sun and almost tripped over a tray of assorted fruit, coffee, and pastries. He grabbed a Danish, nibbled on it gingerly, and took in his surroundings. In the darkness of the previous evening, he'd been unable to appreciate the sheer scale of the mountainside. Behind the resort, volcanic cliffs shot skyward, their steep sides blanketed with purple and orange bougainvilleas winding lazily up the trunks of mango, almond, and palm trees. A silvery waterfall plummeted down the cliff face and disappeared under the resort's raised deck. It was an intimate space, filled with dining tables shaded by grass thatch umbrellas and encircled by the resort's thirty-odd cabins.

Closing his eyes, he inhaled the deep floral aroma. GAPS had consumed his attention for far too long. Life felt simpler here, yet somehow more complete. He resolved to enjoy every minute of it until it was time to return to the corporate world.

Several diners were gaping at him. He glanced down, embarrassed to realize he was wearing only underwear. Grinning sheepishly, he slipped back inside to change for the day's dive.

PALACIO DEL SOL was an intimate location, but its scuba facilities rivaled those of much larger resorts, thanks to Duff's careful attention. Dan exited the resort and traipsed across a fine, white sand beach toward the dive center where he was surprised to find the *Little Diver*'s much larger cousin, the forty-two-foot *Spanish Diver,* dominating the dock. It had been extensively customized for diving, with a low stern that allowed easy access to the water. Bench seats lined both sides, flanked by tubular racks holding the compressed-air tanks.

Duff introduced Dan to Pepé and Mañuel, the two dive assistants, who nodded, then quickly returned to their task of assembling the guests' buoyancy compensators, tanks, and regulators. Under an awning amidships, the other guests were already wriggling into wet suits, unpacking camera gear, or cleaning masks. Dan joined them and began to unpack his mask, snorkel, and fins.

Duff moved to the helm, wearing a black wet suit peeled down to his waist. His ever-present woolen riding cap had been pulled low and tight against the wind. After a quick body count, Duff started the engines and pushed the throttle forward. *Spanish Diver* pulled away from the dock at a rapid clip.

TWENTY MINUTES LATER, Duff checked the GPS, backed off the throttle, and signaled Pepé to drop anchor. Activity picked up. Dan wiped antifog solution in his mask and watched the newlyweds Gary and Camille adjust color-coordinated fins, masks, and snorkels. Ever on guard for the fashion police, Camille had chosen to forego a dive suit, letting her bikini highlight a curvaceous figure. Iris and Ben unpacked myriad lights, cameras, and camcorders from their dive bag, enough equipment to start a movie studio. It amazed Dan that the Silversteins could swim at all with such a formidable inventory. He imagined them sinking to the bottom in a tangled web of cords and straps.

Duff commanded everyone's attention. "We're diving Dolly's Peak today, a reef pinnacle that rises steeply from the seabed sixteen hundred feet below. It's part of the Sierra de Omoa mountain chain, an underwater range rivaling the Rockies in grandeur. We'll swim counterclockwise around the peak. With a bit of Irish luck, we may see a friendly pod of dolphins."

That prompted a chorus of oohs and aahs.

"Make sure to follow dolphin etiquette. Hands off. The males tend to get amorous with the lassies. Just relax and don't panic. Watch for one dolphin with rust-colored skin and a propeller scar on the top of his head. That's Adolpho, our local Don Juan." After he signaled everyone else to enter the water, Duff approached Dan. "I'll be your dive buddy today. Just stay within eyesight."

On Duff's cue, Dan jumped overboard, fins first. Bubbles tickled his skin, then, a feeling of freedom and weightlessness. Through the sparkling clear water, he could see the seamount two hundred feet away. Duff had already opened a lead twenty feet ahead, trailing a school of yellowtails. Dan pursued with long, powerful strokes, delighted to find his sea legs. The old motor skills came back quickly, and soon he was alongside, signaling for an equipment check. Duff flashed an okay sign.

The seamount was expansive, its narrow tip encrusted with a fluorescent canopy of anemones and corals down to about fifty feet. An explosion of life filled every nook and cranny: a rainbow of red gorgonian corals, purple tube sponges, black crinoid coral.

He exhaled to lower his buoyancy and slipped downward. A forest of azure barrel sponges clung to the side of the mount. It was mating season, and large white clouds of sperm spewed from their tops like smoke from a furnace. The cloud coalesced like smog and drifted out across the reef, soon disturbed by a school of sparkling silversides that darted past, turning and twisting in perfect unison. Grouping behavior, Dan mused. Complexity at work. A few feet ahead, a stoplight parrotfish with its distinctive blue-green stripes and parrot-like lip markings hovered under an outcropping of fan coral, scraping algae from the surface for an afternoon meal.

There was a flash of movement at the edge of his peripheral vision as a mass of metal, bubbles, and straps thrashed by. Iris Silverstein was so focused on the fish that she barely noticed him. The parrotfish darted into the shadows, but not before she managed to blind both Dan and the fish with a camera flash.

The diving party had soon spread out across the reef, with divers and their partners exploring the cracks and crevices for interesting marine life. Dan decided to skim weightlessly three feet above the coral and take in the entire vista of the reef.

That's when he saw them.

In the blue distance, a few blurry shapes began to sharpen into six spotted dolphins, gliding in formation. They carried a distinctive pattern of spots along their flanks. The largest one, over seven feet long, had to be Adolpho, Dan realized, sleek and elegant, with deep, rust-colored skin and a wash of multicolored spots. Each of the dolphins peeled off in a different direction, circling, zipping in and out with obvious glee, as if greeting long-lost relatives.

All except Adolpho.

He headed straight for Duff, stopped abruptly, and hovered just inches away from Duff's mask. Duff waved his arms and clucked through his regulator. Adolpho answered back, bobbing his head and chattering with the familiar dolphin squeaks. Duff then twirled his arm with a flourish and Adolpho shot to the surface with a burst of energy, leaping out of the sea, then crashing back in a swirl of bubbles.

The reef soon became a madhouse of activity with dolphins swimming within the group, divers twisting and turning, and Iris churning to try and film the cetacean acrobatics. After each foray into the divers, the dolphins regrouped. They would swim together for a while, caressing one another with their pectoral fins.

Suddenly, Dan heard—no, felt—a series of chirp-like clicks from behind. Before he could turn, Adolpho circled, brushing against him cautiously. He stared into the dark dolphin eyes—eyes that stared back with curiosity—and felt a rush of emotion, a feeling of strange kinship. He reached out to touch, but Adolpho darted away. Realizing his faux pas, he cursed himself, but Adolpho returned a few minutes later as if to say, "Okay, you've learned your lesson."

Camille had been watching the interplay and approached. Adolpho circled her several times, interrogating her with a litany of chirps, clucks, squeaks, and flutters. She let out a few delighted squeaks of her own, sending a cloud of bubbles to the surface. This seemed to excite Adolpho even more and he spiraled in closer. He drifted motionless for a moment, then with effortless grace, slid up the front of her body, tucked his nostrum under her bikini top, and popped it off. She clutched her hands to her bosom a second too late.

Adolpho headed toward the other dolphins, with the bright red bikini top dangling from the side of his mouth. He dropped the top near a sorrel-colored dolphin, a female. She picked it up with her pectoral fin and swam toward one of the gray males, passing it off like a baton. One gray dolphin approached Duff and dropped the top in front of him. Duff grabbed it, kicked several times dolphin style, and relayed the top back to Adolpho. The game continued for several more minutes.

Meanwhile, Camille had cinched up the sides of her buoyancy compensator vest for cover. Several of the dolphins passed within arm's length of her with the top, in what seemed almost like deliberate teasing. After several vain attempts at retrieval, she gave up and headed back toward the boat, husband Gary reluctantly following behind. Sensing that the game was over, the dolphins departed as quickly as they had arrived, except Adolpho, who lingered on the perimeter.

Dan swam out to him for one last encounter.

As the divers' air tanks became depleted, they returned to *Spanish Diver,* leaving Dan as the last to arrive. He always sipped his air and still had half a tank left. On board, everyone chattered excitedly, still intoxicated from the dolphin encounter. Camille had already donned a T-shirt and was sitting away from the others, her face crimson.

Iris dropped her camera gear into the rinse tank and sat down beside her. "My dear, that was the most fantastic thing! Adolpho was hot on you. I caught some great video footage."

"Just my luck." She rolled her eyes. "That's one bikini down the drain."

"Are you looking for this?" Dan grinned broadly. He reached inside his BC vest and held up the bikini top like a prize fish. "You have now been initiated into the cetacean 'booby' ritual. I'd say you and Adolpho are mated for life."

The crowd exploded with laughter, with the lone exception of Gary.

DINNER AT THE resort was served early, in the bar, so everyone could watch the videos from the morning dive. Not surprisingly, Camille's dolphin striptease was the hit of the show. She sat in the shadows trying to look demure, but it was obvious she enjoyed the attention. Not so Gary, who appeared as if he would have a coronary when the video of Dan's ceremonious wave of the bikini top queued up.

It seemed that a camaraderie had already begun to develop among the group, the result of their shared dolphin experience. Dan genuinely liked these people, felt a kinship both to them and to Duff. It was an experience missing from his life.

This must be what family feels like, he thought.

After the videos ended, Duff stood up. "We have a wonderful night excursion planned this evening," he said, rubbing his hands together. "A wall dive along the Bonacca Deep. We'll track an entire reef ecosystem along its vertical drop. This may be the most thrilling dive of the week, so don't be late." He ambled over to Dan's table. "I'll buddy up with you again tonight."

Dan shifted awkwardly in his seat. "I'm uh, not much into night diving, but thanks."

"What? And miss all the fun?"

"I like to see what I'm looking at."

"What's the matter, you don't like my company?" Duff laughed.

"It's not that . . ."

Duff studied him quizzically, looking quite disappointed. "You'd be surprised at the number of things you notice at night in the deep. Besides, I want to show you the coral bleaching I've been talking about."

Dan ran his finger along the rim of his dinner plate. He'd never learned how to say no gracefully.

Duff slapped him on the back again. "Come on, soldier up."

Dan reluctantly nodded. Putting himself in such an uncomfortable position was stupid, but he'd developed a genuine liking for Duff, and didn't want to disappoint him.

"Okay, okay. I'll come, but it's against my better judgment."

HARRY ADLER PREFERRED to take the factory's spiral staircase to the upper level, rather than the elevator. It gave him a good workout and relief from the sterile confines of the robotics department. It also gave him time to prepare mentally for his meeting with the boss. Tomás Martin was a local hire, obviously well connected, mysterious and already in place by the time the chip factory opened. Harry had always thought that was strange, since Martin seemed to know nothing about microchips or robotics. If the man had any useful skills, Harry wasn't aware of them.

Usually when Martin returned from one of his extended business trips, he'd call in every manager for a debriefing. It had become such a ritual that Harry kept his production binder up to date well in advance—stuffed with graphs, reports, and spreadsheets that Martin could scarcely understand. So Harry would inevitably roll out his one-page production summary, which would wrap up everything in a nice, neat bow. It shortened the meetings considerably.

But today was not one of those typical meetings. In fact, Martin had reappeared at the factory just as suddenly as he'd left a day earlier.

Harry reached the top of the stairs and looked into Martin's glass-wrapped executive suite, strategically positioned to allow an unobstructed view of the entire production floor below. Martin was in a heated discussion with Ramon Campas, the manager of the experimental lab. Both men were gesturing with their hands and shouting, their muffled voices barely audible through the thick glass panes. Campas suddenly stormed out of the room, leaving the door open enough for Martin's gaze to land on Harry. Martin waved him toward the office with an energetic motion.

This doesn't look good, Harry thought.

Tomás Martin had the sharp jaw and dark hair of Spanish nobility and he usually carried himself with an air of haughty superiority, but today he simply looked haggard and jittery.

"So, how was your trip?" Harry said in his most cheerful tone.

"Never mind that," Martin said brusquely. "Are we on schedule in robotics?"

So much for pleasantries. "Fifth week in row," Harry said proudly. "Almost finished assembling the sensors for the GAPS line. Next week we start on the AUVs, you know, the autonomous underwater vehicles—"

"Yes, Mr. Adler, I'm aware . . ." Martin fixed his intense eyes on Harry. "What's the status of the disaster recovery robots?"

"Huh? Oh, you mean the ones for DARPA?" Harry replied. "We're still testing the software—"

"How quickly can you have them operational?"

The unexpected question prompted Harry to stop and think. "Well, we still have to install the radioactive shielding—you know, they're headed to Japan for Fukushima, so we've been focusing on the AUVs instead—"

"Never mind that!" Martin said. "I need you to transfer all your resources to the DARPA robots."

"What?" Harry stepped back with a start. "What about the NOAA contract, and all?"

"I didn't ask for your opinion, Señor Adler."

"But the performance penalties—"

"Not your concern."

"But the first delivery for the NOAA contract is imminent! Besides, DARPA doesn't expect their robots for at least another—"

"I'm requisitioning the DARPA robots for another project," Martin said, bluntly. "Can you have them operational by tomorrow? We'll delay delivery on DARPA's contract until you can fabricate another set."

Harry couldn't believe his ears. The GAPS project was supposed to be the number one priority. Maybe Dan was right about Sonny being up to his old tricks. "I uh, yeah, I guess. Especially if we divert resources, but man, Dan Clifford is going to be pissed, especially after I just promised him—"

"Who?"

"Dan . . . Clifford. You know, the *developer* of GAPS."

Martin's stare grew more intense. "Dan Clifford? You broke our communications blackout?"

"No, of course not. When he was here, earlier."

"Clifford was *here*?"

"Yeah, informally, on his way to the Bay Islands, for vacation." Harry wasn't sure he liked having Martin's full attention all of a sudden.

Martin wiped his hand across his mouth. "What did you tell him? Did you mention the benefactor?"

"How could I? I don't know squat about *Mr. Benefactor.* I gave Dan a ramp tour, that's all. We chatted a bit, I told him the GAPS deal was on schedule. Then he left." Harry caught himself twisting his handlebar mustache into a knot. Martin's distraught demeanor was becoming contagious.

Martin leaned forward, his eyes sharply focused. "Listen carefully. You are not to speak to Dan Clifford again. And get those robots ready!"

"Fine." Harry raised his hands defensively. He tried to maintain an air of nonchalance but didn't like Martin's accusatory tone, especially after his exemplary performance over the past months. "What if I divert half our resources? That way I can meet the GAPS deadline, and I can still have the DARPA robots, or whatever they're gonna be called, ready by tomorrow if you don't need radioactive shielding—"

"Yes, yes, fine!" Martin said waving his hand. "We only need the traditional chemical shielding." He had already turned his attention to something else, and was feverishly sorting through papers on his desk. After a few minutes, Martin seemed to regain his composure.

"You're right. Double shifts, cut break time, but just make sure the disaster relief robots are functional by tomorrow. They are critical to our benefactor's project, and he is a man you do not want to disappoint."

The timbre in Martin's voice had the requisite effect. Harry suddenly felt highly motivated. *Mr. Benefactor*'s numerous side projects already had been a royal pain in the ass. The sooner Harry could wash his hands of them, the sooner he could refocus on GAPS. "It'll be tight, but we'll get it done. Have I ever let you down?"

"I'm not the one you should worry about."

Harry had scarcely left the room when he glanced back over his shoulder to see his haughty boss fully engaged on the phone, still looking distinctly out of sorts.

10

MANAGING A CORPORATION'S initial public offering was much like the mastery of a fine watch movement. It required perfect timing, all the gears moving in synchrony. And in the case of the NeuroSys IPO, mastery of all its elements had required a skilled touch. Bradley Gruber fancied himself more than qualified for the task.

He thought back to his childhood in Geneva, where he had been fascinated by the master watchmakers, called cabineteers, who worked with impossibly intricate movements and gears perfectly meshed and engineered toward one singular outcome, the accurate measurement of time. In the Patek Philippe watch museum, he'd spent innumerable hours mesmerized by the intricate timepieces, small worlds of handcrafted perfection.

A perfection he strived to attain. But not in Geneva. He found his artistry in America, studying the ways of influence. Manipulating the whims of finance and politics was an art not so different from the study of time. Both required great patience and a desire to push the boundaries of possibility.

Not satisfied with the simple display of hours and minutes, Swiss master cabineteers added additional functionality or "complications" to their timepieces, mechanisms that could display the movement of the moon, day, or date, set alarms, wind the movement automatically, or chime on the hour. The more complications in a watch, the more difficult it became to design, repair, and maintain. The number of complications spoke to the watchmaker's skill. Watches with grand complications became the ultimate measure of the artisan, the pinnacle of *haute horlogerie,* or fine watchmaking.

Corporate finance, Gruber mused, was similar—a finely crafted movement, engineered with many goals, but with one singular outcome in mind: profit. The corporate entity had been a masterful legal invention that spoke to the ultimate skill of its social artisans.

The name "corporation" was derived from the Latin word corpus for "body," a legal construct that dated back to the Roman Republic. The Roman Senate was the first institutional corporation, with its member senators "joined by law" and ruling as a singular entity.

The ancient Romans obviously understood the power of the corporate machine. Unencumbered by the biases, emotions, and weaknesses of its human members, the corporation could act with great efficiency. Given the right of a "juridical person" by law, the corporation possessed legal personhood. It could sue and be sued, enter contracts, incur debt, own property, acquire assets and transfer them, and raise an army, all without the personal baggage of human frailty.

Soon after its invention, corporations began dealing with commerce and raising capital through shares of public stock or *publicanis* that were traded in Rome's public forum. Like a fine watch, the corporate machine transcended the bodies of its owners, and as such, became immortal. Even after the fall of Rome and two thousand years of social turmoil, the legal foundation of the corporation survived and thrived.

In 1602, the Dutch East India Company or VOC (Vereenigde Oostindische Compagnie) became the world's first internationally traded public company. At its height, the VOC owned five thousand ships and its own army and navy, and it held a monopoly on Indonesia's spice trade. The VOC's might was such that it managed to gain dominion over a colonial territory far larger than its chartering country, the Netherlands.

It was always helpful to reflect on the legacy of one's charge, Gruber felt. The NeuroSys IPO was a much less ambitious project of course, but not without its own special challenges. After several months of work, he had finally put all the parts in place. It would be a tricky operation, a variation on the "pump and dump" market manipulation. Thanks to the NOAA contract and numerous press releases he had fed to the press and social media, interest in NeuroSys public stock had been whipped into a frenzy.

In a matter of days, the initial public offering would make NeuroSys stock available to the unwashed masses on Wall Street. Once the stock price reached its high point, the primary institutional stockholders, the board, and angel investors would "dump" many of their shares with precise timing. The resulting windfall would cover the "incognito leverage" he had negotiated for the chip factory. It would also earn a tidy sum of capital gains for himself, the underwriters, and the angels.

All the gears were moving with precision, the spring wound tight, the chimes set. As with his other projects, he preferred to work in relative obscurity. Better to turn the gears with minimum effort. That technique, he had learned from his mentor. This achievement should surely earn him the distinction needed for the next level.

In anticipation of his future induction, he had allowed himself a guilty indulgence: a Vacheron Constantin Ultra-Thin Calibre 1731 from the Patrimony collection, famous for its simple watch face and alligator band, hiding an intricate movement of 265 parts and 36 jewels. It set him back 275,000 euros, but the masterpiece of understated horology had been worth it. The inner workings of the timepiece were visible only through the sapphire caseback. It had a set of melodious chimes that served to remind him of critical events. His fingers stroked the opaline face as his mind worked through all the remaining tasks of the day.

Unlike the perfection of timepieces, financial machines still required human gears, with their attendant flaws. That required keeping in close contact with all the players. With one last call for the day, he poured a brace of Kona Nigari water into a glass with two cubes of ice, took a sip, and dialed the number.

The shaky voice that answered the other end instantly put him on edge. "Is everything all right?" Gruber asked. "How's production?"

After a long hesitation, the voice finally replied, "I'm afraid we have a complication."

Gruber listened attentively to the details, writing copious notes, his mind racing through alternatives. He'd been expecting the occasional glitch, but this unusual twist caught him off guard. "I'll deal with the aftermath," he said. "But whatever you do, keep this quiet. Don't tell anyone. We cannot afford any public scrutiny at this critical stage."

"But, what about—"

Gruber cut him off. "*Especially* do not tell *him*." He hung up, a wisp of a smile crossing his face.

Time to put his artistry to the test.

11

Dan watched the twin trails of foam splay out at the stern of *Spanish Diver* as it cruised toward the Bonacca Deep, wondering how he'd managed to get himself into this predicament. He wasn't usually one to fall prey to spontaneous idiocy. But here he was, too embarrassed to back out.

At least he wasn't the only one. The dive group had shrunk by half and the other divers seemed more solemn and introspective as well. The darkness did that to people. Dan licked the sweat from his upper lip, leaned against the gunwale, and stared at the others.

Ben was helping Iris attach a second, larger halogen light to her video camera, giving it the appearance of a bizarre fiddler crab. Camille had donned a full-body wet suit, apparently not wanting to risk more encounters with amorous dolphins.

"Hey, wake up!" Duff shook Dan's arm vigorously. "We're here already."

As Dan rushed to don his gear, Duff ran through the night dive procedures with the group: "Head to the tag line and wait there. We've attached a spare tank and light, for a safety stop on the return. We don't want anyone coming down with the bends. If you have problems, head to the light. We descend together, in orderly fashion. Once we reach the reef, I'll signal you to turn off your lights and you'll get a thrill. When your eyes adjust, you'll see luminescent halos shimmering around us, formed by thousands of light-emitting plankton. It's rather . . . ghostly." Duff chuckled demonically.

Great, just great. Dan fumbled with his mask as the other divers began to slip into the black water.

"Señor Clifford, you going in?" Pepé stood by expectantly.

Dan looked up to find the boat deck empty of divers. It felt like only a few seconds had passed. He managed to gather his wits and eased into the lukewarm water.

I'm in. Turn on the damn light!

It was as if he had forgotten everything about proper dive procedure. His eyes adjusted and he could see the other divers already assembled along the tag line like fireflies, beams of light flickering across the inky depths. He could feel the snake of fear slithering up his spine as he became aware of rapid breathing.

Relax, slow down.

This was the same ocean he'd dived in earlier in the day with no anxiety. But in daylight, water was invisible, infinite, like the open cathedral of Tallulah Gorge. At night, it became a thick shroud of hidden secrets.

By the time he reached the tag line, the other lights were streaming out into the distance, their beams swaying left and right like light sabers. He hurried to catch up, humming and counting to himself. *Ten, nine, eight, seven. . . .* He checked his depth gauge. Thirty-five feet and dropping.

Things were getting better, the breathing more deliberate now—

Suddenly, the narrow beams of light exploded into fuzzy halos. Salt water rushed up his nostrils, burning nasal tissue. Groping wildly, Dan eventually grasped the familiar shape of his mask and pulled it back over his head. He cleared the water, then traced the regulator hose from tank to mouthpiece, jamming it back into his mouth. He hit the purge valve too late and choked, coughing up mucus.

Directly ahead he could see the cause of his problem. Iris Silverstein was thrashing away like a pregnant guppy, cameras dangling and swaying as she chased a fleeing manta ray, oblivious to the turmoil she had left in the wake of her fins.

Crap! Dan spun around. His flashlight was tumbling end over end twenty feet beneath him. The other lights were fading rapidly, their luminosity sucked into the darkness. Iris had pulled well ahead of him. *Why didn't you bring a backup?!* Below, the tumbling stopped—the light's beam now silhouetting the razor sharp edge of the reef. Beyond the light, a steep cliff dropped away into the deep.

He could head back to the boat, or try and catch up with the group, or retrieve the light.

If he returned to the boat, Duff would eventually sound the alarm, ruining the dive for everyone else. The light was only forty feet away. With a little luck, he could catch up with everyone before he was missed. He let a trickle of water into the mask to wash away the fog and headed down.

A rush of blood rumbled through his ears as his breathing accelerated. *Imagine an orange glow flowing through your body, warm, relaxing. Visualize an open meadow with cool breezes. Deep breaths—six, five, four, three, two, one.*

Closer now.

He could see the distinct black edge of the precipice. Ten feet to the right and the flashlight would have fallen three thousand feet to the bottom of the Bonacca Deep. A thermocline of cooler water washed over him, sending another shiver down his spine. The light was resting between two vertical rocks, the beam shining up toward his face. *Just a few more strokes—got it!*

He'd strangled the snake, conquered his demon.

As he turned around to leave, something soft brushed against his cheek. He aimed his light and came face-to-face with a pale, bloated mass staring back at him. Strands of dark hair undulated in the current like seaweed, drifting over whitened muscle and sinew. A bare row of teeth revealed a grotesque grin. One tiny white crab crawled from an empty eye socket.

Dan's body became rigid.

The flaccid mass of flesh and bone fell forward, propelling him backward into the reef wall. A sharp pain ripped through the back of his head.

Get out, get out, get out!

The world erupted into chaos. Dan thrashed in all directions, fighting to pull free, kicking, tearing at the coral, pulling up and over the ledge. Spurting upward, he followed the bubbles, passed them, and aimed toward the light on the safety line.

Pain!

His chest burned, reminding him to exhale, lest his lungs rupture. Then something stopped his forward motion. It gripped his leg, clawing him backward toward the abyss. He kicked frantically, as the mysterious force crept up his body and seized his weight belt.

Duff's face appeared from the haze. He removed his regulator and mouthed the word: "Relax." The two of them hovered at the tag line for what seemed an eternity before Duff would allow them to rise to the surface. The two dive attendants dragged them on board.

"What the hell happened?" Duff said. "You okay?"

Dan hacked and coughed up water. "There's a *body* down there! On the reef."

"What? Are you sure?"

"Hell yeah, I'm sure!"

"Okay, I'll check it out." Duff disappeared back into the water.

Dan struggled to his feet and staggered toward the bow, cursing. Pinpoints of light danced in the air like pixie dust. The back of his head throbbed, and when he touched the spot, he felt a swollen lump of gummy hair. He pulled his hand around and stared at a row of glistening red fingers.

The last thing he saw was the green texture of the boat's carpet rushing up to meet him.

DAN AWOKE WITH a start and realized he was still alive, because he wanted to puke.

"My head . . ." He tried to sit up, but the pain stopped him halfway. A hand pressed against his back, helped him the rest of the way.

"Take it easy, Mr. Clifford. You've had a bump."

Dan's eyes focused slowly on a small room, painted pea green and lined with shelves of medicine, bandages, and jars. The table beneath him was cold steel, rimmed with a metal edge, clearly not designed for comfort. Duff was there, standing alongside a diminutive man in a white tunic, with leathery skin dark as teak that stretched over a gaunt face. He looked about sixty, but it was hard to say for sure. A pair of bifocals rested on a thin, bony nose.

"Dan, this is Anastasio Salvatoré," Duff said. "He's stitched you up, good as new."

The doctor murmured softly as he explored the lump on Dan's head with a tongue depressor. "You've got quite the goose egg, Mr. Clifford, a nasty bugger."

"You're British?"

"Oh Lord, no," he replied, smiling pleasantly. "Born and bred on the island, sir. But my grandfather was British, a recalcitrant from the eighteen hundreds."

Dan barely acknowledged him, distracted by a pungent odor—an amalgam of medicinal compounds and fishy putrefaction. Across the room, another steel table contained the source of the odor—a black rubberized bag. He knew its purpose, recognized the indistinct shape within. His first inclination was to run, but instead he found himself morbidly drawn to the crumpled shape.

He studied the items piled alongside the body bag: a pair of shorts, Nike sneakers, a gold pocket watch, and a tangle of waterlogged rope, cut in several places but still attached to a shiny red fire extinguisher, its bright color out of place in the grim surroundings.

But the final item totally riveted his attention: a soggy T-shirt ripped in the center, containing an image Dan recognized with chilling certainty.

12

AN AGONIZING HOWL jolted Dan upright. Disoriented, he scanned the room. The sweaty shadow of his outline lingered on the sheets beneath him. Light was streaming through the teak slats of his room.

Morning.

He probed the lump again, just to confirm it was real. The pain shot up a notch.

His nightmares had returned. Typically, there was no pattern to their arrival and it was the unpredictability that bothered him the most. Therapists insisted that unpredictability was a good thing, which was a lie.

At least this time, he had a good reason.

You would think after so many years, memories would lose their edge. But the images in his mind were as sharp as ever. Therapy, encounter groups—and for what? The only relief came from meditation and tai chi. After crossing his legs, he belly-breathed for several minutes, stepping through a familiar routine. Then, as always, Dan slipped an imaginary cap over the lens of his mind's eye and the visions faded.

By tomorrow he should be back to his old callous self.

He staggered to the bathroom and took a long, hot shower, careful to keep the dressing on his wound dry. Though not eager to see anyone, his stomach protested.

So much for a vacation without a care in the world. . . .

BRUNCH HAD BEEN laid out under the beach pavilion near the water's edge. A flutter of applause rippled through the crowd as Dan padded across the hot sand to the buffet line. Thirty pairs of eyes followed him to the table, low whispers blending with the sound of the surf.

Iris Silverstein gave him a light hug. "How's the patient this morning?"

"Rough night," he mumbled.

She shivered. "I can only imagine. That was too creepy."

Dan sat down in an empty chair next to Duff and took a gentle bite from a crab cake, washing it down with some fresh pineapple juice. "Any information on . . . the victim?"

"Not much," Duff said. His face wore the haggard look of some-one who had been up all night. "Anastasio's autopsy confirmed that the guy drowned sometime in the last few days. He contacted the La Ceiba police, but we've heard nothing back."

"Let me guess." Dan rolled his eyes. "Anastasio is Guanaja's sher-iff and medical examiner?"

"Yep. Versatility is the key on Guanaja."

"Does *Sheriff* Anastasio have any theories?"

"Probably a drug-related killing. Foreigners fly down, think they'll score a load of cocaine and retire. The local cartels steal their money and their lives."

Dan's appetite had returned, and he took another ravenous bite, licking his fingers. "I'll bet you a hundred bucks the guy's an Ameri-can scientist."

Duff looked at him quizzically. "Why do you say that?"

"Look at the clothes. Nike shoes. Hiking shorts, mail order I bet. American all the way. And the T-Shirt. That's the clincher."

Duff frowned. "So who are you? Sam Spade?"

At first Dan couldn't understand Duff's animosity, until he real-ized the reason: murders weren't good for the resort business. "I'm a prediction scientist, Duff. It's my job to notice things—spot patterns." He turned to Iris. "You're a dentist, right? Any way to ID the victim by his dental records?"

"Not likely," Iris replied. "There's no dental database or way to visually search through random X-rays. We have to start with a sus-pected identity and look up that person's dental charts, not the other way around. Lord knows, that guy could be from anywhere."

He turned back to Duff. "How about DNA?"

Duff seemed irritated by this line of questioning. "Guanaja isn't CSI. We're not exactly equipped for DNA analysis. Anastasio's big-gest arrest last year was a guy fishing with dynamite."

"So, how about the police in La Ceiba?"

"They won't be interested unless someone reports a person missing. Otherwise, it's just another random drug death."

Dan dropped the remaining crab cake to the table. "So, nobody can investigate without an identity, but you can't get the identity unless someone investigates."

"Welcome to Latin America," Duff said, and shrugged. He stood up and walked away.

Dan hung around until the other guests began to trickle away. He pondered the victim's shirt: He hadn't yet mentioned it to Duff, but there were only a few hundred people in the world with a T-shirt like that.

There were still several days left on his fictional vacation. There would be no more diving for him, not with a gash in his scalp. Besides, the romance of the sea had suddenly lost its attraction. He stood up and headed back to the bar, finding Duff alone as expected, sipping a beer and reworking the dive schedules.

"Do you have a satellite phone?"

"In my office. Why?"

Dan looked down at his friend. The once proud and jolly old Duff seemed subdued and it made his heart ache. "I've got an idea for identifying our mystery guest—that is, if you're willing."

Duff turned around with renewed interest. "The sooner this is resolved, the better for everyone. We deal in happiness down here. No one is very happy right now."

"I'll need a favor from *Dr.* Salvatoré."

"I'm sure he'd be glad to help."

"I don't know. It's a pretty strange favor."

SEVERAL HOURS LATER, Duff appeared at Dan's bungalow door and gingerly handed him a small dive bag and a satellite phone. "I've got to admit, you've piqued my curiosity," he said. "What the hell are you gonna do with this?"

"Just wait till tomorrow at lunch," Dan said, and winked. "It should be interesting."

"Of that, I have no doubt."

After Duff left, Dan placed the bag on the dresser and stared at it for several minutes. He took a deep breath, unzipped the top, and pulled out the creamy white contents. It seemed so impersonal now, not the frightening image that had haunted his nightmares. Anastasio had done a great job of cleansing and bleaching, removing all traces of flesh and wiring the jaw to the cranium. Dan ran his fingers along the intricate striations that divided the skull into flexible plates. He marveled at the lightness of it, devoid of the brain. *A thinking man's brain.*

He held the skull aloft. "Do I know you?" he implored. "And how did you find *me*?"

Dan placed the skull on the nightstand, fished out his smartphone, and proceeded to capture a series of images, carefully rotating the skull after every shot. When he felt comfortable that he had covered a full 360 degrees, he attached the images to an e-mail, connected his smartphone to the satellite phone's data port, and pressed Send.

THE NEXT DAY, as planned, Dan used Duff's satellite phone for another call, this one to the Federal Bureau of Investigation.

"Vince Peretti, please."

"One moment."

Dan thought back to his first meeting with Vincent Horatio Peretti. Vince was an Italian New Yorker with jet-black hair and the square jaw of a Hollywood "G-man." They had met when Dan was still acting as the NeuroSys sales manager. Vince had been his contact for a critical piece of NeuroSys software.

Peretti was new then, and his path to the bureau had been unusual. Young and energetic, Vince graduated magna cum laude from Dartmouth College with a degree in data processing. Back then, it seemed like an odd major for an FBI hopeful, but Vince had been prophetic in his choice of career path. The modern "cyberterrorism" FBI had been trading in their guns for computers and Internet servers for a while now and Vince had risen quickly through the ranks. He'd recently been appointed as the assistant director of Atlanta's FBI computer crime division.

"Peretti here."

"And Clifford here."

"I wondered when you'd call."

"So you got my e-mail. How's the ForenScan software working out?"

"Frankly? Amazing," Vince replied. "Far faster facial reconstructions than the old clay models. We have a team of jealous sculptors looking for a new skill. We've cleared a backlog of open cases, but I certainly wasn't expecting to receive one from you. What have you gotten yourself into? Where are you, exactly?"

"I'm on vacation, scuba diving in Honduras."

"Since when do vacations include murder and skull reconstructions?"

"Well, that's the weirdest thing. I literally bumped into this guy on a night dive." Dan then recounted the entire series of events, his recognition of the unique T-shirt, and his resulting interest in the man's identity.

When he was finished, Vince drew a long breath, clearly audible over the line. "And why are you getting involved? Let the locals take care of it."

"This is Honduras, Vince. Guanaja isn't exactly a mecca for high-tech police work. I thought you could check your missing persons database."

"And what makes you think he's in our system?"

"I may *know* this guy, and if I'm right, he's definitely an American."

"That would be a hell of a coincidence."

"Exactly. Which is why I feel . . . somewhat responsible, at least to identify the guy. I'm hoping you'll run a facial reconstruction, help us make an ID."

"Check your e-mail."

"You've sent it already?"

"Of course. But I have to say, I received some pretty strange looks when I submitted an unofficial case to missing persons."

Dan's spirits soared. "Thanks Vince!"

"Can I give you some friendly advice?"

"Do I have a choice?"

"Quit trying to solve all the world's problems."

"I know, I just feel connected to this guy."

"Think about it. Whether you know this victim or not, he was murdered, and now you're involved. Quit playing detective."

"But I'm good at it," Dan insisted, with a nervous laugh.

"Dan, this isn't a video game, or some prediction simulation,"

Vince continued. "This is real life, with real-life consequences. Take my advice and go back to your computers. We'll take it from here."

"Yeah, I know you're right," Dan said. "Once this mystery man is identified, I'm officially retired. Promise."

13

THE LONG FLIGHT back to Atlanta had given Dan time to mull over the past week. The last couple of days had been restful but somber. He'd spent most of his time relaxing at the pool and hiking, since his head injury prevented any more diving. Each night, Duff and the guests would assemble at the bar to speculate on their favorite topic—the Enigma Man—their new nickname for the man with a face, but no identity.

An identity unknown to Dan, but not unfamiliar.

Dan knew the face in the rendering from somewhere, but he just couldn't come up with a name. Vince had promised to distribute a missing person's bulletin through the bureau, and Duff had plastered the man's likeness wherever he could, all across the island, even sending copies to the mainland. It was just a matter of time before the mystery would be solved.

Anastasio held a memorial service in Bonacca Town and delivered a short eulogy, unable to say much about the dear departed, except to give his blessing. Between the dolphin encounter and the discovery of the Enigma Man, Duff and his band of tourists had grown close. Dan knew he would miss them. When it was time to leave, everyone vowed to stay in touch, as most people did after the camaraderie of a vacation. But Dan doubted he'd ever see them again.

As soon as the plane touched down in Atlanta, his thoughts returned to the present, GAPS and NeuroSys. He wasn't quite sure what to do with the information he had collected. The mysterious circumstances at the chip factory concerned him, but he was encouraged that the GAPS project would proceed as planned, and that was his primary goal, after all. Once inside the terminal he dialed Rudi Plimpton, eager to catch up on news.

"I'm back. Miss me?"

"I thought you'd never call." Rudi's voice had an unfamiliar edginess to it.

"What's up?"

"That prick Sonny transferred the GAPS software rewrite to Dwayne Clemens, the acne-faced butt-kisser in vision processing. Clemens is a bottom-feeder, a real naught-noggin! He thinks NOAA is an old geezer with an ark—"

"What did you say?" Dan felt his pulse quicken. *Why didn't I check in when I had the satellite phone?* "That's impossible! You're the GAPS software expert—"

"There's more! Sonny's transferring me to a cubicle in administration. Can you imagine me with a bunch of ditsy blond secretaries? I'll go insane!"

Dan leaned against the wall for support. Something was terribly, terribly wrong. "I'll be there in thirty minutes."

"I'd get here sooner if I were you."

By THE TIME Dan swerved into the NeuroSys parking deck, his heart was pounding. He bounded up the stairs to his office and breathlessly swung the door open, only to exchange shocked expressions with a table full of strangers.

He checked the hallway again. It was the right room. "Why are all you people in my office?"

"Pardon?"

"You're in my office."

The man at the head of the table smiled weakly and extended a hand. "I'm sorry, we haven't met. I'm Bill Lassiter. We're with the accounting firm preparing for the initial public offering. This was the office they assigned us."

"Really? *This* office?"

The man lowered his eyes. Dan didn't wait for a reply. He spun around and headed straight toward Sonny's office.

His sudden appearance caught Wilma, Sonny's administrative assistant, by surprise. She sat up with a start. "Welcome home, Mr. Clifford," she stuttered. "Mr. Swyft wasn't expecting you back until tomorrow." She didn't bother with the intercom, just got up and knocked gently on Sonny's door, poking her head inside.

Dan paced, feeling the bile rise in his throat.

Wilma stepped back and motioned Dan in, awkwardly averting her gaze. Sonny was standing at the window, looking out at the Atlanta skyline. He spoke without bothering to turn around. "Amazing about the unpredictability of weather, isn't it? They said it would be sunny and warm this week, and look at it. Another dreary day."

"What the hell's going on?"

"I should be asking you that," Sonny replied, turning around to face him. "Why were you at the Honduras plant?"

"I *told you* I was going scuba diving," Dan said, struggling to maintain an even tone in his voice. Deception wasn't his forte. "I dropped by on the way."

"You just happened by without telling me?"

"Why should I have to tell you anything? I'm the director of the GAPS project."

Sonny held up a hand. "That's the problem. You're always *pushing*, sticking your nose where it doesn't belong. It's time for a new breed, someone who can follow orders."

Dan could feel his anger turning white hot. He chose his words carefully. "How can I do my job without the facts? You've never mentioned the scale of that plant anywhere in my sales briefings. Where did the financing come from? What will the SEC say if they get wind of it? It puts the whole company at risk."

That got Sonny's attention. He glared. "Don't question me, Clifford. I'm way ahead of you. We're leasing that building from the Honduran government."

"For the payments we show on our prospectus? That plant would lease for twenty times that—"

"You still don't get it, do you? Who cares how I made the deal?"

"The public stockholders will care, when you have to pay off the lease."

"You fail to grasp even the most elementary business protocol. I'm the president of NeuroSys . . . you're just a manager . . . or *were*. I've got my reasons for keeping the deal under wraps, and now I'm afraid you've outlived your usefulness here."

Dan tried to speak, but his throat felt as dry as dust. "What . . . you're asking me to . . . *resign?*"

"Resign?" Sonny chuckled. "We can call it that, I guess. Make sure to get all your personal items today, because your keycard will be revoked. Oh, and by the way, details about the chip factory are strictly confidential. I shouldn't have to remind you about the nondisclosure agreement you signed. Are we clear?"

Dan's jaw twitched. Sonny *couldn't* fire him. The board wouldn't allow it, not after all he had done to develop GAPS. "You realize I'll take this up with Neal Johnston."

"Go ahead," Sonny said, grinning triumphantly. He turned back toward the window. "Neal knows already. No loose cannons before the IPO. Besides, why not let us make you a millionaire? You have vested stock options due in two months. If you behave, I might still give them to you."

"You might? I—" Dan sensed that his anger was so out of control that he might do something stupid, so he decided to stop while he was behind. He just stood there, trembling with rage.

"Are we done?" Sonny said with a flip of his wrist. "If so, the door's behind you, where it's always been. I've got work to do."

"HE DID *WHAT?*" Rudi's head shot up from behind the monitor, its glow illuminating him like a ghoul. "Sonny is the *megaprick* of all time. He can't get away with that . . . can he?"

"Sonny says Neal knows already, but I can't believe it. I signed the company's first five contracts. We brought him the GAPS system. He *owes* me, and you, too."

"Face it, executives are assholes by nature."

Dan dialed Neal Johnston's private number, but reached Neal's administrative assistant instead. "Janet, this is Dan Clifford. Let me speak with Neal."

She paused. "He's . . . in a meeting with the underwriters."

"Tell him it's urgent."

Janet sighed. "Neal told me you'd call. He wanted me to tell you how sorry he is for the way things worked out, but he supports the decision. The board can't afford any slipups before the IPO. He wants to assure you that Sonny will give you a glowing reference. You should relax, let the IPO go through, then cash in your stock."

"After all I've done? GAPS is my project!" Dan realized he was shouting into the phone and lowered his voice. "Have him call me anyway. He owes me that."

There was a long pause. "I'll give Neal the message. I'm *so* sorry,

Dan." Janet's voice dropped to a whisper. "Between you and me, I think you got screwed."

Dan hung up and stared at his smartphone. *This can't be happening.* His world had been turned upside down yet again. "Rudi, do me a favor?"

"Name it, partner."

"Poke around and see what you can find out about the Honduras plant. Can you access the prospectus research files?"

"Absolutely." Rudi popped his knuckles. "I can collect an elephantine volume of information."

"Good. Find me something I can use."

14

DAN'S LANDLINE STARTED ringing as he opened the door to the penthouse. He fumbled madly with the lock, wrenched the door open, and dropped his luggage along the way. Rover rolled out to greet him, but Dan slipped to one side and reached the study.

He grabbed the phone. "Neal?"

"*Señor,* do you want to live?"

It was an unfamiliar voice—raspy, as deep as the ocean, and thick with a Latino accent.

"Say again?"

"Let the dead sleep, or you may join them, *comprende?*"

The line went dead.

"What the—" He stared first at the phone, then the answering machine. No messages, after a week of absence. His eyes darted around the condo. It looked the same as he'd left it.

A noise behind him grabbed his attention.

"Hello, my name is Rover. I don't believe I know you. Please state your name—first name then last name, please."

His focus shot back to the darkened foyer. He could see movement in the shadows, beyond Rover's silhouette. He slipped sideways, quietly sliding out a bottle from the wine rack. Grasping the neck, he crept toward the foyer, his breath coming hot and shallow. He paused to collect himself, then lurched forward. As he rounded the corner, his feet hooked the luggage, and his momentum propelled him forward. On the way to the floor he caught a glimpse of shapely legs rising up from a pair of hiking boots and disappearing into the cuffs of khaki shorts. The skin was peppered with small, circular bandages.

"Whoa!" The legs took a step backward.

Dan's gaze followed the legs up the torso to a woman's face staring at him with a mixture of shock and curiosity. She was compact, athletic, and quite attractive, with a blaze of shoulder-length sienna hair. A blue cotton shirt was neatly tucked into the waistband of a pair of khaki shorts. This woman looked as if she could wrestle crocodiles. Dan stood up sheepishly and brushed off his clothes. He gingerly placed the wine bottle on the foyer table.

"Hello, my name is Rover. I don't believe I know you. Please state your name—first name then last name, please."

"Shut up, Rover," he ordered. "Rover, go home." The robot turned obediently and rolled toward the closet. Dan forced a weak smile. "You startled me."

The woman scanned the room and watched as Rover rolled back into his niche. Her sage-green eyes returned to him. "Are you Dan Clifford?"

"Who's asking?"

She smirked. "Do you always greet people so . . . aggressively? And what the hell is *that* thing?"

"Rover? Oh, a house pet of sorts—guard dog. And *you* are . . . ?"

"Rachel Sullivan." She reached out a hand tentatively. Dan took it, marveling at her firm grip. "The FBI gave me your name," she said. "A, uh . . . Mr. Peretti? He said you have information about a missing person."

"Oh, the Enigma Man—I mean, that's what we called him." Dan regretted the term the moment it left his lips. "Sorry for the confusion," he continued, as he checked the hallway. "I'm a little on edge. I just received a death threat."

"Really? Just now?" She stared at him with an incredulous look that said, *yeah right.*

Dan held his hands up. "Look, I apologize. This must seem a bit weird, but I really did get a death threat . . . just now. I'm a little shaken up." He kicked the luggage to one side and motioned her toward the living room. "Please, come in." After she entered, he immediately locked the front door.

As she sauntered through the room, Dan watched her closely, still unsure of her intentions. She didn't seem to be packing any kind of weapon that he could see, but she walked with an air of grace and confidence that left no doubt that she could handle herself in a tough situation.

"Please have a seat. Would you like some wine, uh—beer perhaps?"

She chuckled. "Sure, a beer would be good."

"Rover, two Sweetwater Ales please."

"What kind of death threat?"

"Can you excuse me a moment?" He disappeared into the bedroom to call Vince, just to verify her identity. Then he remembered something and poked his head back out. "When Rover comes back, he'll ask for your name again. Just answer him and he'll go away. If he doesn't respond, just say, 'Rover, go away.'"

RACHEL WATCHED ROVER as he whirred toward the fridge, opened the door, and carefully extracted two beers with his mechanical arms. He placed them on his metal tray, turned back toward the living room, and stopped directly in front of her.

"Hello, my name is Rover. I don't believe I know you. Please state your name—first name then last name, please."

"Martha Washington," she said and grabbed the beers. "Now, get lost."

"I'm sorry Martha. I didn't understand your command, please repeat."

"Rover, go away."

He obeyed.

Rachel took a sip of beer and studied the room's décor, an eclectic blend of early-American, Asian, and contemporary styles. It was obvious to her that the furniture had been meticulously chosen to blend well together. There were hand-rubbed teak shelves along one wall, stacked with a collection of texts: *The Fuzzy Logic Handbook, Mapping the Third Space, The Collapse of Chaos, The Tao of Programming.*

Another shelf contained ancient Eastern classics: *Confucius, Writings of Buddha, I Ching,* and another: *Alice in Wonderland, The Odyssey, The Complete Sherlock Holmes.* The shelves of an old oak apothecary table held an extensive collection of seashells, as well as fern leaves pressed between glass.

But what really piqued her curiosity were two three-dimensional jigsaw puzzles, both partially complete: one of Big Ben, and one of the Earth. Even the walls contained puzzles. Her gaze lingered on a large jigsaw puzzle that had been framed and hung like a picture, labeled MANDELBROT #5. She tilted her head to study it. Branches of psychedelic colors erupted from the edge of two large black circles, like leaves of an exquisite plant.

"Sorry about that," Dan said from the bedroom door. "Had to make a call."

"Checking up on me?"

He grinned sheepishly. "You understand, I'm sure."

She caught him glancing at her legs and smiled. "I know, I've just *got* to change that razor blade more often." Then without a pause, "Quite a place you've got here. It reminds me of the Smithsonian. You know, look but don't touch? It's something I'd expect on the cover of *Architectural Digest*."

Dan's mouth curled into a thin smile. He pulled the September copy of *Architectural Digest* from a shelf and handed it to her.

She laughed a hardy, melodious laugh. "Why am I not surprised?"

Dan wasn't quite sure how to broach the next subject, so he just forged ahead. "You're here about . . . the victim?"

Rachel averted her gaze, the smile dissolving. It was the first hint of discomfiture he'd seen.

"His name is Carl . . . Jameson. How did you get his picture?"

"It's a computer reconstruction."

A look of confusion flashed across Rachel's face. "You're kidding."

Not knowing Rachel's connection to the victim, Dan wasn't eager to explain that he'd used the man's skull for identification. "Digital manipulation. I suppose Mr. Peretti explained what happened?"

"No, not really. He suggested I talk with you."

Dan shifted, unsure exactly how to continue, finally deciding that she was the type of person who would want the news straight, so he blurted: "He drowned."

"Carl, drowned? I find that hard to believe."

"Well, actions were taken . . . to make sure he did."

Rachel's expression flattened. "You mean he was murdered."

"Yes. Someone tied a fire extinguisher to his back and threw him into the sea. I'm sorry."

Her gaze drifted toward the window. Then a look of pain and anger seized her expression, yet no tears came. She seemed lost in some distant place for several minutes, then, just as quickly, she looked back to him, fire again in her eyes. "Who would kill Carl?"

"I was hoping you could tell me. What was he doing in Honduras?"

"Research for NOAA, the National Oceanic—"

"You're kidding." The hairs raised on the back of Dan's neck. Suddenly, the familiarity of the face made sense. They had obviously met on the job at some point. "NOAA is—*was* my employer, and now, my client. My company supplies equipment for their new global weather prediction system."

"Oh, GAPS and the pencil-headed geeks," she said in a gruff tone, appearing almost relieved to replace sorrow with irritation. "The weather geeks waste more money in a week than we spend in a year. Carl and I work for the Oceanographic Research Division. He's a geological oceanographer, I'm a marine biologist. We do *hard* research."

Her emphasis chafed at him. "You don't think there's anything *hard* about weather prediction? I beg to differ."

"No, I mean *hard* as in hands-on. Not so much theoretical stuff."

The mental image that popped into Dan's head triggered a grin he could barely stifle. Her cool demeanor had a way of getting him off track. Recovering his proper indignation, he fired back. "And I suppose hurricanes and tsunamis are theoretical? Tell me that the next time you encounter one."

She must have caught a trace of his smile because she smirked knowingly, but let the argument drop. "Carl was in Honduras doing *hands-on* research of the Chicxulub crater."

"The chick-sa-what?"

"The meteor that allegedly killed the dinosaurs—the KT meteor theory—you know, a meteor collides with Earth at the end of the Cretaceous period. We used to debate it all the time, even had a side bet." She paused and her expression seemed to drift again. "Anyway, the resulting dust cloud would have killed the dinosaurs, or so the theory goes. A few years ago, scientists found evidence of the impact site at Chicxulub on the Yucatan Peninsula. Carl had a grant to examine test drillings from the crater's edge."

Her expression turned cold again. "Trying to save money. We only get seven percent of NOAA's budget, thanks to the geeks. These old mining cores are a poor man's geological sampling. Carl was trying to pinpoint the exact date of the collision."

Dan wondered about her attitude. She had amazing fortitude for a woman who had lost a . . . *who*? Friend, lover, husband? "So, I take it you didn't agree with his theory?"

"Nope. A meteor collision is neat and sexy, but has technical flaws."

"Such as?"

"I'm partial to the birds and the bees, myself," she said demurely.

"Huh?" Her remark baffled him.

"Bees," she continued with a smirk. "We've found ancient tropical bees identical to modern ones caught in amber before and *after* the Chicxulub impact. How could they survive something that killed the dinosaurs? Bees are like canaries in a mine. They're the first to react to environmental changes. Then, you've got the world's other four mass extinctions, earlier in Earth's history. The Permian extinction, for instance, killed ninety percent of all life, but there's no evidence of a meteor impact for that one. So what caused the others? Probably the same thing that caused the *fifth* extinction."

"So, if not a meteor, then what?"

The sudden ringing of Dan's landline startled them both.

"I've got to take that." he picked it up. "Neal?"

"*Hardly.*"

He grimaced at the recognition of Jenifer Coleman's piercing voice.

"What happened?" Jenifer said. "The press release is on all the wires. You've been *fired*?"

It's official then. There would be no reprieve, no call from Neal. GAPS, his life's work . . . gone. "Long story," he muttered.

Jenifer continued to grill him: "You must have found something juicy in Honduras. What was it? *Tell* me."

"I'm not in the mood right now."

"Something big is going on, isn't it? I *knew* it!"

"Thanks for the support." He slammed the phone down, sick of Jenifer's incessant probing, and dropped to the couch, burying his face in his hands. Everything he'd worked for—destroyed.

Rachel touched his arm. "Are you okay?"

"No, I'm *not* okay. This day has gone from bad to horrible. I've lost my career, been threatened—all because of one stupid mistake."

"What do you mean?"

He spent the next several minutes describing his visit to the chip factory and his resulting termination from NeuroSys. It felt strangely liberating to unload this on a virtual stranger. When he was finished, Rachel rolled her eyes.

"That doesn't sound so bad. If you keep your mouth shut, you get rich?"

"You don't understand. It's not the job, it's the GAPS program. My life's work."

"*You* developed GAPS?" Now it was Rachel's turn to look awkward. "Look, I didn't mean what I said earlier about pencil-headed—"

Dan shook his head and smiled. "Hey, don't worry about it. I guess this is the day for comeuppances."

"Look at it this way," she said. "You've got a million new options available to you."

Dan thought about it for a minute. Rachel had a point. Her sudden sympathy left him feeling foolish and self-centered. Here he was whining about his job while she was mourning a death. He was about to apologize when Rachel changed the subject.

"Mr. Peretti said you brought Carl's things back to the States. I'd like to see them."

15

Rachel Sullivan hesitated, running her fingers along the edge of the mahogany box, its polished sides fitted together with seamless precision by a Payan worker at the resort. She raised the lid and removed the items one by one, placing them in a line along the table's edge. There wasn't much: a pair of shriveled tennis shoes, shorts, and T-shirt, all reeking of fish. She unfolded the T-shirt and frowned. It looked as if a small cannonball had been shot through the front. She flipped it over just to make sure, but the back of the shirt was completely intact.

"You're *sure* Carl died from drowning?" she said warily.

"I know, the hole confused me too. I have no idea what it means." Dan had thought the same thing back in Guanaja. "There was no wound corresponding to that tear."

"I've seen this shirt," Rachel said. "Carl wore it all the time."

"That T-shirt, in fact, led me to Carl's identity."

"Really?" Rachel eyed him curiously. "How is that?"

"It's from the Santa Fe Institute. Some of the students commissioned a local Native American artist to draw the design. It's a mnemonic for the seven major tenets of complexity science, or more correctly, what we call syncrenomics. We all had them, and joked that we were wearing our crib sheets to class. When I saw Carl's shirt, I knew he must have attended the institute at some point. I have one just like it."

"I remember," Rachel said. "Carl came back from Santa Fe acting like he'd had some crazy religious experience—said complexity science would change everything. And it changed *him*. Pretty soon, he was talking in riddles. . . ." She looked at Dan. "So, you did know Carl."

"Like I said, not directly. But the Santa Fe Institute has a large

visiting faculty that teaches classes on complexity science every summer. We must have run in to each other once or twice, especially if
Carl attended the syncrenomics presentations. There's only one visiting professor who teaches those classes."

"Well then," she said, looking back at the ruined shirt. "I guess it's
fitting that you were the one to find him. You know, I never understood what Carl saw in all this complexity stuff. It's just a bunch of
theoretical high-end math, right? And what is syncrenomics anyway?"

The last thing Dan expected to discuss on this day was complexity
science, but Rachel seemed genuinely interested, so he forged ahead,
hoping it would distract him from his current predicament.

"It helps to understand a little history," he began. "Chaos theory
and complexity science started out as theoretical high-end math, but
their mathematical principles permeate everything in nature. The
laws of the universe are basically math, after all. Think of syncrenomics as complexity science without the math. One of Santa Fe's, uh,
more *colorful* visiting professors introduced syncrenomics as a way
to expand complexity science beyond the mathematicians, to make it
accessible to the general public. It's a new way of seeing the world's
hidden web that links everything together."

Rachel smiled. "That's assuming ordinary people give a hoot about
complexity."

"They don't, but they should," Dan said. "We deal with complexity every day, in every decision we make, balancing risk against reward, prioritizing our lives, choosing between opposing views, making
sense out of chaos. We simplify our complex world by using rules of
thumb, principles and values, fables, aphorisms, metaphors. In other
words, we boil all that complexity down into a handful of simple
truths, so we can make quicker decisions. Otherwise, we'd all suffer
from 'analysis paralysis.' But simple truths are often a very poor fit to
reality, so we end up making decisions with many unintended consequences. We have 'connection blindness.' We can't see the invisible
threads that connect seemingly unrelated events together, so we often
get surprised."

Rachel looked down at the shirt again, as if trying to puzzle out its
hidden meaning. "If syncrenomics can explain why anyone would
want to hurt Carl, I'm interested. He was just a geologist, minding his

own business." Furrows creased her brow and she wiped her palm across one cheek. She turned her attention back to the box and removed the last remaining item—the watch—cradling it in her palm. "I gave Carl this," she said, "to remind him that time is fleeting." She opened the watch front and examined the salty residue that had crystallized inside. "I suppose it can be restored, can't it?" She gently pried open the rear compartment and stopped short. "That's odd. My photo used to be in here."

"Let's see." Dan slid next to her and peered at a gummy wad of folded paper that filled the compartment.

She picked at the white mass.

"Let's get it under the light." Dan carried the watch to the study, held it under the desk lamp, and examined it with a magnifier. "Looks like Spanish." He could pick out faint images of words ghosting through the translucent paper. He wrote them on the desk blotter:

abismo
la tierra
del cielo

Rachel pulled a chair next to him and leaned in close enough for him to feel her breath on his neck. She wrote the English translation next to each word, then sat back with a puzzled look. "Make any sense to you?"

abismo	abyss
la tierra	earth
del cielo	of the sky

"Not a clue."

"Maybe a geological text? The abyss is a deep ocean plateau."

Dan tried to pry apart the folds of paper with his pocketknife, but the seawater had turned the wad into papier-mâché. "We should send this to the FBI lab. I'm afraid I'll just destroy it."

Rachel rubbed her neck. "Carl obviously saved that paper for a reason." She glanced back at the T-shirt. "And this hole—the edge is rough, almost like *teeth* marks. You didn't find his wallet, a pen, a cell phone, anything?"

"I'm afraid not."

"Why would Carl chew a hole in his shirt? It must mean *something.*"

Dan wondered about that too, but how many murder victims had the wherewithal to leave elaborate clues before they died? "Hold on," he said, and disappeared into the bedroom. He returned a few minutes later with his own version of the T-shirt, holding it up so Rachel could view the symbol in its entirety.

The missing piece only served to confuse her further. "Kokopelli? That's what he removed? What does some flute-playing hood ornament have to do with syncrenomics?"

"A purely whimsical choice," Dan said. "Kokopelli is pasted on practically every tourist item in and around Santa Fe, minus his historically correct phallus of course, censored by the missionaries. But the well-endowed flute player fits into syncrenomics. In Native American folklore, Kokopelli represents a trickster, a common character in mythologies. Shiva, the Chinese Taoist Yellow Emperor, the Greek Prometheus—they were all tricksters. The trickster is a shapeshifter, a symbol for what we now call a black swan. It's the unexpected event that subverts the system and turns the world on its head."

"So it must point to Carl's killer in some way," Rachel said. "Why else go to the trouble of removing it from the shirt? Do I go looking for someone whose nickname is 'the trickster' or some guy named Kokopelli? Or a flute-playing drug dealer? Or a black swan?"

"Carl's reference to Kokopelli could be purely symbolic." *I'm starting to buy in to this,* he thought. "More like an unexpected person or event. You really need to understand the symbol and its seven tenets of syncrenomics to appreciate the trickster's true meaning."

"So explain it," she said eagerly.

"That could take a while." Dan let out a long breath. "To start with, the entire symbol is a Native American medicine wheel. It represents the circular nature of life—from creation to death. The snake eating its tail represents a feedback loop—essential to all nonlinear complex systems. The four spokes point to the four winds or compass directions. The seven-pointed star comes from Cherokee culture and represents not only the four directions, but also up, down, and *center,* or what the Cherokees call 'where you are now.' The center is where truth resides. The other symbols within the wheel represent various other tenets of syncrenomics." Dan turned the T-shirt over so Rachel would read the back side.

FEEDBACK LOOPS
THE BUTTERFLY EFFECT
THE FRACTAL UNIVERSE
BALANCE OF OPPOSITION
THE INTERCONNECTED HIVE
THE UNEXPECTED TRICKSTER
TRUTH RADIATES FROM THE CENTER

Rachel studied the various phrases. "Okay, I'm starting to get it, but why the tie-in to Native Americans?"

"Because they understand complexity better than most cultures," Dan said. "Their world view has always been one of an interconnected world, much like the teachings of Eastern philosophy: martial arts, Chinese philosophy, Buddhism, Celtic and pagan lore, even the Bible in some places. Over two-thirds of the world's population believes in the interdependence of all things. It's the Western reductionist view that's unusual."

"Okay." Rachel leaned forward. "But didn't reductionist science make most of the world's great discoveries?"

"For a while perhaps, but it makes the world's greatest mistakes too," Dan said. "Reductionists study the world by examining its individual parts, like blind men studying an elephant—one feels a snake, the other a tree, another a mountain, and so on—but that seldom explains how the parts fit together. Reductionists miss half the puzzle. Syncrenomics considers the entire puzzle, like a looking glass into the soul of the universe—a web of causality where everything is connected to everything else. You begin to see the world as a *whole,* rather than its *parts.*"

"My, aren't you the poet," Rachel quipped. "You remind me a lot of Carl, waxing lyrical about this new enlightenment. Well, enlighten me some more."

"I'm happy to oblige," Dan said. "Appears I'll have plenty of time on my hands."

She stood up. "Great! So when do we leave for Honduras?"

"Say what?" Rachel's non sequitur caught him off guard.

"Let's go find Carl's killer."

"When I offered help, that's not what I had in mind."

"Dan, you're my only link to Carl in his final days. *You* said it. I need to understand this . . . *syncrenomics* to unravel Carl's clues."

"We don't know if they *are* clues."

"What else could they be?"

"As my FBI friend Vince Peretti reminded me, that's a job for professionals."

"You mean like the Honduran authorities?" Rachel laughed derisively. "They won't do anything."

"I'm sorry, but it would be crazy to go back to the very place I was warned to avoid. Honduras is the *last* place where I should be poking around."

"You're safer here? They know where you live, Dan. Besides, don't you want to know why your NeuroSys buddies fired you? The answer to *that* seems to lie in Honduras too."

Dan couldn't deny that she had him there. His unexpected visit to the chip factory had made Sonny very nervous . . . nervous enough to endanger the GAPS project by firing him. If he wanted to get his job back, he would need to expose Sonny's misdeeds.

Rachel was tapping her foot and staring at him. "What's it gonna be, *geek*?"

"Don't call me that." This strange woman was starting to get on his nerves with her pushy attitude. "I don't know you from Adam and yet you want me to put myself at risk? This is the kind of foolish behavior that gets people killed."

Rachel glared at him. "Someone has already been killed, and you're a part of it now, whether you like it or not."

Dan rubbed his forehead, suddenly wondering if he should have kept his nose out of things, like Peretti had suggested. "There are a million things that could go wrong with this scenario."

Rachel chortled. "Like they haven't already?"

"I'd have to stay out of sight."

"Fine, I'll do the legwork, you teach me syncrenomics."

Dan couldn't believe he was even considering it. This woman was getting to him. He was letting his primitive brain take over, succumbing to pride and anger, and to the kind of stupid mistakes and vindictive actions that felt good for an instant, but seldom lasted. He'd worked hard for twenty years to find more rational and measured solutions. But right now, his only alternative would be to brood in Atlanta, feeling impotent and helpless. That wouldn't do . . . never again. "No direct involvement," he insisted.

"Fine."

"First, there's something I have to do." Dan dialed a number from memory. *In for a penny, in for a pound.*

A familiar voice answered. "NeuroSys, can I help you?"

"Yes, this is Dan Clifford. Tell Sonny Swyft I have to talk to him . . . *now.*"

"One moment, please."

Sonny picked up. "You again? I thought we understood each other?"

"Then understand this, because I'm only going to say it once. I want my glowing reference letter and all my stock options delivered by courier to my condo within the hour. Otherwise, I'll light up every media outlet in the country with details of your nasty little conspiracy in Honduras. Got that?"

He waited for a response, but only heard a grunt and a click.

16

Dan sat at the stern of *Little Diver,* watching the reflections of the setting sun dance across the boat's wake. The trip back to Guanaja had passed in a blur, like a bad case of déjà vu. Sonny Swyft had acceded to his demands, giving him a certain satisfaction in jerking the *jerk's* chain. He felt freer than he had in years, but then freedom is just another word for *unemployed.*

On their way to the airport, Dan mailed Carl's watch to Vince Peretti, in hopes that he could retrieve more text from the sodden note. The trip consisted mainly of Rachel grilling him on every detail of Carl Jameson's death and the time Carl may have spent at the Santa Fe Institute. She was a woman of surprises, fiercely loyal and determined to avenge Carl's death, yet despite her obvious affection for the man, she had not shed a single tear, keeping her emotions tightly controlled.

Dan had a good idea why. Rachel was probably passing through the five stages of grief, a process Dan had experienced firsthand. It would be a difficult journey to acceptance.

He cast a concerned glance over his shoulder toward her. She was sitting near the bow, her legs dangling over the railing, chatting and laughing with Duff. Listening passively, he felt an odd discomfort about the ease with which the two of them conversed.

"I've got *great* news to report," Duff said to Rachel. "The police have found your friend's personal effects at a boarding house in La Ceiba."

"That's a start. When's the next ferry to the mainland?"

"Oh, no need for that, dearie," Duff replied. "You can use *Little Diver* for the length of your stay."

"Why, that's so *very* kind of you," she said, with a coquettish air.

"We'll be glad to bring this mystery to a close," Duff said. "It's been a stressful week here."

"I'll be here until it's done."

"Well, you'll have my support. Anything you need." Duff smiled. "Now, Miss Sullivan . . . that's an honest Irish name. And you have the hair to go with it. You know what they say about red-haired lassies?"

"Of course." She grinned. "And you *should* be cautious. We're trouble, especially us Irish-Italians."

Duff's eyebrow shot up. "My goodness, Irish temper and Italian passion. That must make for interesting discussions around the dinner table. How did that happen?"

"My grandfather flew for the RAF during World War Two. He was somewhat famous as an ace, until he got shot down over Italy. While trying to evade the Luftwaffe, he received sanctuary from my grandmother's family. One thing led to another and . . . it's a long and colorful story." She let slip a mischievous smile. "So, how about you? Judging from your brogue, I'd say you're from somewhere near Cork."

Duff seemed pleased by her insight. "You've nailed the general area. My clan's Black Irish. We moved to Pennsylvania in 1850, but my family has strong ties to the old sod."

"Ah, the Irish potato famine."

"Right again, Miss Sullivan. A most unfortunate time—the starvation, the riots, caskets stacked like cordwood. It's funny how things go 'round full circle, isn't it?"

"How so?"

Duff's expression took on a distant and somber look. He turned his face toward the sky. "In 1588, when storms destroyed the Spanish Armada, the women of Eire took in the poor Spanish bastards, giving them solace and the fruit of their wombs. The Spaniards returned the favor by spreading their seed among many fair ladies of the land, spawning the Black Irish. Years later, their descendants introduced the tuber, brought back by the Conquistadors from this very area. But alas, it came with a terrible price. The blight of the Irish potato spelled our doom, from our total dependence on it. And now, I'm back where it all started, trying to save this small piece of Latin paradise from foreign pestilence."

Rachel laughed heartily. "And my, don't you tell quite the story, Mr. McAlister."

"Oh *please*, dearie, just call me Duff."

Dan tried to focus on something else and noticed that they had already passed the resort off the port bow. Duff had made no attempt to slow down. "Aren't we stopping?"

"You requested a private venue. The eastern tip of Guanaja is my secret hideaway. It's as private and secluded as it gets."

Minutes later, the sandy coastline gave way to volcanic crags and sheer cliffs that discouraged most human settlement. Lava pinnacles stood in naked clusters along the shoreline, the surrounding limestone having eroded away eons ago.

Abruptly, Duff turned the boat and headed straight toward the forest of lava, threading his way deep into the pinnacle maze. He slowed the engines at a narrow channel—barely wide enough for *Little Diver* to squeeze through—and waited until the waves lifted the boat to a gap in the rock. He gunned the engines and *Little Diver* shot through the opening.

On the other side, a glassy lagoon opened up, completely hidden from the outside world. They landed at a tiny pier that connected to a narrow pathway snaking up the steep mountainside.

"This, my friends," Duff proudly exclaimed, "is my *wee* bit of Eden."

Duff grabbed two of their bags and bounded out of the boat with a child's glee. He swaggered up the pathway toward a series of steep switchbacks. Dan and Rachel followed with the rest of their luggage, struggling to keep up. The trail ascended through the deep forest for several hundred yards, ending abruptly at a row of stone steps. Dan stopped, gasping for breath, regretting the decision to bring so much computer gear.

A few hundred heart-pounding steps later, they reached a small, rustic cabin perched on a rocky outcropping. Duff dropped the bags on the cabin's deck and ushered them in. "You'll be safe here. Even the natives avoid this area—they think it's haunted. I do nothing to discourage that belief."

The cabin had three rooms: den with kitchenette stretched along one wall, bedroom, and bathroom. Several rows of shelves sagged with bric-a-brac: a brass diving helmet and canvas suit, old rum jugs, brass sextant, fishing gear, a bagpipe. A large wicker couch anchored the center.

Duff pointed to the kitchenette. "Fresh spring water, electric power from the windmill, gas stove, satellite TV, stereo. There's a composting toilet in the bathroom, and of course, a firkin of Guinness—all the comforts of home. If you need me, use the satellite telephone over there." Duff pointed toward the bar. "Rachel, you've got *Little Diver.* I'll take the skiff back. Think you can find your way out of the lagoon tomorrow?"

"Sure. Hang a left at the first pinnacle, then forty leagues to the bottom, right?"

Duff grinned. "If you get lost, call me."

"Don't hold your breath," she said with a laugh.

AFTER DUFF BID them goodnight, Dan decided to get more comfortable, donning a pair of gym shorts and his own syncrenomics T-shirt, which he had brought along.

Rachel took the hint, sluffed her boots, and changed into a burgundy sun dress.

Dan was captivated by the transformation. Rachel had morphed from khaki jungle girl to chic beach babe in an instant. He watched her as she padded into the kitchen in her bare feet and poured two pints of Guinness, one of which she passed to Dan.

Then, she began prowling the room like a bloodhound, poking around in the corners, finding the boundaries. She opened the kitchen cabinets and noted the foodstuffs, flipped through Duff's collection of Irish books, checked the medicine cabinet. She picked up the old brass diving helmet and set it on her head with the exactitude of someone familiar with the gear. She was boiling over with nervous energy and it took her several minutes to simmer down.

Meanwhile, Dan sipped his beer and took the opportunity to set up his laptop and satellite modem, all the while tracking Rachel's activities from the corner of his eye.

After a final examination of the bedroom, Rachel grabbed another pint of Guinness and plopped down on the couch with a contented sigh, flipping her long curls behind her head. She nodded with satisfaction. "Pretty nice place, and nice of Duff to let us use it. He's quite a character, that guy."

"Yes he is," Dan said. "So, are you going to tell me what *really* happened to your legs?"

She laughed and canted them to one side, putting one hand behind her head in a Vargas pose. "Why sir, you don't like my speckled legs?" She peeled back one bandage to reveal fresh pink skin, then recounted her adventures in Antarctica: her theories about punctuated equilibrium and gene sharing among the local algae, the courting habits of penguins, and her near fatal brush with the lava bomb. Her face grew sullen and distant when she reached the part about Carl's disappearance.

"I'm sorry," Dan said, trying to project the right amount of sympathy, which was hard to gauge with her. "So, how long had you known Carl?"

"Only a short while—a lifetime . . ." She trailed off and jumped back up to refill their glasses.

When she returned, Dan lifted his glass in a toast. "Here's to Carl. May we find him justice."

"Definitely." Rachel slugged her beer. Then she leaned in, gazing at Dan expectantly. "So, Mr. Prediction Scientist, why don't you explain more of this syncrenomics stuff?" She poked at his midriff through the T-shirt. "What's the deal with the fern, for instance? What does that have to do with syncrenomics?"

It seemed that Rachel had already begun to feel the effects of the Guinness, so Dan wondered how much she'd retain, but decided to forge ahead anyway. "All right. The fern represents the fractal universe. Fractals are shapes or behavior that occur at different scales—never exactly the same, but always self-similar. You'll find them everywhere in nature, from the branching of trees, blood vessels, nerves and bronchial tubes, fern leaves, jagged coastlines, patterns on seashells. Once you know where to look, you see them everywhere. And when we say history repeats itself, it's not a cliché. History *does* repeat, like a fractal, because human nature always operates from the same laws of behavior."

"Look, I get fractals," Rachel said. "But what can you *do* with the knowledge?"

"A lot," he replied. "For instance, you can test theories on different scales—that's how engineers can test a scale model of a wing in a wind tunnel before putting it on a full-size airplane. And if human nature is self-similar, then you can use that knowledge to predict future sociopolitical events."

"Sounds like a theory born of too much pot smoking," Rachel said, giggling. She crossed her legs and picked at one of her bandages.

Dan winced. "I hear that a lot, but there's still wisdom hidden in that haze," he said, cracking a wry smile. "Frankly, I'm surprised you don't use fractal theory in your biology studies."

"Sure, I see fractal patterns in nature all the time, but again, how do I *use* that knowledge?"

Dan looked down at his shirt, tracing the fern leaf's intricate pattern with his finger. "Look at it this way: the fern's complex shape is just a simple algorithm repeated many times at different scales—simple rules plus *time* equals a complex fern leaf. You can even draw a fern on a computer with only a few lines of programming code."

Rachel still seemed unconvinced. "It's still math, not too useful in the squishy world of biology."

"Really?" Dan thought for a moment. "What's DNA but a math program for creating a living being? Fractals are a form of information compression. An entire complex organism like a human being comes from a single microscopic DNA molecule. Just add *time*. We're all fractals—collections of self-similar, but slightly different cells, born from the same DNA instructions executed billions of times."

After a brief pause, he continued. "Think about a single genetic mutation in the fern's DNA. That mutation will be repeated countless times as the fern leaf grows, changing the leaf's entire shape, but often in an intelligent way. That mutation will either lead to a dead fern, or perhaps some new species. Maybe the mutation gives the fern a broader leaf so it can gather more sun. If so, the mutation advantage will be passed on to future generations. That's *evolution*. You can use that information to predict the rate of future change. Sounds a lot like your theory of punctuated equilibrium, no?"

Rachel's interest shot up a notch and she leaned closer, smiling. "Pretty impressive, Mr. Prediction. So, why not plug Carl's clues into your GAPS program and predict the killer?"

Dan laughed, not quite sure if she was serious or pulling his chain. "Not that easy of course, but there are a few tricks we can use to improve our chances."

"Like what?"

"We can listen to the butterflies."

"Right, the butterfly effect." Rachel smiled. "The flapping of a butterfly in Tokyo starts a thunderstorm in New York, or something like that."

"More formally called 'sensitivity to initial conditions.' In nonlinear systems, small initial changes multiply over time, making future outcomes completely unpredictable."

"Sounds like it makes your job impossible, then."

"That's what we used to think, but we've learned a lot recently. Many complex systems have a hidden order. All that interaction forms regions of synchronicity that *self*-organize into fuzzy groups called strange attractors—like history repeating itself. We can use this statistical resonance to spot patterns and guess the future. Even roulette wheels are not truly random."

"So why not go to Vegas and clean up?"

Dan smiled knowingly. "That's exactly what a team of Harvard scientists did several years ago. They created a computer in a shoe that could calculate the trajectory of a roulette ball within a zone of probability. They would bet on a quadrant of likely numbers and clean up. Until one nervous guy sweated in his socks and almost electrocuted himself."

It looked like the beer had definitely kicked in. Rachel began to giggle. "Dan Clifford, you're one *strange attractor* yourself," she said, and leaned forward until her forehead touched his. "How did you get interested in this syncrenomics stuff?"

Dan was barely listening. He suddenly felt uncomfortable with his thoughts, like he was interfering with her mourning. "I want to understand how things work, I guess. Isn't that why you study germs?"

She corrected him with a waggle of her finger. "That's microbes, buddy. We don't call them germs."

"Whatever. When we understand complexity, we can better prepare for the future, avoid obvious mistakes."

"I don't *want* to know what the future has in store," she said, her mirth fading. "I might not like it."

"Wouldn't you rather see around the bend? Otherwise you're just stomping around in the dark, wreaking havoc. We live in a world obsessed with control. When you're controlling things, you aren't paying attention to your surroundings. Politicians, religious leaders, executives . . . they think they can make their own future. It's a grand illusion. Meanwhile, invisible butterflies flap at our periphery, ready to upset our perfectly balanced world like an invasive species."

"So butterflies are tricksters," she interjected.

"In a sense, because imperceptible actions can have huge effects. That's the nature of tricksters—and why they're commonly portrayed as clowns, jokers, or feeble old men. Ever wonder why Kokopelli was drawn with a huge phallus, before the missionaries censored it?"

"No, but I'm sure you're going to give me the hard facts," Rachel said, grinning again.

"Well, Native Americans were just as concerned about paternity and adultery as any other culture. The brave warriors would eye one another jealously and compete for the affections of the young women. But away from camp they all had to hunt and fight together. Meanwhile, the flute-playing hunchback with the big phallus stayed at home with the women. It was no accident that Kokopelli was also known as the god of fertility. That's the moral of the story: often the biggest threats come from the most unlikely places."

Rachel sat silently for a while, pondering his comments. "Aren't you trying to change the future with your software? Control things? At least I admit I'm blind."

She had a point. His trip to the chip factory was an effort to take control, and it backfired. "Guilty as charged," he replied. "Prediction is about realizing your role in the grand scheme of things, sometimes becoming the butterfly. That's what GAPS is really about—making us sensitive to our surroundings, so we can identify hidden threats."

Rachel whistled softly. "Control—lack of control. Predicting—unpredictability. Sounds like a bunch of contradictory mumbo jumbo."

Dan laughed. "You have a way of distilling things to their essence don't you? That's balance of opposition, tenet number three."

"That'll have to wait," she said, and patted him on the cheek. "Off with you. I've got to sleep."

"You take the bedroom—"

"No, no—I've got the couch. I'm leaving early."

Dan realized he'd lose the argument and gave up. "Your choice. Check out the deck first?"

"Sure."

They stepped out on the small deck and leaned against the handrail. The smells of nature hung heavy in the air: flowery bougainvillea, spicy fermenting fruit, humus. The forest seemed to vibrate with life, filled with the chatter of birds, insects, tree frogs. Beneath the din of animals came the sound of gurgling water from a small stream spilling down the cliff.

Dan could feel the weight of exhaustion bearing down. After a few minutes' reflection, he ushered Rachel back inside, stopping for a second to study a movement in the cabin light.

A caterpillar was munching lazily on an overhanging branch. On its back hung three white grubs, the eggs of a local predatory wasp. The caterpillar continued to eat, preparing for metamorphosis, unaware of its destiny as nourishment for a completely different form of life.

17

A PARROT'S SCREECH woke Dan from a deep sleep. He checked his watch and realized it was past noon. Still groggy from jet lag, he rubbed his eyes and struggled to the kitchenette. A pot of cold coffee and some dirty dishes lay piled on the counter. From the look of things, Rachel had been gone for hours.

He brewed a fresh pot of coffee, sat down, and stared at his laptop. So this was it—he was unemployed for the first time. He'd been immersed in theory for so long. The stark reality of life hit him in the face.

So, a new career then? But what? Against his friend Vince's advice, it looked to be Sam Spade, detective.

He turned on the computer and placed a Skype call to Rudi Plimpton. The programmer answered with a look of absolute misery. "Rudi, you okay?"

"It sucks here in cubicle hell with the secretarial pool! It's the friggin' center of the SNAFU universe, okay? At least in the dungeon, everybody left me alone. Now, Sonny's minions bug me every day with dumb questions about the NOAA software—hold on a minute." His face vanished from the screen, replaced by his belt buckle. It returned a minute later. "Just checking the maze. Wouldn't want the Gestapo to discover me chatting with you."

"Found anything I can use?" Dan grabbed a notepad.

"Oh yeah. I tapped into the billing files. The NeuroSys chip factory is being leased from a Honduran corporation called Gulf-Pacific Investments. I checked the corporate registry. Guess who's on the board? Senator Nolan Becker."

Dan leaned back in his chair, shocked but not really surprised. *So it's true.* The quick approval of GAPS had been contrived. "Explains why the SEC isn't snooping around. I'm sure Becker is running interference."

"*Correctamundo.* Sonny's got political ties."

Dan let out a sigh. The thought of Sonny rubbing shoulders with politicos curdled his stomach. "Where's the money coming from?"

"Still working on that. There are several holding companies involved."

"Thanks, Sherlock. Keep following the money trail."

"That's getting tougher," Rudi said. "Sonny's pulled the accounting server off the net. Severed the link. You gotta have a swipe-card now."

"You're locked out?"

"Of course not!" Rudi seemed genuinely hurt by the inference. "There are still ancillary documents on the main server. I've unleashed a search-bot."

"I need you to research one other thing for me."

"Anything to keep from going stir crazy."

"You still have access to NOAA's servers?" Dan asked.

"I've got more back doors there than a New Orleans whorehouse."

"Good. Search their files for anything on a Carl Jameson—research papers, Web sites, that kind of stuff. He's the dead guy I found here."

"No kidding." Rudi glanced over his shoulder again. "Give me a few hours."

"Thanks, and be careful."

"Always."

Ending his call, Dan decided to split his search time between Carl Jameson and the NeuroSys plant. He googled the three legible phrases they had found in the watch. The resulting list was depressingly long: references to biblical text, end-of-the-world prophesies, heavy metal bands, ecology papers, Inuit cosmology, Celtic wonder tales, black holes. With three such highly charged terms, his search suffered from a lack of specificity. It would take days to sift through the results. Deciding on a wild-assed guess, he headed to biblegateway.com and searched the King James Bible for "abyss+earth+sky."

After a few anxious seconds . . . nothing. Not a single hit. *So, you expected this to be easy?* His first day as Sam Spade was off to a rough start.

THE PORT OF La Ceiba slowly revealed itself from a shroud of haze clinging to the base of Benito Peak. After a few harrowing minutes in the pinnacle maze, Rachel's trip from Guanaja had gone smoothly. It had given her time to mull over everything from the past few days.

She felt a pang of guilt at having dragged Dan Clifford back to a place where he clearly did not want to be, but she needed his support. At least that's what she kept telling herself. In truth, there was more to it than that.

Dan reminded her of Carl, with his passion for nuances. But *Mr. Prediction* was wound tighter than a winch, something she'd have to work on. The previous night, she had gotten a little too bold, too relaxed. Right now, she couldn't afford any new complications.

Her thoughts drifted back to Carl and a painful memory: the rendezvous they had planned nearby—in Belize—where the *Sea Berth* would have moored on its return voyage from Antarctica. They'd both been eagerly anticipating it—a week on the beach, scuba diving, a chance for them to get to know each other better. Her excitement had grown beyond the boundaries she normally set for herself. Now, instead of sharing time with Carl, she was salvaging details from his last days alive. It was a grueling task she had vowed never to repeat, yet, here she was again, cleaning up after another man, letting another loss take control of her life.

It was too late to do anything about it now, so she refocused on the harbor. La Ceiba was a bustling trade center by Honduran standards. Several large cargo ships dominated the southern quay. The northern end held a patchwork of small fishing vessels, their crews busily loading ice into holds, making repairs to nets and rigging. She backed *Little Diver* in between two small shrimpers, catching the attention of both crews. Their sun-baked faces all turned in her direction. A young boy stopped knotting a frayed seine net, his mouth open. She could feel a hundred eyes on her as she stepped from the boat. Any one of these men could be Carl's killer. The thought triggered a smoldering rage. She scowled back at them, hurried down the crowded dock, and turned left, following Duff's directions to the headquarters of the La Ceiba harbor police.

When she entered, Captain Berto Enrique had his feet propped on the desk and was studying a report. When she rapped her knuckles on the desk, he sat up with a start. The chief was tall and dark, with sharp brown eyes that examined her from neck to knees. He smiled unabashedly and crooned: "Ah, you must be Señorita Sullivan! Duff said you would be visiting." He extended a calloused hand that Rachel shook forcefully. "How may I be of service to you?"

"Carl Jameson's personal effects," she said flatly.

"Ah yes, the drowned American."

"The *murder* victim."

"Yes, yes. I stand corrected." Berto licked his lips. "My condolences. Señora Vasquez owns a boarding house near the docks. When Mr. Jameson failed to pay his weekly rent, she checked his room." Berto stepped around two rusting file cabinets, retrieved a cardboard box from the corner, and, with a satisfied look, placed it on the desk.

It contained scarcely anything of interest: toiletries, several changes of clothes, a small stack of Honduran lempira folded in a money clip, a passport, an electric razor, and a few technical manuals.

"Is this all?"

"*Sí.*"

"No pictures? Lab notes? A laptop?"

"That is all, *señorita*. It appears he was robbed."

"Robbed? They stole his laptop and left his money?" She wiggled the money clip for effect. "What progress have you made?"

Berto's smile faded. "I'm afraid there is little evidence on which to base an investigation, although we have checked the room thoroughly."

"Did you find fingerprints? Fiber evidence?"

"*Sí, señorita.* Fingerprints, yes. Hundreds of them, from previous guests. You must understand, we have no facilities here to filter through such a quantity of prints."

This was exactly what she had expected, and it took little time for her frustration to boil over. "So, this is a closed case for you? Some American is murdered and you turn away, because he's a foreigner?"

"We've done everything—"

"You've done nothing! Do I have to contact the American consulate?"

Berto winced. "There is no need for threats, Miss Sullivan. Your attitude will not help matters."

"What kind of attitude *would*?"

"Please, sit." Berto put on his most diplomatic face. "We will do whatever we can, but—"

The squawk of the police radio interrupted him.

"Excuse me, please." Berto turned his back, lowered the volume, and spoke softly in Spanish. "*Dígame.*"

Rachel listened in on the conversation with a practiced ear for Spanish.

"Captain, come quickly!"

Even over the radio, she could sense the urgency in the man's voice.

"A very bad situation—"

Berto pulled the mike closer. "Hector, calm down. I have a visitor."

The voice wavered. "Captain . . . it's . . . happening again . . ."

Berto's face went pale. He rubbed a hand over his jaw. "Where are you?"

"At your *brother's.*"

"Blessed Mother Mary!" he gasped. The microphone began to shake. "I'm on my way." The captain sat quietly for a few seconds, then whipped around. "*Señorita,* I will investigate your concerns, but now I must leave." He grabbed his gun belt from the table.

She started to argue with him, but saw the futility of it. She picked up Carl's things. "I'll take these."

"No no. That's evidence. I'll need to—" He shook his head in exasperation. "Okay. *Sí,* I'll contact you." He pushed her through the door, followed, and locked it. Before she could say another word, Berto Enrique had slipped around the corner of the building and disappeared.

Rachel headed back to the docks, her sense of frustration growing. The local police were useless, just as she had suspected. She had no constitutional rights here, no political connections. If she wanted justice for Carl's killers, she'd have to get it herself.

Isn't that always the Sullivan way?

Her anger flared as she reached the pier. She scowled at the fishermen again as she stepped aboard *Little Diver.* Suddenly, three young boys burst from the cockpit and darted past her at breakneck speed. Before she could react, they were gone, leaving radios and navigational equipment dangling halfway from the instrument panel. Another five minutes and the young thieves would have stolen the entire array. Rachel threw the box on the floor and kicked the side of the boat, cursing.

The full weight of Carl's death suddenly came crashing down around her. She dropped into the pilot's chair and allowed a few tears

to flow, but they didn't last long. Feeling the eyes of the dock's fishermen on her back, Rachel steeled herself again, cranked the engine, and
roared out of the bay at full throttle, leaving the gawking workers
behind in a cloud of exhaust.

18

BERTO ENRIQUE PUSHED the Land Cruiser to the limit, sirens blaring, corners cut heavy on two wheels, dust billowing. The words turned over and over in his mind:

It's happening again.

What exactly did Hector mean? Berto should have asked more questions. That *Americana* had already caused him to miss the start of his brother's party. Perhaps that was a good thing. His wife and children were still safe at home, awaiting his arrival. . . .

He feared that the ghost ship's secrets had escaped from the depths. At the time, his decision to torch the boat seemed prudent, though he was still baffled by his state of mind on the *Doncella Hermosa*. Still, he told himself, nothing good could have come from telling the Ortega family that their menfolk murdered one another. And what would be his explanation? Satan? No, better to sanctify by burning and tell the Ortegas that their menfolk were lost at sea, an honorable death.

And he had done just that.

Now, the stain of guilt was seeping into his hardened soul. He knew the real reason for his decision. No use trying to deny it. *What have I done?*

He made a hard right onto the town's main street and slammed to a stop a few meters from a crowd of brightly dressed revelers. They shouted obscenities as he beat on the cruiser's horn with his fists.

The Festival of Guadalupe had taken over the streets and the parade was progressing faster than he had expected. He edged past several wheeled booths selling tacos, ice cream, and cups of *atole*. Members of the church congregation stood directly in his path, burdened down with flags, statues, and crucifixes on tall poles, swaying to the tunes of marimba bands.

The local parish priest led the parade, accompanied by a group of colorfully dressed children. The young boys wore the peasant dress of Juan Diego; the girls wore brightly colored Mayan costumes.

He turned around, looking for a way out. Cursing, he backed up several meters, turned left, barreled over the curb, and bounced down an alleyway between two dilapidated buildings. Not bothering with pavement, he cut across a vacant lot, roared through the backyard of the mayor's house, grazed a picnic table. Startled shouts accompanied a barrage of food on the car's back window. The cruiser lurched over a ditch, sending Berto's head into the ceiling. Once again on pavement, he floored the accelerator. The crush of people faded to a trickle as he turned down a narrow side street toward a modest residential district south of town. Moments later he screeched to a halt in front of his brother Delmar's cinder-block home.

He raced around the left side to the backyard and stopped abruptly. Confronted with an inexplicable scene, Berto struggled to retain his professional detachment.

Two tables had been pulled together for the feast, covered in brightly patterned tablecloths. An awning of bedspreads stretched overhead to mute the sun. Delmar, his sister Zita, and his aunts and uncles huddled along the home's back wall, their faces wracked with confusion and horror. His assistant Hector stood a good ten meters farther away.

Heart pounding, Berto forced his eyes along the table. *I do not want to see this!* Death was routine in his job, but this was different. This was *family.* A corpse draped the dinner table like some grotesque entrée. The handle of a large steak knife protruded from the left eye socket. It was the next-door neighbor, Errando. *Not one of us!* He released a guilty sigh of relief.

That relief faded as he spotted Pepito, his sister's son, at the end of the table. Pepito was crouched on his haunches. Bleeding and disheveled, he rocked back and forth, eyes vacant and clouded, face contorted in a mask of hideous glee. He was ripping the tablecloth into long narrow strips, laying them aside in a neat pile.

It made no sense. Berto turned to Delmar, mustering his most professional demeanor: "Tell me what happened here, brother."

"I . . . don't know. We sat down to eat . . . I invited Errando to join us. Everything seemed fine . . . then Errando complained of his stomach." Delmar rubbed his face vigorously. "Moments later, he began circling the yard, yelling that snails were inside his head, eating his brain!" Delmar shook his head. "Whenever we grew near, he threatened. Said the snails would eat us too. We tackled him, carried him to the table; he had the strength of ten men!" Delmar pointed to a gash on his forehead. "Then he just . . . stuck that knife right in his eye. Without a thought!"

Berto winced. He had handled many drug-crazed individuals in his career—people stoked on cocaine or PCP—but nothing like this. "And Pepito?" The mention of his name brought a wail of grief from his sister Zita.

"I don't know. Things were so . . . crazy. Pepito began dancing and laughing, screaming like a wild animal! Next thing we knew, he was on the table, ripping that tablecloth. We feared to approach him, lest he do something crazy like Errando."

Berto stole another glance at Pepito, whose manner seemed meticulous, compulsive. "How long has he been—"

"Fifteen minutes," Delmar said and grabbed Berto's shirt, tears streaming down his face. "What must we do, brother! Are we cursed?"

Berto looked away, his heart filling with shame. *Is this my fault?* "I don't know, but I'll find out. I *swear!*"

Delmar tugged harder on Hector's shirt, sobbing. "And Rosaria! You must find her, and the baby."

"What?" Berto realized he had not seen Delmar's wife. "Where is she?"

"Gone, during the chaos. She was cooking. When things went loco, the two of them disappeared. Find them, *please!*"

"I will," Berto promised, gently pulling Delmar's hand away. "But you must be strong for the family, understand?"

Delmar nodded weakly.

"Give me a minute," Berto said, his composure returning. He signaled angrily to Hector, who shuffled over. "Go inside and find another bedsheet for Pepito, to keep him happy. I don't want him tearing up more evidence."

Hector nodded, his head bowed.

"Then, I want you to get everyone inside, away from this . . . this *mess*! Have you called the ambulance?"

"Yes, but the parade—"

"I know, just get the sheet. Go!" Berto approached the corpse, taking care to stay as far away as possible from Pepito, who remained focused on his bizarre task. Berto examined the area around the body, noting a large bowl of *sopa de caracol* spilled across the table. Large, fleshy chunks of pink conch floated in pools of ivory-hued sauce.

Snails eating his brain?

Berto leaned in. Errando's face glistened with a sweat that gave off a foul, mousy odor. He picked up a spoon, pried the mouth open, and looked inside. Several of Errando's teeth had been shattered by the strength of his convulsions.

A sudden breath of dead air escaped the man's lungs, flooding Berto with a sweet, putrid stench. Through the foul odor, Berto recognized a familiar scent and jerked his head back. He staggered away, grabbed a table. The ground seemed to spin beneath him as a childhood memory surfaced, one of demons entering and exiting through the mouth. He wiped the sweat from his own face. *Get control of yourself!*

Berto turned back to his brother. "When Rosaria left, did she seem . . . different?"

A flash of fear crossed Delmar's eyes. "You must find them! They are everything to me, please!"

"Had she been eating?"

"I, uh, sampling perhaps."

"And the others? Yourself?"

"We had just started to eat."

Berto examined Delmar's eyes, fearful but lucid. He examined the rest of his family and prayed for their safety. As far as he could tell, everyone else seemed normal.

When Hector returned, Berto pulled him to one side. "Listen, you cowardly fool! I saw you hiding in the corner. I've no choice but to leave you in charge. No one touches this table. No one eats or drinks. Get Pepito to the hospital. Take Errando's body to the morgue, have it autopsied. No one but the doctors see this! I don't want panic, or my family implicated. Understood?"

Hector nodded absently, fear heavy in his eyes. "It's the curse, can you feel it? From the boat—"

"Shut up, idiot! Act like a professional for once." He whispered in Hector's ear, "If anyone else starts acting strangely, take them to the hospital, *personally and quietly,* is this clear?"

"Yes, sir."

Berto placed a hand on Delmar's shoulder. "Stay strong, brother." He squeezed reassuringly. "I will return with Rosaria and Maria." Then he bounded down the street, trying to anticipate Rosaria's direction. She had probably panicked and done what any mother would do to protect her child.

He'd panicked too, back at the house, barely able to resist the urge to run away. Even now, he felt a strange paranoia, a sense of being outside his body, yet he pushed on, sucking in great gulps of air. The festival had emptied the streets, making it easy to spot a young woman walking alone. He heard a few faint echoes of laughter from other parties and wondered if anyone else had been afflicted. *Why me?* He could not shake the guilt he felt.

Rosaria was Delmar's prize, the young daughter of a powerful family from Belize. Their roots traced back to Mayan nobility, and it showed in Rosaria's striking beauty. All the men, including Berto, envied Delmar's good fortune. The only thing in the world more precious to Delmar than Rosaria was their nine-month-old daughter, Maria.

His route took him back to the main street, several blocks south of the festival, where he turned left, back toward the Church of the Sacred Heart. Rosaria's deep faith would probably lead her there. A half block away, Berto stopped and hunched over, gasping. The vision of demons rushing in and out of his mouth conspired to suck the oxygen from his lungs with each desperate breath.

Straight ahead, he could see the *espadaña* of the church, the adobe façade designed to give the one-story structure a taller, more majestic profile. His eyes traveled from the twin bell towers down to the ornate mahogany door. It was cracked open. He struggled forward, finally reaching the steps to the entrance. He wobbled up and slipped through the door.

It had been a long time since Berto had seen the church's interior. He was not a religious man. Years of witnessing violence and depravity had drained any faith from him. What caring god would allow such things?

Still, on this day he would have given anything for the comfort of faith.

He walked slowly across the narthex, down the steps, and into the nave, pausing so his eyes could adjust to the dim interior. Below the arched timber ceiling, he could see the two long rows of pews stretching down the length of the church. They stopped a few meters short of an ornate altar screen. Its niches were filled with paintings of saints. Even to a nonbeliever, the decorated expanse inspired awe.

But not like this. The vision before him left Berto questioning his own sanity. He rubbed his eyes vigorously, but the vision remained.

A column of light streamed down from the clerestory, embracing an angelic form, its hands held together in prayer. The air seemed to shimmer and vibrate around her. Gold vases flanked her on both sides, overflowing with bouquets of roses. And on the altar at her feet: a small child wrapped in white cloth. Berto gasped and fell to his knees, the meaning of his vision painfully clear.

I am being punished for my transgressions!

19

THE SLAM OF the cabin door broke Dan's concentration. He turned to see Rachel holding a ragged box, breathing heavily. "How did you sneak up on me like that?"

"Easy," she said, and dropped the box on the floor. "You seemed to be making love to your laptop."

Dan rubbed his eyes, strained from hours staring at the screen. "How was your meeting?"

"A total waste of time, like I suspected," she said with a scowl. "The police chief was more concerned with some local incident than anything I had to say. He practically shoved me out the door to answer his phone."

"And Carl's things?"

"Everything of value stolen, except his money. Doesn't sound like a typical robbery, does it? So, how about you? What have you found out?"

Dan hesitated to discuss his lack of progress, which would only add to Rachel's frustration. "Not much, I'm afraid. My friend Rudi used to work for NOAA and still has a few, uh, back doors, you might say. I had him search through NOAA's servers for Carl's records. They've all been expunged."

"*What?*" Rachel slumped on the couch.

"Research notes, his blog, e-mails, phone messages—everything. It had to be someone with enough computer savvy to sneak past NOAA's security, someone concerned enough to erase all of Carl's personal records."

Rachel grabbed her head and let out a strangled scream. "So we have nothing? How am I ever going to get justice for him?"

"Not exactly nothing," Dan said, joining her on the couch. "You said Carl had a research grant to study mining samples. There's only one mining company with a large warehouse near here: Solá Mining."

"So, that's where we start, then." Rachel brightened.

"Possibly."

"But we'll need proof," she continued. "How do we find any, when Carl's research is gone?"

"We'll have to find a different way. I'm working on it." Dan had been saving one last revelation, hoping it would reduce Rachel's frustration a bit. "Back in Atlanta, do you remember telling me how you and Carl used to argue over the extinction of the dinosaurs?"

"Yeah, but what does that have to do with anything?"

"Humor me for a moment. You never told me *your* theory."

"You mean punctuated equilibrium?" Rachel's eyes narrowed. "I think the dinosaurs died from disease, probably triggered by the Chicxulub impact."

"And how would that work, exactly?"

"The larger the animal, the slower the evolution. If an asteroid struck the earth, there would obviously be a lot of stress on the environment. Stress can trigger punctuated spurts of evolution, but more so in smaller creatures and microbes. No single asteroid is likely to have killed all the dinosaurs, but if they failed to adapt quickly enough, they might succumb to competition from other species, or new diseases for which they had no immunity."

"And Carl disagreed."

"Oh yeah. He thought the meteor impact itself would be sufficient. We had a few knock-down, drag-outs . . ." Rachel wrinkled her brow. "Where are you going with this, because I don't see the point."

"When I said *all* of Carl's personal records were gone, that wasn't entirely true," Dan said. "They forgot one thing, because it wasn't in Carl's records per se, but rather in NOAA's server cache. We found Carl's latest search history. We know the subjects Carl had been researching right before he died." Dan showed her a list of terms he'd entered on his smartphone:

    invasive marine species
    Gaia hypothesis
    network theory
    microbes, punctuated equilibrium, Rachel Sullivan

Rachel stared at the list for several minutes. "He was studying my research?" She seemed genuinely touched at first, then brushed it off. "He was probably boning up for our next debate. But the Gaia hypothesis? Invasive marine species? I don't get it."

"Makes sense to me," Dan said, "if you're researching a *global* extinction. The Gaia hypothesis describes the Earth as a massively interconnected complex system that has its own immune system of sorts. James Lovelock was criticized for giving the theory such a new age name, but the science was sound. Every organism, every weather pattern, every event on Earth is inextricably linked. Carl was seeing your theory through the lens of syncrenomics."

Rachel was back up and pacing the room, deep in thought. "Go on."

"Like an interconnected hive, the Earth's organisms create the conditions for their own survival. Algae and plants create the oxygen in our atmosphere, regulate the Earth's temperature, and recycle our dead. The plants and animals of the food web feed each other, through growth and excrement. All these interconnected systems reach stasis over time, through checks and balances, predators and prey. This duality is represented on the medicine wheel by the yin and yang symbol, because Chinese philosophers realized that opposing forces are not only complementary, but necessary. Everything in nature competes and cooperates at the same time. It's that *balance of opposition* that allows systems to self-regulate, to remain stable and resilient."

Rachel's excitement seemed to intensify. "So you're saying Carl changed his mind? He was agreeing with me?"

"Well . . . it looks that way. If some intruder upsets the Earth's current balance, local ecosystems will either adapt, by killing off the threat, or perish, maybe through punctuated equilibrium, as you say, or some other method. But as you mentioned, larger animals don't evolve very quickly, so they can't adapt. We see this today on a smaller scale. Kudzu invades the south and kills hectares of forest, Apple iPhones turn the computer industry upside down, Asian carp invade the Great Lakes and destroy the fishing industry. Whether it's fish, microbes, or technology, the principle is the same. Invasive species are the very definition of black swan events, or tricksters. They are so destructive precisely because a perfectly balanced system has no defense for the new threat."

Rachel gave him an incredulous look. "And you think Carl left these clues behind to prove a point or something?"

"Maybe Carl discovered evidence of a trickster during his research, some invasive species that could have triggered the extinction of the dinosaurs."

Rachel sat back down and stared intensely at the floor for several minutes. Then she shook her head. "Sorry, that's just crazy. You think Carl would waste time leaving a clue to some theoretical debate about dinosaurs? Right before he's murdered? Besides, why would anyone murder Carl over something that happened sixty-five million years ago? No, it's got to be a clue about his killers, something more imme-diate." Her expression darkened. "Carl's gone, and I'll never know ex-actly what he meant to say. It's like his entire life has been erased!"

Dan gave her a reassuring look. "We'll find more, I promise." Only he wasn't so sure himself.

"I know you're trying," Rachel said, tears pooling in her eyes. "But none of this makes sense."

The two of them fell into an awkward silence. They sat for a half hour, staring out at the sky, as a curtain of gray clouds slipped in from the east, stealing the sun.

Rachel finally stood up and straightened her clothes. "I want to see Carl."

20

NUESTRA SEÑORA DE Guadalupe.

Twice she had appeared to him, first on the ghost ship, and now here in the Church of the Sacred Heart. Berto could smell the roses, their significance clear to him now. Our Lady of Guadalupe had given him a sign on the ghost ship, warning him to reveal the truth.

And he had failed.

He had robbed the Ortega family of absolution, and now his own family suffered. Berto recalled with childlike clarity the famous story of the Lady of Guadalupe:

In the 1500s, the first Catholic missionaries began their religious conquest. Among their converts was Juan Diego. On a chilly December morning, Juan Diego crossed the barren hill of Tepeyac, where once stood the temple honoring Tonantzin, the Earth Goddess, mother of all living things, the giver of life and the devourer. The temple had since been destroyed by the bishop.

Juan Diego was stopped by a blinding light and the sound of heavenly music. Before him appeared a beautiful dark-skinned woman who declared herself to be the Virgin Mary. She gave Juan Diego a message for the bishop. A new church was to be built on Tepeyac hill. It was no easy task for the humble man to be granted an audience with the top prelate, but the persistent Juan Diego was finally admitted. The bishop demanded proof of the encounter.

Confused and fearful, Juan Diego returned to Tepeyac. The Virgin appeared again and commanded him to pick roses from the desolate hill and deliver them to the bishop as a sign. Juan Diego did as instructed. He unfurled his cloak to reveal the miraculous roses and a perfect image of the Virgin emblazoned upon it. Convinced of the miracle, the bishop ordered the construction. After the church was built, millions of Aztecs and Mayans converted to Catholicism, abandoning warfare and human sacrifice for the forgiveness of the Church.

Lost in the wonderment of the moment, Berto stared again at the altar. The boundaries of the apparition sharpened until he recognized the life-sized wooden carving of the Virgin of Guadalupe. This curse had visited his family on the day of her celebration. Was that not a real child at the statue's feet? Arms and legs moving? He was certain that he could hear the sound of quiet sobbing.

The scene grew more surreal.

Berto stared in awe as the Virgin's spirit seemed to rise again from the shaft of light. She hovered for a moment over the child, raising her hands in prayer. Berto shook his head, unwilling to accept the vision that confronted his senses, unable to reject it.

But it is real!

Was it? He rubbed his eyes fiercely again, the truth slowly dawning. *Rosaria!* Kneeling behind the altar, praying. Now she stood over her own child.

With a sudden charge of excitement, Berto stood and approached, embarrassed by his confusion, but relieved. Is this how one finds a vision? An optical illusion? Certainly not the way a man such as himself, trained in professional observation, should behave.

"Rosaria! It's Berto! Are you all right?"

"Berto?"

Rosaria turned toward him. She had been crying, her mascara pooling in the hollows of her eyes. Berto felt a flood of relief. "I've come to take you home. Delmar is worried sick."

"How is he?"

"Fine, fine. Let's go."

"And the others?"

He hesitated, wondering how much of the awful details to reveal. "Why did you leave?"

Rosaria lifted a trembling hand to her face and grimaced. In her other hand she gripped a large crucifix, taken from a stand alongside the altar.

"The others, so horrible!" She crossed herself.

"Everyone will be okay. Let's go home." He reached out a hand.

She backed away. "I can't." Her body tensed.

"Why not?"

She turned and beckoned to the Virgin, as if searching for the answer within the statue's wooden soul. "It's too late," she said, sighing.

"Too late for what?" Berto stepped forward and grasped her loose hand, shocked by the iciness of it.

She jerked it away. "I can't go back. No one can."

Berto felt a sudden weight on his heart. Her pupils were dilated, the whites so swollen and red that they appeared as rivers of blood. He took an involuntary step backward and gasped. *This can't be happening! Not now!* "Rosaria, you are talking nonsense! Come with me."

The woman Berto knew seemed to melt away before his eyes. Rosaria's face cycled through several emotions: disgust, fear, sadness . . . defeat. A stranger fixed her gaze on him.

"We are all going to die."

The certainty of Rosaria's words sent a cold shiver down Berto's spine. "I . . . what do you mean?" He noticed that she was not looking at him anymore, having focused on a point to his left. He turned around to look . . . but there was nothing there.

A whimper escaped her mouth. "Do you see him?" she whispered. "The Jaguar? His eyes, glowing! Can you see his teeth? Slick and bloody?" She took another step back and cowered against the altar screen. "They are at my throat! He wants . . . *everything*!"

Berto stood transfixed, unsure how to react. "Who? Wants what?"

Rosaria rattled out a string of Hail Mary's, spoken in staccato bursts so rapidly that he could barely make them out. Then she mouthed a fury of phrases that sounded Mayan. The words were unrecognizable to him, except for one name—Kinich Ahau, the Mayan Sun god. The Jaguar. Rosaria seemed to be mixing her faiths into a hopeless jumble. It was as if the gods themselves were fighting over her soul.

"Rosaria, listen to me," Berto said calmly but sternly, trying to reach whatever strand of reason remained. "You are sick. We must get you well—"

A hideous screech burst forth. "Stand back! The Jaguar will eat you too!" She doubled over, a gastric moan gurgling from her throat. "It burns!"

"Rosaria, let me help you!"

"No!" she shrieked. "I'm dead, do you hear! *Dead!*" Her body began grotesque contortions, her arms thrashing and gesticulating wildly. "I've swallowed the Sun! It's burning, burning! It will burn you to death!"

The transformation was furious and complete. Berto froze in midstep, unsure what to do. He would rather have taken on an army of drug-crazed maniacs than to see the perfectly rational woman he knew and loved reduced to this . . . horror. Desperate for hope, he cast a glance toward the altar and Maria. The baby seemed normal, agitated but healthy. He made a sudden decision.

Save Maria at all costs.

Berto moved toward the child. Rosaria reacted with lightning speed. Screaming, she swung at him with the crucifix. He tried to duck but she was too quick; heavy metal dug into his scalp, followed by a burst of lights. He bent over, drew his hands over his head defensively. A blow landed on his shoulder and he felt the square edge of the crucifix penetrate muscle. Falling backward, his head hit the sandstone floor with a disgusting *fwap*. Rosaria pounced on top of him, shrieking, swinging the crucifix, her putrid breath washing over him. The world dissolved into a vortex of gray confusion.

He struggled to remain conscious and rolled over on his hands and knees. He could sense Rosaria moving away, her disembodied voice murmuring to someone in the distance.

"Yes, a virgin, pure as the dove! Her blood will quench the Sun!" Then a hideous sob. "My beloved Maria!"

Berto blinked, tried to wipe a bloody film from his eyes. Rosaria's blurry shadow hovered over the baby. She calmly dragged the sharp edge of the crucifix across her wrists, letting the blood drip into Maria's face. The baby cried out. Then Rosaria gripped the crucifix like a dagger and raised it over her head.

"The sacred heart! To bring a new Sun!"

Rosaria's demented intent hit him like a thunderbolt. Memories of Errando . . . *snails eating his brain.* Then, behind her, Berto glimpsed the seed of her delusion. Two paintings on the altar screen: one of Christ cupping his sacred heart to his chest; the other of the Virgin Mary holding out her immaculate heart, knife blade pierced through the flesh. Images he had seen his whole life, never knowing their ancient connotation.

He knew what Rosaria would do next.

Berto gasped, tried to stand, fell back. He fumbled for the familiar knurled handle at his waist, now slick with blood. The pistol came out, wavered in his grip. He could barely see, wiped his eyes with his sleeve, tried to get a bead on her.

Choose!

His arm shook spasmodically.

Rosaria or Maria . . . *choose!*

Berto dropped the pistol to his side with an anguished cry. He stared at baby Maria, sobbing quietly on the altar, reaching out for her mother's comfort—a mother transformed by some terrible evil.

How can I reason with insanity?

Summoning his last ounce of will, Berto forced the gun back up.

Squinting through the blood, he steadied.

Aimed . . .

Squeezed.

He howled in pain as the crucifix arced downward. Through the deafening blast, Berto swore he could hear the dirge of a heavenly choir echoing through the hallowed chamber.

21

RIVULETS OF RAINWATER meandered through the young shoots like rivers through a forest. In the tropical climate, seedlings already blanketed the fresh mound of dirt with a carpet of green. Water streamed from Rachel's hair, joining the turbulent flow as she knelt by Carl's grave. She placed a bouquet of wild flowers at the foot of the grave marker—a mahogany cross with a carving of the Virgin—polished with meticulous care by a local indigenous Payan. With her fingertip, Rachel wiped rain from the Madonna's face.

Dan watched from the porch of Anastasio Salvatoré's office. A steady rain rattled against the tin roof, trickled down the supports. Dual emotions tugged at him as he witnessed Rachel's grief: empathy and jealousy. He found himself surprisingly drawn to her, like a butterfly to the light, and jealous of Carl's access to her, even in death, perhaps because they both had experienced loss.

Anastasio stood by, his wiry frame engulfed by a white frock. The leathery skin of his brow wrinkled like an accordion. "It breaks my heart to watch that young woman. So full of life."

Dan fidgeted and turned away. "Let's go inside—give her a little privacy."

Duff was already there, his feet propped up on Anastasio's desk. He twirled a scalpel between his fingers.

Anastasio snatched it away. "That is not a toy, Duffy," he said.

Duff stuck out his lower lip and proceeded to rummage through a jar of pens and pencils instead.

Dan paced restlessly, frustrated with his failure to produce much in the way of results. It had only been one day, but it already seemed like an eternity. He remembered an old Shaw quote: "To be in hell is to drift, to be in heaven is to steer."

Duff broke the silence. "*Stah-zey*, what are we going to do about this murder? Can we put more pressure on Berto? Get the national authorities involved? I can't have dead guys washing up on the beach."

"Berto's a good fellow," Anastasio replied. "But what more can you expect? No clues, no resources."

A pencil flipped off Duff's finger, hitting a framed medical diploma on the wall. He glanced sheepishly in Anastasio's direction.

Dan continued his pacing along the far wall, examining the myriad books, charts, and medical journals—anything to keep his mind off Rachel. At the end, he turned and spotted a familiar red shape peeking out from behind three green oxygen bottles.

"Anastasio, is that the fire extinguisher from the night dive?"

"*Sí.*"

"You know, it's amazing," he said, bending over to examine it, "how fresh the paint looks after being submerged in salt water for days."

"It's rust resistant, rated for seagoing vessels."

Dan fingered the faded remnant of a yellow tag attached to the cylinder's neck. It sent a strange prickle down the nape of his neck. "Aren't these tanks inspected on a regular basis, to check the charge?"

"Why yes, regulations require it. Why?"

Dan pulled it out, a CO_2 extinguisher designed for oil and gas fires, with a large black cone mounted alongside the cylinder. He turned it upside down and felt a series of numbers stamped into the metal. "Wouldn't the serial number be recorded somewhere?"

Duff and Anastasio looked at each other.

"Master Clifford, that's brilliant!" Anastasio said. "Why didn't I think of that? We have a small inspection firm near the docks in La Ceiba. If the killer's boat is registered locally—"

"—then the police can trace the owners," Rachel declared from the doorway, water dripping from her hair and clothes. Her eyes sparkled. "Finally, something to get the authorities off their butts! Anastasio, can you call Berto?"

"On it!" He turned and disappeared into a small communications room.

"Dan, you're a genius!" She raced forward and hugged him, her wet clothes soaking him through.

Moments later Anastasio yelled from the other room, "Berto is not answering the radio."

"Well then, let's go." Rachel tugged at Dan's arm. "We can visit the registration office."

Dan pointed to himself. "Is that wise? Someone might recognize me. Right now, no one knows I'm here. Let the police—"

"Good grief! Quit worrying. Besides, I need you. Stay on board, out of sight, and guard the electronic equipment from the *banditos.* Hurry!"

Dan threw up his hands. "What the hell . . ."

She grabbed the extinguisher with one hand and Dan with the other.

RACHEL WAS A maniac.

Dan soon became convinced of that after clinging to the console of *Little Diver* for several minutes. His storm jacket provided little protection from the salt spray that lashed his face and ran down his neck. The rain wasn't heavy—more like a fine drizzle—but the speed of *Little Diver* churned the mist into a windblown weapon.

Rachel pushed the boat relentlessly, hurtling blindly over a rough sea cloaked in fog. She gripped the wheel with both hands, her legs braced for stability, her hair billowing behind like a ragged flag.

She was *grinning.*

He had stopped trying to persuade her to slow down. Instead, he squinted through the spray, searching for the slightest change in shade or color. Releasing one hand from a death grip, he checked the time. Five thirty already. The prospect of riding back with her on the speedboat to hell—at night, in the rain—made his stomach churn.

Rachel pulled back on the throttle as masts and cranes began to emerge from the mist. Workers in yellow slickers soon appeared, busily scurrying to and fro, loading two large cargo ships. *Little Diver* coasted into La Ceiba's harbor and drew alongside the second freighter. It loomed over them, spewing out reddish-brown bilge water from its stern. The air here was thick with a sickly sweet odor strangely reminiscent of air freshener and sewage. Dan shuddered.

Continuing farther down the quay, Rachel eased *Little Diver* into a berth alongside a short pier that separated the larger ships from an area crammed with smaller fishing vessels, their crews huddled under tarps, waiting for the rain and fog to lift.

Rachel tied off, grabbed the extinguisher, and waved goodbye. "Make yourself comfortable."

"How long?"

"Not a clue. Hopefully, the sheriff's back in town."

"Rachel—"

"Yeah."

"Be careful."

She winked. "Thanks."

Dan tracked her bobbing yellow slicker down the pier until it vanished behind a large crate. He worried about her safety. Rachel's striking features were enough to attract a lot of attention. But she was also energetic, stubborn, and intractable. That combination would not go unnoticed for long. He was reminded of the mysterious voice on the phone back at his condo in Atlanta.

Let the dead sleep, or you may join them.

He curled up in the cockpit, away from the rain and wind, and mulled over the pieces of an ever-growing puzzle. In a week, he'd gone from the biggest sale of his career to unemployed. Now, he was partnered with a crazed beauty, chasing an unseen enemy with an unknown agenda. Risks were fine, but only if they were *calculated* risks. At home, he always climbed with a safety rope, but here, he teetered on a thin ledge with no escape route or backup plan.

The only thing he knew for certain: Rachel Sullivan would be on that ledge with him. It gave him a feeling of vulnerability and excitement he hadn't experienced in years.

Clunk!

The sound jolted him upright. He locked eyes on a young boy about ten years old, frozen in midstep, his body covered with a coat of oily grime. The boy was gripping a screwdriver in his left hand and waving it defensively. Two other boys clambered around the corner and stopped short.

Dan leapt up and yelled. The youngsters sprang off the boat. He chased them a few feet, then stopped, chuckling at the sight of the three *banditos pequeños* bounding down the boardwalk at escape velocity. He doubted they would bother *Little Diver* again.

Over the youngsters' receding heads, Dan saw a brief flash of the familiar NeuroSys blue-and-yellow logo on a truck that quickly disappeared behind a stack of shipping crates. He followed its motion as it reappeared and continued down the quay, passing the first freighter and eventually coming to a stop alongside the second ship. Grabbing a pair of binoculars from the boat, Dan focused on the truck's rear end, just as a group of bobbing yellow heads opened the doors and began unloading the cargo. He was too far away to identify the contents. Could NeuroSys be shipping product to the States already? If so, why by boat? Their shipments of expensive digital gear had always gone by air.

A little closer and he'd know the answer. *Calculated risks, remember?* He looked around. No one seemed overly interested in *Little Diver.* The fishermen were all too busy preparing to leave the harbor with the receding storm.

Screw it! Dan grabbed his rain slicker and pulled the hood low on his forehead. He headed toward the nearest freighter and began winding his way through a maze of shipping crates, using them as cover. He noted the crate's cargo, mostly agricultural products: bananas, oranges, coconuts. There were several refrigeration containers carrying stamps bearing the names of American cities. Darting around the corner of one refrigerated container, he crouched and examined the open expanse that separated the first ship from the second, where the NeuroSys truck had parked.

A sudden bleat startled him. From behind the slats of a huge livestock cage, the terror-stricken eyes of a young calf peered out. The animals were packed in like sardines, grunting and snuffling as they jockeyed for breathing room. His presence seemed to spook them; they kicked the sides of the container.

He suddenly realized he'd forgotten to leave Rachel a message, but to backtrack now—

A sudden shout from behind startled him. A rough-looking foreman with a hard hat approached, saying something in Spanish. The meaning was clear.

Backward or forward?

Dan began walking, staring straight ahead until he had crossed the open area. Reaching a field of fifty-five-gallon drums, he checked to see if he was still being followed, but the foreman had stopped to inspect the livestock pen. Dan knelt and panned the binoculars across the area, stopping on the second ship's name, painted in fresh white paint.

La Cosecha Abundante.

It was a large cargo freighter with an open deck that was rapidly filling with an assortment of steel drums, Dumpsters, and tanks. A large white structure sat smack in the middle of the foredeck, surrounded by a squad of armed guards brandishing automatic weapons. Dan aimed the binoculars back toward the truck. The workers had unloaded a large pallet filled with blue plastic barrels, all stamped with the familiar interlocking circles that signified hazardous waste. His heart raced.

Maybe Duff was right about the local pollution. The manufacturing process for silicon chips required a lot of toxic chemicals and the NeuroSys factory used quite a few of them. That fact had been emphasized by the numerous showers, chemical antidotes, and eyewash basins he noticed scattered across the factory floor. Chemical waste this toxic would require careful and expensive disposal procedures. The conclusion was clear.

La Cosecha Abundante was nothing more than a garbage scow. Even with his limited Spanish vocabulary, Dan realized the irony of the name: *Abundant Harvest.*

He continued to watch as workers unloaded more barrels, uncovering another item of cargo in the back of the truck—a large wooden crate the size of an automobile. Judging from its size, the container held a large volume of something, but what? Computers? If so, that would be a hell of a lot of processing power. Judging by the sudden appearance of armed guards as the crate was unloaded, Dan suspected that its destination would differ significantly from that of the waste drums.

With the binoculars glued to his eyes, Dan had a severe case of tunnel vision. The impact came without warning, a bright light that exploded inside his head.

Then, nothing.

22

LATE, AS USUAL.

Sonny Swyft checked his Rolex. It was just like the man's self-important attitude to keep him waiting. When you swim with sharks, you're going to meet a few eels along the way. And Bradley Gruber was definitely an eel. Long thin features, velvet voice, and the uncanny ability to slither out of any responsibility when things turned bad.

Sonny both despised and admired him.

Fiddler's Roof was much too public a restaurant for clandestine meetings, but he loved the elegant atmosphere and the lofty view of the Atlanta skyline. For once he wanted to stay anonymous, which must explain why he couldn't get any decent service. This was the worst table in the room, right next to the kitchen.

He managed to flag down a waiter and ordered another Glenlivet on the rocks. He threw back the remains of the last one and rolled the ice around in the glass. Just then, Bradley Gruber stepped from the elevator, his salt-and-pepper hair accentuating a recent haircut, short and parted down the middle. Gruber's narrow head and prominent chin gave his face the appearance of an arrow pointing downward. He looked around the room for a moment, spotted Sonny, and smiled, revealing a row of perfectly capped teeth. Gruber was wearing his usual charcoal-gray suit, white shirt, burgundy tie, diamond-studded cuff links.

Who the hell wears cuff links anymore, Sonny thought, smirking. And that watch of his looked like some cheap Chinese knockoff. *"Braaaddd,* good to see you again."

"That's Bradley, please." Gruber extended a limp hand. "Pleasure to see you again, Sonny."

Gruber had an irritating habit of looking slightly past a person, as if on the lookout for someone of greater importance. They both took a seat and Gruber ordered a bottle of water.

"So, *Braad-ley*. How are Kaye and the kids? How many is it again? Eight?"

"Seven, boys."

"Oh, that's right," Sonny said. "Guess I'm getting ahead of you. Must be a real challenge, feeding all those mouths."

"Don't knock it till you've tried it, Sonny. You need to plan for a wife and family."

"Nah, too busy with my career. Wives are a distraction."

Gruber's gray eyes peered out beneath bushy eyebrows. "Respectability is important in these circles. The foundations of power come from a strong family unit."

"Yeah, I hear that." Sonny downed the second drink and ordered another. "But guys like you don't leave much room for the rest of us."

"Nonsense," Gruber said and tapped the table. "The deadbeats of the world are multiplying at an exponential rate. It's our duty to even things out."

Sonny shrugged. "Okay, so I'll buy a wife. Can we get to the subject at hand?"

"Sonny, it's time to start taking this situation more seriously," Gruber said earnestly, leaning in. "Don't waste this golden opportunity. I've hooked you up with an elite organization, one that wields significant global influence. The members don't like dealing with mavericks."

"Hey, mavericks get things done," Sonny said, his lips curling.

"Yes, and they're unpredictable," Bradley said. "Not a trait you want to emphasize when working with this organization. I've gone to great lengths to coordinate the NeuroSys IPO with our angel investor in Honduras, a man who has invested substantial resources in this deal."

Sonny tried to disguise a look of disdain. It was just like the self-important Gruber to try and take credit. "Hey, everything's running like clockwork on my end. I got the NOAA contract signed, we're receiving product, the PR department has dropped the news to the press like you asked, just in time for the IPO launch. What's not to like? You and the senator ought to be pleased."

"We are, but . . ." Gruber leaned back in his chair and studied his manicure. "You've had your share of slipups, and now Dan Clifford has returned to Honduras."

"What?" Sonny lowered his glass to the table. "I thought your boys were going to scare him off?"

"They're not my boys, Sonny. I'm a *facilitator,* remember? Apparently, Mr. Clifford ignored the strong hint that was delivered. It's just the kind of unpredictability we cannot tolerate at this stage. If you had purged the ranks earlier, when I suggested, Mr. Clifford would have never traveled to Honduras in the first place—"

"Hey! What was I supposed to do?" Sonny said. "The guy was hired by the company founder. He created the damn GAPS program. I couldn't just boot him out the door for no reason. How could I know Clifford would sneak off to the factory on his vacation? Besides, if you'd kept me in the loop more about the factory, and put me in charge of Tomás Martin, I could have anticipated this. I'm the president, after all."

"I've told you this before, Sonny," Gruber continued. "It's better if you focus on issues stateside. It gives you plausible deniability. There are other factors at play here, ones you needn't concern yourself with. But, as I said, if you had followed my original advice, Dan Clifford would have been ancient history, correct?"

Sonny rolled his eyes. "Well, firing the director of your signature program right before the public stock offering doesn't seem too smart to me either. Why risk the bad publicity when you're trying to get investors all warm and fuzzy?"

"That's precisely the problem Sonny, a lack of *trust.* It's my job to keep this complex machine running smoothly. When you go . . . *maverick,* as you say, and make these decisions on your own, unpredictable things happen. You must stick to the plan, which brings me to the real point of our meeting. It's time to release that programmer. He's a friend of Clifford's and pokes his nose into places that it doesn't belong."

"Yeah, but he's the brains behind the GAPS software. Trying to get another programmer up to speed so quickly . . . I don't know."

"Certainly this one person can't be that critical."

"Yeah, yeah, all right—Plimpton's history. It might delay the second phase a little, but that's after the IPO, so who cares."

"We care, Sonny. This project will be a CAFTA showcase. We're counting on your diligence to make that happen."

"And you'll get it." Sonny shifted in his chair, knowing the next topic would be a little awkward. "Well, uh, while everyone is cashing in on the IPO, you want me to stay happy too, right?"

"Sure, Sonny. There's something in this deal for everyone."

"Yeah, well. I've been thinking. I've got a problem. SEC regulations are a real bitch when it comes to corporate officers. We can't blow our noses without filing a damn disclosure report. That includes stock sales."

"So?"

"Well, you know how the market works. A new stock comes out, the investors go crazy, drive the price through the roof. But what about me? As a company executive, I can't sell my stock up front, right? What I need is a surrogate."

"Pardon?"

"A proxy. Someone to buy additional stock for me. Someone who can sell at the perfect time. I'll provide the cash."

"That would cause legal complications," Gruber stated flatly.

A burst of laughter escaped Sonny's lips before he could squelch it. "Well, of course! Should that make any difference? You're a friggin' political lobbyist!"

"I think you misunderstand my position. Integrity, *professional* integrity, is the key to success in an interconnected world. Men of power depend on one another to follow certain, shall we say, rules of play. Predictability, remember?"

Sonny smirked again. "Yeah, I suppose your integrity told you to withhold details of the CAFTA deal from the SEC."

Gruber's face took on a rosy hue. "Integrity is a point of view, Sonny. Sometimes men in power must use inventive techniques to overcome needless regulations that tie the hands of achievers—laws written to protect the welfare state."

"Fine, then," Sonny said. "Those oppressive SEC regulations prevent me from profiting from my own company's success. I'm just trying to overcome that obstacle."

Gruber remained silent for several minutes, stroking his forehead with two fingers. "Okay, Sonny. I'll ask around. I'm sure I can find someone, but it will come at a price."

"Hey, nothing's free in this world."

"You'll take care of the programmer?"

"Consider it done," Sonny said, waving for another drink. "What about Clifford?"

"Don't worry about him. We'll take care of Dan Clifford."

For a split second, Sonny felt a wave of apprehension. Gruber's demeanor had always made him feel anxious. "I hope you're planning something discreet. Nothing violent, right? Promise me that."

"Oh most certainly," Gruber said with a smile. "We abhor violence."

23

"*Uunnngggghhhhh!*"

Dan's voice seemed to reverberate from everywhere at once. He imagined himself alone in a dark room, his arms drawn painfully behind him, his face raw against a rough floor.

Relax, you're having a nightmare.

Only it wasn't a nightmare. When he tried to roll over, an electric pain shot through the back of his head. He gasped, held still for several minutes to gather his energy, and struggled to a sitting position. Incoherent thoughts tumbled through his brain: vague memories of the dock, crates, cargo ship, then gradually, the gravity of his situation. A sudden wave of terror threatened to overwhelm him. *Focus! Deal with it.* Someone must have been following him, and now, he feared that he was captive on the very ship he'd been so eager to investigate.

Be careful what you wish for . . .

The dim surroundings were illuminated by a full moon framed in a small round window like a painting, its light throwing shadows across a tiny room. He could see a toilet and bookshelf, hear the rumbling of diesels, feel the pitch of a ship at sea.

It didn't take a prediction scientist to guess his fate.

But then surprisingly, the engines fell silent. Sounds of sporadic gunfire began to echo through the steel walls. Dan frantically worked his legs underneath his body and pushed himself up the rough wall. Two tenuous steps placed him alongside the porthole. He twisted his head to one side and stared through the glass toward the ship's foredeck. All the ship's lights had been extinguished, making it difficult to see details, but he could make out the dark shapes of workers rolling barrels over the side. Against the glimmering sea, black shapes bobbed in the water like apples.

Pow . . . pow . . . pow.

Two men stood at the edge of the gunwale and fired into the water. One by one, the barrels dipped beneath the surface and disappeared.

Pow . . . pow . . . pow.

With every shot, Dan felt a jolt of panic surge through his body. His throat felt dry and he stumbled backward onto the toilet seat.

God, please make this a nightmare.

Pow . . . pow . . . pow . . . pow.

Several agonizing minutes ticked by as he fought against the panic. He remembered an old and terrible memory, one where the events of the moment had taken on a similar surreal quality. The brain resists acceptance, preferring the comfort of fantasy. But reality creeps in eventually. Then the adrenaline surges, the pulse races, and time slows to a crawl. He was already feeling as if he could live a lifetime in this one moment.

He needed to focus on one objective: *escape.* A quick glance around the room revealed little: porno magazines littering a damp floor, a decapitated toilet plunger. He thought of Carl Jameson, facing a similar fate. Dan's kinship to him was growing in ways he never could have imagined. The idea of history repeating itself pushed his emotions to the edge.

No time for panic. Think! He clung to one hope, an advantage he held over Carl—foresight.

His mind raced through several scenarios. Did he have any bargaining power? No. Any way to break free from his captors? Not likely in his current condition. First things first, then. He slung his arms over the toilet's flush lever and tried using it as a pry bar to stretch the bindings apart. If he could get a knot loose . . .

The firing stopped as abruptly as it started.

The sudden change flushed him with a new sense of urgency. *What are my strengths? Observation . . .*

The clank of keys at the door broke his concentration. Without a word, two men rushed into the room and pulled him through the doorway. They dragged him down a dark corridor that ended at a brightly lit room. He was lifted into a chair, his bound arms pushed over the seat back.

The space was a cramped stateroom, containing a small sink, desk, and bunk. The air smelled of sweat and booze. Through the crack of one door he glimpsed an instrument panel and ship's wheel. *Captain's quarters.*

Then he saw it, mounted in a frame next to the door. He studied its exquisite detail: the lustrous red cylinder, the metal valve painted flat black, a release pin like a hand-grenade, the large black cone arcing down from the tank.

The instrument of his death.

A low grumble from the control room brought his attention back to the doorway. He was totally unprepared for the mass of humanity that leaned over and stepped through. It was a man so tall that his head brushed the ceiling. It took his long legs a single step to cover the distance between them.

"*¿Señor Clee-ford?*" The giant said, his voice reverberating through the cabin like thunder.

The thin man chuckled. "*Sí, Capitán. ¿Gringo estúpido, eh?*"

"*Sí.*" The captain studied Dan for a moment, then leaned over and shouted in his ear. "Señor Clifford! Are you deaf?"

The man's voice rattled his insides. "I am now—"

The captain grinned, exposing a row of yellow teeth. "Funny man, I see. You don't *comprende* too good. We give you a hearing aid." The three men exchanged glances and laughed. Then the captain's demeanor turned sour as he leaned forward to within inches of Dan's face. "Who else knows you are here?"

Dan struggled to remain calm, turning his face away from the blast of fetid breath. "The police. They know of your ship. They'll come looking for me."

The captain seemed to contemplate this reply for a moment, rubbing his jaw with a large hand. "Hmmm, I think not. Our police are not so good. Who else?"

"The American authorities, FBI." Dan knew it would make no difference what he said, but he wanted to divert this man's attention away from Duff and Rachel. "They will be coming to arrest you for the murder of Carl Jameson."

A massive blow whipped his head around ninety degrees, sending daggers of pain down his jaw. Bloody saliva dribbled from his chin onto the floor. The room went funky as his head swayed like a bobble-head doll. In his peripheral vision, he saw the thin man rifling through his wallet. Then the captain's huge fingers clamped down on his ears and squeezed until he thought his brains were going to squirt on the floor.

"Who else? Tell me!"

Stay centered! Ignore the pain. Using his tai chi training, Dan turned inward, trying to remain compliant to additional blows. "Does it really matter what I say? What are you dumping here, anyway?"

"*¡Silencio, cabrón!*" The captain cursed and released his grip, shaking his head in frustration. "I do the talking here!"

Dan tried to think of a way out, but nothing came to mind. This man's intent was not so much to collect information as to suppress it. Dan stared at the red fire extinguisher. "Please don't drown me! I can pay you!"

The captain followed Dan's gaze to the wall and grinned. "I make a mistake with your *amigo*—but not this time. You will sink so deep, only the *hagfish* will find you. You hear that okay, *gringo*?"

"Not the extinguisher, please!"

At the captain's nod, the wiry man stepped out from behind the chair. Dan used the opportunity to push it backward against the wall with his feet. With his arms hidden from view, he struggled against the bindings.

The captain smiled at Dan's futile attempts and nodded to the wiry man. "Make it quick. We must get underway."

"*Sí, Capitán.*" The wiry man reached first toward Dan's arms, pressed up against the wall, and shrugged. He knelt down instead and wrapped several loops of rope around the extinguisher's neck, then around Dan's ankles.

Dan felt a surge of hope. Accepting the inevitable, he closed his eyes and imagined an open meadow. With deep, rhythmic breaths he saturated his lungs with oxygen.

Eyes closed, Dan sensed himself being lifted from the chair. *Stay calm, relaxed. Conserve.* He could hear the sound of waves drawing closer, the breeze flowing across his face. He tried not to think of the dark waters below.

With one last great breath, he steeled himself for the ride down. It seemed to last forever. He hit feet first, slicing through the water like a knife, the fully loaded extinguisher dragging him downward at frightening speed.

Control the panic!

Swallowing to ease the pressure in his ears, he pulled his legs up to his butt, clawed for the top of the extinguisher. Fingers fumbled with the handle and missed.

He tried again, struggled. The panic tensed his body. Finally, he forced himself to relax and his fingers found the circular ring. He pulled it and squeezed the handle. A tremendous roar of icy bubbles engulfed his body.

The world turned into a whirling madhouse as the jet of gas spun him around like a top. But he could feel the tank growing cold as it emptied. His awkward position prompted a sudden and horrible cramp in his hamstrings. He wanted to cry out, but gritted his teeth and clung madly to the handle. An unbearable weight pressed in against his lungs. His thoughts raced back to a child's terror.

I don't want to die like this!

The pain worsened, but he could finally feel the cylinder warming. Just a bit longer. Then, a horrible thought occurred to him. What if the extinguisher had pushed him down instead of up? His lungs began to spasm, desperate to inhale.

It was over . . .

With explosive force, he burst through the surface of the waves and sucked in a lungful of air and water. A wave of coughs threatened to drown him right there at the surface. But he was *alive!* He allowed himself several minutes to catch his breath, then reached down with his bound arms and slipped them under his butt, past his thighs, to the backside of his knees. He took another deep breath, pulled his legs to his chest and managed to slip his arms under his feet and past the extinguisher.

He tilted the cylinder up and grabbed it with his knees, its empty buoyancy enough to keep his head above water. He searched the horizon. The cargo ship had already traveled several hundred yards, out of reach in the rough seas. A few orphan barrels floated by, tempting him to grab hold, but he hesitated to approach their toxic contents. A film of rotten, metallic liquid clung to the surface of the water. The initial thrill of survival faded quickly.

He was alone, at night, in the middle of the ocean.

Maybe a quick death was better. After years of scuba diving, he knew the drill. Fighting the waves would expend precious energy. Salt water would suck the moisture from his skin, bringing dehydration.

Then, even in these temperate waters, hypothermia would set in, draining his will to live as the final hours approached. Breathless and senseless, he would settle beneath the surface, choke and wake up repeatedly, prolonging the agony. Finally, he would drift below the waves for good.

That is, if the sharks didn't come first. He needed to swim for shore, but that would attract predators. The thought of being eaten alive filled him with a new terror.

Swimming would be useless until morning, when he could use the sun for direction. The coast was to the west, but how far? How long had he been unconscious on the ship? There was a story a few years back about a sailor on an aircraft carrier who fell overboard. The guy floated in the open ocean for days and survived. But he was a young man in superb shape—a known missing person. No one knew the location of Dan Clifford.

That's when he spotted the ghostly shape in the moonlight.

Get your hands free! The knot was tied on the underside of his wrists—no way to reach it with his teeth. He tried hooking it on the extinguisher's handle. Water splashed in his face and choked him.

He tried again. It was exhausting work, bringing renewed pain and fear.

A black hump broke the water ten feet away, traveled several yards, disappeared.

Lie still. Don't paddle. He bobbed quietly on the waves for several agonizing minutes, the cold creeping into his bones. Then he began shivering.

A splash of water behind him.

He whirled about in panic, throwing up water and foam, pushing the cylinder in front of him like a shield.

He heard a sound, no, *felt* it—a long, low, mournful vibration that shook him to the marrow, followed by staccato bursts, like a jackhammer, powerful enough to prompt a dull pain in his groin. A mound of black water rose in front of him. The sea went solid, forming a great wave that hissed salt spray into the air.

A monstrous eye the size of a softball stared at him with intelligent recognition. Their gazes locked as they rode the swell together. White barnacles clung to the upper eyelid like an eyebrow. The creature swam in ever-tightening circles, prolonging the encounter.

Its momentum finally spent, the massive shape curled back toward the depths and raised its fluke from the water. It hovered there for a moment, then descended into the blackness. Just as suddenly as it had appeared, the humpback whale was gone. As if in a parting gesture, it let out one last lonely cry.

Dan released a huge sigh. Then he cocked his head to one side, straining to place another sound, this one man-made. A swell lifted him in sight of a small fishing vessel, also running without lights. It could be a scout boat following behind the ship. Looking for witnesses of the dumping, perhaps? At this point, he didn't care. He screamed and slapped the water with his arms.

The boat changed direction. A searchlight flicked on, its beam moving over the water in wide arcs. Dan raised his bound arms above his head as high as he dared. The blinding light found him. He could hear the engines growing nearer.

Then an arm reached over the bow and pulled him toward the stern.

24

"How the hell—"

Rachel Sullivan's voice washed over him like a soothing rain. Dan collapsed on the deck, totally drained of energy.

"Get these ropes off me," he gasped.

Rachel returned with a knife and cut through the thick jute rope. "How did you—that humpback saved your life! I never would have spotted you otherwise."

"They tried to kill me."

"I can see that," she said, and absently wiped the hair away from his forehead. "You look horrible." She gently probed his cuts, stopping at the lump at the base of his skull. One touch brought a worried expression to her face. She left and returned with a wet towel, easing it against the swelling. "Man, the back of your head looks like a battle-field!"

Dan closed his eyes, submitting to her care. "I think I know why they killed Carl," he muttered, and felt Rachel's hand tighten against his arm. "They're dumping waste. Carl must have caught them."

"I figured as much," she said. "The other fire extinguisher was registered to that ship, just like you predicted. When I got back from the inspection office I spotted it, couldn't find you anywhere on the docks. I figured you went to investigate, so I followed it out to sea. I heard the gunshots and feared the worst. You should have left a note or something!"

"There wasn't time—"

"Yes, and you almost died! You're shaking like a leaf." She wrapped a towel around his shoulders and helped him onto the bench seat. "I was frantic. . . ."

Rachel paced the boat for a few minutes, wringing her hands.

Finally, she started the engines and headed in the direction of Guanaja.

"THEY MURDERED CARL because of a bunch of garbage?" With a full night's sleep, Rachel's bitterness and frustration had resurfaced.

"Hooligans, every one," Duff grumbled. He was sprawled across the small couch in the cabin, sipping a beer. "They see the world as their sandbox to play in. I know. I worked for a bunch just like 'em on the oil rigs."

"That can't be all of it," she exclaimed. "Carl wouldn't be snooping around the docks. When he starts a project, he stays focused. He would have been studying core drillings at a lab, not playing the concerned environmentalist."

"Could *you* stand by and watch this paradise being destroyed?" Duff replied. "The currents will carry that poison right to our doorstep! No wonder we've seen a drop in local sea life." He turned toward Dan. "What kind of chemicals are we talking about anyway?"

Dan sat at the small desk hunched over his laptop, squinting at the screen, his left eye swollen half-shut. "NeuroSys waste would be pretty nasty—hydrofluoric acid, heavy metals, dioxins." He tried contacting Rudi for the third time, but was unsuccessful, so he sent an e-mail to his personal account.

"Well, those hooligans picked the wrong sandbox this time," Duff growled.

"What do we know about the ship?" Rachel asked.

"According to Anastasio," Duff said, "*La Cosecha Abundante* comes to port once a month. The crew visits the watering holes, but they pretty much stay to themselves. No one remembers the captain, and from the way Dan described him, he'd stick out like a jackass at a zebra convention."

"I want the man who gives the orders," Rachel declared.

"Here's another connection," Dan said, pointing at the laptop screen. "That ship is owned by Solá Mining. Remember them? Wasn't Carl doing his research at their warehouse?"

Rachel's eyes grew wide. "Yes! That's the one."

"I can tell you some things about Solá," Duff said. "They're a bloody huge company on the west coast of Honduras—mining precious metals and drilling for oil, mainly. When they go into a mining area, *whoosh*—the place ends up looking like the surface of the moon."

"So what's that ship doing on the opposite side of the continent?" Rachel said. "It's going to travel through the Panama Canal, just to dump garbage?"

"Aye," Duff replied. "Strange. Maybe the boat contracts to haul waste—"

"Hold it!" Dan interrupted, reading from the Solá Web site. "The company is owned by Hadan Orcus, privately held . . . estimated net worth, fifty billion." He scrolled down. "They mine ore all over Central America—gold, silver, gallium, copper, iron, platinum, tin. They own several offshore oil and gas rigs."

Rachel stopped pacing. "Carl would have been accessing core samples from their test drills."

"Wait, there's more," he continued. "Hadan Orcus claims to be an environmentalist. He's participating in the CAFTA-DR Environmental Cooperation Program, which gives him preferred trade status. It says here he is spending billions to upgrade his mining operations . . . Solá's per annum yield has doubled . . . *yada, yada, yada* . . . while reducing mercury and cyanide waste byproducts by twenty-five percent. Based on that environmental record, Solá has become a leader in CAFTA's Environmental Cooperation Agreement."

Rachel leaned over Dan's shoulder. "What a liar. He's dumping behind their backs, where no one would look. Now he's going to pay!"

"I'll second that," Duff chimed in.

"Shut up, you two," Dan said. "Here's the ultimate hypocrisy. Orcus is chairing the Earth Summit in Brazil next week."

Rachel leaned in farther. "When he shows up, we'll be waiting—"

"And do what?"

She fell silent.

Dan's concern increased with every article he read: world summits, presidential connections, CAFTA, billion-dollar companies. He decided to go for some fresh air, leaving Duff and Rachel to continue their rants.

His emotions were buzzing—confusion, fear, frustration—and the one he dreaded most, the one Rachel had cornered: rage. Rage made you do stupid things. He understood the depth of Rachel's anger. It came from a feeling of helplessness—when others seize control of your life.

He, too, wanted them to pay, but he needed to counterbalance Rachel's excess, be the voice of reason. Otherwise, they'd both end up dead.

He was alive, and he wanted to stay that way.

Rachel poked her head out the cabin door. "You've got a Skype call coming in, from a guy named Rudi."

"Finally!" Dan stepped back inside, stared at the screen, and realized that Rudi was calling from home. "You okay? I couldn't raise you at work."

"Make room on the unemployment line. I've been canned."

"What?"

"No lie. Sonny did it himself. One minute I'm working on the NOAA satellite tracking subroutine and the next minute I'm out on the street without so much as a 'thank you, nerd.' They practically shoveled my things out the door. That's why I didn't call sooner."

"Rudi . . . I'm sorry. This is my fault."

"Hey, don't worry. I was losing my mind in that place."

Dan described his capture at the docks, the NeuroSys trucks, the Solá connection. As he talked, Rudi's expression changed from surprise to fatherly concern.

"Wait a minute. Repeat the whale guy's name again."

"Hadan Orcus."

"Hold it." Rudi typed something on his keyboard. "Uh-oh. You remember me telling you about Gulf-Pacific Investments, the one leasing the chip plant to NeuroSys? Orcus is one of the partners."

Suddenly, the pieces fell into place. They were looking at one problem, not two. That launched an idea. "Duff, do you have room at the resort for another guest?"

"After Mr. Jameson's discovery, I've got cancellations out the wazoo. Why?"

"Mind if I invite Rudi?"

"You can invite the bloody Marines if they'll get rid of these scumbags."

"Rudi, come to Honduras. Bring your computer gear."

"Me, in the sun?"

"You'll be busy indoors, trust me."

"Why do I get the feeling this isn't a vacation?"

"Just get on the next flight." Dan's mind was racing, but found it hard to concentrate, with Rachel and Duff bickering in the background.

"—let's get Berto involved," Duff argued. "We can have the boat impounded. They can't ignore us now."

"Sure they can," Rachel snapped. "That Berto character is worthless. And we have no solid proof."

"No proof? We've got a victim sitting in the room with us!"

"So what? It's Dan's word against theirs. The captain is small potatoes. I want Orcus."

"How will you do that? The man has an army of lawyers. He's untouchable."

Rachel was seething. "I'll find something. Then I'll go to the Earth Summit and shove it up his worthless—"

"Shut up!" Dan yelled. "Both of you, enough!"

Duff and Rachel fell silent and stared at him. Dan fixed his eyes on Rachel, shook his head, and leaned forward. "You're ready to charge off in a blind rage and get yourself killed."

"So we give up? Maybe you can, but I—"

"No, but I want us to survive this. Otherwise, they win. This conspiracy has tendrils that reach all the way to Washington. If we're not careful, we'll be dead in a week, or in a local prison."

Rachel stared at him intensely. "If you're so afraid, why don't you just run back to Atlanta and hide?"

"You're right, I am afraid. But you act like you don't care if you live or die!"

Rachel's lower lip began to quiver. "Dying is better than living this . . . half life."

Dan immediately regretted his harsh tone. "Look, I know how you feel. I want to see them pay too. But we'll need a better plan. Hit them where it hurts, expose them in a way that will force Congress to revoke their CAFTA privileges. Then, maybe the Honduran government gets involved. If they see their cash cow drying up, they'll investigate."

"So how do we do that?"

He pushed his aching body up from the chair and faced Rachel, gripping her arms.

"By playing the black swan."

25

FIVE HUNDRED YARDS offshore, the *Sea Berth* split the horizon, the upper decks and bridge gleaming white, the hull a dark aquamarine that merged with the sea. Dan hadn't seen a ship this large since his childhood, when he'd toured a battleship with his father.

He and Rachel stood like tourists on the dock, waiting while a large inflatable Zodiac skipped across the waves toward them. Duff and a full complement of vacationing divers were noisily bustling nearby on *Spanish Diver,* prepping for the morning dive. Duff waved at them with a wide grin and a thumbs-up.

Rachel had eagerly embraced Dan's plan, adding her own unique wrinkle by bringing in the *Sea Berth.* Most of the crew would layover in Bonacca Town for some much needed R&R. The quaint town had an adequate hotel equipped to handle visiting crews, sporting its own bar and disco complete with mirror globe and seventies decor. After a month in the Antarctic, the crew—mostly college kids—would be thrilled with any kind of entertainment.

It would also keep them away from the *Sea Berth* and its activities.

When the Zodiac reached the dock, Rachel introduced the pilot, French Culver. He was a tall, lanky man with dark curly hair and sharp features. They quickly loaded their gear and signaled French to open up the twin Evinrudes. With a roar, they surged away from the dock at breakneck speed, covering the distance to the *Sea Berth* in minutes.

"Huge boat," Dan commented, pointing to the gunwales thirty feet above their heads. "How do we get from *here* to *there*?"

"Ship," Rachel corrected. "Anything over a hundred tons is considered a ship. She's thirty-five hundred tons, 274 feet long, with a range of seventeen thousand miles."

Crewmen dropped winch hooks over the side and had the Zodiac topside in minutes. Rachel gave the skeleton crew a quick hug, then dragged Dan along for a tour. The deck vibrated as powerful engines revved to cruising speed.

"She's got the latest oceanographic research equipment," Rachel said, pointing things out like a guide. "Over thirty-five hundred square feet of laboratory space, an integrated computer network, a dynamic positioning system. She's the pride of the NOAA research fleet, one of the few ships to escape congressional budget cuts."

The bow towered a full two floors above the deck. It was reinforced for ice breaking and flared at the top to deflect high waves. Amidships, four huge hydrographic winches sat like circular bales of hay, with cables running up to two large telescoping cranes that could be extended over the sides of the ship. The ship's stern sat much lower in the water, to allow easy access to the sea. A large A-shaped crane was hinged to the fantail, designed to rotate heavy equipment out over the water.

Dan found it hard to believe that just a few days earlier, the great ship had been cutting through icebergs in the Antarctic. He felt a rush of excitement at having this mass of technology at their disposal. Rachel moved comfortably around the ship, exuberantly describing every technical detail.

They were about to embark on what was essentially a rogue operation, one that would be difficult to hide for long. Hopefully, it would be long enough, Dan thought.

AN HOUR LATER, everyone convened in the mess hall. It was a surprisingly small group—French Culver, the ship's engineer; Captain Ryan; Mary Koch; Justin Timmons, the medical officer; Colin Miller, the ship's communications officer; and a few others. Dan was amazed that a ship this size could be managed with such a small contingent.

Carrying a long roll of paper, Rachel approached the head of the table. "First let me say, thanks for volunteering, putting your jobs on the line for Carl and me. I know he would be grateful." She paused. "We tried to keep the group as small as possible. I doubt the NOAA director would be thrilled to know we're spending tax dollars to dredge up forensic evidence."

Mary Koch waved her hand energetically. "What do we say when the others start asking questions?"

"Leave that to me. As chief scientist, I've worked up a cover by adding an addendum to my thesis. We'll be studying the evolutionary changes to neustonic plankton at the surface, seeing how they've adapted to elevated ocean temperatures. It's a logical extension. I'm actually looking forward to the additional data. That will also mean a dive to the abyssal plain to study the oligotrophs as well. It's a thousand-meter dive, straightforward. Shouldn't be any surprises." She paused to gauge the group's reaction. "Anything else?"

French Culver spoke up. "I'm not crazy about this plan. Why not just send in ROVs? Human-powered subs—it's just too dangerous with a skeleton crew."

Rachel shook her head. "Remotely operated vehicles don't have the capacity to collect the evidence we need. Besides, we'll need human eyes to scan the landscape."

"I still don't like it," French said. "It's not standard operating procedure."

"Nothing about this dive is SOP. If anybody feels uncomfortable, you can leave now, no hard feelings." Her gaze circled the room and returned to French. "Are we good?"

French said nothing, nor did anyone else. Rachel seemed to know just how far to push the crew's loyalty. "Fine, let's move on." She unfurled a brilliantly colored map showing the topography of a massive underwater canyon, replete with steep cliffs, plateaus, and embankments. She circled a flat mesa with a felt-tipped marker. "This is the area we're heading for." She slid the chart toward Captain Ryan. "If you can adjust our bearing, we'll prepare the sub."

The captain nodded his assent and left.

"Let's go, people!" She clapped her hands. "We've got less than an hour." The table emptied and she turned to Dan. "Let's visit our mother ship's progeny."

ON THE SEA *Berth*'s fantail, the crew winched the deepwater submersible from its hanger. Dan had expected something more submarine-like, streamlined—bright yellow perhaps—but this oddball contraption bristled with a collection of thrusters, lights, video cameras, hydraulic arms, and tubing that gave it the look of a great mutant insect. Between a pair of black pontoons, a welded titanium frame cradled two identical clear hemispheres hinged apart on one side. When pushed together, the two halves would create a perfect sphere eight feet in diameter.

Dan gingerly leaned into the gap. The interior was stuffed with electronic gear and two cramped passenger seats. A pair of articulated joysticks jutted from the armrests of the copilot's seat. They appeared to be controls for the manipulator arms attached to the front of each pontoon. Letters stenciled across one pontoon spelled: SEAZEE.

"Interesting name," he said.

"It's a diving nerd's name. The 'Zee' stands for the third dimension of Euclidean space—*depth*, this sub's domain. We have a better nickname though," Rachel continued, chuckling. "The human fishbowl."

"So who's your copilot?"

"You are."

Dan waited expectantly for the punch line. "No, seriously."

"I *am* serious."

Inhaling sharply, Dan stepped away from the menacing machine. "Don't think so. Small spaces and I—we don't get along. Besides, I just got *out* of the water."

"Come on." Rachel seemed genuinely disappointed. "With our skeleton crew we have no one to spare. Someone's got to handle the manipulators, and I suspect you've got the talent, right?"

"That's beside the point." He wavered, not wanting to make his discomfort more obvious. Rachel's associates were putting their careers on the line for a plan he had cooked up. He felt an obligation to do his part. The clear globe *did* look less confining.

Dan shook his head. "Let's go then, before I change my mind."

A smile lit up Rachel's face. "Okay, partner, let's get down under."

The next hour raced by in a flurry of activity. French circled the machine, working his way through a long predive checklist. Then he poured bags of lead shot into each pontoon for ballast. Finally, they tethered the sub to the large A-crane.

Rachel handed Dan a down vest. "Here, you'll need this. It gets chilly at the bottom."

Mary Koch appeared, carrying a mesh bag containing two white objects. She handed them to Rachel. "Made to order."

Rachel withdrew two life-size Styrofoam heads, painted with caricatures. "Old diver's ritual," she said. "Reminds us of the power of the deep."

Dan recognized his own caricature, realizing Mary must have painted it over an hour ago. "You sneaky—"

Rachel shrugged and smiled. "I knew you'd come." She urged him into the sub. "Let's go!"

The air inside the sphere felt like a blast furnace. They both broke out in a sweat. Workers wasted no time pushing the two hemispheres together and securing them with two large metal straps. Rachel quickly gave the thumbs-up sign. The crane rumbled into motion and *SeaZee* rose from the deck, rotated over the fantail, and settled gently into the sea.

Rachel called French on the hydrophone. "Request permission to dive."

"Permission granted. Good luck."

The cables released, and *SeaZee* dropped into the water, churning up a froth of silver bubbles. "Bombs away!" she shouted, and flooded the ballast tanks. The sub began to sink slowly.

The transparent shell vanished into the turquoise water, prompting Dan to reach out and touch the acrylic surface. "Cool."

She smiled. "Everyone does that the first time."

A school of blue runners streaked by, separating at the last minute and reforming on the other side. Dan felt a burst of exhilaration. He slid his hands into the finger grips of the joysticks and cautiously moved them around. The manipulator arms tracked his every motion, feeling smooth and natural. Within minutes, he was swiping playfully at passing fish.

"I was right, you're a natural."

"All those midnight hours playing video games."

An iridescent jellyfish pulsated across their path, inviting him to nudge it gently with a manipulator. He was delighted to feel a tug through the control's tactile feedback system. The slightest resistance registered, giving the controls impressive dexterity. Enthralled with his new toy, he failed to notice the water deepening in hue from sapphire to turquoise, then to indigo.

By then it was too late.

He swallowed air. "How deep are we?"

"Six hundred feet," she said. "Twenty-four hundred to go."

The open ocean closed in around him, wrapping *SeaZee* in a veil of darkness.

He closed his eyes and tried to relax.

Not now!

His hands, suddenly clammy, fell from the controls. He slumped back in the chair and closed his eyes.

"Are you okay?"

"Just . . . leave me alone."

Rachel handed him a paper bag. "Here Mr. Wimp, breathe into this."

"I can't help it!"

"Help what?"

Dan seldom uttered the word aloud and it came out as a whisper. "Taphephobia."

Rachel's brow wrinkled. "What? Fear of taffy?"

"Not funny. It's *fear* . . . of being buried alive. Small, dark spaces are the triggers." His voice trailed off.

Rachel's grin vanished. "Sorry, I didn't mean to make fun—everyone's nervous in close quarters."

"You think this is *nervous*?" Dan squirmed in the seat, not wanting to dredge up old memories—not wanting to avoid them. For some reason, he felt compelled to confront the event he had spent a lifetime avoiding, and he wanted Rachel to know about it.

"It happened when I was nine. . . ."

At first the words came slowly, then picked up speed, finally spilling out in a great flood of emotion that transported him back into the memory—a memory as clear and vivid as the day it happened:

THE FEBRUARY DAY is sunny and bright in San Fernando. Light streams through lace curtains, warming the table filled with Mother's buttermilk pancakes, maple syrup, steaming oatmeal. Dad has been working hard to fix up the house. Mother is talking about more work: plumbing, painting, replacing the California prairie grass with new flowers.

She's always talking about the house. Mother loves the old Victorian, saying it was built long ago.

Window light edges across the table and lands on her antique porcelain cups in the hutch, all lined up just so. A breeze catches the curtains and the light scatters in little slivers.

Dad will be leaving soon, making the long drive to Veterans Hospital, out by Pacoima Canyon, to make people well. Dad says we should go fishing on the weekend, in Catalina, to troll for tuna and swordfish. When Dad talks, his eyebrows dance up and down like marionettes.

And then something strange—Mom's cups start dancing on the hutch.

I watch silently as they wiggle and hop across the shelf. They teeter at the edge.

I feel something horrible is about to happen. I try to scream, but nothing comes out. My mouth is numb. Dad looks at me funny.

The floor twists and jerks. The walls heave in and out like dragon's breath. The air fills with sparkling shards of glass.

A piercing scream comes from nowhere and everywhere. The dust tastes dry and chalky. A heavy, horrible, monstrous weight bears down. It's hard to breathe. Mommy cries my name. Where is Daddy? The world becomes darkness and terror, and wrenching, slobbering screams.

A metallic groan throws a shaft of light through the blackness. A few feet away, Mommy's trembling hand reaches out. Why won't Daddy answer?

The light dims, screams fade. The fingers of Mommy's hand spread out like the petals of a sagging rose. There's no feeling, no reality anymore. Only a dream.

Mommy's hand is just inches away, wilted and limp.

"Mommy, I'm right here."

DAN SQUEEZED HIS eyes shut and shivered. It took several minutes before he could bear to speak again. "I was buried in the rubble all night, cracked most of my ribs. It took a month of rehab before I got out of the hospital. Couldn't even go to my parents' funeral. They called it a 'modest' quake—only a six point one. But our old Victorian house was built on a landfill and the soil quivered like jelly. The city should have *never* allowed construction there, but back in the early nineteen hundreds, nobody understood seismology or plasticized soil dynamics. My parents were two of only a handful of fatalities, so everyone forgot—except me, of course."

He pounded the armrest. "Those idiots *still* allow construction on landfills all along the San Andreas! In high school, I read all the literature on quakes, wrote letters to congressmen. Wrote a manifesto on clueless politicians and sent it to local city officials. I tried to make them see the link between their decisions and tragedy. Never got a decent response. . . ."

After a long sigh, he said: "I *hated* them, wanted to blow up city hall." He choked a laugh. "Obviously, I thought better of it—moved to Georgia when I was eighteen and never looked back."

A squeeze of his hand by Rachel tugged him back to the present. The submersible was resting on the bottom, its halogen lights shimmering off a halo of silt. Rachel was sitting quietly, bathed in the nimbus like an angel, her liquid eyes reflecting true empathy.

"Dan, I'm so *sorry*. I had no idea. I would never have pushed you into this if I'd known."

"I should have told you sooner. I haven't talked to anyone about this since . . . well, in a long time."

"You want to head back to the surface?"

He pondered it for a moment, feeling purged, as if the heavy, lingering weight had been partially lifted.

"No, I'll be fine."

26

"Rachel, check in." French Culver's hollow voice reverberated through the hydrophone. "You haven't moved in ten minutes."

"We've made the bottom," she answered. "Checking instruments, over." The haunting echo of her voice returned a few seconds later, reflected back by the ocean's surface. "Frenchie, can you see us on Seabeam?"

"Affirmative. Your target is straight ahead at one-niner-zero. There's a large object, maybe a boulder, in your way. Beyond it, I see smaller blips that could be steel drums, though I can't be sure."

"Thanks, Frenchie."

On the bottom, Rachel studied Dan with concern. "You sure you're okay?"

"I feel fine—really." It was a lie, but he forced a grim smile anyway. He felt a swell of anger at his weakness. *Good*, he thought. *Anger is better than fear.* Feeling a surge of confidence, he wiped condensation from the globe and stared out into the featureless void. "Let's get out of this muck," he said.

"Aye, aye, sir," Rachel replied with a salute. She flicked on a bank of long-range thallium iodide lights. Their greenish beams knifed through the silt cloud. She tapped the vertical thrusters lightly and the sub rose from the bottom. When it had risen six feet, she nudged the ballast valve and buckshot rattled from the pontoons. Soon, she had *SeaZee* hovering with perfect neutral buoyancy. Careful to avoid stirring up more silt, she edged the sub forward.

As they broke free of the cloud, the shadows sharpened, bringing the full expanse of the abyssal plain into focus. It was a barren field, as gray and lifeless as the surface of the moon. A few lonely boulders poked through the layer of mud like warts on a dragon's skin.

"Welcome to *my* world," Rachel said with an air of pride.

"Not much to it, is there?"

"Don't trust your first impressions. There's a thriving ecosystem down here."

Dan watched her as she deftly handled the controls. "You drive this rig pretty well."

She laughed. "All those years flying stunt planes, I guess. Granddad started me as kid, then Dad, who flew commercially. I've been piloting exotic vehicles ever since. *SeaZee* isn't much in the performance category though; flies like a zeppelin. I'd gladly trade her for my Russian Yakovlev. No barrel rolls or hammerhead stalls today."

"Fine with me," he said. "I've had a taste of your piloting skills on *Little Diver,* remember? I'd like to see your more subdued piloting style."

"This is about as *sub*-dued as I get."

"*Punny* girl." Dan grinned at her. "You still fly?"

"Whenever I can, but I gave up the stunt circuit years ago, sold my Yak-55 recently."

"Your dad still flies?"

Her exuberant expression waned. "No . . . Dad's dead."

"Oh, I'm sorry." It was his turn for some awkwardness, he guessed.

The mud flats narrowed, driving them closer to the steep embankment on their starboard side. Soon, there was nothing left to port but a dark void, one that plummeted off the continental shelf into unfathomable depths.

The narrow ledge curved to the right, entering what Dan remembered from the map as a horseshoe valley. The lights disappeared into blackness, the only reflections coming from the cliff and bits of detritus drifting in the water.

Rachel leaned forward. "We must be getting close, but I don't see it." She glanced back down the embankment. "Looks like the garbage scow miscalculated by a few hundred yards. A little farther and our evidence would have fallen off the edge of nowhere—"

"Stop!" Dan screamed.

A dark shape loomed out of the darkness. He instinctively pushed the manipulators forward.

"Crap!" Rachel jammed the thrusters in reverse, pitching up a cloud of silt. "Now I can't see a thing."

"We're okay," he said. "I can feel the embankment."

They waited for the view to clear. Directly ahead, a long row of monstrous ribs receded into the black like the entrance to an underground lair. Slumped at the base of the rib cage was a mound of dark flesh pulsating with slimy, eel-like creatures.

Rachel grabbed the mike. "French, we've got a whale carcass down here!"

French's voice rattled back through the speakers. "Did you say *whale*?"

"Roger that, *Sea Berth*. Humpback . . . a juvenile, over."

"How long has it been there?"

"I'm guessing a few weeks, judging by the decomposition. There's a lot of scavenger activity." She studied the carcass with reverence. "Amazing. A whale carcass is like a biological oasis in the desert, capable of supporting the local ecosystem for years."

"It's a feeding frenzy," Dan said. He marveled at the writhing creatures with a mixture of fascination and disgust as they fought over the rotting flesh.

"Hagfish," Rachel replied. "No jaw, head, or eyes—just a single tooth in the middle of a suckering mouth. They love to crawl up the anus of their prey and suck out their body fluids." She looked at him with a mischievous grin.

Dan shuddered, thinking of the captain's last words on the garbage scow: *You'll sink so deep, only the hagfish will find you.* "What do you think killed it?"

"A disease or parasite, likely." She seemed to have a revelation. "Then again . . . this is near the dump site. It could be chemical poisoning. Let's take a biopsy." She looked at Dan expectantly. "We'll need fresh tissue from deep inside the carcass where the decomposition is slower."

"You want me to cut it open?"

"Piece of cake. We've got the tools."

Rachel showed him how to operate the saw attachment, a small circular blade with hoses snaking back to a hydraulic pump. Once attached to the manipulator, the blade tore effortlessly through the thick skin of the whale, sending up a cloud of red particles as creamy white blubber drew away from bright-red musculature.

His stomach churned. "It looks so fresh."

"Now, jam the sampling pole in deep. It's got a hollow tip, like a big biopsy needle."

He thrust the six-foot pole into the flesh and felt it glide in with a squish, then pulled it out and dropped the plug of flesh into a sample jar, relieved to be done. He wasn't sure if his stomach could take much more.

Rachel watched him with keen interest. "You handled that like an expert."

"Maybe I should put in for a new career." He grinned. "Master manipulator."

"Ouch! Now who's the punster?" Rachel grimaced. With a fleeting grin, she gave the whale one last look, and maneuvered *SeaZee* out onto the expansive plain.

FRENCH CULVER HUNKERED over the Seabeam's video monitor, waiting for the latest image to materialize. The Seabeam's bathymetric scanning sonar sent narrow pulses of sound to the bottom, assembling the echoes into three-dimensional images. With it, French could track *SeaZee*'s progress along the seafloor with amazing clarity. As sophisticated as it was, Seabeam was still just fancy sound, and it took a minute to sweep the entire scene.

French called *SeaZee*. "Rachel, request that you halt. I need a fix, over."

"Roger. Going full stop."

French watched the image inch its way up the monitor. The whale carcass that looked like a boulder took shape in the lower right corner, then the oval shape of *SeaZee*. "Rachel, you're wandering too far west. Target area is at one-seven-zero. Distance, three hundred meters. I see a large distribution of rectangular objects."

"Roger, *Sea Berth*. Turning to one-seven-zero."

Colin Miller, the ship's communication's officer, slid in behind French to watch the action. "How's our intrepid crew doing?"

"They found a whale corpse."

"You're kidding. Rachel's got the Irish luck, hasn't she?"

"And the stubbornness," French mumbled. On the next scan he noticed an elongated black smudge in the upper right quadrant and pointed it out to Colin. "What the hell is that?"

Colin studied the ephemeral shape. "Hmmm, pretty big. Looks

like an echo from the embankment. See if it's there on the next scan."

A moment later, and the smudge had vanished.

Colin turned to leave. "See? Nothing to worry about. Sonar is squirrelly as hell."

DAN GAWKED AT the full expanse of the dumping field, a large semi-circular bowl bordered on three sides by steep banks. Thousands of drums lay in varying stages of decay, funneled into the area by the surrounding cliffs. Blue drums of inert plastic looked as if they had been dumped yesterday, but the steel barrels had disintegrated in the salt water, leaving nothing but rust and the ghostly shadows of their former shape imprinted in the mud. A smattering of newer drums, their paint still fresh, mingled with the others. Most had imploded on the way down.

A scowl flashed across Rachel's face. "No lack of evidence, that's for sure."

Dan realized that the volume of material far exceeded the amount that could be explained by a few toxic byproducts smuggled out of NeuroSys, or from several factories for that matter. "Look for the freshest barrels," he muttered. "Ones with lettering, or logos."

"Right." Rachel shook off her trance and coaxed the sub forward, crisscrossing the field in a grid pattern. Every few minutes she would stop to take photos and Dan would flip over the barrels with the manipulators, keeping an eye out for the familiar NeuroSys logo.

Much to Dan's dismay, the barrels were blank or had long since lost their markings. Hadan Orcus had gone to great lengths to hide his activities. Then Dan noticed something missing from the debris field: those featureless crates he'd seen at the docks. Judging from the security detail on board, *La Cosecha Abundante* had other responsibilities besides garbage detail.

After twenty minutes, Rachel stopped alongside a crumpled metal drum with a single bullet hole. "This one looks new. Let's get a sample."

Dan reattached the saw blade and sliced a fist-sized opening through the thin metal, inserted a sample bottle, and swished it around. He withdrew a glob of brownish muck.

"What the hell is this stuff?"

"Not a clue, but look at this." He lifted the drum slightly. Stenciled lettering clearly revealed the name of Solá Mining spray-painted on the side.

"Finally! The bastard got careless."

Dan began cutting around the logo. His activity scattered a swarm of small, shrimp-like creatures about four inches in length that scurried about on long, spindly legs, their heads crowned with eight writhing tentacles.

"What the hell?" Rachel sat up with a start and studied the bizarre creatures intently. "I've never seen a species like that—they look like a hybrid between a shrimp and a squid. What are they eating down here?" She followed one creature with her lights as it moved to another cluster of drums a few feet away, noting the thick blanket of white fluff draped over them like freshly fallen snow. "Bacteria," she mumbled.

Scanning deeper into the field with the long-range lights, she discovered more of the flocculent, teeming with thousands of the bizarre octopods. She screwed up her brow. "We've assumed this cargo was toxic, now I'm not so sure."

"How so?"

"These octopods, aren't just surviving, they're *thriving*."

"Should we gather more samples?"

"Absolutely. I want to dissect one of these things back at the lab."

Dan had grown adept with the sampling equipment and quickly filled more bottles, eager to get out of the graveyard and back to sunlight. He was chasing one of the octopods around with a slurp gun when he was distracted by a dark mass sliding past the edge of his peripheral vision.

FRENCH CULVER'S ANXIETY returned along with the mysterious smudge on the Seabeam.

It had shown up two more times, prompting him to run a full diagnostic of the system, which showed nothing out of the ordinary. Without sonar guidance, Rachel and Dan would be flying blind, but he hesitated to worry them needlessly before he had a firm grasp on the problem. The anomaly seemed to appear every third or fourth scan, always in a different location, as a wispy blur. Finally, he settled on a different tactic: a low-resolution scan. It would show less detail but would execute four times faster, giving him a sharper image to work with.

Technical problems such as this reminded him of the folly of this whole operation. He sipped his coffee, struggled with a nagging feeling of dread, and waited for the new image to resolve itself.

It came up quickly, the mysterious smudge solidified into a distinct shape he recognized immediately. And it was only a few yards from the *SeaZee*. The coffee mug fell to the deck and shattered as French shouted into the hydrophone. He waited, desperate for a response, but heard only the feeble echo of his own pleas.

27

DAN TWISTED AROUND to follow the shape, but it had vanished beyond the sub's illumination. "Did you see that?" he sputtered. "There's a *whale* swimming down here!"

"Nonsense," Rachel said. "Whales don't dive this deep, unless you saw a blue, which I seriously doubt—"

"I'm telling you what I saw!"

She peered out into the darkness more from obligation than curiosity. "See? Nothing."

The words barely left her lips when a mighty fluke swept out of the void and crashed into the sub with enormous force, driving it sideways through the muck. It careened through a pile of barrels and lurched to a stop with a blinding flash that knocked out half the lights.

"He's coming around again—hold on!"

The second impact threw them forward into the instrument panel.

Dan stared in horror as the whale circled for another pass. It slammed into the superstructure. A shower of sparks threw the sub into total darkness, shrinking their world to a tiny circle of amber in the middle of the instrument panel.

FRENCH CULVER GRIPPED the table, his eyes glued to the Seabeam, not sure whether to believe what he was seeing. The image of the whale had vanished again. The small speck of *SeaZee* remained, silent and unmoving.

"*SeaZee*, this is *Sea Berth*! Please acknowledge, over."

Five minutes passed without a reply. But that could mean anything—electrical failure, a blown fuse, or a broken antenna. Thankfully, the tiny image was still intact. If the sub had imploded there would be nothing left to see.

"*SeaZee*, answer me, damn it!"

Nothing.

"They're dead in the water," French muttered to himself. "I don't get it. What's a humpback doing that deep?"

Colin Miller had heard French's screams and reappeared, only to stare at the image, dumbfounded. "Maybe it's the juvenile's mother. The family ties . . ."

"At three thousand feet? She wouldn't last long." French licked his lips. "We need eyes and ears down there. Go launch *Li'l Toot*."

Colin's face lit up. "Yes, sir!" He scurried out the door and headed toward the equipment hangar.

French took another look at the flickering image and cursed himself for letting Rachel talk him into this foolhardy mission. They should have used the robot in the first place. Now, their skeleton crew would have to contend with a genuine emergency.

On an unsanctioned mission.

He slammed his fist on the counter and shouted: "No more crazy ideas, Rachel!" Trying the hydrophone again, French wished desperately for the chance to chew her out personally.

THE BLACKNESS SUCKED the life out of him. Dan sat perfectly still, barely breathing, alert for the faintest sound. Without the noise of machinery, he could hear the din of underwater life: mournful sighs, wails, ticks, scratches. They came from nowhere and everywhere, like the chattering of restless souls.

Once his eyes adjusted to the dark, he was relieved to find the bottom brighter than he expected. Light from the millions of luminescent octopods shimmered through the debris field in a strangely coordinated manner. Their bursts of light rippled in pulses that seemed organized, intelligent, like swarming behavior.

"Where's the whale?" Dan whispered.

"It won't be back," Rachel said, already at work on the instruments. "It's got to return to the surface for air. Let's get the lights back on—"

He pressed his palm against the acrylic and felt a series of sharp echolocation clicks. "It's still out there. We need to get the hell out of here, *now*."

"That's not possible, it's got to—"

Dan grabbed her arm and pointed.

An elongated shadow drifted slowly across the field of flickering lights, obscuring the illumination like a black hole. It paused for a moment and then arced upward.

Rachel flipped circuit breakers in a desperate attempt to bring the thrusters back online.

Mesmerized, Dan watched as the shadow slowed, turned, and headed straight toward their position. Before he could scream, a sickening thud propelled the sub backward. He heard the soft slap of flesh against metal and a loud curse from Rachel. Then the sub slammed to a halt once again.

"You okay?"

"I think so." After a few more minutes of struggling and cursing, she managed to reset the breakers. Light flooded the enclosure.

Rich, luxuriant, wonderful light. Dan took a breath and steadied himself until his eyes had time to focus.

Dead ahead, the two surviving halogens threw a fan of light over the leviathan, twisted grotesquely, belly up, its fluke invisible in the murk. Its monstrous eye was pressed against the glass just inches from Dan's face. The former white flesh surrounding the pupil had turned a brilliant red, a demon eye. He jerked back reflexively, noting the familiar barnacle pattern over its brow. The two of them stared at each other with mutual recognition. Dan saw something else in that eye, something strangely foreign in such a majestic animal.

A look of stark terror.

"It dove straight into the ground," he muttered. "Like a suicide mission."

Rachel tugged at his arm. "Forget the whale for a minute." Her attention was riveted on the other side of the sub. "Look—"

The rear edge of *SeaZee*'s port pontoon hung precariously over the edge of a drop-off. "We better hope our friend wakes up," she said, and fidgeted with the directional controls. "We're pinned, the hydrophone's busted, and the thrusters on this side are trashed."

Dan turned back in time to see the last flicker of life drain away. "It's the whale that saved my life," he said. "And it's not going anywhere." He checked the manipulators, which seemed to be in perfect working order. "Could we cut ourselves out with the saw?"

"Even if you could cut away the flesh, how would you extract it?"

"Surely the *Sea Berth* knows something's wrong by now."

"True, but it will take days to get a rescue sub down here. There aren't many vehicles capable of launching a mission this deep. We might as well settle in for the long haul."

Dan swallowed. "*How* long?"

"We have power for twelve hours, air for three days. There's more emergency oxygen under the seats. It will get very cold and dark. I'm cutting everything but the CO_2 scrubbers and the dash lights to conserve power."

The thought of enduring the darkness for days inside the tiny globe, perhaps even dying in the crushing depths, seemed unbearable. With memories of the earthquake still fresh in his mind, Dan blurted: "So much for *your* world!"

"I'm sorry," she said, as she switched the instruments off one by one.

He immediately regretted his outburst. "I didn't mean that."

"Not a problem," she said. "I got you into this mess."

"No, you didn't. We got *ourselves* into this mess, and we'll get out of it . . . together."

Rachel turned away, hiding the wetness on her cheek. "I've been thinking. The strange behavior, first the dead juvenile, then the adult. Whatever's in the water here, those octopods are probably absorbing it, then passing it up the food chain to the whales."

"You think the whales are eating them? I thought you said they don't usually dive this deep."

"This one sure did—"

A low rumbling sound sent a shudder through the sub.

"Uh-oh." Rachel stared at the dead whale. "This is bad." A frothy stream of bubbles rose out of the whale's blowhole. "The lungs are collapsing."

The whale let out another mighty burst of bubbles. The huge body rolled toward the sub as its buoyancy changed. The tremendous weight ground against the frame, triggering a screech of twisting metal.

Then, *SeaZee* popped off the boulder, shot upward a few feet, and sailed over the edge of the abyss.

"We're free!" Dan yelled.

"Yeah, and headed in the wrong direction." Rachel pointed at the depth gauge. The numbers shot past thirty-four hundred feet and continued downward. She flipped the ballast switch, but there was no response. "Not right, not right—we should be neutral," she moaned, flipping the ballast switch repeatedly. She tried the thrusters. One lone motor simply sent them into a spin.

Thirty-eight hundred feet.

"Do something!" Dan shrieked.

"I'm trying! Let me think." Her face took on a determined air and she braced herself against the pilot's chair. "Hold on to something," she shouted and applied full power to the thruster. The sub began spinning madly, drawing ever closer to the cliff.

"We're going to crash!"

"That's the idea," she said calmly. At the last moment, she threw the thruster in reverse, dragging the starboard pontoon along the cliff wall. The ballast door wrenched open and lead shot spilled out.

The change in the center of balance canted *SeaZee* to port, throwing Dan into Rachel's lap. She pushed him away. The sub was listing twenty degrees, and he had to cling to the chair frame.

Rachel checked the depth gauge again. "We've slowed, but we're still falling. This doesn't make sense!"

Forty-six hundred feet.

"Damn!" She slammed her fist against the instrument panel. She tried the same trick with the left pontoon, unsuccessfully.

Then a faint sound, like crumpling cellophane.

Dan heard it first and looked up. He could see feathery lines creeping out from the rubber seal between the two hemispheres.

Rachel followed his gaze, watching with resignation as the small cracks crept out like icy fingers. "We're past our rated depth of forty-five hundred feet. That's crazing in the acrylic—the beginning of structural failure." She slumped into the seat. "It won't be long now."

Dan stared at her in disbelief. "You're giving up?"

"There's nothing more I can do."

"Yes there is." With a sudden surge of energy, he grabbed the manipulator controls. "Get us back to the cliff edge."

"That won't help—"

"Just do it!"

She applied power to the thruster, sending *SeaZee* into another spiral. Dan waited for the wall to draw perilously close.

He thrust the sampling pole into the cliff like a sword.

There was a satisfying *thump* as the pole penetrated the soft mud all the way up to the gripper. The reactive force checked their momentum and left them dangling from the cliff face.

As the sub leaned to starboard, Rachel fell into his lap. She held still, inches from his face, not wanting to risk jarring them loose. They huddled together for a few tense moments, sharing breaths.

Seeing no further movement, she slipped back into her seat. "Nice work. You've delayed the inevitable, now what?"

"Now we examine our options." He cast a wary glance toward the gossamer crazing that continued to creep steadily across the acrylic.

"Let's see. We were neutrally buoyant with both pontoons full, now one's empty and we're still too heavy." Rachel grabbed the video controls and aimed the camera toward the lower pontoon assembly. "There," she said. "Our slide across the sea floor packed the subassembly with mud and rocks. We'll need to remove it, or we're stuck here. The *Sea Berth* would never find us on this cliff."

Dan felt the weight of a mile of ocean bearing down on him. He forced himself to focus on solving the problem, finding something they had overlooked, but he came up empty.

Rachel turned to him, her eyes glistening. "Before it's too late, I want you to know how much—"

He held up a hand. "I don't want to hear it. We're *getting out* of here." He stared at the video screen, willing his mind to wander. *Think outside the sub*, he thought. He allowed himself to relax and just breathe, as precious minutes ticked by.

"Ditch the pontoons," he said finally.

"How? They're *welded* to the sub."

"Yes. By these four welds here. We have a saw."

"You want to trash *SeaZee*?"

"It's already trashed."

Rachel studied the screen and shrugged. "I suppose it's worth a try."

"Better than waiting to die."

Dan watched his progress on the video monitor as he moved the saw to the front left weld. The screech of grinding metal sent clouds of metal billowing off the blade. After fifteen minutes, the weld broke loose with a thud and the pontoon sagged. The sampling pole slid halfway out of the cliff face.

"This had better work," he said nervously, as he repeated the procedure on the right weld. The operation was taking longer as the blade was beginning to dull. Suddenly, the assembly broke free, ripping the sampling pole completely out of the cliff face.

They were falling again. The pontoons sagged beneath them, rocks and mud clinging tenaciously to the diagonal framework.

"Damn it! The rear welds held," he said, devastated. "I thought they'd snap for sure."

"Now it's my turn." Rachel threw the lone thruster into reverse, sending the sub into another tailspin. Like an ice skater in a pirouette, the sub accelerated, slinging mud and pontoons around wildly. There was a sudden, sickening sound of rending metal, a jolt, and the *SeaZee* heaved upward.

The pontoons fell away, carrying the batteries with them. The sub's interior plunged into total darkness.

"Not *again*," Dan said, groaning.

THE SEABEAM'S LAST image had thrown French Culver into a panic. *SeaZee* had vanished. Refusing to accept the possibility of their demise, he raced down the stairs to the ROV hanger and burst through the hangar door. "Rachel's off the Seabeam!"

Colin looked up, startled. "How—what?"

"We need this fish in the water, now!"

They dragged *Li'l Toot* out to the deck and hooked it to the portside boom crane. Tethered to the mother ship by ten thousand meters of fiber optic cable, the ROV could be remotely controlled. Colin had already prepped her for the dive, attaching an extra video camera and an auxiliary 120 kHz side scanning sonar.

French raced up a flight of stairs to the control room as Colin ran down to deck three, where *Li'l Toot*'s cabling had to be attached to the hydrographic winch. French, still panting, watched as Colin struggled to hook up the cabling. It was a two-man job. They should be doing this with a full crew.

Finally, Colin gave him the thumbs-up. French lifted *Li'l Toot* from the deck and swung the crane out over the gunwale. He lowered the ROV into the water, suddenly realizing that someone would have to disconnect it from the crane's hook. French searched for Colin, but he was already heading up. The ROV was bobbing wildly in the open sea and needed someone to cut it loose immediately. He'd have to do it himself. Scampering back down to the deck, he lowered the smaller Zodiac over the stern and jumped in.

28

NOTHINGNESS.

That was the open ocean at three thousand feet. No light, no way to tell up from down.

Away from the bottom, the water held nothing but fear, and Dan was drowning in it. Recounting the horror of days buried in rubble, he realized what he hated most about the dark. There was no frame of reference, no way to note the passage of time. His mind told him they were heading to the surface, but his psyche refused to believe it.

"Talk to me," he said.

"About what?" Rachel's voice pierced the darkness.

"Anything."

Dan felt the pressure of Rachel's hand gripping his. "Well, let's see. Word games? Nah, too boring. Hmmm, what can we do in the dark? We could always make out."

He laughed in spite of himself. "I'm afraid I'd tongue your nose or something."

"Oooh, kinky. Sounds promising." Her laughter helped put him at ease. "You handled things pretty well back there."

"You too. We make a good team." Dan leaned over cautiously until he could feel her moist breath on his face.

"Did you hear that?"

"What?" Dan cocked his head. At first, it was an indistinct sound, almost a whisper. It grew louder, hissing like bacon in a hot pan.

"What *is* that?"

He shifted in his chair. A stabbing pain sliced through his right foot. "Something just *bit* me!" His instinct was to jump up, but he was unsure which way to move. "We need light in here, damn it!"

Rachel let go of his hand. He heard her shuffling about, then several sharp raps. An explosion of green light erupted from two rods in her hand. "Here," she said, handing him one. "I almost forgot about these. Cyalume—bioluminescence." She held her light over him and gasped.

The tip of his tennis shoe had been sliced off cleanly at the little toe. Blood oozed from the gap. "How in the hell—"

Rachel jerked him toward her. "We've got a *leak*!"

A silvery glint caught his eye and he traced it back to the sphere's seal near the side hinge. Propelled by tons of water pressure, a needle thin jet of water had cut its way through the crazing and was slicing through the metal frame of the instrument panel near where his foot had been resting.

Rachel began throwing loose items in front of the stream. "Help me! It'll eat a hole right through the globe."

Dan grabbed a clipboard and thrust it into the stream. The laser-like jet cut through it like butter. He eyed another glint and jerked backward. "New one!" It sliced through the edge of his seat. Rachel threw a broken monitor in front of it. A fine spray of dark water erupted from the metal box with a sizzle.

"Another one!"

As the sphere continued its ascent, the cracks expanded in the lessening pressure, opening up new water jets every minute. Soon, there would be nowhere to go.

"Get up high!" Dan shrieked.

They scrambled up on the seats, balancing tenuously between the jets. He wrapped his arms around her, knowing one wrong move could mean amputation. Rachel twisted to face him. They were so close their noses touched.

She was *grinning*.

The streams quickly multiplied, splaying out like sunbeams across the enclosure, locking them into a survival embrace. Rachel's arm slipped and caught a jet. She yelped and looked down, expecting to see blood, but found only a welt. "It's losing force," she yelled. "We've just got to ride this out."

Like gymnasts playing a demented game of Twister, they contorted themselves into nearly impossible positions, trying to avoid the brunt of the spray. Exhausted, Dan could feel Rachel's chest heaving in time with his own. They held on several minutes longer, until the jets widened into gushing sprays. Then they fell into a pool of icy water that had risen to the seat cushions.

Rachel gasped. "Damn, I *hate* cold water!"

"How much farther?"

"Don't know, but I see light." She began shaking uncontrollably.

Over the next few minutes the surface continued to brighten.

Dan waited eagerly for them to cover the last hundred feet, but the minutes seemed to drag on forever. "We're not going up anymore."

"N-n-no more buoyancy." She took a deep breath and slipped under the surface. He groped for her, thinking she had gone mad. A froth of bubbles hissed out from underneath the seats.

He could feel pain building in his ears and pinched his nose to equalize the pressure.

She popped back up. "Spare oxygen."

As the pressure rose inside the sphere, he could see bubbles streaming out through the cracks.

"Lean that way," she ordered. They both climbed up the side of the globe, rotating it until the crazing disappeared under the interior water level.

They waited, hoping the air pressure would force the excess water out through the cracks.

FRENCH REACHED *Li'l Toot* and pulled it alongside the dinghy. In his haste, he had forgotten to let out extra slack on the tether. Now, with the choppy seas, he had to time his motion and unhook the tether as a swell passed. After several unsuccessful tries, he fell back into the dinghy, exhausted.

He had failed them, unable to launch even the simplest of operations with his tiny crew.

Despondent, he struggled up for another try. But before he could, the ocean boiled up around him. *SeaZee* bobbed to the surface like a cork. Inside, French could see Rachel and Dan treading water in the dome like fish in a tank.

29

THE FACE STARING back at him from the mirror told a story of narrow escapes and physical trauma. Dan's cheek was swollen and a black welt had started forming under one eye. He could feel a goose egg throbbing on his neck, next to the stitches from his former injury. The dive had also added a brand-new bandage on his little toe.

But he was *alive*. Happily, gloriously alive.

These close calls were beginning to feel like a habit, desensitization therapy better than any he'd gotten from psychologists. Dan felt a rush of exhilaration, similar to what he experienced rock climbing. But that had never been this intense, or as intoxicating. Strange how the mind discriminated between fears. Some people thought nothing of driving to an airport, only to break out in hives when boarding a plane a hundred times safer than their automobiles. He never thought twice about scaling a granite rock face, but that dive? He shivered.

Rachel had seemed unfazed by it all, smiling at death like a true adrenaline junkie. What pushed her buttons? He wondered what fears lurked under her iron façade.

He finished dressing and left the cramped berth, stopping at the handrail to let the warm sunshine penetrate skin, muscle, and bone. On the fantail, he saw the shattered corpse of the sub resting on a pair of wooden timbers. Several crew members worked over it like thieves stripping an old car. Colin was working to retrieve the electronic equipment and sample containers.

Dan headed toward the mess hall and found it deserted, save for Rachel. She sat slumped over a table, her face cradled in both hands, studying the foam in a glass of beer. Four cans were lined up in front of her like tin soldiers.

"Why the long face?" Dan slid into the seat next to her. "You should be celebrating. I feel great!"

She kept her eyes trained on the glass. "*You* don't have to explain to the director of NOAA how you trashed their fifteen-million-dollar submersible on an unsanctioned mission."

He tried to intercept her gaze. "You couldn't help that. Nobody could. We're alive! And we've got the evidence we needed."

"*Please,* no bedside manner," she replied. "I'd rather be on the bottom."

He decided to drop the issue.

A few minutes later, French appeared and slid a small note across the table. "It's a message from Mañuel, one of the dive masters at the resort, I think. He wants you two to meet *Spanish Diver* at the dock at four o'clock. He sounded pretty upset, but didn't elaborate." French stood by, waiting.

Rachel seemed to be in another place altogether.

Dan read the note and nodded. "We'll do it."

French turned to leave, then remembered something and reached into his pocket. "I thought you two might want these." He placed two small objects on the table.

Dan stared at the familiar foam caricatures. The tremendous water pressure had crushed them both to the size of golf balls.

As THE *SEA* *Berth's* skiff approached the dock in Guanaja, Dan could tell that something was amiss. The *Spanish Diver* had docked and was unloading. The guests still on board milled about, grim-faced. Several women appeared to be sobbing. To the west, several hundred yards out, Dan could see Anastasio Salvatoré's small skiff bouncing over the waves, closing in on their position.

At the very end of the dock, Dan recognized a familiar profile standing amid a mound of crates, wearing a large black safari hat, tie-dyed shirt, black shorts, scruffy beard, and righteous smirk.

Rudi Plimpton.

The Zodiac bounced off the dock and tied up near Rudi's crates. Dan hopped out. "Jeezus, Rudi, you brought half the computers in Atlanta with you."

Rudi pulled off a pair of Day-glo-green sunglasses and grinned.

"Hey, you told me to bring my stuff. I've got a NeuroSys Model 5000, a couple of PCs, server, umm, digital scanner, another satellite phone—one can't have too many datalinks—oh, and a few toiletries too. I figured I'd enjoy myself in paradise."

Dan introduced Rachel. "She works for your old employer, NOAA."

Rudi extended a hand. "Ah, one of the squids from oceanographic."

Rachel glanced past Rudi toward the crates for a moment, then back toward the diving boat. She walked off in that direction.

Rudi whispered in Dan's ear, "Hmmm, ice lady, I see."

"Give her a break," Dan said softly. "She's had a pretty lousy day."

"Judging by your looks, so have you."

"A lousy week, actually."

A loud moan drew everyone's attention toward *Spanish Diver*. Ben Silverstein was stretched out across one of the benches, his head in Iris's lap, grimacing in pain. A large black bruise was beginning to form below his rib cage. At that moment, Anastasio's boat slammed against the dock and he leapt out with his medical bag and rushed to Ben's aid. Meanwhile, Rachel had already jumped on board, heading toward the stern, where a large spotted dolphin lay with a spear poking from its head.

Adolpho.

Duff McAlister sat on the dive bench staring blankly into space, an empty speargun still dangling from his right hand.

Dan approached Duff. "What happened?" he asked.

Duff said nothing. Mañuel hopped out of the captain's chair and pulled Dan to one side. "So glad you're here, Señor Clifford. We were diving with dolphins like always. Then, Adolpho goes *loco*, rams into the divers. I think Señor Silverstein, he has broken ribs, no? Adolpho, he keeps coming . . . we tried to push him away." Mañuel cast a sorrowful glance toward the stern and shook his head. "Duff—he loved that animal."

Rachel had knelt next to Adolpho's carcass. When she heard Mañuel's description she looked up. "What about the other dolphins? Were they acting strangely?"

"No. They swam away, circled at a distance."

Rachel glanced back at Dan. "That's two cetaceans in one day. I'd like to take Adolpho to the *Sea Berth* for analysis."

"*Sí, sí.* That's why I called."

Once the guests had unloaded their gear, French helped Rachel roll the dolphin onto a tarp. Everyone pitched in to load the 450-pound carcass into the Zodiac. Rachel and French climbed in and, with a cursory wave, roared away toward the *Sea Berth,* leaving Dan, Rudi, and Mañuel standing awkwardly on the dock.

"So that's the lady you've been bragging about?" Rudi shook his head. "A real bubbly personality, that one."

Dan watched as the Zodiac skipped across the waves, then turned to Rudi. "Come on, we've got work to do."

THE *SEA BERTH'S* wet lab was not for the squeamish. The combination of fishy odors, formaldehyde fumes, and ocean turbulence could turn even the most rugged seaman into a whimpering blob of puking humanity. For that reason, Rachel was grateful for the opportunity to work in the sheltered port of Bonacca Town, where ship movement would be at a minimum.

She found it hard to concentrate after the day's events, particularly after her aloof behavior on the docks, which left her with a tinge of guilt. She knew Dan only wanted to help, and she had treated him like dirt. Now, everyone was mad at her: the crew, NOAA, Dan. Perhaps that was the way she wanted it.

Alone was better; it meant less chance of hurting others.

Resentment and sorrow welled up inside her. So much loss, all because some SOB was too lazy and selfish to properly dispose of his garbage. She was almost certain of a connection between the toxic dump and the bizarre behavior of the two cetaceans. Now, she just needed to prove it.

Refocusing on the job at hand, she scanned the dolphin from tail to nostrum. Adolpho was truly a magnificent specimen, with deep rust-colored skin and multicolored spots. He was large for a wild dolphin, well fed, his body extending well past the ends of the stainless steel table.

She had only time enough for a few noninvasive tests. The autopsy would have to wait for tomorrow, and since the ship's refrigerators couldn't handle a dolphin this large, she'd have to work fast. At best, she could lower the lab's temperature to fifty degrees to slow decomposition. She cranked down the thermostat and slipped on a sanitary gown, mask, and latex gloves.

One oddity immediately caught her attention. The fatty bulge on Adolpho's head used for echolocation seemed disproportionately large. She pushed a finger against it and the tissue sprang back stiffly. It looked like edema, which would indicate toxic chemical poisoning.

Pulling a large serum syringe from the drawer, she attached a three-inch needle and slid it firmly through the soft tissue into the pocket of cerebrospinal fluid around the brain. A chill ran through her as bright red liquid squirted from around the puncture, filling the syringe rapidly. The appearance of blood indicated a hemorrhage of some kind, but she was certain the deadly spear had penetrated well behind the brain stem.

The fluid was milky, typical of an infection. She filled two vials, then picked up one and wafted her hand across the top, sniffing its contents. Most bacterial infections had distinctive odors. Some smelled sickly sweet, like gangrene; others had the familiar rotten odor; and some, an aroma like grape juice.

When the odor hit her, she jerked her head back. This smelled entirely foreign, strangely floral. In all her years as a biologist, she had never encountered anything quite like it.

30

JENIFER COLEMAN GLANCED at her watch for the third time. Traffic on Atlanta's International Boulevard had slowed to a crawl. "Can't you squeeze around? I'm already late!"

The cab driver turned around slowly. "Whad'ya want me to do lady, drive on the sidewalk?"

"That would be nice," she replied without hesitation. "Listen, I mean it. I've got a weather forecast to do."

The driver shrugged and tapped lightly on the steering wheel.

"Look, it's only a block away! Just scoot around these cars straight ahead."

"No ma'am. Got a license, see? I wanna keep it."

"Here, then." Jenifer threw a twenty in his face, jumped out, and ran across the intersection, eliciting a chorus of honks. She jogged through Olympic Centennial Park toward the CNN building, working up a serious sweat.

DEE JOHNSON DROPPED his chin accusingly as Jenifer burst into the makeup room. He pointed a finger. "My my, girl. You're shaving it awfully close today, aren't you?"

"No time for wisecracks." Jenifer started dialing the control room on her cellular. "Just slap on some base to hide the sweat. I've got ten minutes to—hello, Frank? Jen—I know! Look, don't start with me now. I'm in makeup. Just get the blue screen ready, will you? I'll be down in five."

Dee spread the thick studio makeup across Jen's cheeks and rubbed briskly.

"Ow!" Jenifer winced. "Not so hard."

"Honey, we've got to seal those pores, or you'll be sweating on the carpet." Dee kept rubbing. "You're just on a tizzy tantrum today." He hummed and reached for the highlighter pencil.

"Skip the eyes."

Dee dropped the pencil, picked up a powder puff. "Okay, *hon,* but I've got to do something to that shine on your face, or you'll light up like a beacon."

Jenifer waited impatiently for Dee to finish. *Four minutes left.* She jumped up, raced down the corridor, turned left, and scampered down a flight of stairs. She slipped into the main newsroom, catching a stern glance from Cynthia, the show's producer. Pausing to compose herself, she strolled casually toward the studio, but Cynthia's voice rang out across the noisy room.

"Jenifer!" Cynthia signaled with a curling finger. Jenifer pointed at her watch, but Cynthia continued the finger wag.

The newsroom was particularly busy, vibrating with the tap of several computer keyboards. Once the heart of the world's collective consciousness, CNN had suffered of late, but the public still expected the weather forecast, complete and punctual—a forecast she was dangerously close to missing.

She tried to smile.

"This isn't funny, Jen," Cynthia barked.

"I didn't mean—"

Cynthia raised her hand. "I don't want to hear it. I covered your butt this time, but don't let it happen again. I've got a lead-in that'll buy you an extra five minutes. Frank's loaded the weather images for you."

Jenifer left, feeling the heat on her cheeks. Frank intercepted her at the door and clipped a small microphone to her lapel. "Jen, where have you been—"

"Don't *you* start with me!"

"Okay, okay. The National Weather Service images are loaded in the usual order. West Coast first, then the U.S. forecast—"

"I know the drill." She glanced at the anchor desk where Ike Winter, CNN's silver-haired veteran, was wagging a finger at her too. Ike always looked for any opportunity to horse around on the set. Still, he knew precisely when the cameras were on and could switch personas in a split second. Ike had an eye for the "tally light," the red beacon that marked the on-air camera. It bounced from one camera to the next, carrying the attention of millions of viewers.

Jenifer gave Ike a scowl, checked the commercial clock. Ike grinned, his crown of silver hair glowing in the floodlights. The instant the break ended, Ike straightened up.

The tally light switched to camera two, and Ike began reading from the teleprompter with his mellifluous baritone voice.

"From the CNN Center in Atlanta, this is . . . Primenews. Forecasters say there's more severe weather on the way. El Niño is back, sooner than expected. El Niño means 'Little One' in Spanish but its effects have been anything but petite."

Ike turned to watch a canned news clip on the monitor.

Jenifer checked herself in a small mirror. Her jet-black hair always seemed in place, and the makeup was holding. She tugged at the edges of her red suit and checked both ears for her gold earrings. Then she took several deep breaths and slipped into the weather studio. It was a small niche eight feet from the news desk, built more as an afterthought, Jenifer felt. The back wall was painted blue to allow her television image to be combined with the weather images.

She studied the first map on her private monitor positioned offstage. It was an ocean temperature map, and she struggled to remember the precise effects of El Niño on the Americas, gave up, and watched the news clip for hints. Ike was leaning back in his chair, off-camera, sipping an espresso as images of flooding and devastation played across the studio monitor.

"Residents in the United States may enjoy milder weather this year, but farmers in Peru will likely suffer through floods, while Asia braces for the worst droughts in one hundred years. All because of the weather phenomenon known as El Niño—a cyclical event that threatens to become an extreme affair. El Niño's effects have drastically altered global weather patterns, causing billions of dollars in damages over the last decade. And now it's back. Scientists from the National Oceanic and Atmospheric Administration say this year could prove to be the worst El Niño of the century. NOAA is developing a global monitoring system to predict changes in ocean temperatures. They hope that early warning will help reduce the damaging effects. But for now, few scientists believe the disastrous effects can be avoided.

"Marv Jackson, CNN, reporting."

Ike straightened up, hiding his espresso.

"Coming up, a new outbreak of drug-resistant *E. coli* bacteria at a popular fast-food chain. On Wall Street, the Dow Jones Industrials dropped another sixty points. We'll have the opinions of top analysts, up next. But first, here's Jenifer Coleman with the world weather report."

Ike turned toward her, still sporting his no-nonsense persona.

"Jenifer, are we seeing any effects of El Niño in U.S. forecasts?"

Jenifer smiled and pointed toward an imaginary point on the blue screen. The tally light switched to camera three.

"We should see increased precipitation, Ike, especially in the southwestern and eastern United States. This could bring drought relief to the West Coast."

She waved her hand across the blank wall with a flourish, using her side monitor to guide her movements. As she continued, Ike made faces, picked his nose, stuck out his tongue—anything to fluster her. She wondered why he bothered. She had long since learned to stare past him.

". . . let's take a look at the weather in that area."

Jenifer pressed the clicker that controlled the images on her side monitor, and a map of Southern California appeared, complete with a three-dimensional animation of rain clouds moving across the Los Angeles area. She slid her hand across the middle of the blank wall.

"There's an area of low pressure in the Pacific that's producing rain all along the West Coast. Los Angeles is reporting three inches . . ."

She could feel herself calming down. Having done this a thousand times before, she knew how to read the indicators. Another press of the clicker. An animated map of the U.S. popped up.

"We move now to our forecast weather map and put it in motion."

She slid her hand in a broad swipe along the virtual East Coast.

"You see the frontal system pushing toward the Northeast—"

The monitor suddenly went blank.

"Well, we could look at it, if the computer cooperates."

She stared at Frank, who was frantically typing commands. The monitor sprang back to life, but now it showed a map of Central America. She stared blankly at the foreign image. It contained no weather symbols at all.

"Well, uh, we seem to be having some technical difficulties, so—"

The map zoomed in to a red circle fifty miles southeast of Honduras. Next to it, a murky photograph containing a field of rusting oil drums. Under the image, a message appeared in large block letters:

ILLEGAL DUMPING OF TOXIC WASTE!

Then a different image appeared: the rotting carcass of a whale.

MASS POISONING OF SEA LIFE!

Jenifer turned back toward the cameras.

"We'll, uh, be back after this commercial break."

She stared at the control room, but Frank signaled her to keep going. She froze. They always kept a commercial ready, just in case, but Frank had left her hanging, defenseless. *This has to be some sick joke.* The glow from the tally light seemed to bear down on her like a spotlight. Beads of sweat erupted as she swore silently to exact terrible revenge on the person responsible. She forced a smile and muttered:

"Looks like El Niño is messing up more than the weather."

The seconds ticked by like hours. Ike was laughing silently, his face turning red with suppressed laughter. Stupefied, she searched for something more to say, but her mind was a blank. She glanced back at the monitor just in time to see a fresh set of images, all with subtitles.

LA COSECHA ABUNDANTE, A GARBAGE SCOW
CARL JAMESON, MURDER VICTIM!

Jenifer glanced from monitor to camera, camera to monitor, mouthing a string of senseless words, struggling for some witty statement, a way out.

Nothing. Not a damn thing.

Then the screen went black and a final message scrolled across it like teletype.

WHAT DO ALL THESE THINGS HAVE IN COMMON?
HADAN ORCUS, OWNER OF SOLÁ MINING & CHAIRMAN OF THE
EARTH SUMMIT.
STOP THE SENSELESS DESTRUCTION!
BROUGHT TO YOU BY THE CHAOS CONTINGENT.

Jenifer spun back around. The tally light was off.

She stormed off the set, raced past the anchor desk and into the control room. Cynthia and Frank were both hunched over the control board.

"I've never been so embarrassed in my life! How could you do that—"

Cynthia placed a finger to her pursed lips, then pointed to the bank of monitors with news feeds from competing stations. The same scene was playing out on every monitor, the weather personalities all ad-libbing through the disruption.

Jenifer's jaw dropped.

"We couldn't go to break," Cynthia whispered. "This is *news*."

"What?" Jenifer's brow puckered. "You made a fool of me so it would be newsworthy?"

"Jen, calm down. The wires are going crazy—" A news writer handed Cynthia a printout. She scanned it quickly. "Jen, this just played on half the stations in the country, all during the weather forecast."

"You mean this wasn't a joke?"

"We'll talk later." Cynthia jabbed at the break clock, just seconds away from the live feed. Jenifer slumped into a chair and watched the rest of Ike's newscast.

"We have a breaking story. Minutes ago, an unknown individual or group breached the security of news stations across the country, commandeering broadcast time. If you were watching, you no doubt saw our own meteorologist, Jenifer Coleman, as she encountered this cyber invasion."

The control room queued up a short outtake from the weather report. Jenifer winced and buried her face. Ike continued:

"Teenage hackers? Computer terrorism, or worse? Here's Christine Wilkins with more."

"Thank you, Ike. We know little at this time. What we do know is that this attack is a nationwide phenomenon, with each studio's blue screen computer hacked during the weather report."

"Christine, what do we know about the message?"

"Very little so far. Hadan Orcus is owner of the Solá Mining Company and chairman of this year's International Earth Summit. An Internet search indicates that the alleged victim, Carl Jameson, is a scientist working for the National Oceanic and Atmospheric Administration. Our contact at the FBI has verified that Mr. Jameson was reported missing several days ago, so there may be foul play involved. But the FBI has declined any further comment."

"Christine, how could someone infiltrate different computers, at independent studios, all at the same time?"

"Ike, we don't know, but we're calling in experts to examine computers here at CNN."

"Thank you," Ike said. He directed a stern gaze at the cameras. "We'll be back with more after the break."

Jenifer stroked her chin. "Frank, replay my video clip."

He shrugged and queued the digital clip. She ran through it several times, studying the locations in the images. Then she smiled. "Where did Cynthia go?"

"Back to her office, I guess. Why?"

Jenifer barged into the office without knocking and pushed Cynthia's phone away from her ear. "I want to cover this story as a *news* reporter," she blurted. "And I want to start *right now*. I won't take no for an answer."

Cynthia placed her phone on mute, a flash of irritation crossing her face. "We've been through this a thousand times. This is not the time to—"

Jenifer leaned closer, a sly grin lifting the corners of her mouth.

"What if I could deliver the mysterious computer hacker to you . . . exclusively?"

31

RUDI'S TROJAN HORSE had galloped across the country like the Fifth Horseman of the Apocalypse. The program was devilishly simple, yet virtually impossible to trace. Using one of his many back doors into the National Weather Service computers, Rudi had hidden his payload inside the day's meteorological images, buried like parasites among countless millions of bytes. When the news networks downloaded the files for their weather forecasts, they unknowingly infected their systems. It seemed flawless.

Even so, Dan felt a jab of apprehension—or possibly remorse—as he watched Jenifer's desperate floundering on Primenews.

"All right!" Rudi flipped through the channels. "That's what I call a cyberdeluge of *epic* proportions. Did you see the look on Jenifer's face—"

"That's enough," Dan said, tired of watching. "You sure this is untraceable?"

Rudi shot him a disdainful look. "*Dan,* come on. We're talking hacking 101 here."

"For you perhaps, but what if they find the original pieces?"

"They can't. Encrypted and hidden in other files—steganography." Rudi grinned. "The only program capable of putting Humpty Dumpty together again erased itself after executing."

Dan wiped a bead of sweat from his brow. Rudi's cramped bungalow hummed with computers. Without air conditioning, the room had turned into a sweatbox. "Well, let's hope so, because we've stirred up a hornet's nest."

"That was the idea wasn't it?" Rudi muted the TV. "I can't wait to see how Orcus handles this."

Dan was worried about his quirky friend. Rudi was not accustomed to public scrutiny. "You're a prime target now."

"Me? Nah."

"You don't exactly fade into the woodwork. All those crates at the dock attracted a lot of attention. You'd better head home tomorrow."

"What, and miss all the fun?" Rudi browsed the Internet for more news stories. "Besides, Duff has two of the groundskeepers watching me, just in case. I feel safe enough."

"Whatever." Dan's initial adrenaline rush was wearing off and he felt a sudden wave of exhaustion. "I'm heading back to the cabin."

"All the way back there? Why not crash here tonight?"

Dan looked around. NeuroSys computer servers filled the floor, dresser, and closet. Rudi had stacked the empty crates in the bathroom shower, leaving a narrow path to the toilet. He wondered if Rudi intended to bathe.

"No, I need some quiet time. And I feel a sudden urge to sleep for days." He left Rudi's room and skirted the pool area, hugging the bushes. When he reached the bar, he noticed Duff sitting alone, nursing a drink and gouging holes in the table with a diving knife.

Dan placed a hand on Duff's shoulder. "You okay?"

Duff barely flinched. "How'd the computer thing work out?"

"Incredible, really." Dan sat down. "Hadan Orcus is the man of the hour."

"Some of the guests are leaving tomorrow."

"I'm sorry, Duff." He gently reached over and placed the knife flat to the table.

"I've known that dolphin for seven years. Never hurt a fly, that one . . ."

"Things will get better."

"They won't get better, if we don't make them better. I won't sit by and watch my paradise turn into a cesspool."

"We're doing all we can. Give it time."

"Yeah." Duff picked the knife back up, jammed it into the soft mahogany, and walked away.

AN INCOMING SQUALL churned the bay, tossing the small skiff about like a float. The horizon had vanished into a band of gray, lit sporadically by flashes of lightning. Dan considered turning back, but he was already a mile offshore. Instead, he turned the outboard's throttle to the stop. The motors whined and the bow lifted.

It was risky piloting a small boat alone in these rough seas, but he'd been taking risks all week. In the heat of the moment, their plan to expose Orcus had seemed like a great idea, but now he was having doubts. He held no illusions about keeping their involvement a secret. The details would eventually lead back to the *Sea Berth*, especially with the loss of *SeaZee*. But with Orcus's henchmen trying to kill them, it seemed better to have the glare of the media spotlight shining on them. He only hoped they could stay hidden long enough for Orcus to get what was coming to him. Dan wanted Rachel to get her justice.

As he neared the pinnacles, he slowed as a few fat drops of rain pelted the skiff. The cliffs loomed in the dark shadow of the storm, whitecaps crashing against their base. A faint buzzing permeated the air and raised the hackles on his neck. With a brilliant flash of light, a ragged bolt of lightning struck the nearest pinnacle, showering the water around him with bits of rock. He gunned the motor again and cut through the maze with frantic abandon. The starboard bow caromed off a rock, scraping off a swatch of paint. He hunkered down and drove forward. Squirting out the other side, he let out a whoop of excitement.

Maybe a few cheap thrills were warranted.

When he arrived at the dock, he tied off the skiff at both ends and scrambled up the darkened trail. Halfway up, the rain caught him, turning the trail into a torrent of mud and debris that rushed past his legs with surprising force. He slipped a few times, cursing and laughing.

The brunt of the storm hit just as he reached the cabin. He scrambled up the steps and through the door, locking it behind him. Inside, the air was pleasantly warm. He stripped off his clothes, flinging water and mud on the floor. After drying off, he slipped on some sweats and collapsed on the couch. His bandaged toe throbbed, but he welcomed the freedom of bare feet.

The floorboards groaned under the force of the wind. Sheets of rain pummeled the tin roof as shadows danced across the walls in the storm light. Despite the fireworks outside, his exhaustion drove him into a restless sleep.

THE SOUND OF scuffling cut through the chorus of raindrops, stirring Dan awake. He checked his watch. An hour had passed. Still hungry for sleep, he struggled to clear the haze from his mind.

There it was again.

He tensed, the grogginess gone. There were footsteps across the deck and a sudden thumping that startled him into action. He sprang toward the door and tore back the curtain. A flash of lightning illuminated the silhouette of Rachel, her palms splayed out against the glass.

"What the hell?" He flung the door open and pulled her inside.

With no raincoat, her drenched clothes clung to every curve. The exertion of the climb had left her breathless, chest heaving. Dan glanced down, watching a puddle form on the floor.

"Are you crazy? It's insane to be traveling through the storm like that."

"Never mind that," she wheezed. "I . . . have news." Rachel hugged herself, trembling like a wet cat, her face ashen, eyes red and puffy. "And could you find some painkiller? I've got a *terrible* headache."

"Hold on." Dan headed to the bedroom and returned a moment later with a towel, T-shirt, and sweats. "First, you need to get out of those wet clothes." He draped the towel over her shoulders. "Here, put these on while I look for some aspirin."

"Something stronger, if possible."

Dan rummaged through Duff's medicine cabinet and discovered an old prescription bottle of Vicodin. At the door, he hesitated, giving her time to change. Through the crack, he could see the curves of her back rippling in the storm light as she slipped the shirt over her head. He felt a twinge of guilt about invading her privacy, but something else too—an ache of desire. When she was dressed, he brought her the pills and a glass of water. "Take these."

She swallowed them in one gulp.

He led her to the couch. "Couldn't this have waited till morning—"

"No!" A grimace of pain flashed across her face. Her next words came as a soft whisper: "I just . . . needed to see you, that's all." She squeezed his hand and shuddered. "All afternoon I've been having these visions of something terrible crawling out of that dump site. I couldn't bear to be alone in the lab another minute."

The tone of her voice sent a chill down his spine. "What do you mean, something terrible?"

She tilted her head back, rubbed the back of her neck. "It's Adolpho. He didn't die from chemical poisoning after all."

"No toxins?"

"Oh, there were plenty of toxins all right—cyanide, dioxins, heavy metals—just not in high enough doses to be fatal. Adolpho died from a massive infection in his brain. I'm familiar with most cetacean diseases, and I've never seen symptoms like these before. I scoured the journals, but I kept coming back to those strange mats of flocculent at the dump site."

"I don't understand."

"Neither do I!" She pinched the bridge of her nose, eyes squeezed tight, then relaxed. "That dumping field should have been a wasteland, but those microbial mats seemed to be *consuming* the waste."

"Consuming what, exactly?"

"I'll know more tomorrow when I grow a culture, but the dolphin's infection, the crazy whale, and the strange life at the dump site have to be related."

Dan's brain was still scrambled, the exhaustion dulling his mind. "So, the dumping field has nothing to do with Adolpho's illness?"

"No, I didn't say that." She grimaced in pain again, whispered: "I think . . . the toxins at the site triggered the emergence of some new cetacean disease."

To Dan, it seemed like Rachel had decided to speak in riddles. "Poisons causing new diseases? How does that work exactly?"

"It's punctuated equilibrium, using a mechanism we call doomsday genes. The bacteria must have evolved a way to feed on the toxins at the dump site. Then they infected the dolphins and whales. I've seen stressed algae in Antarctica adapt to changing conditions in just a few generations."

"Doomsday genes?" Dan laughed nervously. "I'm not sure that's funny."

"It's not meant to be funny," she said. "Doomsday genes are dormant master genes that are activated when an organism is under extreme stress: lack of food, a change in environment, or *toxins*. It's a survival mechanism. Mutations increase tenfold but in an ordered way, allowing microbes to search for genetic solutions to a problem. Take antibiotic-resistant bacteria, for instance. What doesn't kill them makes them stronger. That's why you should always take all the antibiotics in a prescription, so you don't leave any survivors. Or the next time, the bacteria will have evolved resistance."

"And you figured all this out from looking at Adolpho's blood?" Dan couldn't suppress a grin.

"I know what I'm talking about," she sputtered, her lower lip quivering.

"I'm sorry, it just sounds like a lot of speculation, even for you." This new emotional side of Rachel bothered him, though he wasn't sure why.

She continued: "Doomsday genes are capable of incredible biological changes. Take the slime mold, *Dictyostelium,* for instance—a common single-celled amoeba. When it's stressed by a food shortage, it looks for other slime molds. They gather together and transform into a worm that can travel in search of food. If the worm fails, it changes into a fungus and grows a stalk that releases spores into the wind. All these genetic changes are made for survival. Multicelled creatures may have evolved this way billions of years ago."

Dan listened carefully, trying to put her statements into context. It sounded a lot like hive behavior. Sometimes the group is superior to the individual for problem solving. He thought back to the medicine wheel. "You know, shape-shifting is part of trickster lore. Your microbes sound like shape-shifters. Maybe *that* was the clue Carl intended."

Rachel pulled her knees to her chest. "I thought we'd find Carl's murderers and that would be the end of it. But if this is an outbreak . . . I don't even want to think about the ramifications."

"Well, at least it's not infecting humans."

She rested her chin on her knees. "It's all so overwhelming, I feel like I'm going insane!" She began sobbing deeply and moved to lean her head on Dan's shoulder. "Carl *knew.* He must have."

Dan put his arm around her and drew her close. They huddled together for a long time, watching the thunder and lightning.

"I don't know what's gotten into me," she finally said, sniffling. "I'm just . . . *scared.*"

Dan wiped a tear from her cheek and gazed into her eyes, suddenly so deep and fragile. The merest touch of her hand against his back unlocked an overwhelming desire. He pressed his lips to hers, inhaled the scent of her skin, felt hot tears against his cheeks.

Suddenly, their hands were everywhere, probing, grasping.

Dan reveled in her passionate response. They stumbled backward into the bedroom and fell across the sheets. He rolled on top of her, pressing his weight against her thighs. She moaned and opened to his advances.

They found each other in the darkness, as the storm lashed and swirled around them.

32

THE NEXT MORNING, Dan rolled toward Rachel, only to find empty sheets. He lay there awhile, basking in the memory of the prior evening.

Despite all that had happened, despite Rachel's disturbing revelations, he felt at peace.

It was a strange and unfamiliar sensation.

In the kitchen, he found Rachel's mark, as usual—a pile of filthy dishes stacked in the sink. How could one woman go through so much china, just for breakfast? Grinning, he cleaned up, made a fresh pot of coffee, and checked his watch.

Rachel would be starting her autopsy soon. Now, it was his turn to do his part.

Rachel's theory about doomsday genes continued to haunt him. It made sense in a strange way.

Had Carl Jameson made the same connection?

If Dan could gain more insight into Carl's research, then he might have a better understanding of his clues. To do that, he needed to contact the source, the one person in common who tied their two destinies together: their Santa Fe syncrenomics instructor.

That would not be an easy task.

The man was notoriously difficult to reach, was isolated, and eschewed many of the world's modern conveniences. He had a cell phone but seldom checked it.

Dan could only try.

To Dan's shock and amazement, he got an answer on the first ring.

"Hello, mouse! What took you so long?"

Dan chose to address his mentor by his formal designation. "Professor Proudfoot, how did you know it was me?"

"A thunderbird landed on my windowsill yesterday and told me you would call."

Dan shook his head. *Here we go.* "So I take it the weather's been bad in your area?"

"A mere shower. Nothing like the storm that threatens your future—"

"Uhhh, how do you know where I am, exactly?"

Ben let out a signature cackle. "My boy, how do you think I take measure of the world? The weatherman has much to share."

Dan swallowed hard. Ben had figured out everything already. If his and Rudi's handiwork had been so transparent, he may have miscalculated their window of anonymity. "Was it that obvious?"

"To the eagle, yes. To others, I cannot say. I am truly sorry for your loss. My heart is heavy with sorrow for dear Jameson. He was one of my favorites, next to you, of course."

"Thanks, but I barely knew the guy."

"Ahh, but that is not true. You two share a cosmic link. After all, you are the Hero Twins. Gucumatz, heart of sea, and Hurricane, heart of sky. Your destinies were always ordained to merge. I knew that from the first time I met you both."

It seemed like Ben was laying it on a bit thick. "I'm sorry, professor, I don't feel very godlike right now."

"That comes from actions, not thoughts."

"Whatever. What I *can* tell you is that I'm trying to learn more about the man. These recent events and Carl's death are linked, and he tried to leave clues. Ones I'm trying to decipher."

"Then how can I help?" Ben replied.

It was obvious to Dan, even through the satellite phone, that Ben's lighthearted tone had taken on more weight.

"Did Carl happen to contact you recently? Anything that might help me to understand his mood or the work he was doing?"

"I heard from Carl only once—a few weeks ago—another age. He seemed very excited about his research—eager to share his parables."

Dan felt his pulse quicken. "Really? What did he have to say?"

"Oh, he had uncovered some deep mystery, hidden for eons before the age of man. Carl joked that we might witness the dawn of the seventh sun."

Dan waited patiently for Ben to continue, but the man remained silent. Dan remembered the old Aztec tale of the five suns, or six suns, depending on the version. He'd heard Ben recite it often enough. Obviously, so had Carl Jameson.

But the seventh sun?

"What did Carl mean by that, exactly?"

Ben's answer seemed to take an eternity. "Ahh, the Earth always speaks in riddles."

"So, that's it? He didn't provide any details?"

"Oh, he promised more, but Earth Mother reveals her secrets in her own time."

Ben Proudfoot wasn't making things any clearer. Dan was certain of one thing: Carl Jameson knew he had discovered something of great significance, and he wanted to communicate it to someone.

"Thanks, Professor. If you think of anything else that helps, will you call me?"

"Of course," Ben replied. "Just know this. You are Hurricane, the bringer of change. You have found the Arrogant Imposter. Continue your brother's task."

"I'll try."

"Oh, there is one more thing," Proudfoot said, almost as a side note. "Carl left another riddle, one I do not fully understand."

Dan chuckled at the irony of Ben Proudfoot admitting confusion over a riddle. Yet he knew that riddles served a purpose. They forced a person to look beyond one's own biases, to open the mind and see familiar objects in a new light, to "think outside the box," in modern parlance. It seemed somehow fitting for their conversation to end on a riddle.

"So what is it?"

"Carl said that he had found Earth Mother's medicine wheel."

AFTER HIS CONVERSATION with Ben Proudfoot, Dan was more confused than ever. But at least he had something to work with, if he could decipher its meaning.

The chirping of Dan's Skype account broke his concentration. It was Rudi. His patented smirk was conspicuously absent, replaced by a look of concern.

"The honeymoon's over," Rudi said, typing as he spoke. "We've got trouble. Watch this." A new window appeared, playing a news clip of Jenifer Coleman standing in front of Duff's resort.

". . . Bay Islands Honduras, where vacationers and scuba divers come to enjoy the pristine waters of one of the world's largest reef systems. But there may be more under the surface. Is this an idyllic vacation paradise, a toxic waste dump, or a hotbed of computer terrorism? The Weatherman Virus points to alleged activities just a few miles from here."

The video switched to an image of Duff leaning awkwardly against the bar's entrance.

"Mr. McAlister, is it true the body of Carl Jameson was discovered here last week?"

She handed Duff a photograph. He glanced at it, his expression vacillating between discomfort and anger.

"Yeah, that's right."
    "And how has that affected you?"
    "How do you think? It's hurt our business. Guests are concerned. But the dumping—that's worse, much worse. We've seen fish kills and the reefs are dying, but . . . it's still a diving paradise here. The toxic dumping has got to stop—"
    "Have you actually seen these dumpings?"
    "Who, me?"

Duff's eyes darted around.

"Not personally, but—no I haven't, but I can see the results."
    "What can you tell us about the involvement of Dan Clifford in the cyberattack?"
    "Who?"

Duff's expression took on an air of wide-eyed innocence.

"Dan Clifford."

"Oh yeah, he was a guest here once."

"He discovered Carl Jameson's body, correct?"

"Why yes, I think you're right—"

"Have you seen him lately?"

"I don't keep up with my guests."

"Even ones who find corpses?"

"Especially ones who find corpses."

"Is he staying at the resort now?"

"No, he's not. Now young lady, don't you have something better to do than interview an old goat like me?"

"Do you know his whereabouts?"

"No! I've got a dive to host, thank you."

Duff tried to walk away. Jenifer followed him.

"What can you tell us about the computer virus?"

Duff turned and scowled.

"Nothing, not a bleep-bleep thing! You want to investigate a virus? How about the virus of corporate greed? Investigate Hadan Orcus, why don't you? Goodbye."

The clip switched back to the front of the Hacienda.

"Dan Clifford, a citizen of the United States, has become the prime suspect in this case. CNN has learned that he flew to Honduras on a commercial flight four days ago. Illegal dumping, computer viruses, murder. What steps will the Honduran government take to get to the bottom of this mystery?

"CNN has also learned of several deaths in the Honduran city of La Ceiba, from a mysterious illness that is causing widespread panic among the populace. Is this related to the illegal dumping? Dan Clifford may hold the answers to these questions.

"This is Jenifer Coleman, reporting exclusively for CNN."

"What'll we do?" Rudi pleaded, his composure fraying. "We're all over the news! Jenifer's out poking around the resort and looking for the NOAA ship . . . Dan? You there?"

Dan was already out of the chair, pacing. "What was that about deaths in La Ceiba?"

"I don't know. The rumors are that townspeople started wigging out during some festival, attacking each other—it's bedlam! Guests are all leaving."

Doomsday genes.

"Rudi, stay in your room. Draw the curtains. Don't let Jen see you." Dan rushed to get dressed and found a note in Rachel's hand lying on the dresser:

> *Dan, thanks for the wonderful evening. I feel much better today. See you soon.*
> *With love, Rachel.*

He stuffed the note into his pocket, scurried down the trail to the skiff, and churned through the pinnacles at breakneck speed.

As RACHEL BEGAN scrubbing up for the autopsy, she pondered her behavior the night before. After promising herself not to get involved, she had succumbed to a moment of weakness. She couldn't remember a time when she had felt more vulnerable, and Dan's intimacy had left her yearning for more. She knew that getting involved with him was a bad idea. It would only complicate matters later.

Best to cool things off now, she decided.

What had gotten into her? She felt embarrassed by her weakness and petty fears. Maybe the pain of Carl's loss had finally caught up with her. She needed to get her head back in the game.

The doomsday theory was still in play. It seemed less convincing to her this morning, but she couldn't shake a lingering sense of doom. Enough so to prompt her to use level-two biosafety procedures during the autopsy—just to be safe—two pairs of gloves, full plastic scrubs, viral face mask, and a splash guard.

The day before, she had iced down the dolphin to retard decomposition. Now, the ice had melted, leaving behind limp bags of meltwater and a sizable puddle on the floor. Taking care not to slip, she removed the flaccid bags, pulled a surgical tray next to the table, and laid out the cutting tools.

Performing a full autopsy on an animal this large could take all day. She was primarily interested in the brain area, and decided to start there. The swelling around the cranium had increased significantly overnight, distending the dolphin's head to twice its normal size. She poked a scalpel into the fleshy area between the dolphin's eyes. With such swelling, she expected a spurt of cranial fluid, but none came. Instead, decomposition gases sputtered out of the incision like air from a Whoopee cushion. In five seconds, the dolphin's head had deflated to its original size.

Rachel began breathing through her mouth, anticipating the onslaught of rancid fumes. She placed the scalpel at the blow hole and pulled it downward smoothly but firmly in a continuous motion, all the way to the dolphin's nostrum. The blade easily sliced through the white fatty tissue, splaying it out and exposing the reddish musculature underneath. That was strange too, she thought. It should be stiff and leathery; there had been ample time for rigor mortis to set in. She made another pass through the incision, cutting through the cranial musculature and exposing a narrow strip of ivory skull.

The bone saw came next. She hated this part—the sound of metal rasping on bone. She reached for the power blade and pulled its trigger a few times, eliciting a familiar piercing whine.

She swung back around to the table and screamed, dropping the saw to the floor.

The impossible vision on the table filled her with elemental terror. She backed away, whimpering, hands out defensively. "*No, no, no,* this is not possible!"

It was her father, his cold gray skin tired and wrinkled.

She had sawn off the top of his skull.

The once-firm folds of his brain sagged onto the table in a mass of gelatinous pulp. Recoiling in disgust and self-loathing, she tried to regain her composure, but the solid world had melted away. She struggled toward the door, her footsteps sinking into quicksand. Demons hovered overhead, their grim claws reaching out to pluck folds from her brain.

A guttural scream poured forth as she lunged, swam, slid through the muck.

33

THIRTY-FIVE THOUSAND FEET above the Isthmus of Panama, Hadan Orcus sat in the media room of his private Gulfstream jet, his gaze fixed on a flat panel screen. Across from him, Bradley Gruber squirmed silently.

Orcus carefully studied the taped broadcast. Then he flicked off the monitor and slid back into the recesses of a massive baroque armchair. The room fell quiet. The plush upholstery, thick carpet, and ancient tapestries on the walls smothered any extraneous noise, leaving only the faint hiss of air rushing past the fuselage.

Gruber had learned not to interrupt Orcus, so he sat quietly and studied the man. Orcus was an imposing figure, rugged, though a bit too ostentatious for Gruber's taste. He filled the smoking chair with his six-foot-two-inch frame. Surprisingly muscular for a man his age, his skin was tanned and wrinkle-free. His salt-and-pepper hairline had receded long ago, but it had been revived somewhat with several hair transplants. It was combed straight back and held in place with copious amounts of mousse. Square cheekbones framed a pair of intense blue eyes—eyes that could bore a hole through a man.

Gruber mused over the décor, a hideous collection of overwrought European antiques—a reflection of Orcus's heritage. Born Hagan Luis Othmann in Salzburg, Austria, he had played along the banks of the Salzach River, in the shadow of the Hohensalzburg fortress and a stone's throw from Mozart's birthplace, during the aftermath of World War II.

After the fall of Berlin, the Othmann family fled to Argentina in a U-boat, settling with other refugees from the Austrian aristocracy on the cattle ranches. When anti-German sentiment grew in the fifties, a young Hagan Othmann fled northward to Honduras, reportedly with most of the family fortune, changing his name to the less Germanic

Hadan Orcus. He invested heavily in the mining industry, cutting roads into the ancient forests of the Honduran mountains. There, he founded Solá Mining Industries and the boomtown of Soluteca. Now, he controlled a multi-billion-dollar empire that spread halfway down the west coast of Central America.

It was an extravagant story and one Gruber had been forced to endure from Orcus innumerable times. But Gruber also knew the hidden details, the ones Hadan Orcus kept to himself: that Orcus's father had been an intelligence operative in the German SS; that he had smuggled a cache of gold and priceless art objects on board the fugitive U-boat; that the crew and the U-boat had mysteriously disappeared off the coast of Argentina. Yes, Gruber knew it all, and he knew that soon, he would be expected to hang on every word Hadan Orcus spoke.

Orcus revived, his voice cutting the air with a strength and timbre that concealed his anger. "Forty years of work to build this company. All threatened by some faggot with a computer! The Earth Summit was a disaster. You assured me you'd take care of the rogue programmer."

Gruber inhaled sharply. "Mr. Orcus, we proceeded exactly as you requested. His termination backfired, unfortunately. He had more free time to help his friend Clifford. You know the saying, keep your friends close and your enemies closer."

Orcus raised a wagging finger. "Let's dispense with the truisms, shall we? I've been plagued by incompetent fools lately. My imbecilic captain can't clean up his own mess. If this leads back to our other activities—"

"It won't," Gruber said. "My contacts in Washington are already working on damage control."

"The damage is *done*. This is a constant danger when dealing with outsiders. They're unpredictable, sloppy."

"You can't expand without them. We must develop plans for contingencies—"

"Gruber, I don't need a self-help lecture from you. I need competence. What if Clifford exposes our connection to the NeuroSys plant?"

"He won't," Gruber said. "We've cut off his link to company information. He has everything to lose by destroying this deal: stock options. We're only a few days away from the IPO. Clifford could lose millions if anything comes out beforehand."

"My dear Bradley, renegades do not behave logically. You should know that by now." Orcus kept his eyes trained on Gruber. "They've played right into the hands of my enemies. The U.S. president and his band of militants have been trying to derail my CAFTA privileges for years. Now they have an excuse to do so."

"With all due respect, sir," Gruber said, returning Orcus's gaze with cool indifference, "you are vastly overestimating the talents in Washington. I work with these men every day. Most politicians are just greedy little men with small ideas and huge egos. They are not capable of such a conspiracy, and for what purpose? They support CAFTA and globalization, after all."

Orcus's expression became more distant. "Never forget this: the most dangerous conspiracies are formed in the minds of envious little men. Devoid of reason, disorganized, creating havoc at every turn—*that* is what makes them so dangerous. Rome—the greatest empire in recorded history—fell to a horde of barbarians."

Orcus lowered his head and seemed to drift away. "I've been barraged by the media, my reputation impugned, all over a few harmless barrels of garbage dumped in the vastness of the sea. It seems to make no difference to them that I have put food in the mouths of thousands—primitives who would otherwise be scrounging for their next meal. I want these renegades *eliminated,* only this time, I'll take care of it myself."

Gruber listened quietly, stroking the opaline face of his wristwatch with his thumb. "Your reputation is still sound. American politicians are experts at withstanding attacks on their reputations. Violence is not the answer. It will only focus more attention on your operations. We need a diversion instead, something to redirect the public's attention. The media has given us an opportunity with their coverage of the weather report cyberattack. And we need some good old-fashioned lobbying, to spin goodwill before the NeuroSys IPO. Remind them where their loyalties lie."

"I can't tolerate any more unpredictability," Orcus said. "Can you guarantee the success of your plan?"

"Nothing is guaranteed, of course," Gruber replied. "But let me do my job as facilitator. You can always keep your methods as a failsafe."

"And another thing," Orcus continued. "Tell those idiots at Neu-roSys to complete the other end of their bargain. I need that equipment, now more than ever. I cannot afford to lose this opportunity and neither can you, my dear friend, *Bradley*."

Gruber understood the threat all too clearly. It was his job to absorb such threats, he supposed. "I've never failed you before, have I?"

Orcus chuckled. "Gruber, you're a slippery toad, but I clearly remember who introduced me to this cadre of clowns."

Gruber felt the anger rise in his chest, but he concealed his emotions behind an opaque expression, honed through decades of political maneuvering.

Go ahead, Orcus, and show your bluster. But don't get too close. This toad is lethal. "Don't worry, Señor Orcus," Gruber continued. "It's my job to direct the clowns, and I'm very good at it."

34

STILL RUNNING THE skiff at full throttle, Dan threaded it through the seaside shanties of Bonacca Town. The locals, friendly as ever, waved at him as he passed, but he didn't wave back. Wary of the press, he kept his head lowered and eyes focused straight ahead.

The outline of the *Sea Berth* finally slid into view.

Its bright profile gleamed against the muted tones of the harbor. The ship would be a magnet for any video crew. Not seeing any activity, he allowed himself to relax a bit. He'd arrived ahead of Jenifer.

Pulling alongside the pier, he tied off and jogged up the *Sea Berth*'s ramp. At the fantail, he saw French working on some diving equipment.

French grinned. "I didn't expect to see you here."

"You've got to get the hell out of here. The media have invaded the island."

"Uh-oh. When? How?"

"No time to explain. There's some sort of pandemic in La Ceiba. It could be related to the dumpsite. I've got to warn Rachel."

"Pandemic? From what?"

"Don't know. Just get ready to leave. Where is she?"

"The wet lab, behind you, on the right."

"Thanks." At the door, he found a large white sign:

NO ADMITTANCE
Autopsy in progress.
Absolutely NO interruptions.
Lab is sealed—Rachel

Dan figured the interruption was warranted and rapped on the door. No response. He knocked more forcefully, then cracked the door open and peered in. He recoiled from a bizarre but faintly famil-iar smell, like flowers and sewage. A jolt of fear surged through him. He took a breath and stepped inside.

"Rachel? You in here?"

His eyes fell on the autopsy table. The dolphin was there, a bright-red seam of flesh visible along its head. Tools were strewn across the floor, broken glass everywhere. Where was Rachel? Scanning the room anxiously, Dan gasped at the sight of her in the far corner.

Her face was red and drawn, her rigid arms and legs stretched backward like a bow. Her eyelids fluttered spasmodically, caught in the clutches of a grand mal seizure.

"Rachel! Oh my God!" He raced over, slipped his hand under her head, and pulled her gently toward him. Foamy saliva dribbled from the side of her mouth. He absently wiped it away and let out an an-guished sob.

The room started spinning. His eyes and cheeks burned, as if someone had hit him with pepper spray. Blood pounded behind his eyeballs. He wrapped his arms around her and struggled to stand, bumping into the walls like a drunkard. He staggered to the door and wobbled out into the afternoon sun.

Suddenly, he was racing across a field of heather, the limp body of his mother held tightly in his grasp. Behind him lay the smoking ruins of the old Victorian, its shattered timbers raking the sky. He stumbled in the wet grass, found his balance again, and pushed forward toward a line of flashing lights. At the edge of the field a man in a white frock waited, his arms outstretched.

Dan cried out. "Father! Help her, please!"

"It's important we talk to the chief," Jenifer Coleman said, putting on her most persuasive face. "We need an official statement."

Hector tried to edge Jenifer and the news crew back out the door. "*Señorita*, the captain is not talking to no one right now, *comprende*? Death in family."

Through the window she could see the man just sitting there.

"Look, I know of the tragedy," she said as politely as possible. "Shouldn't he speak to the press about the incident, the current situa-tion? It's his responsibility as chief . . . and it will take his mind off his personal affairs."

Hector pushed again, more forcefully. "Not today."

Jenifer's cameraman saw an opportunity to slip past the officer and began filming the inside of the office.

"No!" Hector jerked the camera down. "Leave!"

Berto turned toward the ruckus and signaled him to let them pass.

Jenifer squeezed into the tiny office. The camera lights came back on. Berto looked like he hadn't slept in days.

"Captain Berto, we've heard about your tragedy. My sincere condolences."

"It's *Enrique,* Captain Enrique." Berto stared down at the desk, looking as fragile as a gossamer. "It is the devil's work . . . ," he mumbled.

Jenifer smiled, relieved to find the man's English fluent. "So how many people have been affected by this incident? A poisoning?"

"I don't know," Berto said. "Ask Hector."

Captain Enrique was obviously in shock. Jenifer felt a jab of pity for this man of authority, but this was *news.* "There are accusations of toxic waste dumping by a ship called *La Cosecha Abundante.* Could this be connected to the tragedy?"

Berto shrugged. "That is for the medical doctors to decide."

"I'm sure you've heard of the terrorist incident in the United States. About a man called Dan Clifford. Have you heard of him?"

"No."

Jenifer sensed the chief's patience was waning, but she pressed on. "What can you tell us about the recent murder of Carl Jameson?"

Berto sighed and leaned back in the chair. "If I talk, will you leave me alone?"

Jenifer shrugged. "Sure. We're just looking for the truth."

"Very well," he muttered. "Señor Jameson. Yes. We have heard of him. And the ship. But no Señor Clifford. Only the American woman from, how you say, Noah?"

"You mean NOAA?" She spelled it out.

"*Sí.* She came around asking about Jameson."

"Who is this woman?"

"I don't know. Señorita Sullivan, or something."

Jenifer slumped. "What did she want to know?"

Berto rested his elbows on the desk. "Why don't you ask her yourself?"

"I'd love to," Jenifer chirped. "If I knew where she was."

"She and her ship, I think they are in Guanaja."

"Really?" Jenifer felt a jolt of excitement. "Is this a big ship? We were there earlier today. I don't remember it."

"It is *muy grande*. It would be docked in Bonacca Town. Now, if you'll excuse me . . ." Berto wheeled the chair around and fiddled with some papers.

"Thank you, Captain *Enrique*. I hope you feel better soon."

35

DAN AWOKE WITH an excruciating headache. Any sudden movement resulted in a jolt of pain. *This is getting old,* he thought. Pushing through a fog, he began to orient himself. He was in the visitors' quarters of the *Sea Berth.* His clothes had been replaced with a green medical gown. Wires were running up one sleeve. A harsh beep pinged from a monitor next to the bed.

What happened? Turning carefully, he peered out the porthole toward a bizarre vehicle with twisted wings and huge propellers painted in U.S. Coast Guard colors. He recognized it as a V-22 Osprey, a tilt rotor airplane that could hover and land like a helicopter. Normally, he'd be fascinated by such a slick gadget, but not now.

Some important thought was fighting its way back into his consciousness.

Almost on cue, a gentle tap came on the door and a man entered, dressed in an orange biohazard suit.

"Mr. Clifford," the man said thinly, through the mask. "My name is Dr. Philip Goodson. I'm from the Centers for Disease Control. How are we feeling?"

"A bit punchy."

The man checked Dan's pulse, aimed a digital thermometer in his ear. "Hmmm."

"What happened?"

"You don't remember?"

Vague, horrifying images of Rachel suddenly rushed to the forefront of his consciousness. *"Oh god!* Is Rachel all right?" He tried to get out of bed, but Dr. Goodson pushed him back.

"Relax, my boy. She's in the next room. Before we talk of her, tell me about yourself. What do you remember?"

He struggled with the question for a long moment. "The lab, seeing Rachel . . . then I picked her up, and . . . nothing."

"You don't remember talking with anyone?"

"No."

"Arguing with French?"

"No."

"Well, they had to wrestle Rachel away from you. You've been sleeping for hours."

Dan grabbed the man's arm. "Is she okay?"

Goodson pulled away gently. "Rachel is comatose, but stable. We're doing everything we can."

The words were like a punch in the gut. What did fate have against him? "I should have stopped the autopsy."

"From what I understand, you saved her life."

Did I? "Is she going to be all right? I want to see her."

"That's not a good idea," Goodson said. "If this illness is contagious, we can't risk you coming in contact with her."

"But I've already been in contact with her!"

Dr. Goodson studied him for a moment. "You have a point. Wait here." He left, locking the door behind him.

MINUTES LATER, GOODSON returned with a green cap, face mask, and gloves. Dan waited impatiently as the doctor helped him carefully don the scrubs. He had to see her, to erase the last image of her tortured expression from his mind.

Goodson led him down the hallway and as he entered the room, Dan was shocked by the scene that confronted him. Rachel was lying like a corpse, wires and tubes running everywhere. Two more men in biohazard suits stood by like aliens, assembling a large, transparent, coffin-like structure.

Rachel's anguished grimace had faded. Now, she just looked . . . *blank.* Try as he might, Dan could sense nothing of her vibrant personality through the empty visage. He held her hand and squeezed, hating the layer of latex between them. "Is she going to wake up?"

Goodson hesitated. "We don't know. Her condition is stable, so that's a good sign. She's fighting."

"Fighting what?"

"We're not sure yet. We should know more after we've tested her blood and have a chance to examine the victims in La Ceiba. We were hoping you could shed some light on the subject."

"I'll gladly do anything I can to help," he said eagerly.

"Then tell me everything you remember from the past few days."

Dan took Goodson through the story of the garbage scow, their dive to the abyss, the death of the whale and dolphin. But when he got to the part about Rachel's theory of doomsday genes, Dr. Goodson waved him off dismissively.

"Nice theory, but we don't see that type of spontaneous evolution over such short periods of time. Let us grow some cultures first, to see if we can identify any known pathogens. That will take some time."

Dan looked back at Rachel, his mind racing through all the latest chaos.

Time did not appear to be something Rachel could afford.

JENIFER COLEMAN TRIED to protect her hair behind the boat's windshield, to no avail. The wind whipped it into a mass of knots. She strained with anticipation as the motorboat neared Bonacca Town.

When they rounded the island's tip, Jenifer squealed with delight. She could see a large gray ship with a strange, twisted airplane parked at its stern, the only one of its kind in the small harbor. And it looked like something important was happening.

"Quick!" she yelled to the cameraman. "Get a shot of that!"

The cameraman climbed on the bow and began filming. Jenifer focused a pair of binoculars on the airplane. Two orange-suited men struggled toward it, carrying what looked like a glass coffin. She yelled in the pilot's ear: "Dock over there! Hurry!" The boat banked to the right, almost throwing the cameraman into the water.

"Are you getting that? Up there, by the plane! Zoom in."

The motorboat hurtled toward the Sea Berth. At the last minute, the pilot whipped the stern around and slid into the pier. Jenifer was out in a flash and racing toward the gangplank. A sign read:

NO ADMITTANCE UNDER ANY CIRCUMSTANCES
THIS SHIP IS QUARANTINED BY ORDER OF THE CDC

"Excuse me, I'm Jenifer Coleman with CNN," she shouted to a man standing guard on the ship. "What's going on here?"

"Sorry," he yelled back. "Can't help you. Official government business."

Jenifer started up the gangplank. "Is this related to the toxic dumping off the coast of Honduras? Do you know the whereabouts of Dan Clifford?"

The man smiled and shrugged. "Sorry, no comment."

"Look, I'm with CNN! We have a right to know what's going—" Suddenly, the airplane's engines came to life, the whine from their overly large blades rising in pitch. Two more men in orange suits exited a side door and trotted toward the plane. She raised the binoculars and yelled. When they turned, she glimpsed a familiar face and started back up the gangplank. "Hey! Dan Clifford! Stop!"

The guard on the ship stepped forward and blocked her way.

Jenifer could only watch as the orange suits climbed inside. As the props of the plane picked up more speed, it suddenly lifted off the deck with a mighty roar. The ship rolled, and Jenifer fell to her knees.

"Damn, damn, damn!"

36

THE FLIGHT TO Atlanta had been miserable. Locked inside a biohazard suit for the entire trip, Dan was hot, sweaty, and claustrophobic. They called it a bunny suit, but no bunny would be caught dead in one of these. Bright orange and disposable, the material crinkled like cellophane. The thick rubber boots and gloves were sealed at the openings with duct tape and the tight hood was fitted with a full-face mask connected to filter canisters protruding from the front.

The CDC team members were all wearing their suits as well, to protect them from contamination.

Dan wore his suit to seal in any contamination.

There was nothing to do but stare at Rachel's isolation pod across the aisle. The doctors hovered over it, monitoring her vital signs.

Dr. Goodson left her side and sat down next to him. "How do you feel?"

"Miserable."

"Any change in your symptoms?"

"I'm hot, thirsty, wet, and nauseous. Otherwise, great. What if I hurl in this contraption?"

Goodson gave him an empathetic smile. "Please don't." He pointed out the window. "Just a few more minutes."

The campus of Emory University came into view, nestled in a forest of dogwoods. The plane veered left and headed for a cluster of nearby buildings covered in shiny white tiles like an inside-out shower stall. The Osprey slowed as the engines began to tilt upward for vertical landing.

They touched down in the parking lot and were immediately swarmed by another team of suited doctors who rushed Rachel's isolation unit out of the plane and up a long, white tunnel. Dan followed, struggling to keep up, his rubber boots scuffing across the concrete.

Shortly, Rachel's unit headed one way, while Goodson tugged Dan in the opposite direction.

"No! I want to stay with her."

"I'm sorry, that's not possible." He gestured toward a pair of doors. "Go through and remove your clothing. Push the red button on the wall and wash thoroughly in the shower. You'll see a fresh hospital gown there."

Reluctantly, Dan did as instructed, relieved to get out of the sweltering suit. He stepped out of the shower, dressed, and entered an enclosure that hummed with fluorescent lights. Dr. Goodson's voice rasped through an intercom. "Okay, straight ahead."

He walked across the stark white room. It was sparsely furnished, with a bed jammed up against a wall of glass and a toilet directly opposite with nothing but a curtain for privacy. *You could get snow blindness in here,* Dan thought, *if you didn't go crazy first.* He heard the faint clunk of an electric dead bolt behind him.

On the other side of the glass window, Goodson motioned toward a pair of black rubber gloves that projected through the wall like a pair of ghostly arms. After slipping his hands into the gloves, Goodson opened a pass-through drawer filled with medical equipment and began inserting intravenous lines into Dan's arm.

A few minutes later, Dan felt like a cyborg, with multiple tubes, wires, and sensors dangling from his arms, chest, and scalp.

"Hook the IV lines and sensors into their color-coded wall sockets," Goodson said. "We'll be able to draw blood samples and monitor your condition continuously. If you need anything, push the button. There's satellite TV imbedded in the wall, so just settle in and relax."

Dan felt like a lab rat. "Would you be relaxed in here?"

Goodson smiled, anticipating Dan's next question. "I suppose not, but if anything changes with Rachel, I'll let you know immediately."

"You better." Dan leaned against the glass and watched as Goodson crossed the rotunda and approached another windowed enclosure. Through the crowd of doctors, nurses, and crash carts, he caught a flash of auburn hair behind the glass, bright against the white background. He had visited the ER with his father once, watching the frenzied activity, comforting embraces, busy hands . . . saving lives. It was a cherished memory.

He had to trust that these doctors were equally effective.

Dan sat on the bed, his stomach churning. Was it a symptom of the illness? What if Rachel didn't make it? The thought seemed incomprehensible, unbearable.

What if *he* didn't make it?

He imagined Carl Jameson sitting in the rusting hulk of the garbage scow, pondering precisely the same things as he tore holes in his shirt.

Unable to help Rachel now, Dan resolved to fit the pieces of the huge puzzle together. What did Carl mean by the seventh sun? Did that imply a tragedy, or a new age of enlightenment? Ancient medicine wheels? And how did Hadan Orcus figure into Rachel's doomsday scenario? Was she correct? What about NeuroSys and those mysterious crates? What about the victims in La Ceiba?

He thought of other victims in history—of ancient Pompeii, the Asian Tsunami, 9/11, swine flu—all of them had been living ordinary lives the day before their tragedies, blissfully ignorant of what tomorrow would bring. He'd spent his career developing software to predict black swans. This should be his domain, but the work had always been theoretical, a set of calculations on a computer.

When fate singled you out, life didn't feel so theoretical anymore.

GOODSON STOOD AT the window of Rachel's isolation ward—unceremoniously called the slammer—and watched her vitals trace a steady line. He wondered if she needed isolation at all. A third set of blood tests had turned up negative results for infection.

It made no sense.

Goodson returned to his office and placed a call to his cohort at Ft. Detrick, Colonel Clarence Peterson, director of USAMRIID, the U.S. Army Medical Research Institute of Infectious Diseases. It was the Army's version of the CDC and had once been the country's chemical and biological warfare branch. That time had passed and USAMRIID's new calling was to develop antidotes to modern weapons of mass destruction.

So they say, Goodson thought.

"Peterson here."

"Clarence, this is Goodson. Our two guests have settled into their quarters."

"I saw your great escape on the evening news. Quite exciting. How's the girl?"

"Still alive."

"Clifford?"

"Resting under tight security. He seems fine, which is perplexing."

"I gotta give you a gold star for your detective work," Peterson said. "The president and the OHS want to know if this cyberattack and the outbreak are some kind of coordinated bioterror event. When can we question this guy?"

Goodson doodled with a pencil on a legal pad. He was not quite sure how to proceed. "Frankly, I don't see Clifford as a cyberterrorist, more like a whistle-blower. And I certainly don't see him as a bioterrorist. It's his girlfriend who's ill, after all."

"Girlfriend, or fellow terrorist," Peterson said. "What do we really know about their relationship? If Clifford *is* involved in bioterrorism, it would serve him right. He's lucky more people haven't died."

"There's something odd about this disease, if that's what it is at all," Goodson said, as he continued to pencil in a question mark wrapped around a doctor's staff. "The test results are very contradictory. I left a team in La Ceiba to collect additional samples. They're reporting a host of very different symptoms. Some of them look like infectious disease. Others indicate poisoning. We'll know more when the samples get here. In any case, I recommend we mobilize for an outbreak. This may be the perfect time to field test our new toy."

"Forget it, Phil. I'm getting resistance from the Hill to that idea, unless this is a bona fide outbreak. They're focused on the computer hacker and bioterror angles. Besides, we're not ready to launch. You know that. Let's let the outbreak run its course, figure out if it's toxic chemicals or something more serious. If it's illegal dumping, then that's not our job. We're not environmental watchdogs."

"I thought our job was to save lives," Goodson replied. "How many deaths does it take to get Washington's attention?"

"Look, I'm just following orders. I gave up long ago trying to figure out why politicos do what they do." Peterson paused. "I'll try and keep the pressure on, but we'll need more definitive answers. Your index of suspicion should center on Mr. Clifford, in my opinion. We need a debrief before Justice gets their claws into him. They want to press him on the hack attack. Send me tissue samples and we'll work the toxin angle."

"Already on their way," Goodson said. "The Osprey left an hour ago."

AFTER SEVERAL HOURS in the slammer, Dan had grown weary of watching himself on television. He'd seen the news clip narrated by Jenifer showing him boarding the Osprey in Honduras. Other reports focused on his hack attack. They were calling it the Weatherman Virus. There was hardly any mention of Hadan Orcus or *La Cosecha Abundante*.

The world had turned inside out. Hadan Orcus was the victim, Dan Clifford, the criminal. He felt numb, his only solid emotion a desperate longing to see Rachel survive.

The news began to mention more deaths in La Ceiba. He was about to push the service button again when he heard the click of a dead bolt. The door swung open and Dr. Goodson entered, wearing only doctor's scrubs.

"Feeling better?" Goodson asked.

"I thought I was under quarantine."

"Well, it seems there's nothing wrong with you. Your blood profile is perfectly normal."

Dan felt a mixture of relief and confusion. "And Rachel?"

Goodson sighed. "No change, I'm afraid."

"I don't understand. Why am I okay, and she's not?"

"We're not certain, but we think you two were exposed to some type of chemical fumes in her lab. She's sicker because she received a larger dose."

"But she was sure the dolphin was suffering from some kind of pathogen."

"Perhaps for the victims in La Ceiba and the dolphin, but not Rachel. Our initial cultures have come up negative."

Goodson turned to leave, but stopped, having remembered something. "We have noted one distinct symptom on Rachel's brain MRI that probably explains her coma."

Dan felt another tinge of hope. "What's that?"

"We're seeing a high level of activity in Rachel's prefrontal cortex and amygdala. These areas are primarily associated with the brain's fear response and creativity. We think her coma is protection against overstimulation. In other words, she was *scared* into a coma."

"So can you treat it?"

"Our spectrographic analysis shows trace substances in Rachel's blood. Once we isolate the specific compounds, perhaps. Just be patient."

Patience had never been one of Dan's virtues.

AN HOUR LATER, Goodson returned again, carrying a bundle of Dan's clothes, freshly laundered. He wore a look of regret. "You need to get dressed. You have visitors."

Dan knew immediately what was coming and felt a knot tighten in his chest. "I can't leave Rachel behind."

"I'm sorry, I miscalculated." Goodson rubbed his temple. "The Justice Department moved faster than I expected."

"Doc, you've got to make her better," Dan said. "I'm putting my trust in you."

"I'll do my best," Goodson replied.

Once dressed, Dan followed Goodson to the lobby where two men in dark suits awaited, their faces stern and unmoving. He immediately recognized his friend, Vincent Peretti.

Vince was not happy to see him. Shaking his head subtly, Peretti approached, flashed his FBI identification, and pulled out a pair of handcuffs. "Dan Clifford, you're under arrest for violation of the Patriot Act. You have the right to remain silent. . . ."

37

UNLIKE DAN'S TRIP to Atlanta, the flight to Washington had been quiet. Too quiet. Vince Peretti waved off all of Dan's attempts at conversation, his demeanor icy cold. When the private jet landed at Dulles, it was met by a featureless black limousine. They drove into the heart of Washington, past the Jefferson Memorial and toward what Dan expected to be FBI headquarters in the Hoover Building. But instead, the car turned right onto Independence Avenue.

"Where are we going?"

"Russell Building," Vince said brusquely. "Senate hearing on cyber-terrorism."

"You're kidding."

Vince's expression made the answer clear.

They cruised past the Smithsonian and the National Mall. Tourists milled about, enjoying a crisp fall day. Farther away, in the distance, Dan could see street vendors plying their wares in the Ellipse, and beyond, the hazy outline of the White House. It was another carefree day in America. People were going about their usual routine, oblivious to a tragedy unfolding a thousand miles away.

The enormity of his situation began to sink in. He had never desired notoriety, certainly not the infamy of a criminal. He thought of Rachel and everything he had to lose.

They took a quick turn onto First Street. Through the trees, the Capitol loomed at the crest of the Hill. At a cluster of Senate office buildings, the car slowed and pulled in to a small recessed parking area. A pair of muscular guards checked Vince's identification.

After a pass through metal detectors, Vince led Dan and two other agents up three flights of stairs to a wing of guest rooms. He ushered Dan inside the first one and stationed the other two men outside as guards.

Small, but elegantly furnished with Colonial Williamsburg antiques, the room smelled of old leather and shellac. A four-poster bed and walnut armoire were set against one wall, a small television and wet bar on another.

Once they were alone, Vince's demeanor changed. He paced across the Persian rug, rubbing his neck. "For chrissake, Dan, what the hell were you thinking? Cyberterrorism?"

Dan sat on the edge of the bed. "It seemed like a good idea at the time."

"A good idea?" Vince snorted. "Hacking into TV stations? Couldn't you be more discreet?"

"The idea was to call attention to the situation."

"This is a federal offense. Everyone in Washington wants a pound of your flesh, and then I have to tell my boss the perp is a friend of mine. Me! The assistant director of the Cyber Division. You owe me one hell of an explanation, buddy."

Vince's demand raised Dan's hackles. "How come no one's interested in Hadan Orcus? The death of Carl Jameson? The dead citizens of La Ceiba? Who's looking out for them?"

"That's in another country. You attacked America."

Dan stared defiantly at his old friend. "Hadan Orcus killed Jameson. He almost killed *me* . . . and now Rachel is . . ." The words caught in his throat. "You don't think this affects America?"

"You have any proof of all this?"

"Damn it, Vince, we stirred the pot so someone would *get* proof."

"Still trying to save the world, huh, Dan?" Vince loosened his tie. "Here are the facts. Without direct evidence linking Hadan Orcus to this dumping, he's untouchable. He will hide behind the Honduran government. The American people don't give a damn about deaths down there. What they *do* care about is terrorism in their living rooms, weapons of mass destruction on their doorsteps. They want to live their lives in safety. Your little terrorist scheme gave them the perfect target for their angst, and now the government is going to make an example of you."

"And what about the pandemic?"

"A few deaths in Honduras do not make a pandemic."

Dan couldn't restrain his anger any longer. "Rachel Sullivan's in a coma! And you could just as easily be next!"

Vince's expression softened. "Look, I'm sorry about your friend or whoever she is, but face it. Epidemics in third world countries happen all the time. Do you have any reason to think this one is different?"

"Maybe. Rachel thinks the toxic waste they've been dumping triggered a new disease. That's what's attacking dolphins and humans. I'm guessing Carl Jameson witnessed the dumping, which is why he was killed. When I witnessed it, they tried to kill me too. This could get a lot worse—" The look of disdain on Vince's face stopped him cold.

"What has happened to you?" Vince shook his head. "The Dan Clifford I knew was a logical scientist, committed to reality. Now you're spouting drivel like some madman."

Dan knew his ranting sounded preposterous. He had to slow down. If he couldn't convince his friend . . . "Vince, I've told you this before, black swan events always seem preposterous before the fact. That's why they're ignored until it's too late. Who expected anyone to fly planes into the World Trade Center and the Pentagon? If reality sounds mad, do we just ignore it?"

"You'll have to sell your story better than that."

"*Smith Thammasaroj,* ever heard of him?"

"Smith *who*?" Vince looked at him with tired eyes.

"He was chief of Thailand's weather forecasting department. He insisted on the need for a faster tsunami warning system, because a killer wave could sneak up on the country with little warning. Government leaders called him a crackpot, fired him for fearmongering. Said he was hurting the tourist industry in Phuket. Now there is no tourist industry in Phuket anymore, thanks to the Asian tsunami. And Fukushima? Who expected the worst earthquake in Japan's recorded history? Sometimes reality sounds crazy. If politicians had listened to Smith, *two hundred and fifty thousand* people might still be alive."

They stared at each other as Dan tried to calm himself. "Any progress on that note I sent you? The one from Carl Jameson's watch?"

"You never give up, do you?" An exasperated smile crept onto Vince's face. "It seems I've been distracted by a cyberterrorist. Have you heard a word I said?"

"That note could be the key to this whole thing."

"It'll have to wait." Vince glanced toward the door and spoke in a whisper. "You may have a way out of this mess. I've heard Senator Becker wants to strike a deal. Whatever they offer, you *take it*. Understand?"

Dan laughed bitterly. "That SOB is part of the damn conspiracy!"

"So what? Be pragmatic for once. You can't save the world if you're in jail."

A knock came on the door. Vince opened it and admitted a slim man in an expensive silk suit.

"Agent Peretti," the man said. "It's a pleasure to see you again. May I have a word with Mr. Clifford in private?"

Vince nodded and started for the door, then turned. "Dan, don't forget what I said, okay?"

"Yeah. Thanks."

The man walked over, offered a slender hand. Dan shook it, and was immediately put off by its limp muscle tone. He spoke with an effeminate silkiness, yet he seemed to exude total confidence. Right away, Dan didn't trust him.

"Mr. Clifford, my name is Bradley Gruber. I'm an emissary of sorts. You've made quite a name for yourself on Capitol Hill. So much so that the Senate Committee on Computer Affairs has called a hearing. They've subpoenaed you to appear and testify as to your involvement in the recent cyberattack."

"I don't know what you're talking about," Dan said.

Gruber's expression hardened. "Let's not play games, okay? We have assembled enough evidence to put you away for a long time. Do you know the current penalty for computer terrorism? It's a federal offense now."

"No one's been harmed by my actions."

"Hadan Orcus might disagree. We realize you intended no serious harm, however misguided were your actions. So, in the interest of improving our defense against future attacks, Senator Nolan Becker has authorized me to offer a plea bargain."

"Ah yes, Senator Becker." Dan leaned back on the bed. "Another conspirator. Does Orcus work for him, or the other way around?"

Gruber's left eyebrow twitched and the faintest ghost of a smile flickered across his face. "I don't know where you received your information, but Hadan Orcus's business practices are beyond reproach."

"Oh really?" Dan snapped. "I can tell you about his garbage scow firsthand."

"Mr. Orcus is an international paragon of virtue, a supporter of the environment. He is appalled that one of his vessels could be involved in illegal dumping and has apologized publicly, suspended the captain, and launched his own investigation. If your accusations are true, then the men responsible will be dealt with."

"Uh-huh. And the attempt on my life?"

"Let me ask you something. Do you have any proof that Mr. Orcus was aware of this activity?"

Dan said nothing.

"No, I didn't think so. What if you're wrong? Think of the damage you've done. His corporation provides jobs for tens of thousands and vital raw materials for Americans. He's a key dignitary at the Earth Summit."

"Can we cut to the chase, please?"

Gruber's demeanor suddenly changed. He grinned broadly. "Mr. Clifford—may I call you Dan? I find your direct style quite refreshing. A man in my position hears it so seldom, you understand. So let me be quite direct in return. Senator Becker is working hard to protect the United States from computer terrorism. If you share your knowledge of the computer attack, plead guilty to the charges before you, admit to unfounded accusations against Mr. Orcus, and restrict your testimony *only* to the computer issues—then Senator Becker will petition for complete amnesty. You walk."

"And if I don't?"

"I'll be blunt." Gruber crossed his arms and rubbed his finger across his watch. "The Justice Department will bury you under the jail. Twenty years in federal prison, and for what?"

"I need time . . . to think about it."

"Certainly Dan, I understand."

"It's *Mr. Clifford* to you."

"Very well." Gruber turned and checked the time. "You've got one hour, *Mr. Clifford*. Think hard."

BY THE TIME Bradley Gruber reached the Senate banquet room, Senator Becker was working the buffet line, chatting with constituents, shaking hands, laughing at their stale jokes. Becker spotted Gruber and pulled him to one side. "So, what's the verdict?"

"I gave him the rundown," Gruber answered. "He's thinking about it."

Becker's eyes grew large, but he held his casual smile. "What do you mean, he's *thinking* about it? The president would like nothing better than to jerk Solá's CAFTA privileges. And then we've got the NeuroSys IPO tomorrow. We're cutting it close with this hearing as it is. You know how many favors I had to call in to schedule it this quickly?" He strolled down the buffet and wolfed down two large shrimp. He leaned closer, whispering forcefully in Gruber's ear. "Get the SOB on board, or—"

"*Please* Senator, calm down." Gruber grimaced, then said gently, "You needn't worry. Didn't I say Clifford will turn? You should have more faith. The man may be volatile, but he's no fool."

The senator from Alabama walked past and pasted on a huge smile. "Nolan, how *are* you?" He nodded toward Gruber. "Bradley."

"Buck, good to see you again," Becker crooned. "So how do you like Solá's little spread? Orcus flew in his own private chef and the best seafood in Honduras."

"It's mighty nice, Nolan. Orcus knows how to put on the dog, I'll give him that."

"Yes, he does," Becker replied. "Buck, we owe the man a great deal. Campaign contributions are up and Solá Mining had a lot to do with it. Can I depend on your vote?"

"We'll see. I'll be watching your hearing."

Becker laughed it off as the senator walked away. He turned back to Gruber. "See what I mean?"

"Look," Gruber said. "You court the votes here. You're so good at it, Nolan. I'll take care of Clifford."

Becker dragged another shrimp through a mound of polenta and popped it in his mouth. "Don't let me down, Gruber. Neither of us can afford to have this thing go south, especially you."

Gruber managed a thin smile but remained silent.

DAN RECLINED ON the bed, his hands behind his head, and gazed blankly at the television. The latest CNN report featured footage from the docks at La Ceiba. There were shots of sobbing women and a mob of protesters fighting among themselves. Several people lay wounded on the street.

The mysterious outbreak was spreading.

The video of the Osprey's departure from the *Sea Berth* ran again. He saw himself again in the bunny suit, leaving the *Sea Berth* crew and everyone else behind to fend for themselves. His thoughts drifted to Duff, Rudi, and the guests. Had the epidemic spread there?

He switched off the TV set and turned to Vince, who had rejoined him to wait for the hearing. "This is what I'm talking about. People are dying and no one cares. They want me to pretend this isn't happening? What would you do? Would you lie to save yourself?"

Vince drew back from the question with a wary look. "That's a tough one. Under most circumstances, no. But this is different. As I said, you're no good to anyone if you're in jail."

"I'm no good to anyone now."

Vince seemed to take on a compassionate demeanor. "Fight and run away, then fight another day, that's what I say."

Dan wanted to do the right thing, but he also wanted to survive. When it came down to it, Vince was right. Survival was the only thing that really mattered. He would be no good to Rachel in jail. And the thought of prison, of being treated like a common criminal . . .

"Vince, call 'em," he said finally. "Tell Gruber I'll accept the offer."

TEN MINUTES BEFORE the hearing, Vince escorted Dan downstairs to one of the many rooms used for such proceedings. A cluster of reporters rushed over, thrusting microphones in his face as they peppered him with questions. Vince fended them off and pushed into the committee chamber. Bradley Gruber stood to one side and nodded. A C-SPAN camera sat on a large tripod in one corner of the room.

Dan's stomach rolled into a knot as he thought of what he was about to do—lie on national television. It made him feel terribly small.

Several rows of chairs had been meticulously aligned with an aisle down the middle. Only about half of them were occupied, mostly by reporters, judging by the preponderance of laptops and tablets. The rest probably contained legal aides, advisors, and lobbyists.

A long folding table draped in cheap fabric dominated the front of the room. This was where members of the investigating committee would sit like judges, which, in a sense, they were. Judge and jury for anyone unfortunate enough to cross their path.

Directly in front sat the witness table crammed with a knobby mass of microphones.

The Senate Subcommittee on Computer Terrorism was a group of senators who were supposed to have at least a cursory knowledge of computers, which Dan doubted. Only three members had seen fit to attend the day's hearing, judging from the seats at the table. It had been hurriedly convened—intentionally, Dan guessed—to cut down on the attendance.

Dan and Vince sat in the first row of chairs. A voice in the back shouted. "All rise!"

The senators filed into the room and sat down, all except Nolan Becker. He stopped at Dan's chair and leaned over, his face only inches away. Dan could smell his breath—a sickly sweet odor of aftershave and alcohol. It turned his stomach.

"Are we working off the same page today, Mr. Clifford?"

"I think so."

"You've been fully instructed about topics that are off limits, correct?"

"Correct."

"Then keep your answers short, stick to the agenda, and this will be over soon."

Dan took a deep breath. "Right."

The senator stared at him fiercely, as if trying to decipher some deeper mystery within him. Dan returned his gaze. Becker's expression had an odd intensity about it. Dan expected confidence, but instead saw something akin to terror, although Becker tried to disguise it. His eyes darted back and forth nervously.

A sudden hazy memory re-formed in Dan's mind, back at the autopsy on the *Sea Berth*. It triggered an instant of absolute clarity and the puzzle pieces began to fall into place.

He and Becker were both standing on the edge of a precipice, and it would be Dan's responsibility to provide the final push.

38

SENATOR BECKER MOVED to the committee table and the hearing
began. An aide signaled for Dan to approach the witness table, where
he was sworn in. Dan sat down and pulled the chair close, leaning
into the microphones.

Senator Becker sat in the center seat. To his left sat Senator Gra-
ham Carter; to his right, Senator Stuart Nelson. Before the testimony
began, each senator gave a brief speech about terrorism. Becker's prepared statement was by far the most melodramatic, alluding to the
destruction of liberty, happiness, and life as we know it, if our lives
were compromised by the thoughtless acts of terrorists.

Finally, the three men turned their attention to him.

Senator Becker started the questioning. "Mr. Clifford, is it true
that you masterminded the recent computer terrorist incident known
as the Weatherman Virus?"

"Yes, that is correct," Dan said, as he watched Becker repeatedly
ball his hands into fists.

"And are you aware that your actions violated federal statutes?"

"Yes, I am."

"How were you able to breach the security of the weather service
networks to accomplish this act?"

Dan took his time and explained the process in detail, describing
the creation of the Trojan horse and the infiltration of Weather Service
images. He took pains to describe the events with the authority of a
man who knew precisely how the job was done. He wanted to leave
Rudi and Rachel out of the situation entirely.

Senator Carter asked the next question. "I'm no computer genius,
mind you, but I can get my e-mail and surf the Internet pretty well.
Mr. Clifford, I'm curious—how does one *learn* how to manipulate
software like this? Did you learn it from other hackers?"

"No, Senator," Dan replied. "I learned on the job. I am also a former employee of NeuroSys. The company specializes in high-tech computing and simulations. One of the company's clients is the National Weather Service. I used my knowledge of their networks to breach security."

"Hmmm, I see." Senator Carter smiled and glanced toward Becker. That seemed the extent of his curiosity.

Senator Becker rubbed his temples.

It was Senator Nelson's turn. He grumbled to himself for a minute and flipped through a stack of papers. "I'm having trouble understanding, Mr. Clifford," he began. "You seem to be an articulate and reasonable man. Why do this? What did you hope to gain?"

Dan stared at Senator Becker, trying to gauge his reaction. The man was sweating now, but alert. What if his guess was wrong? He'd rot in some prison for twenty years. He'd never see his friends again, Rudi or Duff . . . or Rachel, assuming she survived. He thought back to his youth, so innocent, so optimistic. Then, after the fall . . . he'd fantasized about making a difference, talking sense into the politicians. Politicians, these men who flippantly turn the gears of fate that control the lives of so many people. But he was just a dreamer, a theorist . . . until he met Rachel. Now, he was experiencing life up close and personal . . . and it was scaring the shit out of him. But then, fear of loss means life is important. Too important to waste. Maybe, he could actually *accomplish* something for once. The opportunity was sitting right in front of him; all he had to do was choose. . . .

"Mr. Clifford . . . must I repeat the question?"

Oh well, in for a penny, in for a pound.

Dan locked his eyes on Becker as he spoke. "Senator Nelson, I did this because I wanted to save lives. I wanted to expose a conspiracy by Hadan Orcus and NeuroSys to conceal evidence of the intentional poisoning of the Honduran sea, the murder of Carl Jameson, and an attempt to defraud American investors. I did this because it needed to be done."

A sudden murmur passed through the crowd. The reporters sat upright and started typing madly on their laptops.

"Mr. Clifford!" Senator Becker interrupted, his face crimson. "Those accusations were untrue though, weren't they? Weren't you just bitter over losing your job at NeuroSys?"

Senator Nelson stared Becker down. "I believe I have the floor." He turned back to Dan. "Is what Senator Becker said true?"

"No, sir," Dan stated flatly. "I never mentioned NeuroSys in the Weatherman Virus, although I now believe them to be deeply involved in the conspiracy. In fact, I have evidence directly linking NeuroSys and Solá Mining."

"What kind of evidence?" Nelson asked, his eyebrows going up.

"I saw toxic waste drums from NeuroSys dumped from the cargo ship *La Cosecha Abundante*. I myself was a victim of attempted murder. But, my true motivation was to bring attention to deaths—"

"I thought you—" Becker blurted. "I mean, this hearing is about computer terrorism! You don't have any proof of these accusations—"

"Becker!" Senator Nelson shouted. "Please let the man speak and *please* allow me my time on the floor."

"All the proof you need," Dan continued, his voice rising, "is on the evening news, Senator. People are dying in Honduras of a mysterious ailment. Someone I care about deeply is lying in a coma right now. All because of the toxic dumping by—"

"You're out of order!" Becker shouted, spittle spraying from his mouth. "You agreed!"

The other two senators turned his way, their mouths agape.

"Agreed to what?" Nelson asked.

"He means me," Dan interrupted. "Senator Becker is also involved in this conspiracy and asked me to lie to this committee about Hadan Orcus. But I won't. A mysterious disease—or toxin—is causing deaths in Central America, and could spread here as well. That's why I created the Weatherman Virus. To alert people to the truth—"

"Shut up, shut up!" Becker's teeth clenched into a grotesque scowl. He glanced nervously around the room.

"Trying to sweep this under the rug," Dan continued calmly, "isn't going to make it go away—"

"You're trying to ruin me!" Senator Becker stood up suddenly, knocking his chair backward. He leaned over the table and gripped his midriff. A long, low belch rumbled out of his throat, eliciting a chorus of gasps from the audience. He wobbled for a second and stared down at his suit, his eyes growing wide. "My clothes! Where are my clothes?" With a shriek of terror, Becker lurched across the table.

Everyone else in the room froze in place, except for two aides who grabbed Becker as he fell to the floor, fighting and spitting.

"Get your filthy hands off me!"

"Sir?" one aide replied, astonished.

"Quit staring at me!" Becker let out a bloodcurdling howl. "Get away!" He tore loose from the men and ran past the witness table before stopping suddenly. His head jerked to one side in a severe spasm. His right hand curled into a ball as the arm drew up tightly against his chest.

"What . . . what's wrong with me?" The words dribbled from his mouth in a stream of spittle. He bent over and vomited, his jaw snapping shut with the sound of a cracking bat. A pink mass of tongue fell to the floor, eliciting more gasps from the audience. His lips drew back from his teeth in a bizarre grin. A thin hiss of air exited his lungs and he fell to the floor in a writhing mass.

The room erupted into chaos.

"Call 911! Call 911!"

Aides tried to pin the senator's arms and legs. Becker's back arched a foot from the floor. Someone tried unsuccessfully to place a rolled-up handkerchief in his mouth.

The C-SPAN cameraman jerked the camera from the tripod and waded into the fray, slamming the camera into bystanders in a desperate attempt to film the action.

GRUBER HAD BEEN watching the events from the back of the room. Clifford's admission and Becker's sudden, bizarre behavior caught him completely off guard. He stood stunned for several minutes, trying to process the situation, then he slipped out the door, raced down the hall, and whirled into a side corridor. He noted a slight tremor in his hands as he dialed a number from memory.

"Yes?"

"This is Gruber. There's a problem. Unload the NeuroSys stock, now!"

"What? Before the IPO? Why? That will tank our profits."

"There won't be any profits. No time to explain," Gruber urged. "Just sell! To anyone you can, at any price! You haven't a moment to lose."

"Gruber, this was your plan, your responsibility. You better have a good explanation for this!"

"No time to explain now, just sell!"

There was a long pause, before the voice continued. "I'm disappointed in you, Bradley. Maybe my confidence in your abilities was misplaced. Should we take another look at your induction?"

"Just give me a little time . . . I'll fix this somehow. I always have before, haven't I?"

"I will be eager to hear your explanation for this mess."

"I fear we have an overzealous partner," Gruber said. "But for now, the priority should be to limit our losses."

Gruber hung up and leaned against the wall, trying to catch his breath. Was he losing his touch? All the careful planning, relationships, timing—they were starting to unravel. And yet, that lying asshole, Dan Clifford, appeared to anticipate Becker's breakdown. *What am I missing?*

Gruber realized that it would take considerable effort to rehabilitate this deal. And he was the only one capable of doing it. But first, he needed to make a call to his own broker.

"Sell all my stock in NeuroSys, immediately," he said. "Take whatever price you can get."

Then Gruber straightened, smoothed his suit, and headed toward the airport.

REPORTERS AND GOVERNMENT workers outside the committee room had been watching the events on C-SPAN. The incident served as a magnet, pulling everyone in the building toward the action. Security guards and ambulance personnel had to struggle through a crowd of curious onlookers.

Dan watched the gruesome scene with detached horror, thinking of Rachel and the wet lab.

Vince grabbed him. "Let's get out of here." He pulled Dan against the far wall and slid along the room's perimeter until they reached the door. They attempted to reach the stairs, but their escape route was blocked by a horde of onrushing reporters.

Microphones lanced forward from every direction. Vince tried to lead Dan away from the onslaught, but Dan turned back to the group, indicating a willingness to talk. He spotted Jenifer, who was struggling to the front of the crowd. Questions came from everywhere at once.

"Mr. Clifford, what happened inside the hearing?"

"Is Senator Becker all right?"

"What did you mean, about a disease spreading here. Is that what happened to the senator?"

Jenifer positioned herself directly in front of him, wearing what looked like a triumphant smile. "Mr. Clifford, does this have anything to do with recent events in Honduras?"

"It has *everything* to do with Honduras." He looked across the crowd of reporters and video cameras. "We are all members of a global community. Events in other countries are destined to affect us, eventually. Something terrible is happening in Honduras, and it will spread. I believe Senator Becker is a victim of this scourge."

Jenifer spoke earnestly. "What do you think is happening?"

"I'm not sure. But there is one thing I'm sure of. Senator Becker will not be the last American affected unless we take immediate action."

39

SONNY SWYFT SIPPED his drink and watched as the sunset lit up the spires of Atlanta's skyline. His favorite seat at Fiddler's Roof afforded him an excellent view of the city. The restaurant was like a shrine to him: quiet, classy, and exuding the aura of power. Only the gentle murmurs of private conversations and the subtle clinking of silverware disturbed the sanctity of his temple. It seemed the perfect place to celebrate his rise to the upper echelon. Sonny downed the last drops of his martini and checked his watch. Where was the damned waiter anyway? He headed to the bar. "Martini, dry. Double olives."

With a quick flourish, the bartender filled the glass and slid it across the granite surface. Sonny took a sip. Out of the corner of his eye, he spotted a familiar image on the television behind the bar.

"What the hell?" He asked the bartender to turn up the volume.

It was a recap of Clifford's interview with the press. CNN showed clips from the congressional hearing: Senator Becker was lying on the floor, medics hovering around him.

Sonny's throat suddenly felt as if an olive had lodged there.

He spotted the stock prices scrolling across the bottom of the screen. The video clip switched from the events on Capitol Hill to the developments on Wall Street. Both the Dow and the NASDAQ had plummeted in value. He waited for the NeuroSys numbers to scroll by, the proposed issue price for tomorrow's offering. The lump in his throat grew even bigger.

Sonny's brain went blank. The chirp of his cellular phone broke the trance. No one there. It was the bartender's phone. The man's expression turned to stone and he disappeared around the corner. Another chirp, and then another. The restaurant erupted in a chorus of cellular phones wailing for their owners. Diners dropped their silverware.

Sonny snapped to his senses and dialed his broker. He waited for the familiar ring, but heard a prerecorded message instead.

We're sorry, all our representatives are busy now. Please leave a message or try again later.

He tore across the room, hoping to find a rare pay phone. He brushed past several tables, felt them shudder in his wake, and heard the shouts of disturbed patrons.

All that mattered was to *sell, sell, sell.*

A line of callers had formed next to the restrooms in front of the lone public phone that had occupied the restaurant for years. Sonny pushed his way toward the front. "Excuse me, excuse me. This is an emergency!"

Someone grabbed him by the collar and jerked him backward. "Screw you, buddy! My pension is on the line. You'll wait your turn like the rest of us!"

"You don't understand!" Sonny pleaded. "I've got to talk to my broker now!"

"You and every other damn investor in here!"

The restaurant, normally a bastion of calm decorum, had turned into a madhouse. Gray-suited men rushed about aimlessly. Plates of caviar and pecan-crusted salmon fell to the floor. Sonny abandoned the phone line and joined a struggling crowd of people at the elevators, fighting to be one of the fortunate few to make it on board. It was no use. The doors closed while he was still several feet away.

"No, no, nooooooo!"

THE DINING ROOM of the Russell Senate Office Building was a jumble of orange-suited men and women, medical kits, and laboratory instruments. Colonel Clarence Peterson scanned the aisles of serving tables, still covered in silver and crystal, and half-eaten food. He let out a huge sigh, fogging the inside of his MOPP suit. He was still breathing heavily, having rushed from a strategy meeting.

This was only the second time in history that a Senate office building had been quarantined, the first time having been during the anthrax scare years ago. He wanted to take no chances and hoped like hell this wasn't going to become an annual event.

"How can you be sure it's the shrimp?" he asked.

"Take a look for yourself." Marilynn Archer, a specialist in communicable diseases at USAMRIID, led Peterson to the buffet table. "Check the third bowl from the left."

The mound of steamed shrimp was still bright red, except for a cluster near the top, stained the color of black cherries. Their flesh was beginning to dissolve into slimy ooze.

Peterson gasped.

"This decomposition happened since the senator's death," Marilynn continued. "Now take a look at this one." She pointed to another tray filled with a gray liquid. "This *was* shrimp with wine sauce. The other dishes are clean."

"How long ago were these dishes cooked?"

"The chef insists no more than four hours."

"Somebody's lying. Nothing decays that fast."

"That's why I thought of a toxin," Marilynn said. "The heat of cooking would have accelerated the destructive process. But then, I noticed this." She lifted a few boiled shrimp with forceps. Below them, strands of decay were spreading into the neighboring shrimp.

"Crap. Cellular migration pattern," Peterson said. "Not good."

"Right, and we've already got visible growth on blood agar plates."

"Why were so few affected? We had fifty senators dipping into these dishes."

"The only thing I can think of is that someone planted the infected shrimp *after* the buffet was set, *after* the shrimp was cooked."

"Deliberate poisoning?" Peterson stood silently for several minutes, juggling the clues. A horrible thought occurred to him. "Where did the chef buy these shrimp?"

"They were brought on Orcus's private jet, from Honduras."

"And where were they harvested?"

"Don't know, but I'll find out."

"Do that." Peterson was halfway out the door when he turned back. "Marilynn, freeze those samples, pack them up, and get back to Detrick, *stat*. Then pack for a trip."

"Sir?"

"Just do it!"

He bolted from the room, passed through the decontamination area, and called the CDC on his cell phone. "Goodson? You may get your wish, after all."

40

THE NEXT MORNING, Vince Peretti brought a stack of newspapers and a tablet to Dan's room. "You're going to be a busy man today."

Dan read the first headline and drew back in shock.

Senators Dead from Unknown Causes

"Senators?"

"Becker died last night," Vince said. "Senator Jackson a few hours later. Two congressional aides are dead. It's been a madhouse. Practically every agency in Washington is swarming over this place like flies on carrion."

"They're *dead*?" Dan struggled with the thought. "What about—"

"Rachel's the same." Vince tapped the paper. "Read up on current events, especially the article at the bottom. You'll be having visitors soon."

Dan barely had time to skim the paper when a knock came at the door. A man in a military uniform entered, although he was not Dan's idea of a soldier. He looked to Dan as if time had thickened his frame, though he was far from unfit. He was surprisingly short, with a round face, piercing green eyes, and something Dan had never seen on a modern military officer before—a closely cropped salt-and-pepper beard. He removed his hat and shook Dan's hand firmly.

"Mr. Clifford, I'm Colonel Peterson, U.S. Army. Let me get right to the point. I work for USAMRIID, the U.S. Army Medical Research Institute of Infectious Diseases. Mr. Peretti here"—the colonel glanced toward Vince—"has briefed me on your story. I've studied your testimony on the Weatherman Virus. It appears you've become somewhat of a social media celebrity overnight. The president wants this outbreak stopped quickly, and I would like your help."

"Help?"

"We want you to show us the precise origin of this outbreak, tell us everything you know about the dumping. You've been aboard the garbage scow, right?"

"Yes, quite recently."

"Good. Then I'm authorized to grant you full immunity from prosecution in exchange for your cooperation."

Dan's jaw dropped. Of all the scenarios running through his mind during a restless night of nonsleep, this was certainly not one of them. "You want me to go back to Honduras?"

"Yes."

"And if I cooperate, I'll be absolved of all criminal responsibility?"

"That's what I said."

He stared blankly for what seemed like minutes. Finally, he smiled. "I'll be glad to cooperate, but I have conditions."

"Oh?" Peterson's eyebrows shot up. "You're not exactly in a position to negotiate."

"I beg to differ. They're minor, but I won't cooperate without them."

"And they are . . . ?"

"A friend of mine, Rachel Sullivan, is at the CDC right now, sick with whatever is causing this disease. I want assurances that she will be given the best medical care available."

"Anything else?"

"I may have had some help, uh, conjuring the Weatherman Virus. I want anyone else associated with it granted immunity as well."

The colonel's expression hardened for a moment, then relaxed. "You're a lucky man, Mr. Clifford. I can grant both of your requests. In fact, Ms. Sullivan is already on her way to Washington to join us."

"What, really?" He felt a sudden surge of hope.

"She will receive the most advanced medical care in the world."

"She's coming with us? How?"

The colonel smiled for the first time. "On the President's latest toy, MOBIDIC."

"What the hell is that?"

Colonel Peterson's eyes lit up. "You'll find out soon enough."

41

Esrom Nessen plunged the sampling pole deep into the steaming waters of Sapphire Lake, one of a hundred hot springs dotting the landscape of Yellowstone Park, like boils on the skin of Mother Earth. The springs were the lingering scars of a cataclysmic event that had decimated Yellowstone 600,000 years earlier, a fantastic eruption that covered most of North America in a blanket of pumice several feet thick.

Even now, the scene around the lagoon recalled the ancient devastation. A border of bone-white trees stripped of leaves leaned precariously over the shoreline. Named for its brilliant turquoise waters and reddish sediment, Sapphire Lake looked pristine, except for the steam clouds rolling off its surface. One dunk in the water would prove fatal.

Esrom gingerly lifted his pole from the lake, careful to avoid the scalding water. He filled a stainless steel thermos with the valuable liquid. He was a fisherman of sorts. His catch contained extremophiles—ancient microbes that could survive in waters as hot as 199° F, a temperature that would kill most common bacteria.

The extremophiles lent the hot springs their distinctive colors: bright reds, browns, and brilliant greens. Knowledge of their existence would have languished in scientific journals as a curiosity if not for another discovery: most extremophiles manufactured powerful enzymes—enzymes with scientific and commercial value.

Most of Yellowstone's other springs had been "fished out" long ago, including the one that had started it all—Mushroom Spring, which had harbored the bacteria *Thermus aquaticus*. Years earlier, it had spawned an entirely new industry—genetic engineering. The *Taq polymerase* enzyme extracted from the bacteria had made the process of splitting DNA possible. Now, Sapphire Lake remained his last and best hope for new discoveries.

As Esrom packed away the last sample, he cast one last glance across the prairie. Two buffaloes grazed contentedly nearby. The diversity of life in the park never failed to amaze him. From the depths of the forest to the cauldron of a boiling spring, life managed to find a niche.

As revolutionary as *Taq polymerase* had been, Esrom needed ever more powerful enzymes, ones that could work at higher temperatures. Higher temperatures meant faster genetic processing, more effective results, larger profits. Sapphire Lake was the hottest spring around.

Picking up the last of his supplies, Esrom ambled around the shore to test his latest toy, supplied by an old Air Force buddy. It was an aluminized inflatable raft that had been designed for water rescue. His friend claimed it would stand up to the searing heat of an aviation fuel fire. Esrom laughed nervously, because he was about to bet his life on that claim.

He glanced across the steaming waters, smooth as a sheet of glass. Calm was good, because his next destination would be Dead Man's Island, a mound of minerals near the center of the lagoon, forested with pipes of calcium-carbonate formed by gases spewing up from miles below. Clouds of steam poured from their tips like smoke from a furnace.

It was virgin territory. No one had sampled the island's greenish mud. The clay should harbor the toughest of all extremophiles.

Esrom steeled himself for the trip and eased into the raft. He slipped on a pair of thick rubber gloves and pulled the brim of his hat down over his pale forehead. Gripping the paddle securely, he pushed off from shore. The raft floated atop the steaming surface like a bird on the clouds.

This was risky, very risky.

He waited several anxious minutes and checked the sides of the raft. The seams held fast. *Thank you, Air Force.* His confidence growing, Esrom paddled gently across the lagoon, taking numerous glances around the raft's perimeter. The air took on a still quality. The incessant chirping of swallows had stopped, as if the birds were holding their breath while he drifted across the hellish surface. The bow of the raft nudged gently against the soft clay and stopped. *There, that wasn't so bad.* Esrom checked the raft again and assembled the sampling pole. Bubbles of gas streamed up from below, squeezing out through channels in the clay.

Mother's got gas today. He chuckled. *Smells like it too.* A low, throaty growl echoed from deep within the columns, a sound far deeper than the lowest note on a pipe organ. It was a sound you could *feel. Shame on you, Mother!*

Esrom searched for a soft spot in the clay and pushed the sample pole in as far as he could, being careful not to rock the raft. He pulled out a glob of steaming clay, opened the top of a thermos, and dropped it into the container.

One down, several more to go. What he really needed was a sample from the heart of the pipe, where the temperature was the hottest. But how to punch through the hardened clay? He wouldn't have time to figure it out. The wind picked up suddenly, sending choppy waves across the lagoon.

"What the—?"

A fine spray of scalding water started pelting him. He raised his arm defensively and spotted the cause of the wind gust. Beyond the plateau, a huge set of whirling blades seemed to erupt from the landscape. A large Air Force helicopter rose and loomed over him, the blast from its blades pushing the raft back out into the lagoon. The spray of water turned into a monsoon.

"Get out of here!" Esrom screamed at the top of his lungs. With one arm shielding his face, he waved wildly at the intruder with the other. As the helicopter drew closer, the raft rocked back and forth, threatening to tip him over into the boiling waters.

42

Colonel Peterson's military caravan motored through Andrews Air Force Base toward a large, nondescript hanger. Its huge doors had been pulled open, disgorging a transport plane from its dark recesses. Dan immediately recognized the profile of a Lockheed C-5M Super Galaxy, the largest airplane in the American fleet. Dan had seen the Galaxy from afar many times as it flew to the Lockheed plant in Atlanta, but he'd never seen one from this vantage point before. It was truly an intimidating sight.

Longer than a football field and towering six stories high, the plane had wings that seemed woefully inadequate to lift the bulbous fuselage off the ground. Soldiers worked feverishly loading crates through the Galaxy's rear hatch, large enough to accept an M-1 tank.

The plane was painted solid white with a large blue medical cross emblazoned on its side. Dan smiled at the obvious reference. "MOBIDIC, right?"

"Correct," Peterson said. "The MOBile Infectious Disease Interdiction Center."

The Humvee screeched to a halt alongside a massive wheel. Peterson led Dan up a shallow ramp alongside the plane to an elevator that took them to the upper deck, a large conference room with plush blue carpet and white walls. Several rows of chairs and conference tables bolted to the floor acted as flight accommodations, complete with seat belts.

"Quite impressive," Dan remarked. "I expected a more spartan interior in a cargo plane."

"Oh, MOBIDIC is far more than a cargo plane, Mr. Clifford. It's a mobile hospital and biolab." Peterson introduced Dan to staff members while pointing out the plane's high-tech interior: satellite telecommunications, computer network, a large flat screen display dominating the front wall. "This is our nerve center where we hold staff meetings. It also doubles as our mess hall."

As Dan examined the surroundings, the irony of his situation began to sink in. His world had turned upside down again. Yesterday, he was public enemy number one. Now, he was being ushered around like a dignitary. Did they really need his help, or was he the government's latest media trophy, to be trotted out when needed? Whatever Peterson's plans for him, Dan had his own agenda. Fate had given him another chance to make things right, and he fully intended to use it.

In the galley, soldiers loaded foodstuffs into every nook and cranny. At the far end sat a lanky man wearing khakis, sandals, and a long-sleeved flannel shirt hanging loosely on his gaunt frame. His clothes were covered with white stains. The man's freckled skin lacked much pigmentation, as did his hair—wispy strawberry-blond locks. Looking like a painter who had just finished whitewashing a fence, he was gingerly holding a bag of ice to his forehead.

Peterson patted the man on the back, eliciting a yelp of pain. "Dan, meet Esrom Nessen," he chuckled, "the driving force behind MOBIDIC."

"That's *ez-rum nes-sin*," the man said in a European accent Dan couldn't quite place. He held up a swollen hand covered in ointment. "Pardon me if I skip the handshake."

Peterson's face broke into a wry smile. "Glad you could make it."

"You're lucky I'm here," Esrom growled. "Your flyboys almost parboiled me."

"I do apologize, Esrom," he said. "But the president wants MOBIDIC in the air. You wouldn't want to miss her maiden voyage, would you?"

Esrom rearranged the cubes in his ice bag, exposing a large blister on his forehead. "Luckily, I had collected most of my samples."

"Dr. Nessen here," Peterson said to Dan, "works at Argonne Labs. But you can't take the boy out of the man. He still loves to play in the mud."

"That *mud* has spawned a multi-billion-dollar industry," Esrom snapped. "But that wouldn't interest you, Peterson. You get your kicks devising new ways to kill people."

The insult elicited another chuckle from Peterson. It became apparent to Dan that these two men enjoyed a certain level of spirited banter. "Argonne?" Dan said. "My former employer, NeuroSys, works with them. Telepresence robotics, right?"

Esrom stared at him. "You're from NeuroSys? Well, I'll have some questions for you. Their equipment causes me no end of frustration."

Peterson broke in. "You gentlemen can socialize later. I need to settle Mr. Clifford into his quarters."

"No," Dan said. "I want to see Rachel Sullivan first."

Peterson nodded. "I can understand that," he said. "Follow me."

They headed deeper into the plane, past an air lock door that opened into a wider corridor. A row of U-shaped niches lined both walls, each of which held three sealed chambers, each containing a bed and patient monitor. The clear windows featured a pair of the familiar rubber gloves dangling from their center.

"This is our level-three facility." Peterson pointed to ducts running along the ceiling. "Our doctors can operate in here with relative safety when treating contagious diseases."

Dan wasn't listening. Right now, he had one thing on his mind. He spotted Dr. Goodson in a distant niche and rushed forward, pressing his palms against the Plexiglas.

Rachel Sullivan lay beneath white sheets, her complexion waxy.

"Is she any better?"

"Honestly? No," Goodson said. "But she's no worse, so you can take comfort in that."

Dan slipped his hands inside the gloves and picked up Rachel's hand. Even through the rubber, he could feel the rhythm of her pulse tapping steadily against his palm. That pulse had anchored him during their dive to the abyssal plain. Now, she seemed frail, a shadow of the vibrant, sassy woman who had pushed him beyond his limits. He squeezed her hand and watched the rise and fall of her chest, experiencing a moment of clarity.

He was not going to let her die.

AFTER SETTLING INTO yet another small, white room similar to the one at the CDC, Dan headed back toward the conference room where a meeting of the plane's personnel had been scheduled. The room was now full, buzzing with energy from a hodgepodge of scientists, soldiers, and doctors.

Dan sensed a subtle tension forming between three distinct groups, like opposing teams feeling out the competition. Peterson and his cohorts from USAMRIID, which Dan had met earlier—Ian Morris and Marilynn Archer—commanded a position near the front of the room, wearing their Army uniforms.

Then there were the CBIRFs, an elite squad of Marines, more soldiers than doctors, who wore standard-issue camouflage and spit-polished boots. They sat near the back of the room with the alert posture and silent swagger you'd expect from members of the "Corps." Dan had learned about them during the Atlanta Olympics in 1996 when a bomb had been detonated during the games. The acronym "CBIRF" stood for the Chemical/Biological Incident Response Force, the Marines' version of paramedics.

Dan had chosen to sit with the CDC team, hoping to grill Goodson on Rachel's progress. This group, which also included Michael Odom, Esrom Nessen, and a few other new faces, had all changed into Hawaiian shirts, shorts, and sandals. They laughed and joked like tourists on vacation, which had the effect of irritating Peterson and the CBIRFs. According to Goodson, the CDC doctors had long since developed an appreciation for comfortable attire, after years of working in third world hospitals and primitive backwaters.

The conversation died down on the announcement that MOBIDIC was ready for departure. Everyone took a seat and strapped in. Soon, the plane's four General Electric engines were whining like a chorus of banshees, rattling coffee cups in their holders. As the sound grew louder, the C5-M rumbled down the tarmac, turned onto the runway, and began its takeoff roll. Despite the Super Galaxy's size, it rose from the runway with surprising ease and pulled into a steep ascent.

Colonel Peterson waited for the plane to level off before addressing the group. He stood and studied each face in turn. "For those of you unfamiliar with MOBIDIC, I'll start with a little background. This mobile hospital is our newest weapon in the war on terrorism. You were handpicked to be its frontline troops. The past few epidemics have caught us unprepared, quickly overwhelming local hospitals in the hot zone, even in major cities. Developing countries seldom have the proper facilities at all. MOBIDIC is capable of reaching anywhere on the globe in less than twenty hours and is designed to bring the

mountain to Mohammed, so to speak. It's the latest in medical intervention—"

"—*and* a SNAFU waiting to happen," Esrom Nessen said, leaning forward in his chair, his blistered face glistening with lotion.
"MOBIDIC hasn't even completed a shakedown cruise, I'm still
struggling with the computers, the staff is untrained, safety procedures aren't finalized . . ."

Peterson bristled at Esrom's breach of protocol. "This plane was
your baby, Esrom. You want to pass on her because she's got a few
wrinkles?"

"A few wrinkles?" Esrom said. "Half the team was chosen yesterday, by *you*."

"That's right, mate," chimed in Michael Odom. "This was all news
to me, and then I'm drafted. What do I tell my wife and kids?"

Peterson forced a smile. "I apologize to everyone for the short
notice, but you must appreciate the need for swift action. The American public is terrified, and the president wants results. As for you,
Dr. Odom, Goodson recommended you because of your expertise in
Latin American field operations."

Odom cast a sideways glance at Goodson, unsure whether to be
flattered or angry. "What's so special about this white whale anyway?"

"MOBIDIC contains a biosafety level-four laboratory—bleeding
edge—no sweating in grimy hospitals. We can research and treat in
relative safety and comfort, and we hope, be much more productive—
but frankly, we don't have time for pleasantries. Everyone will have to
learn on the job."

Peterson glanced at Dan. "In the last few hours, Dr. Goodson has
made some progress identifying the threat that caused Senator Becker's death. Here's what we know—it's a rapid-acting, food-borne
pathogen of great toxicity. We've tracked it to shrimp served at a buffet,
provided by Solá Mining and flown from Honduras on Hadan Orcus's
private jet. It was harvested from waters near La Ceiba, Honduras.
There have been multiple fatalities there, with symptoms like the ones
exhibited by Senator Becker. There's a full summary in your information packets, along with specific assignments."

Peterson displayed a slide on the multimedia screen and aimed a
laser pointer at the accompanying flow chart. "Odom, I want you to
autopsy Senator Becker. Esrom, debug the DNA equipment. Marilynn,

get us a picture of this thing so we know what we're dealing with. Oh, and instruct the rookies on procedures in the BSL4 lab. Major Paxton and the CBIRF team will head up patient care and crowd control. Goodson, you're running the onboard hospital. We'll be picking up fuel and additional supplies in Guantanamo Bay, then we depart for La Ceiba. That gives us only a few hours, so get to it."

Everyone quickly gathered their things and left for their respective jobs, leaving Dan and Colonel Peterson alone in the room. "So, why am I here, Colonel?" Dan asked.

"Esrom Nessen will want to talk to you about NeuroSys," Peterson said. "But first, I'd like a debriefing."

"If you've talked with Goodson, you should know everything already."

"I'd like to hear it directly from you."

Dan walked Peterson through the details of the submersible dive to the dump site, the sickened dolphin and whale, and the parts of Rachel's autopsy that he still remembered, which wasn't much. It was a long story that took some time. Peterson kept interrupting him with a barrage of questions, but Dan resisted the urge to mention Carl Jameson's mysterious clues.

Judging from Vince Peretti's reaction to that narrative, he would lose all credibility with Peterson. That was information he had decided to keep to himself for the time being and instead, focus on keeping Rachel Sullivan alive.

When Peterson seemed satisfied, he rose from his chair. "Let's see if you can give Esrom a hand, and I'll show you the rest of the plane."

THEY VENTURED FARTHER back into the bowels of MOBIDIC, past the onboard hospital, to a balcony that overlooked the rear half of the Galaxy's fuselage. It was open and unfinished, a remnant of the plane's original function as a cargo hauler. The CBIRFs were scurrying about in a labyrinth of bizarre machinery, unpacking and organizing.

Two vehicles caught Dan's eye: bizarre hybrids of troop carriers and all-terrain vehicles. Several menacing barrels protruded from gimbals on their roof. "What's with the guns?"

"Those are minifoxes," Peterson said. "Sealed against contagions and hazardous chemicals, giving us free movement in the theater of operation. Those weapons are all nonlethal, for crowd control."

"And those?" Dan pointed toward two large vans bristling with antennas and satellite dishes.

"Mobile Medic Mentoring Vehicles, or M3Vs for short. They employ telemedicine robotics. Doctors can perform remote surgery and treatment without ever leaving the plane, via remote controls." Peterson led Dan down a set of stairs to the bottom level and reversed course, back toward the front of the plane. A narrow corridor flanked a large cylinder, eight feet in diameter and thirty feet long. It crowded the fuselage, leaving barely enough room to get by.

Peterson patted the metal affectionately. "This is our BSL4 lab. We can handle the world's most lethal diseases inside it, with safety. It's made from two inches of titanium, using submarine technology, completely sealed with interior HEPA filtration. If we were to . . . um, have an unfortunate event such as a plane crash, the structural integrity should be sufficient to protect against any breach."

"Comforting thought, I guess," Dan said with a nervous laugh. He moved to a nearby high-definition monitor that gave a view of the chamber's interior. Inside, he saw a man's naked body sprawled on an autopsy table, the chest cavity split by a long Y-shaped incision. The upper flap of skin had been folded back over the corpse's head like a death shroud. A figure in a blue biohazard suit was digging deep inside the cavity with a pair of scissors.

Without seeing the corpse's face, Dan knew it had to be Senator Becker.

It was strange to see the politician displayed so unceremoniously— reduced to his essence—a mound of flesh and host for microscopic life. Dan hoped that flesh would yield a clue to Rachel's coma.

Peterson pushed an intercom button. "Anything interesting?"

Michael Odom's Aussie accent hissed over the speaker. "Bloke's a friggin' mess. Look at this liver." Odom held up an oily black mass that dripped stringy globules into the chest cavity.

Dan felt the bile rise to his throat.

"Christ," Peterson murmured. "Incredible decomposition."

"And look at this." Odom pulled the chest flap away from Becker's grossly distended face. "When I got here, the entire body was puffed up like the Pillsbury Doughboy."

Despite the grotesqueness of the corpse, Dan forced himself to stare, the scene reviving a faint memory from Rachel's dolphin autopsy.

He suddenly remembered that he'd left out a critical detail during his debriefing. "Colonel, ask Odom if he smells anything . . . *peculiar.*"

"Odom can't smell anything but his own sweat," Peterson replied. "His air supply is isolated and filtered."

Which explains why he's not affected, Dan thought. "Back in Rachel's lab, when I found her on the floor, I remember a strange floral scent, sort of like . . . fishy roses. It's the same smell I recognized on Becker's breath. That's how I knew he was infected."

Peterson's eyes grew wide. "Why didn't you mention it earlier?"

"At first, I just thought it was a symptom of the infection. But I just realized something. That smell permeated Rachel's lab, I remember gagging on it. Goodson thought it was some toxic chemical, but now, I think it explains why Rachel and I survived."

That prompted a skeptical look from Peterson. "Oh really? How so?"

"What if it's the decomposition gases *themselves* that are noxious? Rachel could have inhaled them during her autopsy. I did too, but for a much shorter time."

Peterson smiled condescendingly. "Nice idea Mr. Clifford, but we've never experienced pathogens creating gaseous neurotoxins . . . except—" He stopped in midsentence, his jaw sagging slightly.

Dan took the pause and ran with it. "I'm no doctor, but I know rotting flesh creates hydrogen sulfide, and that's lethal in large doses. Why couldn't some bug mutate to create a gaseous neurotoxin? How else can you explain Rachel's symptoms? If I've learned anything as a prediction scientist, it's that answers often come from unexpected sources. In fact, our own expertise and knowledge of past experiences can make us blind to the occasional anomaly."

Peterson seemed to be barely listening. His expression had changed to a peculiar frown. "Worth checking out." He pressed the intercom button again. "Michael, pull a sample of that gas from Becker's face and run it through the mass spectrometer—compare it against the hazardous materials database."

"Will do, mate."

"Meanwhile, let's find something more to your liking, Mr. Clifford." He moved down the cylinder to another monitor. "Recognize them? They make good use of cramped space."

Dan was dumbfounded to see two NeuroSys robots—descendants

of the Rover prototype—moving quietly along a row of scientific in-struments. One robot deftly plucked a lab rat from its cage and poked it with a syringe. The other one seemed to struggle, its arms moving drunkenly.

"Amazing how things come full circle," Peterson said, chuckling. "Becker himself recommended the NeuroSys robots. Ironic, no?"

Peterson's cavalier attitude seemed odd at first, but Dan realized the need for gallows humor as a coping mechanism for men constantly surrounded by death.

"Bad advice too," Peterson continued. "This NeuroSys equipment has been nothing but trouble."

Dan knew nothing of these sales contracts. "Who handled this account?"

"Came straight from Honduras, a Tomás Martin, if I remember correctly. Tech support has been abysmal. But now *you're* here. We could use your NeuroSys expertise."

Dan couldn't help but feel some smug satisfaction. "I'm no techni-cal genius, but I know someone who is."

"Really?" Peterson said. "Who?"

"And he'll soon be a stone's throw away—"

"Damn it all!" The voice of Esrom Nessen echoed from the end of the hall.

"Temper, temper, Esrom," Peterson said as he approached a war-ren of cubicles nestled directly in front of the BSL4 chamber.

Esrom was struggling with two control arms, his blistered hands barely touching the controls. The robot inside the BSL4 lab struggled to place a small black square under the lens of a video microscope.

"I can help with that," Dan said, and slipped into an adjacent chair. "You mind?"

"Be my guest."

Dan grabbed the controls, and the robot's movements became fluid and graceful.

"Damn, Esrom. Clifford's making you look bad," Peterson quipped.

"I've had a lot of practice with these arms," Dan said. He studied the small square at the end of the robot's manipulator, barely the size of a postage stamp. "What is that?"

"The latest in genetic technology," Esrom said proudly. "A gene chip, fabricated by Argonne. It's a silicon device capable of identifying fifty thousand discrete DNA alleles in less than five minutes. Imagine drawing a drop of blood and screening for hundreds of diseases at one time, all at a cost of a few dollars. That's how it's supposed to work anyway. Only it's *not* working. GeneScan, the NeuroSys software that runs the pattern matching, is full of bugs. And your tech support staff won't answer our phone calls."

Another surprise, Dan thought. The idea of all this NeuroSys activity going on behind his back riled him up even more. "Why would NeuroSys supply software for this *gene chip,* anyway?"

Esrom shrugged. "The software's the biggest challenge with this chip. NeuroSys offered assistance, since we already had the robotics contract."

"I'll get you some better tech support soon," Dan said. If this GeneScan system used pattern matching, it *had* to be based on GAPS software. Sonny Swyft must have been diverting the GAPS code to Honduras behind his back. He suddenly thought back to the garbage scow and its mysterious crates.

"How is this gene chip made, exactly?" Dan asked.

"It's standard silicon technology, with a 3-D twist. We fabricate them at Argonne."

"And could these gene chips be fabricated in a standard computer chip factory, one equipped with 3-D technology?"

Esrom gave Dan an odd look and shrugged. "I don't see why not."

43

SONNY SWYFT CROUCHED in his car seat a mere hundred yards from the NeuroSys building. It was midafternoon, and he had been watching from the parking garage for hours as a line of FBI agents filed out the door, carrying a long line of boxes filled with files and hard drives.

They're stealing my future, he thought.

Sonny twisted a lock of hair on one finger as a wheeled cart of backup tapes bounced over the threshold on its way toward the back of a large black panel van.

What do I do now? He'd sunk his entire investment portfolio into NeuroSys stock options. And judging from the stock ticker on his phone, their value was shit. NeuroSys stock was fifty dollars below the original issue price and still dropping. Nobody wanted to touch the IPO with a ten-foot pole.

Sonny slammed his palm on the steering wheel, thinking of the board and all their promises. And especially that limp-wristed asshole Bradley Gruber. He swiped through his contact list and placed another call, his fourth in the last two hours. The sound of Bradley Gruber's silky voice on the other end caught Sonny off guard.

"It's about time!" Sonny growled. "I've been calling for ages."

"As you can imagine," Gruber replied, "I've been quite busy the last twelve hours."

"Well, I'm sitting here watching the feds clean out the NeuroSys office," Sonny said bitterly. "A little advance notice would have been helpful. Then I wouldn't be watching my future get flushed down the crapper."

"I was as surprised as you were, Sonny. This incident with Senator Becker has caused quite a stir in Washington."

"Ya *think*? What's all this about murders and toxic waste dumping?

And what the hell is that asshat Tomás Martin doing down there, anyway? If only I could have put my own man down there, none of this would have happened. . . ."

"Sonny, calm down," Gruber said. "Can't you see that keeping you out of the loop has limited your liability? Need to know, remember?"

"Yeah, well, now I need to know what the hell's going on! When I signed up, this was supposed to be a sweet financial deal, not some turf war with murderers, or whatever the hell this is."

"No one knows what happened yet," Gruber said. "So far, it's just Dan Clifford and a lot of baseless accusations."

"And yet, Senator Becker is dead," Sonny said. "Doesn't sound baseless to me, and what about my money? Get your investor guy to send it back."

"Do you really think there's any money left?" Gruber said. "Everyone has taken a loss in this deal."

Gruber's flippant response pissed off Sonny even more. "Damn it, I've got the feds on my ass now. They've been calling, wanting an interview. What am I supposed to tell them?"

Gruber let out a long sigh. "Sonny, you may be right. Tomás Martin has clearly followed his own agenda, against our wishes. Perhaps I should have listened to you. But, you need to calm down and focus. First, did you move out all the technical files, as I originally requested?"

"Yeah, yeah. I sent the servers and all the files, even the backup tapes, to Honduras, just like you said. But that means Tomás has access to them."

"Let me worry about that," Gruber said. "Are you sure there is no paper trail connecting the NeuroSys corporate office to our special purpose entity?"

"Nothing, wiped clean, just like you asked."

"Good, good. Then, things aren't as bad as you think. We can fix this."

"How?" Sonny's spirit rose a bit. "What do I tell the feds in my interview?"

"You won't tell them anything," Gruber said. "Listen carefully. Go back to your apartment. Do not answer any more phone calls, especially from the FBI. You're the president of an American corporation.

The FBI won't push for an interview until they have ample evidence, and if you're correct, they won't find any. I may have a solution to your complaints. We'll meet late tonight. I can put you out of reach of the FBI and give you a chance to make things right at the same time."

"Good," Sonny said, feeling a swell of satisfaction. "Gruber, you got me into this mess. You better get me out, or I swear—"

"Just relax," Gruber said in a most soothing tone. "I'm heading your way. We'll clean up all the loose ends, I promise you."

BATHED IN THE glow of a monitor, Colonel Peterson sat alone in the darkened conference room, browsing through hastily drafted protocols of MOBIDIC operations. He'd been at it for almost an hour and his eyes were glazing over. Despite years of experience, his job as mission commander was oddly uncomfortable. He was a medical doctor, after all, not a military tactician. The collar of his uniform cut into his neck and he tugged at it, wishing he could join the other doctors in casual attire, but the media in Honduras would expect a uniformed officer, and the façade of authority.

Enough policy crap, he decided. *Time to get back to the critical items at hand*. He placed a video call on the plane's internal network.

Michael Odom's face appeared. "I've got those spectrometer results."

Peterson tensed. "And?"

The timbre of Odom's voice had a strange edge to it. "Well, there's definitely a match between Rachel Sullivan's blood samples and the decomp gases from Becker. It looks like some type of nerve gas. I can only assume it's being generated by the microbe. That's a new one on me."

So it's true. "Any matches to the hazardous substance database?"

"Not exactly. . . ." Odom hesitated. "I had to go to the military database to find anything. We've got a partial match to a substance marked top secret."

Peterson knew why. A line of concern crept across his brow. "Thanks, Michael. Would you download the results onto the network? Oh, and keep this to yourself for the time being, okay?"

"Yeah, but—"

"We'll talk later, thanks."

Peterson examined Odom's graph, running it against another

database, one off limits to Odom and the rest of the crew. Within a few seconds, the computer displayed a match.

> Spectrometer pattern match with sample: 87%
> Matched compound, Detrick file: 11456-EK-7
> Information classified, enter access code:

With trembling hands, Peterson typed the password and waited several agonizing seconds for the file to display, then scanned the report. He closed the file, hurried from the conference room, and took the elevator down to MOBIDIC's pharmacy. When he reached a particular locked cabinet on the back wall, he passed his ID card through the reader and punched in another access code. A steel door hissed open, revealing shelves stacked with labeled trays. He worked back through the rows of drugs, stopping on a tray marked DET-EK-7. He removed a vial, dropped it into his pants pocket, and quietly slipped out.

DAN FIDGETED WITH restless energy. He had taken the GeneScan DNA software as far as he could, fixing a number of bugs, yet it still turned out gibberish. There was a problem with the algorithms that needed Rudi's expert touch.

In a gesture of trust, or perhaps desperation, Esrom had given him his own research cubicle and access to all but the most confidential material in MOBIDIC's database. That trust weighed heavily on him as he trudged through the program's source code.

He had been so deeply invested in the GAPS software for so long that he felt lost for the first time in years. The GAPS program would probably die with the demise of the NeuroSys IPO. That was something he had failed to anticipate in the heat of the moment and there was no one to blame but himself.

What was he supposed to do now? He'd have to adapt, evolve into someone with a new purpose. The GeneScan project had provided a temporary distraction, but his thoughts always kept returning to Rachel. There had to be more he could do. She'd want him to keep working on Carl's clues, and that realization made him feel resentful— why, he didn't know. But first, he needed to put all the pieces of the puzzle together, to back away and see things from a distance.

His thoughts returned to the mysterious crates on the La Ceiba docks, guarded so carefully. They must hold some serious computing power, maybe even gene chips for all he knew. Why else would Hadan Orcus invest so heavily in a factory that seemed to have nothing to do with Solá Mining's core business? And how was that related to this outbreak?

Try as he might, he couldn't finger a connection.

Dan looked down at his computer screen and realized he had the perfect research tool right in front of him. He took a sip of coffee and dove in to MOBIDIC's medical reference library, browsing through news articles and research papers, speed-reading as he went along. There *were* patterns in the data. Frightening ones.

There had been an explosion of disease outbreaks over the last twenty years: Hantavirus transmitted by mice after a bumper corn crop in the Four Corners region; AIDS jumping from apes to humans in Nigeria, then spreading through international travel; the sudden appearance of a new virus in human settlements along the Ebola River in 1969; accidental creation of the Marburg virus in a German lab; equine encephalitis jumping to humans after the destruction of a Brazilian rainforest; mad cow disease erupting in Britain after sheep offal was fed to cattle; the creation of new influenza strains due to the Chinese farming technique of allowing pigs and ducks to feed and defecate together in the same rice paddies.

They all had two things in common: human intervention and genetic adaptation.

And now, this new disease had evolved for the same reasons . . . but from where? He was deep in thought when a sudden touch on his shoulder jerked him upright. "Crap! A little warning would be nice."

"A little touchy there, aren't we?" Colonel Peterson said, chuckling. "You look like you've seen a ghost."

Dan caught his breath. "Something like that, actually."

"Well, I have news you'll want to hear," Peterson said, grinning. "Ms. Sullivan is awake."

44

THE STERILE ENCLOSURE around Rachel's bed had been disassembled, revealing a startling change in her appearance. Her complexion had warmed from a pale gray to ruddy pink. Her eyelids were still closed, the bulge of her pupils visible underneath, darting back and forth. Dan turned to Goodson expectantly. "I thought she was awake."

Goodson looked up from a sheaf of brain wave graphs. "She's been drifting in and out of consciousness."

"Is that good?"

"Oh, most certainly," he said.

Dan felt a burst of elation. "How? I mean, what changed?"

"Actually, Mr. Clifford, it was something you suggested to Colonel Peterson."

"What suggestion was that?"

"You'll have to ask the Colonel," Goodson said with a wry smile. "He'll be sharing the information with the team soon. In the meantime, Rachel could use some tactile stimulation, to help her wake up."

Dan took Rachel's hand and squeezed. When he felt a return in pressure, he leaned forward and touched her cheek, whispering softly, "Time to wake up."

Her eyes fluttered. Deep furrows creased her brow as her eyes opened, then squeezed shut again. She whimpered.

"Rachel, can you hear me?" Dan looked at Goodson. "What's happening?"

"A nightmare, perhaps. Sign of an active brain."

When he looked back, Rachel was staring wide-eyed at him.

"Where am I?" Her voice rasped through dry vocal cords as she glanced around suspiciously, gripping Dan's wrist tightly.

"Hey, take it easy," he said, gently peeling her fingers away. "Remember me?"

She struggled to sit up. "Why am I wearing this gown?"

"You've been . . . asleep for a while. Do you remember the accident at the lab?"

"Accident?" She grimaced and rubbed the back of her neck. "What's wrong with me?"

Dan laughed heartily, overwhelmed by relief. "Judging from the scowl you just gave me, I'd say nothing."

Rachel spotted Goodson. "Who are you?"

"A long story," Goodson said. "What's the last thing you remember?"

She puzzled a moment. "A dolphin . . . dead. Adolpho."

"Yes, that's right," Dan urged her. "Anything else?"

"I remember the dock, and the *SeaZee*." She groaned. "Oh no!"

"Don't worry about that now," Dan said. "Do you remember visiting the cabin . . . the night of the storm?"

"Storm?" She was distracted by everything in the room, but soon she fixed on the IV line in her arm. Frowning, she pulled it out. "Where's the bathroom?" she muttered. "I gotta puke."

"Down the hall, on your right," Goodson said.

Before Dan could stop her, Rachel rose unsteadily and bumped into the wall with a curse. He tried to help her, but she pulled away and stumbled down the hallway, oblivious to the gap running down the back of her gown. He caught himself staring, and gave Goodson a sheepish grin.

"I think she's going to be just fine."

COLONEL PETERSON HURRIEDLY called a meeting of the entire staff. Dan was the last one to arrive, having been reluctant to leave Rachel's side. Eager to learn more about her recovery, Dan sat at the front and surveyed the room. Fueled by adrenaline and coffee, the medical team buzzed with excitement. They knew something important was afoot.

Colonel Peterson entered, wearing a smug grin. "I'm sure you've all heard about our breakthrough. Rachel Sullivan is awake, lucid, and with apparently few side effects, except some short-term memory loss."

An excited murmur rippled through the crowd of doctors.

Marilynn Archer waved her hand immediately. "Was this a fluke? I hate miracle recoveries."

"Not a fluke at all," Peterson said, nodding in Dan's direction. "Actually, a suggestion from Mr. Clifford and some good detective work led to the cure." He paced the room excitedly, talking with his hands. "We now understand *why* Rachel Sullivan survived. She never contracted the Becker Bug. Instead, she inhaled neurotoxins released in gaseous form from the dolphin corpse. The effects were immediate. Senator Becker, on the other hand, became directly infected when he ate the contaminated shrimp. After an incubation period, the pathogens multiplied, creating a dose of toxin a thousand times stronger than the one inhaled by Ms. Sullivan. Becker had no chance for survival."

Marilynn scrunched up her face. "A microbe that creates nerve gas? I've never heard of such a thing!"

"Unusual, yes," Peterson said. "But not unprecedented. I found at least three historical incidents of corpses outgassing lethal poisons."

Marilynn seemed unconvinced. "Okay, that may explain the cause, but how did she recover so quickly?"

"I was, uh"—Peterson shifted uncomfortably—"inspired to try an experimental treatment, one of many we have in MOBIDIC's pharmacy. It worked, extremely well, I might add. I've ordered more serum flown in by fighter jet to meet us in Guantanamo. We'll be fully equipped by the time we reach La Ceiba. With luck, we'll have this epidemic under control in no time." He finished with a satisfied grin.

Esrom Nessen tilted his head to one side. "What kind of neurotoxin, exactly?"

Peterson fidgeted with his jacket. "We found . . . a strong resemblance to *Pfiesteria* toxin." His statement elicited a number of blank stares.

"*Pfiesteria* doesn't produce gaseous toxins," Nessen said.

"No, not *Pfiesteria*, something that produces toxins *similar* to *Pfiesteria*."

Dan raised his hand. "Colonel, what the heck is *fist-eria*, for us laymen?"

Peterson seemed relieved by Dan's interruption. "*Pfiesteria* is a protozoan that grows in coastal estuaries. Ships spread it around the world in their bilge water. We call it the Devil Bug. It incapacitates marine animals with a variety of toxins, then devours them. Pretty sophisticated for a one-celled organism. It's decimated fisheries along the North Carolina coast. The scientists studying it have reported strange mental problems—short-term memory loss, abrupt mood swings, hallucinations—you see the connection."

"I've got a question," Esrom said. "Since when do we have an antidote for *Pfiesteria* toxin?"

Peterson pressed his lips together. "USAMRIID's been working on that for a while. It's experimental, mind you."

Esrom locked his pale eyes on Peterson. "Perhaps you should explain *why*."

Peterson glared. "There are national security issues at play here."

"Yes, and we've all got security clearance."

"Not everyone."

Esrom nodded in Dan's direction. "Mr. Clifford helped find this cure. I think he's earned your trust. If we're to function effectively, we must work as a team."

After moments of nervous silence, Peterson seemed to make a decision. "Okay, fair enough. I agree we need open dialog. But if this gets out—"

"It's already out, and it's killing people."

"Point taken." Peterson sucked in a deep breath, then let it out. "A few years back, Detrick caught wind of a procurement of *Pfiesteria* by Middle Eastern sources. It appears they tried to purify its toxins into a gaseous form, as a WMD."

"Jesus bloody Christ!" Michael Odom exclaimed. "So this outbreak is some bioweapon you've engineered?"

"No!" Peterson snapped. "*We* didn't engineer it. But you can't defend against a weapon without studying it. Detrick was working on the *antidote*, not a weapon. And luckily, the citizens of La Ceiba stand to benefit from that antidote. I think that's pretty damned exciting."

"So what are we looking at here?" Marilynn said. "An attack on American senators by terrorists?"

"I doubt it. That wouldn't explain the deaths in La Ceiba."

"A test, perhaps?"

The colonel gave a quick shrug. "Frankly? I don't know, but we don't have time for speculation. We're refueling in Guantanamo in a few minutes. We'll arrive in La Ceiba at dawn. The primary mission of MOBIDIC is containment and we'll need a treatment plan. We can identify the source later."

45

BRADLEY GRUBER SAT quietly inside the limousine, staring up at the red granite façade of the Residence Imperial Hotel, silhouetted against the late-evening sky by a bank of sodium vapor lights. His mind was tired, yet restless, having struggled nonstop since leaving Washington, DC.

Gruber rubbed the sleep from his eyes as his mind searched for order and structure. He was unaccustomed to failure, especially in such spectacular fashion. The details kept rolling around in his mind, yet he could make no sense of it. He understood the incompetence of the Washington elite; in fact, he depended on their reliable incompetence. But these latest events made no sense to him—the actions of idiots operating outside their own best interests.

Hadan Orcus was a man Gruber could understand, but Dan Clifford was a mystery. Clifford, somehow, had anticipated Becker's death and seemed to know more about the situation than he did, and that left Gruber feeling at a distinct disadvantage. With time, he'd fill in the missing pieces. But first, he had to regain control of the situation, and that would start with Sonny Swyft.

The Residence Imperial Hotel and its adjoining condominium apartments struck an impressive sight. Gruber had to grudgingly give Sonny Swyft credit for his taste. The condominium tower was built above one of the most exclusive five-star hotels in Atlanta, and exuded status. Several actors, sports icons, and musicians called the address home. The ready availability of hotel services and furnished rooms made it attractive for celebrities who traveled for a living and needed constant attention. Unfortunately, that celebrity status would pose a problem for him on this night.

Celebrity meant security.

Any visitors to the Residence Imperial had to check in at a security desk and submit to an advanced biometric fingerprint scanner. Security cameras covered the hotel area like a blanket. The doormen and service staff were all well trained to observe visitors with security in mind. Gruber could not allow himself to be filmed, either entering or leaving the building. He was accustomed to handling things from a distance, and this was far too intimate for his taste. But it couldn't be helped.

Thankfully, the habits of celebrity clientele presented an equally viable solution to his problem. Celebrities loved to host late-night parties and other questionable activities that necessitated a certain amount of back-door discretion.

That required a private means of entry and exit.

Gruber leaned forward and instructed the limousine driver to drive them around to the back of the building. He then stole a quick glance toward his cohort, who had been sitting quietly in the seat next to him, taking in the surroundings. The man was every bit of six foot three, dark and muscular with a quiet, professional demeanor. He was well dressed in suit and tie.

"I might need your help convincing Mr. Swyft of this latest strategy," Gruber said to the man. "So I'll need you to reinforce anything I say. Just follow my lead. I'll signal with a subtle nod when it's time for your role."

"Just make sure the signal is clear," his cohort said tersely.

Gruber had never worked with this man before, but so far he was impressed. The definition of professionalism was knowing precisely when to speak up, and more importantly, when to say nothing.

The limo finished a circuitous route that ended up behind two large Dumpsters. Both men exited the car and approached the hotel's rear service entrance, their eyes making determined sweeps across the parking lot for any security activity. Gruber knocked lightly on the service entrance door.

A young woman in provocative dress opened the door from the inside. Gruber handed her a wad of hundred-dollar bills in exchange for a passkey.

"Thanks, my dear," he said. "Please remember . . . discretion."

She looked at him with incredulity. "Sugar, discretion is my profession." She turned and left the way they had come.

Since the Residence Imperial was foremost a five-star hotel, its full services were available to the condominium tenants, with concierge and room service. That required a separate service core that traveled the full height of the tower. Gruber hoped that at this hour, activity would be at a minimum.

Using his new passkey, Bradley and his cohort entered the service elevator. Gruber punched the button for the twenty-third floor.

On the ride up, his cohort spoke for the first time since leaving the limo. "You think it's wise leaving a loose end with the escort?"

Gruber smiled. "Relax. I have extensive experience working with her. She can be trusted to keep her mouth shut."

"Okay, it's your call, but I'd handle it differently."

"Well, I wouldn't." Gruber grew silent and watched as the floors ticked by on the service panel. He worked through the next few steps in his mind, only to be surprised when the doors opened all too soon.

Once at Sonny's apartment's entrance, he tapped gently three times.

A disheveled Sonny Swyft jerked the door open. "Where the hell have you been? It's almost three in the morning." Sonny waved them in dismissively and staggered toward the kitchen.

Bradley took in the surroundings. The apartment reflected the style and good taste of a professional interior decorator, with muted colors and tasteful furnishings, but Sonny had obviously added his own personal touches, to the detriment of the overall decor. The living area was strewn with clothing, empty glasses, and food containers. An eighty-inch flat screen dominated one wall, with a mass of wiring leading to a set of video game controllers strewn around the couch.

Sonny appeared to be several sheets to the wind already.

Good, Bradley thought. That should make things easier. He guided Sonny toward the dining-room table. "Let's all sit here," he said. "I've got some paperwork to go through."

"Who's this guy?" Sonny drawled.

"Our corporate lawyer," Bradley said. "Mr. Otis. Max Otis. He's here to answer any legal questions you might have." Gruber opened his briefcase and pulled out several contracts and a paper bag containing a pint of Glenlivet, which he held forward. "Here, Sonny. Something to celebrate your rebirth."

Sonny quickly removed the bottle from the bag, unscrewed the top, and poured a generous amount into his glass. "Want some?"

Bradley waved his hand dismissively. "You know I don't drink."

Sonny laughed bitterly. "I figured you'd make an exception, considering the shit-storm you brought down on us."

Bradley stiffened. *You insolent jerk,* he thought to himself. "This is not my doing. I can't control the actions of foolish men."

"Foolish men?" Sonny took a healthy draw from his glass. "You never said there would be killing involved. Who's this Jameson guy they talked about on the news, and did you really try to kill Clifford?"

"Sonny, I already told you," Bradley said more firmly. "I can't control the actions of everyone involved in this deal. I'm a facilitator, remember? Besides, Dan Clifford's accusations are just the bitter ramblings of a man who has lost everything."

"And I haven't?" Sonny sputtered. "Who is Jameson—"

Bradley cut him off and looked down at his watch, stroking the face a couple of times. "You can speculate later, but right now, we are on a timeline. I've just spent a good portion of the day and half the evening trying to save your future."

Sonny sighed and rubbed his temple. "Sorry, just tell me the plan."

"As you know, your NeuroSys stock is now worthless, *but . . .*" Bradley pushed his stack of papers toward Sonny. "I've put together an alternate arrangement that will give you an opportunity to recoup your investment and come out a hero. Since the IPO failed to meet funding, NeuroSys is dead in its present form. But our special-purpose entity still lives, far from the reach of the FBI. You'll find the Honduran government to be a much less demanding partner. We'll need to assign all the NeuroSys intellectual rights, patents, computer programs, and assets to the chip factory, in full payment to the angel investors for all liabilities incurred. This also serves to protect our financial interests by moving NeuroSys assets out of the reach of the U.S. government."

Sonny's brow wrinkled. "But how does this help me? All my money is tied up in NeuroSys stock! I've got debts, obligations. You have any idea what this condo is costing me?"

"Let me finish," Bradley said with a forced smile. "This second contract protects you." He pushed another stack of papers toward Sonny. "This gives you a twenty percent stake in Gulf-Pacific Investments, our special-purpose entity and the holding company for the chip factory. Mind you, this was a tough sell. I had to call in several favors, but I convinced the board that you were the only person who had followed through with your obligations. The misfits in Honduras have caused all of our problems."

Bradley studied Sonny's expression carefully. The man looked stunned and on the verge of tears.

"You did this for me?" Sonny said, his eyes reddening.

"Of course," Bradley said. "I reward dedication."

Sonny stared down at the table for several minutes, clearly at a loss. Then he looked up. "I appreciate this, but how do we stop these screwups from happening again? Tomás Martin is clearly out of his league. If I could have placed my own man down there in the first place . . ."

Bradley patted Sonny on the arm. "Yes, you've made that abundantly clear, and you'll get that chance . . . by moving all authority to the chip factory, with *you* in charge. You'll issue a transfer directive, along with the assets. Then, you can fly to Honduras and take over operations. You can fix the gross negligence that caused this nightmare in the first place."

"What? Move to that backwater?" Sonny moaned.

Bradley edged the papers forward again. "Sign these transfer papers. Send an e-mail to the employees, transferring power. Then you'll need to pack, and quickly, because your last chance to leave the country in advance of the FBI will be departing soon—" Bradley looked down at his watch again for emphasis. "Orcus's private jet leaves Peachtree-Dekalb airport in an hour."

For the first time since the conversation began, Sonny acknowledged Otis at the table. "So Max, you agree with this strategy? I gotta move to Honduras?"

Max stole a quick glance toward Gruber, then back to Sonny. "I can't think of any other alternative. So far, the FBI has not restricted your movements, but that will likely change if they find discrepancies in your records. It's best to put yourself out of harm's way while you can. Once you have everything in control in Honduras, we can revisit your options."

"Honduras, huh?" Sonny ran his hand over his bald pate and stared at the papers. "I guess I can tolerate a little Latin influence for a while." He picked up the pen and started signing.

Bradley stroked his watch again and stood up. "Okay, one more thing before you leave. Let's draft that e-mail to the management staff, transferring authority to the chip factory. Once you get to Honduras, you can decide who on the Atlanta staff you want to transfer."

Sonny nodded, rose unsteadily from the table, and shuffled toward his office.

Bradley followed and watched carefully as Sonny opened his laptop and logged into his corporate account. When prompted, Sonny swiped the fingerprint scanner, typed another password, and opened a new e-mail. Once Sonny began typing, Bradley nodded toward his cohort. "Max, why don't you go over and help Sonny with all the legalese?"

"Sure," Max said, and positioned himself behind Sonny's chair.

Bradley Gruber turned away and walked toward the apartment's terrace. He took a deep breath, exhaled, and admired the breathtaking view of Atlanta's skyline, glowing in the distance like a jewel. Sonny Swyft had done well for himself, Bradley thought, considering his station in life.

Beyond the terrace's edge, Gruber could hear the heartbeat of the city drifting up from below: the occasional honk of a car's horn, the hum of engines, and a steady breeze that moaned through the building's façade.

It wasn't quite enough, he realized.

He winced at the sound of gurgled screams and the thump of flailing legs against the wall. Several agonizing minutes passed before Bradley Gruber turned back around, just in time to see his cohort removing the leather garrote from Sonny's neck. He walked back in and stared down at the crumpled form. Sonny's tongue had grown purple and bloated and hung from one side of his mouth like an appendage.

Bradley looked at his cohort and nodded toward the terrace. "Set it up out there, if you please, while I do a little editing."

His cohort took a step back from the scene, breathing heavily. "Max Otis? Really? That's the best you could do?"

Bradley shrugged and allowed a thin smile to form. "What can I say? My inspiration came in the elevator."

His cohort shook his head and laughed. Then he grabbed Sonny Swyft under the armpits and unceremoniously dragged him out the door.

Bradley Gruber calmly reached into his suit pocket and removed a pair of blue nitrile gloves. After slipping them on, he sat down at Sonny's laptop, highlighted the existing text, and pressed the Delete key. Then he began to type an altogether different message.

46

DAN STOOD AT the far corner of MOBIDIC's cargo bay, his vision focused on a video monitor showing an aerial view of the La Ceiba airport taken from the plane's wing as it approached to land. Daybreak was still a half hour away. A western squall line had dumped several inches of rain on the airfield. Judging by the hectic mood of the medical teams, Dan wondered if they had failed to anticipate this type of weather—it didn't seem like the best conditions for introducing MOBIDIC to the world.

So far, everyone had tolerated his presence and he hoped to keep it that way. He remained quiet and watched as CBIRFs and CDC doctors raced back and forth, completing last-minute preparations. Gradually the two groups coalesced into distinct lines, spread along either side of the cargo bay.

Nearest the bay door, the Marines grasped long telescoping crowd restraints that would extend horizontally as they rushed from the plane. Two minifox vehicles were idling directly behind them, ready to haul out trailers carrying the inflatable field hospitals. The preparations seemed more appropriate for a military siege than a mission of mercy.

Farther back in the cargo bay, the two corresponding lines of CDC doctors began to wedge themselves into webbed seats along each wall in anticipation of landing. Colonel Peterson walked up and down both lines, checking through a list of deployment procedures. The CDC team would make up the second wave to leave the airplane, once the barricades had been placed. Peterson and the USAMRIID scientists would stay on board, manning the labs and onboard treatment center.

The contrast between the CDC and CBIRFs was striking. Unlike the CDC's bright orange, almost clown-like biohazard suits, the

CBIRFs' MOPP 4 isolation uniforms bore a dark, camouflage pattern. Their headgear consisted of black rubber face masks with hoses snaking from narrow snouts to backpacks designed to filter out contagions and biochemicals. It made the CBIRFs look like great menacing insect creatures with Coke-bottle eyes.

Dan wondered how the beleaguered victims of the outbreak would react to such bizarre apparitions swarming out the back of a plane like enormous ants of war.

The answer would come all too soon.

MOBIDIC's undercarriage suddenly hit pavement, sending a shudder through the cargo bay. When the plane reached the end of the runway, it turned and taxied toward a large open field where a crowd had gathered, and rolled to a muddy stop. A collective moan rippled through the team as they watched the video monitors. Hundreds of desperate townspeople began streaming from the shadows with their sick and dying in tow. The infected were easy to identify by their eccentric behavior. Many were restrained by family members or tied to makeshift stretchers. Others appeared to have succumbed to deep comas or perhaps, death.

The CBIRF's commander, Major Paxton, brusquely approached Peterson, his face marked with concern. "Colonel, you didn't apprise me of the crowd's size."

"The outbreak must have expanded during the night," Peterson said. "Can you handle it?"

"Do I have a choice?"

The pilot cut power to the Super Galaxy's engines, throwing an eerie hush over the cargo hold. The wind howled outside, punctuated by the occasional thunderclap or scream. Major Paxton returned to his men to finish last-minute preparations, and the CDC doctors fidgeted in their seats. Peterson stared intently at the strange scene unfolding on the monitors.

As the engines wound down, the crowd edged closer, jostling for position near the bay door. Far from having a calming influence, the presence of MOBIDIC seemed to agitate the onlookers. Remembering Senator Becker's scented breath, Dan became uncomfortably aware that the victims and their families were crowding together ever closer, sharing breaths.

Major Paxton shouted out last-minute orders: "Move quickly, extend restraints. Keep the crowd outside the secure zone until field hospitals are deployed. Watch your backs, people!" He looked toward Peterson and got a thumbs-up.

Dan suddenly realized what was about to happen. One small misstep—

He rushed forward and grabbed Peterson's arm, pointing toward the monitors. "You've got a riot about to explode out there."

"Not now, Mr. Clifford! I'd appreciate your staying out of the way."

"You're about to make things worse! They're packed too tightly. The neurotoxin—"

Peterson glared at him. "Leave this operation to the professionals with expertise in—"

"This *is* my area of expertise! The crowd is inhaling the neurotoxins from the victims, creating an amplified feedback loop. They're paranoid already. The sudden appearance of the CBIRFs could tip them over the edge."

"So what would you have us do?"

Dan started to speak, but it was already too late.

Paxton's palm slammed down on the red hatch release. The cargo door swung down with a groan, bathing the anxious throng in hatch light. The sodden air whipped inside the plane as a wave of CBIRFs streamed out, pressing the crowd back with their barricades. The CDC doctors followed. A chorus of anxious screams rippled through the crowd.

Dan watched helplessly as Michael Odom waded into the fray, his orange suit towering over the shorter Hondurans. Chattering in Spanish, he worked to find the sickest individuals. He approached one family and pulled out an inoculation gun filled with antidote.

The threatening device triggered a panicked reaction from the crowd.

Odom disappeared under a crush of bodies. The sudden burst of violence sent the rest of the mob into chaos. The CBIRFs realized what was happening a moment too late. People lunged over the barricades, grabbing at the soldiers.

Suddenly, thunderous explosions and brilliant flashes brought howls of pain. The mob parted like the Red Sea, leaving Odom and several Hondurans writhing in the wet mud. A Marine grabbed Odom under the arms and dragged him toward the cargo bay. Holding the barricades before them like shields, the CBIRFs retreated back up the ramp. With another screech of metal, the cargo door slammed shut.

"I'm exposed!" A cursing Odom clambered out of his ripped biohazard suit. Blood streamed down his face. "I need the antidote!"

Peterson rushed over to Paxton. "Stun grenades? This is a rescue mission, for God's sake!"

Major Paxton ripped off his MOPP hood. "Unavoidable. They're painful, but harmless."

"Harmless? Look at the panic! We're supposed to be helping these people!"

The major's eyes flickered with consternation. "I'll not put my men in harm's way without some defense, sir."

Peterson struggled to regain his composure. "I'm still in command of this operation, Major!"

"Then what do you suggest, Colonel?"

"Whatever you do," Dan yelled over the din, "you better do it quickly." He pointed toward the monitors. "There are more victims out there, bleeding, outgassing toxins. Before long, you won't have any control at all."

Peterson's expression softened, almost pleaded. "Paxton, don't you have anything more . . . *benign?*"

"We've got a wide variety, sir."

"Anything that won't frighten the crap out of these poor souls?"

Paxton stopped and thought for a minute. "The minifoxes are equipped to spray crowd-control foam. We can use it straight up, simply to disorient, or we can mix in a mild sedative to calm the crowd."

"We'll need to reach the infected victims quickly, or they'll die." Peterson cast another glance at the regrouping mob.

"We could dart them," Paxton said. "With the antidote. From a safe distance."

Peterson's eyes brightened. "That might work." He nodded. "Do it!"

Paxton issued commands to a contingent of Marines. One team quickly loaded semiautomatic dart rifles with a fast-acting sedative and a dose of antidote. They then moved toward an access tunnel leading to the top of the wings. Another team rushed to the minifoxes, medical supplies in hand. The hospital trailers were disconnected and the foam guns loaded with the mild sedative mixture.

Paxton barked orders into his radio. A flurry of muffled reports echoed from the top of MOBIDIC's wing. Bodies began dropping to the ground, eliciting a new chorus of shrieks from the disoriented crowd. At that precise moment, Paxton reopened the cargo door.

The two minifoxes roared out and broke in opposing directions, their guns spewing sedative-laced foam around the perimeter of the mob as if they were giant cans of shaving cream.

By midafternoon, Dan was standing alongside Colonel Peterson at the tail of MOBIDIC, gazing across the field of mud and sodden grass. The sun had broken through the clouds and baked much of the moisture from the earth, driving up plumes of vapor. In a few harrowing hours, the airport had been transformed from a riot scene into an orderly tent city. A line of helicopters, including several military Hueys and three commercial Bells from the media, had joined the entourage, and were parked several hundred feet away from MOBIDIC alongside the runway.

Dan marveled at how quickly conditions had improved since dawn. Considering how things had started, the Marines had done an admirable job of subduing the riot and erecting the two field hospitals. Once a semblance of authority and trust had been established, the crowd seemed eager to cooperate.

Such was the nature of mob mentality, with the help of a few drugs.

Within hours, the infected victims had been identified, treated with antidote, and quarantined in one hospital. Everyone else had been assembled in the second hospital, to be examined for effects of the neurotoxin. It fell to the CDC staff to calm the ragged nerves of the uninfected and brief them on the nature of the illness.

Dan was turning to go back inside the plane when Jenifer Coleman's familiar face appeared in a crowd of reporters. They had been swarming the mobile hospitals since midmorning and when they caught site of Dan and the colonel, they descended on the cargo hatch.

Jenifer thrust her microphone in Dan's face. "Mr. Clifford, what are your thoughts on the current crisis?" She flashed him a grin and winked. He backed away, uncomfortable with the absurdity of it all and the notion that his opinion mattered. Then again, maybe it did. It gave him an idea as scary as it was exciting. "I believe the MOBIDIC team has everything under control," he announced, smiling.

"Is this connected to the toxic dumping by Hadan Orcus?"

"I'm sure of it. But you should really be talking to Colonel Clarence Peterson . . . here. He's in charge of the operation." The reporters took the cue and swarmed the colonel. Dan used the diversion to back into the shadows. One of the Marines tapped him on the shoulder.

"You've got a guy over here asking for you."

Dan found Rudi Plimpton hiding in the shade under the cargo hatch, wearing his ever-present black outfit.

"Why it's Dan Clifford, the media sensation," Rudi quipped. "I've been watching you on the tube. Did I just see Jenifer?"

"Yep. She's moving up in the news world."

"Yeah, thanks to us." Rudi shook his head. "You're one lucky guy—we're *both* lucky. We came out smelling like a rose."

Dan thumped his finger against the brim of the large sombrero engulfing Rudi's head. "Where's your black hat? This ruins your ensemble."

"A gift from the island folk. They said I'd fry my brain in a black hat down here."

"How's Duff?"

"Not good. Two guests came down with the screaming meemies last night. Everyone else packed up and left. Duff's burning on a long, slow fuse."

The thought of Duff, the cheerful old Irishman—moping in his bar, digging holes in the table with his dive knife—left Dan feeling depressed. Duff had a dark side that worried him. The man needed something to keep him occupied and out of trouble.

"Hey! I hear the ice queen awoke from her slumber. Is she a princess now?"

"Hey, give Rachel a break. She's had a tough time."

Rudi twitched an eyebrow. "Why Dan, what's up with you? Is Rachel your 'umfriend' now?"

"What's that supposed to mean?"

"You know, when you introduce that special someone. 'This is my, *umm* . . . friend.'"

Dan ignored the remark, focusing instead on the pile of familiar crates nearby. "I see you brought your toys along."

"Well, the jarheads said my computing prowess was needed, so I came prepared."

"Good. I need your help with some NeuroSys software: Gene-Scan. Ever heard of it?"

"Yeah, I've seen references to it on the company servers. What is it?"

"Something you wrote, I think. Part of GAPS, repurposed."

"If so, I should recognize my handiwork."

"Good. The crew needs your help and I've got a lot to share with you. There's more going on here than you know."

Rudi shivered. "This situation gives me the creeps already."

Dan went through the situation with the GeneScan software, then he told Rudi of his latest plan, one still forming in his mind.

Rudi's irreverent grin faded. "That's insane, even for you! Why?"

"Because no one else is going to do it. I've got to know what Hadan Orcus is up to. Are you going to help me or not?"

Rudi shrugged. "If you're determined, I doubt I'll change your mind." He pulled out his laptop and searched for the information Dan had requested. When he found it, Rudi wrote it on an old business card. When they were done, Dan led Rudi into the belly of the plane, past the BSL4 chamber, to Esrom Nessen's cubicle.

"Reinforcements have arrived," Dan announced.

Esrom grinned and pushed away from the computer. "Just in time." He shook Rudi's hand gingerly. "I understand you know this DNA software."

"May I?" Rudi gestured toward the screen.

Esrom nodded.

After a few minutes, Rudi looked up from the screen. "Yeah, I wrote most of it. However, some peabrains have screwed it all up. These idiots must have slipped into the gene pool while the lifeguard wasn't watching."

Dan stood to one side, studying the absurd image of Rudi in his black clothes, black beard, and sombrero, and Esrom in tropical clothing with his freckled complexion and flaxen hair. *Salt and pepper.* "I'll leave you two to get acquainted," Dan said, chuckling under his breath. He needed to get away, find some time to think. His next move would be critical.

Perhaps Rudi was right. This idea was his craziest ever.

47

EARLY THE NEXT morning, Colonel Peterson strolled down the aisle of the field hospital, the shoes of his biohazard suit scuffing across the muddy floor. Sanitation had been a joke, but he suspected that the Becker Bug, as they were now calling it, wasn't contagious anyway. It seemed to be transmitted by ingestion only. There had been a few early fatalities from inhalation of the neurotoxins but the bodies showed no sign of infection. Just like the Sullivan girl and Clifford.

Still, he was taking no chances, especially with the media lingering outside. Everyone wore full biohazard gear, despite the terrifying effect the sight had on those still suffering from hallucinations. Several patients had torn through their plastic isolation units before the antidote could kick in.

He checked in on Goodson in the patient ward.

"What's the current fatality count?"

"Only twenty, incredibly." Goodson was unpacking more vials of antidote from a heavily padded case. "Most of them died before we arrived. Looks like we got here just in time."

"Maybe that'll be it," Peterson said with a relieved sigh.

Buoyed by the good news, Peterson headed to the communications center and placed a call to Esrom Nessen. "Anything interesting to report?"

"This microbe scares the hell out of me," Esrom said.

Peterson was partially taken aback. "How's that?"

"Well, as you said, it's not *Pfiesteria*, exactly. Our immune systems seem capable of defeating it, if the toxins are neutralized. But if the host dies, it reproduces rapidly."

"What's the scary part?"

"I ran a temperature analysis. This protozoan is a heat lover, Colonel, and I mean sweltering. When the chef cooked the shrimp at the lobby dinner, he actually *triggered* accelerated growth. By the time Senator Becker swallowed them, the toxin concentrations were off the chart."

Peterson knew of only one other human pathogen—Creutzfeldt–Jakob disease, a.k.a. mad cow—that could survive high temperatures. And it wasn't even technically a living thing, but a prion, or primitive protein. "You have an image of this thing yet?"

"In an hour or two."

"I want to see this for myself."

He felt a lump in his throat as he left the communications room. A food-borne pathogen that wasn't killed by cooking? That would spell disaster for the local seafood industry. What were the locals supposed to eat?

Peterson's ebullient mood crashed.

VINCE PERETTI SLIPPED on a pair of polypropylene overboots and walked through Sonny Swyft's apartment toward the terrace, brightly lit by the early-morning sun. Trent Hockaday, a young homicide detective with the Atlanta Police Department, stood over the corpse, examining the grisly scene.

Vince introduced himself and shook hands. "Thanks for meeting with me," Vince said.

"No problem," Trent replied. "But I'm not sure why the cyberterrorism branch of the bureau would be interested in this case."

"Have you been watching the news lately? The deaths in Washington?"

"Sure," Trent said.

"Well, Sonny Swyft was implicated by Dan Clifford in his Weatherman cyberattack," Vince said. "I had intended to interview him today." Vince looked down at Sonny's corpse, which the forensic team had laid out on the stone floor. A twisted braid of wires ran from Sonny's neck to the balustrade of the apartment's terrace. The source of the wires, a video game controller, was still attached, dangling below Sonny's neck like a strange necklace.

Vince's gaze reconnected with Trent, his head shaking. "Well, so much for that interview."

"Ah, I wouldn't worry. He left you plenty of info, believe me," Trent said. "We found him hanging over the side of the terrace. Initial liver temp puts the suicide at about three A.M. last night. You can imagine the flurry of calls we received this morning during rush hour."

"So, you're saying this was a suicide."

"Oh yeah," Trent said, nodding his head. "Most definitely. Neck injuries are consistent with a violent hanging. Vertebral dislocation at C2 and C3. Besides," Trent continued, leading Vince back into the main living area. "The guy e-mailed a full confession to his employees right before his death, from this laptop," he said, pointing. "The guy should have been a writer. The confession is a virtual manifesto. Best written suicide note I've ever seen."

Vince's brow wrinkled. "Can I get a copy of this?"

"Sure, I'll get you one on a memory stick," Trent said.

"No chance this was staged?"

"Not that I see," Trent said. "No other fingerprints, signs of struggle, or obvious fiber evidence, though that will have to wait for forensic analysis."

"Anything on the security cameras?"

"Nothing out of the ordinary, oh, except one thing. One of the hotel's perimeter cameras caught the fender of a limousine out back about the time of the suicide, but as you can imagine with these tenants, this place is crawling with limos at all hours of the night."

"You mind?" Vince pointed down at the wireless keyboard and mouse the forensic team had attached to Sonny's laptop to avoid disturbing fingerprints on the original keyboard. "I'd like to read the confession."

"Knock yourself out," Trent said.

Vince leaned over and paged through the entire confession. Trent was right. Sonny Swyft had eloquently confessed to the attempted murder of Dan Clifford and the hiring of a Honduran ship captain to dump toxic chemicals from the NeuroSys chip factory near fishing lanes. He expressed regret for his actions and hoped to atone with his death. It all seemed too neat and tidy. When Vince finished reading, he glanced down at the patina of white residue that had settled on the laptop's keyboard, left over from the forensic team's fingerprint dusting.

"Hey, Trent," Vince called out. "Your team didn't actually lift prints from the keys?"

"Nah," Trent said, approaching. "Too messy and imprecise. They prefer to use side light and photographs."

"And you only found Sonny Swyft's fingerprints?" Vince said. "No one else's?"

"Correct."

Vince pulled out a magnifying loupe from his pocket and examined the keys carefully. Several of the less-used keys exhibited distinct fingerprint ridges, but the more often-used keys appeared smudged, indistinct. He turned to Trent. "This is just a suggestion, but if I were you, I'd have your forensic team take another look at these keys."

"Oh really? Why?" Trent leaned over and looked for himself.

"Because I'm betting that if you do a distribution analysis of the so-called suicide note, you'll find that all the letters used in the message will have smudged keys, while the unused keys will be the ones with Sonny's actual fingerprints. Exactly what you would expect to find, if a person with gloved hands typed it instead."

48

HADAN ORCUS STOOD on the balcony of his mountainside compound, carved from the southern flank of Mt. Cosigüina. His eyes traveled across the Gulf of Fonseca to Conchigüita, Cosigüina's sister volcano, then down to the Pacific Ocean. There, nestled in the bay, was the city of Soluteca, gleaming in all its brilliance.

His city.

It had grown into a thriving metropolis, the envy of Central America. Every day, tons of precious metals, raw materials, and food left for the markets of America and Europe. Even now, Orcus could see workers scurrying about the harbor like ants, filling the holds of cargo vessels.

Twenty years ago, this area had been nothing but a sleepy fishing village, filled with illiterate laggards wasting their lives away on worthless pursuits. Now, the city pulsated with energy. Skyscrapers raked the horizon.

He'd been able to negotiate many concessions from the cash-strapped Honduran government, and now he operated free from wasteful bureaucracy, import duties, and restrictive labor legislation. The fledgling port was modeled after the ancient Roman free port of Delos in Greece, and was growing rapidly.

Soluteca was Central America's first "special economic zone" and would soon rival the best of Singapore or Dubai.

That is, if he could quit hemorrhaging money. The city's rapid growth consumed capital and resources faster than he could unearth them. He needed more.

For that, Orcus looked farther north, his eyes tracing fingers of red clay that extended out into the emerald forest. The entire coast along this stretch of beach was volcanically active, and his trench mines smoldered like the breath of a beast. Thousands of company-owned shanties clung to the cliffs above the mines, hastily constructed to house his army of cheap laborers. The structures were spartan, but a far cry from the squalor that existed before his arrival. He proudly provided the locals with good, solid employment, unlike the subsistence farming and drug crops the locals had grown before.

It was a wonderful sight, one he relished each morning, until recently. Now, everything he had worked for was being threatened by the actions of a few jealous fools.

No longer.

He picked up a secure satellite phone from the nearby table and dialed a familiar number. "Give me a status report," he said brusquely.

"It's not good, I'm afraid," Bradley Gruber said, his voice dripping with irony. "Capitol Hill is in a state of shock, which is only feeding the media's frenzy. The president has enacted food import restrictions—"

"Restrictions that are ruining my exports!" Orcus spat. "I've got shipments of food rotting in the holds of ships. My net worth has dropped by the billions, thanks to the NeuroSys failure, all because of your empty promises. I distinctly remember you assuring me that Dan Clifford would play along. What, exactly, am I paying you for?"

"My dear Orcus," Gruber said tersely. "Things might have gone according to plan if you had warned me of your intention to poison Senator Becker."

"What?" Orcus jerked the phone away from his ear and stared, as if it were a foreign object. His voice rose an octave. "You mealy mouthed prick, I did no such thing! My enemies obviously planted that poison to frame me. I worry about your loyalties, Gruber. If you didn't come so highly recommended, I would deal with you myself!"

There was a long pause that made Orcus wonder if the connection had been lost. When Gruber spoke again, his voice had grown more tense. "I suggest you dispense with the threats. I've been putting out brush fires as fast as you can light them. It was *your* responsibility to eliminate Dan Clifford, and you failed. Meanwhile, I have been rehabilitating your reputation. The NeuroSys president, Sonny Swyft, has conveniently provided you with ample cover, having taken responsibility for your failures."

"How dare you talk to me like that!" Orcus roared. "You're no more than a hired hand."

"Yes, and I seem to be the only hired hand of yours capable of fixing things." After another pause, Gruber's voice turned mellifluous again. "Relax, your CAFTA deal is protected, I assure you. And your net worth may be higher than you think. Thanks to the 'transfer-on-death' clauses in Becker's and Swyft's contracts, Gulf-Pacific Investments now owns all of the chip factory as well as the main assets of NeuroSys. That *doubles* your equity, if my math serves. I assume that was your intention with Becker's death. In addition, all of the NeuroSys intellectual property has been transferred to Honduras. I assume the chip factory is still providing for your needs. So you see, things are looking up. It just takes patience, and more importantly, *full disclosure*." Gruber paused again for effect. "Tell me, is there any credence to Clifford's accusations about this outbreak?"

Orcus struggled to calm himself. He took a deep breath and exhaled. He had to admit, Gruber *had* made some legitimate points. "I fail to see how a few barrels of waste could have anything to do with some peasant outbreak. The entire idea is preposterous."

"Let's hope you are correct," Gruber said, "since there's a team of American doctors in La Ceiba right now. That will only draw more media attention to your activities. The increased scrutiny may make it more difficult for you to continue with your operations."

"A delay is not an option," Orcus said. "With this scrutiny, my window of opportunity will soon close. There must be a way to get the Americans out of the area."

Gruber sighed audibly. "What about your Honduran connections? Surely you can wield some influence in Tegucigalpa. Create a diversion. I'll fulfill my obligations here in Washington."

"You'd better—" Orcus began again, but Gruber had already hung up on him.

Orcus cursed out loud. He didn't trust the man. Gruber was a political whore, lacking the legacy of heritage. But Orcus had to admit, the man was usually effective. That counted for something.

AFTER SEVERAL STRATEGIC calls to his friends in the capital, Hadan Orcus felt his confidence returning. There was just one more critical phone call he had to make: to his incompetent lackey, Tomás Martin.

"Good afternoon, Señor Orcus," Martin answered with a cautious tone. "What can I do for you?"

"Do you have any idea what your failure to deal with Dan Clifford has cost me?" Orcus said.

"I'm so sorry, sir," Martin said. "The ship captain—"

"A cowardly excuse! It was your responsibility to shut Clifford up, especially after his surprise visit to the chip factory."

"It's been hectic here, and now this outbreak—"

"Have you been talking with Bradley Gruber?"

"What? Uh no, of *course* not, sir. I only talk with you! Why? Has he said something to the contrary?"

"Are you sure? When was the last time you talked with him?"

"Uh, I don't know, sir. The time of our last meeting, perhaps? When he informed us of activities in the States. Why? What has he said?"

"Just checking. Because if he ever contacts you, I would expect an immediate call."

"Of course, sir. I would never—"

"My next shipment," Orcus continued. "Is it ready?"

"Umm, not quite. The outbreak . . . it's affecting our productivity. The family members of some of our workers have gotten sick."

"Well then, double the shifts. And quit using this outbreak as an excuse for your incompetence. It's only a matter of time before our operations come to light and I cannot tolerate any more delays. Do you understand?"

"No, I mean, of *course,* sir," Martin said, his voice quavering. "It's just . . . we're working as fast as we can. Another day or two."

Orcus enjoyed the disorienting effect his call was having on Martin. *Serves him right.* With all the ineptitude, Orcus needed to exact his pound of flesh, make Martin think twice before acting again in such a slipshod manner. Perhaps he should have fired the fool weeks ago, but with his degree in biochemistry from the Universidade de São Paulo, Tomás Martin was uniquely qualified to manage the chip factory. Still, at some point, the man needed to prove his worth.

"And the other project?" Orcus continued. "Where are the latest results?"

"I'm, uh, afraid we've had a number of setbacks there as well," came the nervous reply from Martin's end. "The software has bugs."

"More excuses!"

"But sir," Martin said, his voice pleading, "the main programmer was recently fired—"

"Well then, hire him back!"

"We can't," Martin replied. "Frankly, we don't know where he is right now."

"And you can't find a replacement? What good are you, then?" Orcus was beginning to wonder if Martin's qualifications even mattered anymore.

"Well, uh, there's another problem."

"Oh? What now?"

"Yes, well, uh . . . you see, there was a serious incident, totally unexpected, you understand. We've lost two of our key biologists."

"Fired as well?" Orcus grew very still, sensing another ruinous bit of news. "Go on."

"Not fired, dead." Martin paused for a moment. "I, uh, haven't had the opportunity to inform you. There was an accident of some sort in the lab—acidic cyanide. It poisoned the breeders, contaminated everything, killed the men. But we've completed the cleanup and we'll be starting up again very soon, once I hire replacements— I'm searching madly for qualified individuals, I assure you."

Orcus was stunned. "What kind of accident, exactly?"

"We do not know, Señor Orcus. It is a mystery."

Orcus closed his eyes and pinched the bridge of his nose, as if trying to squeeze the frustration from his mind like a pimple. "This incident, did it happen prior to the outbreak?"

"Yes, sir," Martin said weakly. "But it is not connected to the outbreak. This was a chemical accident."

"But we don't use cyanide." Orcus struggled to quell an involuntary rage. "The one thing I've demanded of you was *full disclosure*," he said, "and you keep me in the dark?"

First, Becker's poisoning, then this. Orcus pondered the situation for several quiet moments, finally regaining his composure.

"So, we must have a . . . saboteur."

"Apparently so," Martin replied. "It's the only explanation that makes sense. We've doubled our security, but I suspect the culprit was the scientist, Carl Jameson. We found him wandering the halls immediately after the incident. As you know, we took care of that problem."

"And created a host of new ones," Orcus said.

Lacking the energy to chew out Martin any further, Orcus hung up. This new revelation had him more confused than ever. He needed time to clear his mind, to make sense of all this betrayal. Carl Jameson was a saboteur, planted . . . by who? Apparently, he had underestimated the cunning of his enemies. Perhaps he had grown complacent with his recent successes. That made a redoubling of efforts more critical than ever.

Orcus stood up again and moved along the balcony of his compound. He reached the open courtyard, tiled in peach-colored Saltillo, where his army of waist-high flowerpots—cast in the likeness of Mayan figureheads—stood like sentinels. Erupting from the pots were his prize-winning rosebushes, adorned in every imaginable color like giant headdresses. Orcus approached the nearest bush and drew a flower to his nose, inhaling the intense aroma, in the hopes of calming his pounding heart. A thorn punctured his thumb and he drew back in surprise, licking away the crimson liquid.

The bitter, metallic flavor lingered on his tongue.

49

AT THE NEXT staff meeting, Rachel Sullivan seemed unprepared for her reception. Applause and cheers greeted her as she ambled in with Dr. Goodson. Blushing, she shuffled over to Dan's table.

Dan noticed that the intensity had begun to return to her eyes. "How do you feel?" he asked.

"Shaky," she replied. "With the hangover from hell." Then she did something surprising—she leaned over, touched his ear with her lips and whispered: "You're my hero. Dr. Goodson told me you saved my life."

Her words left him feeling like an awkward teenager. "I have a lot to tell you. . . ."

Esrom Nessen walked over and hugged her.

She responded with a grin. "Dr. Nessen! I didn't expect to see you here."

"You two know each other?"

"Dr. Nessen was my genetics professor at Johns Hopkins," she replied.

Esrom gave Dan a sheepish grin. "Sorry I didn't mention it to you earlier. It seemed prudent to wait until we knew the, uh, prognosis." He turned back to Rachel. "I'm just relieved you're okay."

"I'd like to help with your research," Rachel said.

"You think that's a good idea? You shouldn't rush things, my dear."

"Goodson's caught me up, and I have more experience with marine organisms than anyone else here. Besides, I feel fine, really."

"Well, we'll see . . ."

Colonel Peterson moved to the front of the room and addressed the group. "We have a new, pressing issue." He nodded toward Esrom, who projected an image of the Becker Bug on the big screen, color enhanced to highlight its interior details.

Dan marveled at the organism, amazingly complex for something so tiny. He'd never thought of a single cell having so many individual parts. It resembled a fried egg, sunny side up, with myriad multicolored shapes surrounding the cell's dark central nucleus.

"As you can see," Esrom said, "the Becker Bug is a protozoan, a eukaryote."

Dan leaned over and whispered in Rachel's ear, "You-carry-*what?*"

"Eukaryote," she whispered back. "A cell with a nucleus, where the DNA is stored. It's the cellular structure of all higher animals, including humans. *Pro*karyotes, bacteria, are simpler, with no nucleus. Their DNA floats around inside the cell like alphabet soup."

"I thought most diseases were caused by bacteria or viruses."

"Not always. Many of the world's biggest killers—malaria, chaga's disease, cryptosporidium, leishmaniasis—they're all eukaryotes. Their complexity makes them harder to treat—"

Colonel Peterson cleared his voice. "Can we have everyone's attention please? This isn't Biology 101."

Dan sat up straight like a scolded student.

Esrom Nessen stood and began a clinical summary using a laser pointer. "The cell has an unusual combination of organelles—mitochondria—here." He aimed at several oblong shapes. "Endoplasmic reticulum, golgi apparatus, ribosomes and surprisingly, chloroplasts. A structure similar to algae, but also with cilia. You know what that means."

"That it's mixotrophic," Rachel replied. "A chimera, part plant, part animal."

"Correct. It's capable of surviving in the ocean through photosynthesis, but can invade a host and feed off it. That makes this thing terribly efficient. But that's not the biggest surprise." Esrom took a long pause, his expression strained. "The Becker Bug is also an *extremophile*."

The last statement elicited a chorus of gasps.

"It's unlike any creature I've ever seen," he continued. "The shrimp eat it, get infected, and pass it up the food chain. Cooking won't kill it. Think of the traits—resistance to heat, creates a toxic gas, survives in the ocean, infectious—almost as if designed as a bioweapon." He turned to Peterson. "Is this what Fort Detrick has been working on?"

Peterson's face reddened. "We've been through this already. I'm on your side, for Christ's sake! There is no bioweapons program producing anything like this that I know of. This is more likely an unfortunate evolutionary quirk. But if you're so eager to expose a conspiracy, then get that damned DNA scanner fixed. We need a genetic profile to trace the creature's origin."

"We're working on it," Esrom snapped.

"Then work faster."

"What about Hadan Orcus?" Dan practically yelled over the din of the crowd. "He's certainly financially capable of bioengineering. Didn't you say the DNA software came directly from the NeuroSys chip factory?"

"Yes, and the damn thing doesn't work," Peterson said.

"Our copy perhaps, but I'm trying to understand why Orcus would invest in DNA software without a good reason or equipment to run it on. The crates I saw loaded on the garbage scow could hold gene sequencing equipment, right?"

"For what purpose?" Peterson said. "Orcus is into mining."

"Who knows?" Dan said. "Maybe he developed it to eliminate his enemies. We won't know if we don't investigate."

"This is a medical mission, Mr. Clifford, not a military one. We don't have the authority to investigate."

"So Orcus gets away with it?" Dan persisted. "How can you stop this outbreak if we don't stop the source? It all started on his garbage scow."

"So you keep claiming," Peterson replied, "but I think you may be blowing things out of proportion."

"Am I?" Dan said. "Tell that to your victims in the field hospital."

Peterson stared at Dan intensely. "Why don't you leave the medical research to the experts? I don't need you telling me how to do my job."

Dan felt his anger spinning out of control. "In case you forgot, I predicted this outbreak, and your victim riot. You've admitted this creature is enigmatic, something you didn't expect. That's *my* domain—black swan events. You've got your eyeballs jammed so far up your microscopes that you're missing the bigger picture."

Peterson's face flushed, the veins on his neck pulsing. He seemed at a loss for words.

Dan could feel his own face reddening. The other members of the team stared at him in stone-cold silence, some with their mouths agape. Esrom Nessen's face wore a bemused expression. Dan regretted his comment. Peterson was bullheaded, but so was he. Making it personal like this was not the way to go about it. He tried to take a much calmer tone. "Look, all I'm asking is that we research the chip factory, go on a diplomatic mission, anything to find out the game Orcus is playing. Otherwise, he'll stay one step ahead of us."

Peterson kept his own fury bottled up with military discipline. "Mr. Clifford, I've already contacted the proper authorities about the possibility of a terrorist incident. In the meantime, the focus of *our* mission, MOBIDIC's mission, is to understand and treat this disease. *Period.*"

Dan realized he'd screwed up. Peterson was not a man who would tolerate being dressed down in front of his peers. Now it would take a herculean effort to get Peterson back on his side. For that, he'd need concrete proof, and he knew only one way to get it.

AFTER THE MEETING broke, Rachel asked Dan to escort her outside for some fresh air. He led her down the corridor toward the cargo hold, giving her a short version of the MOBIDIC tour. She walked gingerly, taking in the sights with muted interest, the strain of her ordeal still evident in her unsteady gait. When they reached the plane's exit ramp, Dan slipped his arm around her waist. She leaned in, the warmth of her touch rekindling memories from their night together. He wondered how much she remembered.

They reached the tarmac. The scent of asphalt and freshly trodden grass lingered in the humid air. A muddy path snaked up the hill to the hospitals. A handful of people strolled about in the distance, oblivious to their presence.

She turned her face toward the sun and closed her eyes momentarily. He could feel a shudder travel up her spine. "The nightmares I've had . . . so terrible. And then to wake up, surrounded by doctors, in La Ceiba, to *this.*"

She opened her eyes and scanned the field with its domed structures, helicopters, cars, media tents. "What did Carl witness that caused all of this?" She took a sharp breath and turned away, dragging her sleeve across her face. "Sorry," she said, sniffling. "The toxins must still be messing with my mind."

"No need to apologize," he said. "You're alive and improving, and that's good enough for me."

Blushing, she replied, "I have you to thank." She fixed her gaze on him and smiled demurely. "What has happened to my *strange attractor*? You've been kicking ass lately. I thought you and the colonel were going to trade blows."

He chuckled. "I have demons, my dual nature, I suppose. My teenage years were bitter times. It's taken a long time to suppress that anger. It sneaks out occasionally."

She winked. "I sort of like it. Dan Clifford, strange attractor and ass kicker."

They stared at each other for a while.

He marveled at how beautiful she looked, even now, without a shred of makeup. Solitude had always been his preference; in fact, most relationships seemed to pass him by like scenery beyond a glass window. But in Rachel's presence, he felt something different, more like a need than a desire. "Do you remember our last night together?"

The corners of her lips curled and she looked away. "A little. Why don't you refresh my memory?"

He chuckled. "You were paranoid, very scared that night."

"Me, scared? Nah."

"Oh yes, and soaking wet. I couldn't believe you made it to the cabin through that storm. I tried to calm you down."

"Did it work?"

"Hardly." He grinned.

"*That* sounds more like me. Must have been those toxins. You had quite the bedside manner, if I remember correctly."

He pulled her close and slid his hands into the small of her back. "It seems your memory has improved." She met his embrace and leaned her head against his chest, lingering there for several minutes, her breath hot against his neck.

He finally succumbed and lifted her chin. His lips grazed hers, lightly at first, then more forcefully as he sensed a willing response. She pressed herself into him, her arms sliding up his back and into his hair. His heart pounded against her chest and he pulled her closer, feeling an emotional abandon more powerful than anything in his adult life. The worries of the world seemed to fade into insignificance.

This is life, he thought.

And then, just as suddenly as the moment had begun, it was over.

Rachel gently pushed him away. They stood in awkward silence, breathing hoarsely. "Let's go in now," she said and averted her gaze. "I've had enough excitement for one day."

Only he wasn't ready for the moment to end. "Maybe I should catch you up on Carl's situation first." At the mention of Carl's name, Rachel's eyes brightened and he knew he'd lost the moment for good.

"Did you decipher his message?" Rachel asked.

"Not exactly," he said. "What with all the ass kicking—"

"But what about your FBI friend? I thought he was going to analyze the wad of paper."

"Things have been moving too fast. I haven't had a chance to check with him yet."

"Right." Rachel flashed a look of disappointment.

"But I have learned more," he said. "Do you remember Carl's research into invasive species? The search history we talked about back at the cabin?"

Rachel thought for a moment. "Vaguely. Those memories are all jumbled."

"I talked with Professor Proudfoot, the man who knew us both. It seems that Carl called him before he died, hinting of a great discovery, and joking about a new age, the coming of the Seventh Sun."

Rachel rolled her eyes. "More mythology mumbo jumbo? What the hell is the Seventh Sun?"

"Before I explain that, you need to understand an old Aztec creation legend," he said. "Before the dawn of man, four suns were created and destroyed, marking the four cosmic ages—the Jaguar, Wind, Rain, and Water. Each age ended with total destruction of inferior beings that did not meet the expectations of the gods. In other words, *mass extinctions*. From each destruction, the world would be reborn. Then, the god Tonatiuh ushered in the fifth sun of man, and with it, an age of prosperity. This was the golden age of the Aztec Empire."

"Okay, I'll bite," Rachel said. "So where's the *sixth* sun?"

"Ahh, that's the point I'm getting to," he said. "Many Native Americans, both from North and South America, believe that the Conquistadors ushered in the sixth sun, leading to the mass extinction of indigenous culture. In other words, the sixth sun is the age of the white man." He paused to gauge Rachel's reaction.

She seemed to be listening intently. "Okay, and this is relevant . . . how?"

"Think of the Conquistadors as an invasive species. Colonial Europeans have invaded and destroyed hundreds of indigenous eco-systems. We're like a kudzu vine, creeping into every nook and cranny. But the Conquistadors brought along another passenger, an invasive species more deadly than themselves—smallpox. In fact, smallpox did most of the conquering, wiping out entire cultures. Later, the American military learned how to use it as a bioweapon, handing out smallpox-laced blankets to Native American tribes to cull their pop-ulations."

Even in her weakened state, Dan could see the wheels in Rachel's head beginning to turn. "So you're thinking Hadan Orcus is the trick-ster? That he's developed some doomsday microbe to what—cull the herd?"

"Maybe, maybe not. It could be unintentional, but in any case, Orcus is an invasive threat. His mining operations move into pristine areas, destroying natural habitats. Native microbes will either die, or evolve. The trickster in this case could be Orcus, or man himself."

"Another crazy theory." Rachel's deflated look stung him. "That doesn't get us any closer to understanding Carl's clues. We're still no closer to the truth."

"That's why we need answers from Orcus, and soon."

"But Peterson already shot you down."

"I'm working some angles," he said.

Rachel stared at him warily. "What kind of angles, exactly?"

He realized he'd said too much. "I'm still thinking through things . . ."

"I hope you're not planning something stupid or reckless, some-thing that might get you killed."

"You're warning me about recklessness?" He let out a derisive laugh. "The crazy woman who wanted to, what was it you said, 'con-front Orcus and make him pay?'"

"That was different. I'm better equipped to—"

"Do what, exactly?" Rachel's hypocrisy set him off. "Get *yourself* killed? What is it with you, so flippant about risk? But with me, it's different, right? Why do you care what happens to me, anyway? I'm not Carl."

"What does that mean?" Rachel's eyes turned cold. "I *do* care what happens to you. You just don't understand—"

"Understand what?" He stepped closer to her. "There's something you're not telling me. Why won't you let me in?"

Rachel pushed him back forcefully. "You'll *never* understand." She turned back toward the plane and hobbled away in silence.

50

THE NEXT MORNING ushered in a bright, sunny day with limitless possibilities. That's the attitude Dan chose, because to think otherwise might weaken his nerve. He'd had a fitful night of sleep, thinking about Rachel and her curious behavior. Had he conjured a relationship that didn't exist? Her initial response had not been faked, he felt, but she still stubbornly kept her emotional distance. He understood how the loss of Carl Jameson would affect her. He'd been through loss himself. The pain could linger. But now he felt his own unique, unrequited pain. She was right there, but just outside his reach. It was maddening, and he knew he'd handled the situation poorly.

But for today, he would have to put her out of his mind. There hadn't been time to work up a flawless plan, so he just decided to forge ahead. After changing into the suit Vince Peretti had gotten him for the Senate hearing, Dan headed down to the communications room to run off a few key items on the printer.

He was about to leave, then decided to check his e-mail. He scanned down a long list of consolation messages from friends about his firing at NeuroSys, then, an even longer list of congratulatory messages after his Senate hearing. One message near the bottom caught his eye: an e-mail from Vince Peretti.

Sonny Swyft was dead.

The news hit him in the gut. Yes, Sonny was a jerk, but the man didn't deserve to die. According to Vince, Sonny had taken responsibility for Dan's attempted murder and the toxic dumping, which Dan clearly knew to be false. Then, Vince warned him of the possibility of a staged suicide. That realization made his next move far more dangerous than he had anticipated. And yet, there was a certain serendipity to the moment. If he hadn't checked his e-mail, he could have walked straight into a trap unprepared.

After several minutes thinking through the ramifications, he made some last-minute tactical changes to his plan. Then, forcing himself forward, he left MOBIDIC and stepped out into the harsh light of the airfield. He searched for transportation and found Tito's familiar Toyota sitting at the far edge of camp, its warped trunk door still tied down with rope. Dan walked across the airfield quickly and slid into the backseat. The old man reacted with shock.

"*Hola,* Tito! I need a ride."

"*Señor Cleeford!* You bring doctors here, I see you on TV." Tito forced a smile.

"I need to visit the NeuroSys plant again."

Tito's smile disintegrated. "Is no good idea, *señor*! Is not safe to travel so far, and the plant *es muy peligroso*!"

"Dangerous? Why? Doesn't your daughter work there?"

"*Si.*" Tito stared at the floor.

"She's all right, isn't she?"

"*Si.* She is protected inside from the curse."

"Well, regardless of the danger, I need to get to the plant. It's important."

With more urging, Tito agreed to cooperate. The squeaky Toyota sprang to life and retraced the path they had followed on his first visit. Had it been only a week? It seemed like a lifetime ago. The vibrant market area had been transformed into a ghost town. The streets were deserted, littered with the flotsam of quick retreat.

So this is how a civilization dies.

The car reached the dirt road sooner than he expected. He refocused, ran through several scenarios in his head, plotted alternate strategies. Improvising left him feeling exposed, vulnerable. Much as he hated the limelight, his newfound celebrity could be leveraged, especially with Sonny's death all over the newswires.

Tito turned onto the paved highway leading to the security checkpoint. The car slowed at the gate and the security guard stepped out, stern-faced as usual. Dan flipped out his old NeuroSys badge.

The guard broke into a broad smile.

"Señor Clifford, so good to see you again! Thank you for bringing attention to our plight."

"Glad I could help." He felt genuine warmth from the guard, which made his next lie all the more difficult. Forcing a stern smile, he said:

"I've been sent by the Board of Directors to see how things are holding up down here."

"Really?" The guard seemed pleased, hopeful. "We are doing okay, sir. We have our own food supply. But the workers are worried for their families."

"Don't worry. The American medical team has things under control. I'll let Atlanta know that everyone at the plant is doing well, oh, and since this is a surprise visit, please keep my arrival confidential."

The guard flashed a knowing grin. "Certainly, sir." He opened the gate without hesitation.

Dan urged Tito to drive on. "Tito, what's your daughter's name?"

"Juanita."

"Is there anything you can tell me that would be helpful?"

Tito remained silent until he had pulled in front of the main entrance and parked. Then he turned around. "It is no good, this place. Beware of Señor Martin, my friend."

"That, I already know." He laughed. Tito looked particularly distraught, so Dan handed him a fifty-dollar bill. "It's *muy importante* that you stay here and keep the engine running until I return. Okay?"

"*Si.*"

At the reception desk, he recognized Benita Rosales from his last visit. Managing his best smile, Dan stepped forward and reached out to shake her hand. "Well, good morning, Benita."

She glanced up from her magazine and straightened up. "Señor Clifford! How did—"

"I hope all is well with you."

She blushed and accepted his handshake with a broad smile. "Why, thank you, sir. These are trying times, but you have given us hope."

It was his turn to blush, though it was not the impression he wanted to make. *Celebrity opens doors.* "I wanted to surprise Harry Adler. Call him for me, would you?"

Benita seemed perplexed by his request. "I'm sorry, but Señor Adler is on temporary leave. Shall I call Señor Martin?"

Dan struggled to hide his disappointment. That meant he'd have to fall back to plan B. He *hated* plan B. "No, not quite yet. I have other business here." From his jacket pocket he pulled out the business card he had printed that morning and handed it to her.

Benita stared at it for a long time, then looked up. "You're the new *president?* Congratulations, sir!"

"Yes, after the fiasco in Washington and Sonny Swyft's untimely death, the board thought it best that I come here to straighten things out. Oh, and I'll need an executive assistant. I'd like you to be that person."

Benita's smile broadened into a Cheshire grin. "Me? Why I would be *honored,* Señor Clifford!"

"Please, call me Dan," he crooned. *Amazing what a fake business card and promotion could accomplish.* His brash lie created an unavoidable reaction. Beads of sweat started erupting on his forehead. With a flourish, he grabbed the edge of the desk, pulled out a handkerchief, and dabbed the sweat away. "Please excuse me, this is a bit embarrassing. The terrible conditions in La Ceiba have left me feeling a bit queasy."

Benita instantly switched into her new supportive role. "Oh I understand, Señor Clifford . . . I mean *Dan.*" She smiled. "Can I get you anything? Contact our company medic?"

"No, no, that's not necessary," Dan smiled weakly. "You'll make a wonderful executive assistant, I can see. I just need time for my stomach to settle." He leaned in and spoke softly. "Let's keep my arrival a secret, shall we? I'll freshen up and then we'll start anew. Where is the men's room?"

"Oh, just down that hall and to the left," she said, pointing.

"Good." He held his stomach for effect. "When I get back, we'll buzz Mr. Martin and I'll make a formal announcement."

He followed Benita's directions and turned the corner, hoping no one else recognized him. Relieved to see the hall empty, he continued past the bathroom to the employee locker room.

Empty as well. *So far, so good.*

His celebrity had gotten him into the building; now he needed to regain his anonymity.

Dan rifled through the lockers, looking for the right size bunny suit. He found a medium white one in the third locker and donned it hurriedly. Benita might grow suspicious after fifteen minutes or so. That left barely enough time. After sealing the coverall, he pulled on the white overboots, and hesitated at the hood. It was his second time in one of these oppressive suits; his throat tightened as he slipped the hood in place. It couldn't be helped. No one entered the production floor without being covered from head to toe to preserve the clean-room environment.

Luckily, the bunny suit gave him a strategic advantage. Once inside, he would become invisible.

After checking the seams, he headed to the air lock door and stopped cold. His hand paused at the security keypad. There was still time to take the suit back to the lockers, find some excuse to hightail it back to the cab, and get the hell out of there. Closing his eyes, he took a deep breath and listened as the air wheezed through a filter pack on the back of his belt.

He examined the security system. As expected, access relied on a passcode. There was no fingerprint scanner, voiceprint analysis, or iris scanning, since everyone was wrapped up like a Popsicle.

But did he still have security access?

According to Rudi, the security systems had been mirrored off the Atlanta servers when the plant was moved to Honduras a year ago. His ID and passcode should be on file. It had been active on his last visit, but it could have been purged since then.

He was betting on human inefficiency. The sound of scuffling foot-steps pushed his fingers to the keyboard. An excruciating few seconds passed. No alarms sounded. Instead, he heard the sweet *thunk* of an electric dead bolt.

Dan stepped through the air lock and walked onto the floor of the massive clean room.

BENITA ROSALES FIDGETED in her seat like a child five minutes before recess. She felt as if she would explode with pride at any minute. *Executive assistant.* That would bring a hefty raise and a move to a *real* office. No more sitting in the hallway like an outcast while her friends worked in their glassed-in suites above. She'd be looking *down* on them, from an executive suite! She couldn't believe her luck, and soon that bitch Juanita would be eating her words. She was so sick of hear-ing that tart brag about her fancy clothes, her fancy office, her fancy job working for that sleazebag manager Tomás Martin.

Her boss, the famous Dan Clifford, was about to change all that!

She would have traded her rosary for a chance to see the look on Juanita's face when the news got out. Benita chuckled at the mental image and tapped her fingers on the desk. What was taking Señor Clifford so long? Smiling to herself, Benita picked up the phone and dialed Juanita's extension. Her whiny voice came onto the line almost immediately.

"Señor Martin's office," Juanita said in that haughty voice.

"It's me. Can you keep a secret? You won't believe the promotion I just got. . . ."

51

MAKING HIS EARLY-MORNING rounds at the hospital, Colonel Peterson was pleased to see that conditions had improved considerably overnight. There had been no more deaths and some of the early victims were almost ready to be discharged. The families who had accompanied them to the airfield were a different story, however. Housed in the second field hospital, they were quarantined in row upon row of plastic stalls like livestock. The rooms afforded no privacy, since they were covered in clear plastic to allow monitoring without contact, and were horribly small and barren. He scribbled some notes: *Install video monitors for entertainment. Bring movies, happy ones. Toys for children, easily disinfected.*

Learning on the job like this was awkward, but it beat the alternative, he supposed. Still, the antidote had succeeded beyond everyone's wildest expectations. He looked forward to sending everyone home in another twenty-four hours.

That left only the issue of new infections. He had issued a public decree to avoid all seafood, cooked or not, knowing that it would only be a temporary reprieve. The local economy depended on fishing, and the temptation to slip back into old habits would be hard to resist, despite the risk. People had to eat. The medical team would need to develop a permanent strategy of containment—and quickly—before the Becker Bug could spread farther down the coast.

In that sense, Dan Clifford had a point. The man certainly knew how to get under his skin, but Dan also had the irritating tendency to be right. Before they could stop the outbreak for good, they would need to know the Becker Bug's origin, understand its life cycle.

In a perfect world, Peterson would have had the authority to search out the truth, but that wasn't the world he lived in. Government agencies followed protocol. Bureaucrats had to place their stamp of approval on every detail.

Meanwhile, people died.

Washington was already breathing down his neck to complete the mission. Nevertheless, he allowed himself the luxury of basking in MOBIDIC's success, at least for now.

He pushed his concerns to the background and continued his rounds. His attention was soon diverted by the sight of Dr. Goodson running toward him from the other field hospital, out of breath and perspiring heavily.

Goodson grabbed his arm. "Colonel, there's something you need to see."

"Fine, I'll be over just as soon as I finish—"

"I think you should see this first."

A FEW MINUTES later, Colonel Peterson was standing over a portable containment unit, staring at a patient inside. The man stared back at him with desperate eyes, his body as rigid as stone. The man's clothing had been removed, except for a pair of filthy boxer shorts. Peterson noticed a faint yellow cast to the skin. A deep red hue glowed from underneath, classic signs of inflammation.

"Who is he?"

"A crew member from the garbage scow *La Cosecha Abundante,*" Goodson said as he checked the man's chart.

"The ship Clifford keeps talking about?"

"Right," Goodson said. "The local police captain, Berto Enrique, brought him and another crewman in two hours ago and impounded the ship." He pointed toward a slumped figure in the corner. "That's Berto."

"And he's been sitting here all this time?"

"Yep, quiet as a church mouse."

Peterson refocused his attention on the terrified man in the bubble. "So, this guy doesn't have the Becker Bug? What's his story?"

"I interviewed him when he came in," Goodson said. "He started itching three days ago, and by this morning it had become unbearable. That's when he asked the police chief to bring him here. The other crewman exhibits similar symptoms, though not nearly as far advanced. We have him in the onboard treatment center."

Peterson leaned over and studied the man's skin. The surface was flaky with striations that covered it like the grain of an oak table. "Damned if I've seen anything like this. You?"

"No, unless it's the world's worst case of psoriasis."

"Humph, an allergic reaction to the antidote?"

"He hasn't been given the antidote."

"No other drugs?"

"None he's admitted to."

"Then it must be unrelated to the outbreak. Ask him how he feels now."

"He quit talking an hour ago," Goodson said, a look of concern darkening his face. "Earlier he said it was too painful to move his mouth. I knew you'd want to see this."

"So how do we make a diagnosis?" Peterson pointed over toward Berto Enrique. "How's his English?"

"Pretty good."

Peterson walked over and introduced himself. The skeletal face that stared up at him gave Peterson a start. The man's eyes were sunken and lifeless, his back slumped in a way that brought an old cliché to mind. The police chief looked like he was carrying the weight of the world on his shoulders. "Captain Enrique, are you all right? My name is Colonel Peterson."

A hoarse whisper left Berto's lips. "What do you want?"

"What can you tell me about the men you brought in?"

"They're from the devil ship."

"Devil ship? Why do you call it that?"

"Because they do Satan's work, and now God is turning them to salt."

The bizarre response caught Peterson by surprise. Law officers were usually pragmatic, jaded. This guy sounded like a holy roller. Peterson needed to keep the conversation factual. "So what was this ship's port of origin?"

Berto sighed deeply as if every word was a burden. "Soluteca. The men worked the mines, until Hadan Orcus replaced the ship's crew. The bad publicity, no? He says his friends are sick too."

"On the ship?"

"No, in Soluteca."

"Is anyone else sick on board?"

Berto sat silently for a long time before speaking. "What does it matter?"

Peterson's frustration was growing. "Why would you say that? Things are getting better here. Let us help these people."

Berto's eyes grew more intense. "Do you not understand? We are all going to die."

The certainty in Berto's tone sent a shiver down Peterson's spine. He laughed nervously. "We all die sooner or later."

"Not like this," Berto said. "I was once faithless like you, steeped in my own greedy affairs, but I've seen the horror with my own eyes, witnessed the innocent carrying out the devil's work. The ancient legends are true. A new age is coming, one without man. We will all die a horrible death." Berto buried his face in his hands, sobbing. "And it is my fault!"

Peterson tried to console him, but this was not his forte. He was trained to heal the body, not the mind. "You can't blame yourself for this."

"I sold my soul to Satan!" Berto croaked between sobs. "I've known about the dumping for months. Hadan Orcus paid me to look the other way. I thought nothing of it until I saw men turned into butchers. Still, I ignored the signs, even from the Virgin herself. I burned the evidence. So many have died!"

Peterson backed away, unsure how to handle this inconsolable man who was now sobbing like a child. He moved out of Berto's earshot and whispered to Goodson, "Have we tested this guy for the Becker Bug?"

"Tests were negative," Goodson replied. "He's grief stricken. Several members of his family died in the outbreak."

Peterson ran his fingers across his forehead. "So he's got post-traumatic stress, manifesting as religious delusion. That's all we need. Pathogens aren't enough—now we've got to worry about biblical curses. Let's keep this Berto guy under observation. Give him some sedatives. I don't want him spreading panic among the other patients."

After collecting himself, Peterson returned to the sick crewman, who had remained perfectly still and unmoving—so still, in fact, that he looked like a statue, if not for the desperation in his expression. His eyes were bloodred, big as marbles, and darting wildly back and forth.

"Let's see if we can make sense of this," Peterson said, as he slipped his hands into the isolation unit's gloved ports. "Phil, pass some swabs and sample bottles through the air lock, will you? We need to get them to Marilynn for analysis, stat."

Peterson took a swab from the tray and gently ran it down the man's arm, eliciting a groan of clenched agony. The tip seemed to slide along the surface, hardly making an impression.

"This is so strange," he muttered, as he lifted the man's arm to take a swab from underneath.

The man screamed, convulsed, and exploded.

The skin burst open like a phyllo pastry, the bloody flesh underneath pushing out through the cracks like raspberry filling. The man gurgled, thrashed about uncontrollably, each movement tearing open new wounds. Peterson jerked away but his hands snagged inside the gloves. He fell backward, dragging the isolation unit off the gurney with the man still inside, jerking and twisting madly.

52

THE LAST TIME Dan had visited the chip factory, he had viewed the production floor from above. Now, seeing the activity from ground level made the scale of the plant seem even grander. He stared up at the executive skyboxes rimming the interior of the dome. For all he knew, Tomás Martin was looking down on him at this very moment, ignorant of his identity. He was just another faceless bunny suit walking the floor. That thought sent a surge of adrenaline though his body. It felt good, like a release of frustration suppressed for far too long.

This time, he was the hunter.

Dan walked briskly down a wide aisle that separated two long rows of enclosures. The glass-clad enclosure on the right contained the assembly line he had watched on the earlier visit. He was astounded to see it manned with a full complement of workers. Judging by their frenzied activity, they were oblivious to the crisis unfolding just a few miles down the road.

The left enclosure piqued his curiosity. It was taller and windowless, hiding its contents from prying eyes. He needed to find a way in there.

But first things first.

He ducked into an empty cubicle containing a low-tech production schedule on one wall, scribbled with permanent marker on a plastic sheet. Dry-erase boards were forbidden in clean rooms, their dust a contaminant. The schedule listed one hundred NeuroSys servers due for delivery in ninety days. The delivery date had been crossed out and replaced with a question mark. Dan hissed. Less than a week had passed and the GAPS contract was already delayed.

Underneath the server timeline, a new schedule had been added: *AUM modules, ASAP!! Double shifts.*

The acronym, AUM, meant nothing to him. But production had

started the day before, so it must be important. He took a cautious glance out the doorway and checked his watch. Already, seven minutes had passed. He slid into the chair and fired up the computer, working with renewed urgency.

His security login was valid, but what about data access? Probably limited. A quick browse through the directory revealed only rudimentary files, as expected. Score one for the security geeks. The employees' forum had several images from a party, news articles in Spanish, and portraits of beaming employees holding plaques. There was a menu from the cafeteria with one glaring item missing: seafood.

He browsed some more but found nothing of significance. The critical files must be hidden beyond his clearance level. That would mean using Rudi's back door. He started typing in the commands to grab root access, growing more anxious with every passing minute.

Something was wrong.

He heard muffled shouts and glanced down the hallway. One look toward the skybox confirmed his worst fear. Tomás Martin stood at the glass, screaming into a radio and gesturing at someone below. Hurried footsteps echoed down the hallway as a white-clad worker rounded the corner fifty feet away. Two security guards in orange bunny suits were pursuing him. Dan watched in horror as they pulled out handguns and fired. Two loud pops sent the running man to the floor in a convulsive heap.

No blood stained the white suit. Instead, sparks danced from projectiles that clung like burrs to the material. Dan recognized them as "sticky stunners," fired by compressed air and similar to ones used by the CBIRFs for crowd control. They were effective at close range and far cleaner than firearms, especially important in an ultraclean environment.

The guards pummeled the man with nightsticks. Only then did they turn the man over to study the face beneath the visor. They looked up at Martin and shook their heads.

Dan realized what had happened. *Benita Rosales, you're fired!*

Despite nonlethal weapons, the guards' intentions would be deadly serious. Dan fought a sudden urge to run. That would be the worst possible move.

No, he had to remain invisible in the herd of faceless white suits. Dan stepped back into the office, grabbed a clipboard from the table, and walked out, keeping his face downcast. He glanced back to see a crowd gathering around the fallen man.

The guards were up again, working their way through the group, staring into faceplates and moving on. They would have no problem recognizing the face of Dan Clifford, so recently plastered all over the evening news. He caught himself speeding up and forced a slower gait. *Remain calm, deep breaths.*

He slipped into the windowed production building and ambled down the line, pretending to inspect the work coming down the belt. They looked like control modules for the GAPS ocean AUVs. He traveled a hundred feet and exited right, heading toward a warren of office cubicles. More guards joined the hunt, conspicuous in their bright orange suits, like a pride of lions. He stopped at the edge of the cubicles and studied the main floor.

The guards were wandering through the crowd examining faces and moving on. There seemed to be no pattern or order to their actions. It seemed inefficient. They might examine the same person time and again. So what was their game?

He stared at the front air lock, guarded now by two men. At the rear of the building were two larger air locks designed for the transfer of product. Guards were posted there too. Dan suddenly understood the logic of their actions. They were beating the bushes, trying to flush their prey out into the open. And they could do it all day long, knowing he was trapped inside.

One guard randomly grabbed a worker only twenty feet away and stared into his faceplate. It was all Dan could do to stand his ground. He turned away and tried to look nonchalant. If they stumbled onto him, it was game over.

Only this wasn't a game.

He felt like a pheasant under glass. He started walking again, heading straight toward one of the emergency wash stations. Harry Adler had described them as large shower stalls with powerful water hoses, designed for decontaminating workers in case of a chemical spill.

An orange blur entered Dan's peripheral vision. A guard was heading his way, picking up speed, forcing him to speed up as well. Finally, the guard broke into a run, so he did too.

Flushed!

He threw the clipboard like a Frisbee, darted around the corner and into the wash station. He grabbed a high-pressure hose off the wall. As the guard rounded the corner, gun in hand, Dan twisted the valve all the way open. A jet of water shot through the open door and hit the startled guard with surprising force.

His gun discharged. The sticky stunner hit the floor, sending sparks of electricity up the legs of the guard's wet bunny suit. Dan dropped the hose and leapt over the stunned guard. The sudden spike of humidity in the clean room triggered alarms.

Screaming Klaxons sent a mob of white suits scrambling toward the air locks.

53

Rudi Plimpton examined the DNA chip with satisfaction. Its etched squares shimmered with iridescence like an alien chessboard, signaling matches with strands of DNA. The whole of life was made from this molecule's four basic proteins—guanine, cytosine, adenine, and thymine. They allowed four possible pairings: GC, CG, AT, and TA. The spiral ladder of the DNA molecule—the genome—was like an ancient codex, a diary of life's evolutionary history written in nature's four-letter language. How similar to a computer's binary language, Rudi mused, which used 0 and 1 to spell out everything in the digital universe.

Identifying a specific gene with this chip was simple, really. And far quicker than the PCR machines used for traditional forensic analysis. The computer took the genetic "hits" from the chip, and searched for pattern matches in MOBIDIC's genetic database, which held gene sequences for the world's deadliest microbes, for humans, and for thousands of other creatures. Even he was impressed by the technology.

"Okay," Rudi said. "She's up and running." He pressed a button. The laser printer dropped out one short page:

NeuroSys GeneScan Search
Calibration Sample
Reported: 1 hit

Classification	Percent	Common names
Escherichia coli	100%	E. coli, intestinal bacteria

Esrom picked it up and smiled. "Good work, Rudi! This is outstanding."

"Are we ready for the real thing?"

"Let's do it," Esrom said, rubbing his hands together lightly. He loaded a new DNA chip impregnated with samples of the Becker Bug.

Rudi typed a command and sat back, humming an off-key tune under his breath. Waiting was the part of computing he despised. "Okay, there it is."

Esrom eagerly grabbed the printout and stared at it, his face contorting. "This can't be right . . . you're sure the software is working?"

"Absolutely, positively, dead on," Rudi said confidently. "I'd stake my life on it."

Esrom let the paper fall from his hands. "This isn't possible—"

Colonel Peterson burst into the room wearing a blue biosafety suit with the hood folded back. "Does that thing work yet?"

"What the hell happened to you?" Esrom stared at Peterson's swollen left eye.

"Never mind that, does this thing work or not?"

"Uh, maybe. Yes—"

"Well, I need a scan of this sample. Now!" Peterson held out a sample vial. "We've got problems."

"We sure do, I think you'd better look at this—" Nessen held up the printout.

"Save it. . . ." Peterson's voice trailed off as he waddled away, looking like a fat Gumby. "If you need me, I'll be doing an autopsy."

DAN USED THE confusion from the alarms to merge into a crowd of white suits jostling for position at the front air lock door. He was anonymous again. With a little luck, he might slip past them unnoticed. The guards were holding fast though, pointing their stun guns at the crowd and refusing to let anyone through. He was now committed to the front entrance. Any attempt to leave the safety of the mob would only draw attention to himself again.

His optimism took a nosedive. How did he ever imagine this would work? The chaos had only postponed the inevitable. He needed another way out. More orange suits converged on the air locks. Tomás Martin was still standing overhead, looking down on the scene like a hawk on his perch.

He'd have to sprout wings . . .

If you can't go out, go up. Dan turned and stared at the chip camera, with its Eiffel-like tower stretching upward from the center of the dome. A gangway ran from its apex to an air lock at the skybox level.

If he could reach it . . .

Pushing to the edge of the crowd, Dan took a deep breath and ran, hoping for a few seconds' lead. He reached the tower, scrambled around the left side, grabbed the railing, and vaulted himself backward, up and over. His feet landed solidly on a huge image. It was the drawing of a computer chip the size of a basketball court. A few feet away, a plotter inched along, laying down square grids like the blocks of a city. The steel tower loomed directly overhead.

The guards reached the platform and surrounded it. One man stepped forward and spoke in English: "Señor Clifford, why don't you step down off the platform?"

"Why should I?"

"That's very expensive equipment. Do you really want to damage things? Make it worse on yourself?"

"Your guns make me nervous."

With a wave of his hand, the guard signaled the others to lower their guns. "There, is that better?"

"Yes, now back away," he ordered.

The man's smile was evident through the face mask. "You're not in a position to negotiate."

"No? And what if I just tip this machine over?" Dan moved toward the plotter.

"Stop!" The guard lurched forward, thought better of it, backed away.

Dan paused at the boundary between wet and dry ink. It suddenly dawned on him that he could be leaving his footprints on a chip that would be reduced to the size of a postage stamp and copied thousands of times. A small signature of defiance from Dan Clifford to Hadan Orcus, he mused.

"So it looks like I have a bargaining chip after all," Dan shouted. He sensed movement behind him, a guard trying to get a clear shot with the sticky stunner. It would be a shame to mess up something attached to the GAPS project, but this image didn't look like a Neuro-Sys chip to him. He watched as the English-speaking man nodded almost imperceptibly toward the man behind him.

Time to act.

Dan used the plotter as a first step and leapt toward the tower. Two distinctive pops came from behind, but he was already moving through the framework with lightning speed, climbing over, around, and under the steel trusses, keeping himself out of the line of fire. The guards still seemed hesitant to risk damage to the high-tech equipment. A quick glance down showed that he had gained fifty feet in height. The orange suits were circling the tower like maypole dancers, searching for a clear shot. He kept climbing with reckless abandon, trying not to think about falling. The words of Ben Proudfoot echoed in his mind.

Move like the mouse, nose down, one hold at time. Don't think, just climb.

A sticky stunner clanged on metal a few feet away.

It felt as if every neuron in his body fired at once. His hands went spastic and he fell several feet, jamming his groin into a junction between two trusses. A fiery pain shot through his midsection and he spewed a string of profanities as he rolled to the other side of the truss. He wavered for a second, then fought through the pain and continued on, driven by adrenaline.

Before he knew it, he was at the access ramp, clambering along its narrow track toward the upper air lock door. The orange suits had given up the hunt and were streaming out the lower air lock on an intercept course.

He could make it! He had a lead on them. If he could get to the cab . . .

He reached the spiral staircase and searched for Tito's car.

Gone!

Dan slumped to the railing and felt his energy drain away. Tito had double-crossed him, or panicked. Three stories below, a line of orange suits snaked their way up the stairs. *No use feeling sorry for yourself!* He turned and headed in the only other direction, toward the executive offices, where Tomás Martin was waiting.

The exertion fogged his faceplate. Dan ripped the hood off and gulped in sweet, cool air. Shouts echoed from behind as he raced forward.

Tomás Martin seemed intent on stopping him, a twisted grin plastered across his face. He had lowered himself into a crouch like a football player preparing for a tackle. Martin was a large man, but out of shape. This was one confrontation Dan felt confident he could win.

At the instant before they collided, Tomás leapt forward, aiming for Dan's waist. Dan timed his steps perfectly and planted his knee squarely into Tomás's jaw. The man's head snapped back, sending Tomás sprawling across the floor, out cold.

Two more pops sent stunners over Dan's head. He ducked and hurtled left around a corner. A short hallway ended at a door marked SALIDA.

He threw the door open and a blast of hot air and sunlight hit him in the face. A long, winding fire exit clung to the outside curvature of the dome. Dan ran down the steps as fast as his feet would allow, only it didn't feel fast enough. He leapt up and wrapped his arms and legs over the top of both handrails, riding them downward like a slide. By the time he heard frantic voices above, he had disappeared around the curve of the dome.

The ground loomed up suddenly as Dan jumped off the handrail and slammed into a chain-link fence. He struggled up and surveyed the area, his few seconds of lead time ticking away.

To the left, a grassy field curved downward toward a line of barracks, employee quarters, he figured. That would leave him exposed, an easy target. To his right, a stone retaining wall dropped thirty feet straight down to a loading dock at the back of the plant.

It was an easy choice. He ripped off his white booties, Italian loafers, and socks and stuffed them inside the bunny suit so as not to leave a clue to his route. Then he scrambled over the railing, dropped to the retaining wall, and slipped over the edge. It was sheer, but the wall's rough stonework provided ample foot and handholds. *This is easier than the climbing wall back home,* he thought.

He down-climbed smoothly, dropping the last six feet just as the guards reached the bottom of the fire exit. He crouched at the base of the wall. Their voices faded away down the hill. They hadn't even considered this option. With a great flood of relief and satisfaction, Dan slipped his shoes back on and turned back toward the dome.

Two green NeuroSys delivery trucks were parked at the loading dock, the same ones he'd spotted at the pier an eternity ago. They looked ready to leave.

Dan ducked behind a barrel and waited. When the dock was empty, he darted across the concrete, hooked a left into the first truck, and collided with the side of a large wooden crate. Voices approached. He squirmed into the gap between the crate and the sidewall. A leathery dockworker holding a shipping manifest grabbed the truck's rear door and pulled.

The grind of rollers on metal echoed through the walls as the packed enclosure fell into darkness.

54

PETERSON FINISHED HIS autopsy in the BSL4 chamber and washed up. He was stepping out of the air lock when Major Paxton appeared. "You're wanted outside, Colonel. We have another . . . situation."

"What now?" He climbed out of the still-dripping suit and followed Paxton outside. He was shocked to see a long line of military vehicles winding their way down the mountainside toward the airport.

"*Buenos días, señor!*"

Peterson turned to see a baby-faced Honduran man in his late twenties leaning against a nearby jeep. He was wearing a white lab coat, his arms leisurely crossed, his eyes peeking over a pair of horn-rimmed glasses. The man cheerfully extended a hand.

"It is truly a pleasure to meet you."

Peterson did not return the gesture, but studied the caravan closely. There were several heavily armored jeeps and personnel carriers mixed with a hodgepodge of vans and trucks, over thirty vehicles in all. "What the hell is this?"

"I am Dr. Dominguez from the National Medical Institute in Tegucigalpa," the man said. "We have come with our medical staff to lend aid to your operation. I must say, it is quite impressive, your MOBIDIC."

"We don't need any help."

Dominguez smiled innocently. "Ah, but you will. Your American team has done an *outstanding* job in controlling our epidemic, but we are here to relieve you."

"You want us to leave?"

"*Sí,* that is the understanding." Dominguez fished out a crumpled pouch from his pocket and offered it to the colonel.

It was an official government document transferring jurisdiction and authority to Dominguez and his team. "We're not done here," Peterson said. "You have no idea of the seriousness of the situation. We've got problems—"

"There is no problem," Dominguez insisted. "We are trained in the latest medical techniques. Just supply us your research data and I'm sure we can follow up quite well."

"We have no intention of leaving until we understand what's going on."

Dominguez seemed hurt by Peterson's outburst. "I'm sorry, but you must." He waggled the diplomatic pouch and then glanced over his shoulder at the approaching caravan. "You see, Colonel, we simply cannot have American soldiers firing their weapons at our citizens. It has caused a national uproar, no? The Hondurans here will be more comfortable, more *trustful,* of physicians from their own country."

"That couldn't be helped!" The man's thinly veiled insult boiled Peterson's blood. "We *saved* these people. Our weapons were nonlethal." He nodded toward the armored jeeps. "And what about *your* weapons, doctor?"

Dominguez simply stood and waited as if he could stand there forever, that infuriating smile welded to his face.

AN ENGINE COUGHED to life and Dan could feel the truck moving away from the dock. He should have been thrilled, knowing exactly where the truck was headed, but he was focused instead on a fresh wave of panic. Despite his daring escape from the chip factory, he was still a little kid trembling in the dark. Had he gained nothing during the past week?

This is insane!

A seething rage overtook him and he kicked the side of the crate. It felt good. Anger was good, better than fear. He kicked it again, harder this time, and felt a new flood of relief at his newfound control.

With his second kick, there was a crack of splintering wood. He bent over, his rage overtaken by curiosity. He jerked a loose board away, creating a gap just large enough to fit his arm through.

He knelt down and groped inside, like a blind man interrogating an object. What he felt was definitely not a computer. He ran his hand up and down the familiar shape, hardly believing his own senses.

This was the last thing he expected, and it changed everything.

"THEY WANT US to leave?" Michael Odom blurted. "We've barely scratched the surface!"

"We have little choice," Peterson replied. His confidence deflated, he paced restlessly in front of the media screen. "We were invited, after all. They can uninvite us anytime they wish."

"Those ungrateful blokes," Odom muttered. "We take the risks, they get the glory."

By now, the entire team had encountered the Honduran officials as they imposed their authority over every operation in camp. Frustrated and angry, they were forced to retreat to the sanctuary of MOBIDIC. Seventy-two hours of exhausting work had taken its toll on everyone except Rachel.

With another full night's rest, she felt amazingly refreshed, and eager to *do* something. She glared at Peterson. "Colonel, you can turn tail and run if you want, but I'm not leaving until I get to the bottom of Carl's murder."

"Do you think I have a choice in this matter?" Peterson said grimly.

"Yes, I do." She leaned forward defiantly. "Let me remind you of the dead senators. That's tantamount to a declaration of war."

"Ms. Sullivan, if you think you can change the president's mind, by all means try, but for now, we haven't the authority."

Rachel scanned the room, hoping for Dan's support, but he was nowhere to be found. She worried about his comment the night before: *I'm working some angles.* If another man in her life came to harm . . . she tried not to think about it, turning her attention back to the team. "Dan was right. This has the stink of Hadan Orcus all over it. He has the Honduran authorities under his thumb and he wants us out of here."

"Ms. Sullivan, I sympathize with your frustration, I really do, but we've got bigger concerns. Where's Nessen?" Peterson searched the room to no avail. "Well, I'm not waiting any longer." He sat down at the nearest terminal and typed a command. A man's nude corpse filled the monitor screen, crisscrossed with scores of ragged lacerations.

Peterson stood back up and faced the group. "I'm afraid we are confronted with a new disease." He aimed a laser pointer toward the corpse on the screen. "Cause of death was massive fluid loss and shock. This man's epidermis was totally desiccated, as brittle as a dried leaf. My autopsy indicates a fungal infection."

"I've seen fungal infections in the Amazon," Odom said. "But nothing like *that*."

"The fungus appears to attack the oil glands. Dries the skin out completely."

"Two unrelated diseases in one week?" Odom threw up his hands. "What the hell is going on?"

"I don't know—"

"You're *both* wrong," Esrom Nessen said as he entered the room. He placed a printout on the overhead projector. "Both diseases *are* related. Look at these GeneScan results."

NeuroSys GeneScan Search

Becker Bug Analysis
Reported: 6 hits

Classification	Percent	Common names
Pfiesteria piscicida	36%	predatory algae
Aquifex aeolicus	13%	extremophile bacteria
Methanococcus jannaschii	07%	extremophile bacteria
Homo sapiens	16%	human
Rosa odorata	08%	wild rose
Unclassified	28%	unknown

Unidentified Fungus Analysis
Reported: 6 hits

Classification	Percent	Common names
Pfiesteria piscicida	09%	predatory algae
Thiobacillus ferrooxidans	13%	oil oxidizing bacteria
Epidermophyton floccosum	27%	athlete's foot fungus
Methanococcus jannaschii	07%	extremophile bacteria
Homo sapiens	16%	human
Unclassified	28%	unknown

Peterson stared quizzically at the printout. "This can't be right. You still don't have this software working—"

"Oh, it's working. We've triple-checked it. These microbes share much of the same genetic structure, and what a collection! *Aeolicus* and *jannaschii* are extremophiles found in hot springs. And *odorata* is a plant, a wild rose. There are even human genes! Both microbes are laboratory chimeras, transgenic eukaryotes."

Peterson blinked, his gaze darting around the room. "I don't understand."

"Dan Clifford was right. These microbes *have* to be man-made," Esrom said. "Only a world-class genetics lab could mix this many genes together into a functioning organism." He fixed a fierce gaze on the colonel. "I ask again. Is this a Detrick experiment gone wrong? Or is Hadan Orcus developing some weapon of mass destruction?"

Peterson's jaw dropped. "I'm as surprised as the rest of you, and I resent your implication! We're on the same side here."

"How do you explain two diseases in one week?" Esrom's voice grew more strident. "Look at the genes in this latest disease: part Becker Bug, part oil-eating bacteria, part athlete's foot fungus. To me, it looks like a well-designed bioweapon."

"Why would Orcus murder Senator Becker? And all the other citizens of La Ceiba? They're just collateral damage? It just doesn't make sense."

"Perhaps to steal Becker's share of the booty," Esrom replied. "Or maybe Becker knew too much."

"Senator Becker's death was most likely an accident," Dan Clifford said.

Everyone's attention turned toward Dan, standing at the back of the room, breathing heavily and wearing a white bunny suit.

55

DAN FELT EVERY pair of eyes in MOBIDIC's conference room trained on him. Even Rachel was staring, her mouth agape. He'd caught the last part of Esrom's presentation and knew he would not be speaking to a friendly audience.

Peterson stared at Dan's clothing. "Where the hell have you been?"

Dan realized he'd forgotten to remove the bunny suit. "The chip factory."

"What?" Peterson's face reddened. "Without my authorization? Why did you—"

"Stop right there!" Dan held up a hand defiantly. "*Someone* had to get answers, so I did. I don't think Hadan Orcus is the engineer of these microbes, not directly at least."

"Weren't you the one accusing him earlier?" Peterson sputtered. "Make up your mind!"

"So I can't change my mind with new evidence? Frankly, I *hoped* Orcus was running some clandestine genetic experiment. We can stop one man, but the alternative frightens me much more." Dan paused to catch his breath, knowing the next words out of his mouth would sound ridiculous to these pathologists.

Peterson ran a hand over his closely cropped hair. "What alternative?"

"That Orcus has triggered a spontaneous outbreak of new diseases. I've read the studies in the MOBIDIC database. New diseases pop up every time humans invade a pristine ecosystem. Hadan Orcus may have done the same, and the ecosystem is fighting back."

"Back to Hadan Orcus again," Peterson said. "I didn't realize you'd become a medical expert."

"I understand complex systems," Dan shot back. "Every biological ecosystem is interconnected through a complex food web. Its creatures conspire to preserve the conditions for their own survival. If humans invade and upset the balance, microbes will fight back. The Ebola virus first emerged in Zaire after humans disrupted the local chimpanzee habitat with intense development. Ebola then jumped from chimps to humans."

Peterson's expression morphed into amusement. "Thanks for that biology lesson, Mr. Clifford. But the Ebola virus mutating is a far cry from what we're seeing here."

"Dan has a point, Colonel," Rachel interrupted. "You've heard of doomsday genes? They can trigger huge genetic changes in stressed organisms. Why not an entire ecosystem?"

"This conversation is absurd," Peterson said. "You're saying there's some local conspiracy by microbes to snuff humans out? To have a conspiracy, you need forethought. Microbes don't think."

"Mutual habits and behaviors create conspiracies," Dan said. "No conscious thinking necessary. A microbe's survival *habit* is to defend itself against invasive species. Carl Jameson left a series of clues that Rachel and I have been trying to decipher, and one of them points to his knowledge of humans triggering a doomsday event. After all, humans are the most invasive species on the planet."

"Fascinating theory," Peterson said. "There's one problem. As Esrom pointed out, it's impossible to have this level of gene sharing in a natural environment. It would be like ants and elephants deciding to crossbreed. To get this level of interchange, you'd have to have a gene-splicing laboratory."

"Things are impossible, until they're not," Dan said. "That's the essence of a black swan event."

"Colonel, you and Dan may *both* be right," said Rachel as her gaze focused on the GeneScan printout. "Look at the extremophiles on the list."

Peterson turned and stared, his expression blank. "What am I missing?"

"Several of those organisms are used for bioleaching," Rachel said. "Biological extraction of minerals from ore. Mining companies have been experimenting with them for years. What if Orcus is running his own bioleaching operation?"

"Rachel has a point," Esrom said. "Many of the extremophiles I've collected over the years have been licensed to the mining industry.

The higher the temperature, the more bioactive the microbe. If Orcus's mining operation is experimenting with bioleaching, who's to say what new chimeras he might have cooked up?"

"And these new chimeras could be exchanging genes," Peterson said, his expression registering a new understanding. He turned back to Dan. "You still haven't explained how you thought up this theory of yours in the first place."

"Part of it comes from Carl's clue," Dan said. "The rest comes from the NeuroSys chip factory. Hadan Orcus has been shipping large crates to some unknown destination, using his garbage scow— the same scow that triggered this outbreak."

"And what's in them?"

"Robots," he said. "NeuroSys robots."

"Robots?" Esrom said. "If he's using lab robots—"

"No, not laboratory robots," he replied. "Think bigger. Ten times bigger."

"I'm afraid you lost me."

"The large robots I saw, or rather felt, must be designed for one thing—mining—in places too dangerous for human workers. Like a volcano, a hot spring, or somewhere filled with noxious gases or pathogens. I'll bet there's a place like that near Soluteca."

Esrom's pale face turned a shade paler. "The west coast of Honduras *is* an active fault line. It extends all the way to Alaska, part of the Ring of Fire."

Colonel Peterson nodded almost imperceptibly. After an inordinate length of time, he spoke. "Major Paxton, how long before MOBIDIC can be packed and ready to go?"

"A few hours, sir."

"Good. I want everyone prepared to depart ASAP. Meanwhile, I have a call to make." He turned and headed toward the communications room.

AFTER THE ROOM emptied, Dan walked tentatively over to Rachel's table.

She gazed at him intensely. "I should be totally pissed at you. How could you take that risk without telling me?"

He shrugged. "I didn't want you trying to talk me out of it."

"And I would have succeeded," she said. "At least you made it back in one piece. Are you going to wear that stupid bunny suit all night?"

Dan peeled it off, revealing the infamous T-shirt, which he had worn under his suit as a defiant gesture. His coat, tie, and dress shirt were still hanging in a locker back at the chip factory.

"How did you get back?"

"Hitched a ride to the shipping docks, then had Berto's deputy drive me back."

"You'll score more points with these scientists if you rephrase your new age mumbo jumbo in more scientific terms."

Dan let out a sigh. "These *are* scientific terms. Unconventional perhaps, but no less real."

"Try being more conventional, then."

"Maybe they should be more open-minded," Dan said, frowning.

"Do you really believe your theory?"

"More or less."

"It sounds so . . . melodramatic."

"The unimaginable usually does. It demands flexible thinking." Dan looked down at his shirt. "That's the point of the medicine wheel. The truth radiates from the *center*, where many different ideas come together."

Rachel looked at him thoughtfully, smiled. "There you go with double-talk again." She placed her hand on his chest and traced the medicine wheel. "Duality," she said. "We must be yin and yang, then."

"Opposites need each other to survive. Balance of opposition, remember?" He smiled, then grew quiet for a moment. "Look, the way we left things—"

Rachel drew her finger to his lips. "Don't." She met his gaze, her expression a peculiar blend of affection and sadness. "I can never be what you want me to be."

He felt the stab of disappointment. "Don't you think Carl would want you to move on?"

She placed her hand on the side of his face, cupped his cheek. "Poor Dan. And you call yourself a prediction scientist? You know nothing."

"I know . . . enough."

"Do you?" She smiled a weak, sour smile. "Carl Jameson is my brother."

"What?"

"Well, half brother anyway." She took a long breath. "My father was a lady's man. You know, commercial airline pilot and all that. I didn't know about the affair—neither did my mother—until he mumbled something on his deathbed. I did some searching. Carl and I only knew each other for a few months. We tried to make up for a lifetime apart."

Dan was stunned. Despite all his prediction training and supposed insights, he had missed the obvious truth that had been staring him in the face. He'd let his own personal bias blind him. But the revelation posed a new question. "So then, why are you so distant?"

She squeezed his hand. "No man has ever cared for me like you, but we can never be together. I'm no good for you."

Her words pressed on him like a great weight. "I don't understand."

With that, she stood up to leave. "I don't expect you to."

DAN WAS STILL sitting alone in the conference room, trying to make sense of Rachel's cryptic statement, when Colonel Peterson burst out of the communications room, the swagger back in his step. "Mr. Clifford, it seems you'll get your wish. We're heading to Soluteca."

"How did you swing that?"

"The threat of multiple pandemics finally tipped the balance," Peterson said, his expression holding a sardonic smirk. "It appears our friend, Mr. Orcus, is getting a taste of his own medicine. This new fungal disease is spreading rapidly through his mines in Soluteca. The president called the Honduran consulate and threatened a permanent food embargo. We've been given provisional authority to investigate this new epidemic."

Peterson hurried out to tell the others, prompting Dan to visit the communications room himself. The colonel was right about one thing: MOBIDIC employed doctors, not detectives. Orcus had outmaneuvered them in La Ceiba already and Dan couldn't allow that to happen again in Soluteca.

He needed to call in an insurance policy.

56

THE SOLUTECA AIRPORT seemed a world away from the dreary coastal village of La Ceiba. It was equipped with a futuristic control tower and international terminal, both clad in acres of black glass. Airplanes of all sizes dotted the landscape, the runways long enough to accommodate the largest commercial jets. Before MOBIDIC had even rolled to a stop, a line of yellow Humvees undulated across the tarmac like a python.

Esrom Nessen and Rachel entered the conference room, dressed for hot weather. Esrom was almost invisible underneath a billowing white shirt and straw hat. Rachel, wearing her khaki shorts, seemed energized, showing little evidence of her recent illness. She met Dan's gaze for a split second and looked away toward the video monitors.

Peterson soon joined them, wearing full dress uniform. "You guys look like you're going on a safari."

"We are," Esrom replied. "We're on the prowl for microbes. The hot springs along the coast could provide sanctuary for these heat-loving microbes."

"Any progress on a treatment for the skin fungus?"

"As a matter of fact, yes," Esrom said, beaming. "Clotrimazole. We mixed up an aerosol and misted the surviving crewman from the garbage scow. He's shown marked improvement."

"Marvelous news!" Peterson let out a sigh of relief. "We've been damn lucky so far. Both diseases have responded to treatments in our arsenal."

"Let's hope our luck holds out then," Nessen said. He grabbed Rachel's arm. "Come on. We won't find answers by sitting around."

"I agree." Peterson tucked his hat under his arm and followed them toward the elevator. "I have an appointment with the infamous Hadan Orcus."

Dan stood up. "I'm coming with you."

"I don't think that's wise."

"Why not? Orcus tried to kill me, remember? I should have the right to confront my enemy."

Peterson gave him a bemused look. "You're constantly surprising me, Mr. Clifford. Can I trust you to control your temper? This is a fact-finding mission."

"I know more facts about Orcus than anyone."

Peterson appeared to consider Dan's words. "True. Perhaps your presence will throw the man off guard."

As soon as they stepped off the plane, Dan and the colonel were greeted by a contingent of Solá representatives. A stiff man in a dark suit waved them toward a shiny yellow Humvee with the logo of Solá Mining emblazoned across its side. Peterson waved him off. "We have our own transportation."

"Mr. Orcus insists," the man said coldly. "You are our guests. I will ensure you safe passage to his residence." He opened the passenger door.

Peterson shrugged. "Come on. Our chariot awaits."

The Humvee wound its way out of the airport and along the coastal highway, taking them past rows of million-dollar condominiums. The white sand beach must have been shipped in, because Dan could see the native shoreline farther north: an ugly black volcanic pumice. In the distance, faint wisps of steam drifted out to sea from hot springs.

Soluteca itself was a cluster of glass- and steel-clad skyscrapers, packed into a narrow valley like crystalline shards. None of the buildings were more than a few years old. Dan could scarcely imagine the wealth required to construct such a metropolis, wealth that must have come from Hadan Orcus's mines.

The jeep left the cityscape behind and turned toward the fenced entrance of a large harbor crammed with container ships, sailboats, and yachts. Across the bay, Dan spotted what had to be Orcus's compound, nestled halfway up the slope of an ancient volcano, blazing bright yellow against the verdant green of the forest. It was impossible to miss.

The jeep jerked to a stop and let them out alongside an eighty-foot yacht. The driver led them through a security checkpoint onto the foredeck. He motioned toward an elaborate mahogany bar. "A drink perhaps?"

"I'll take a scotch, straight up," Peterson said. "Dan?"

"Nothing for me, thanks."

Ten minutes later, the yacht had reached its destination and tied up at a pier blasted into the base of Mt. Cosegüina. Dan and Peterson climbed into a small electric cart that quietly labored up a winding road toward the compound, passing several guard posts along the way.

The narrow track eventually opened onto a wide vista filled with gardens, topiary, and elaborate fountains. But the compound itself commanded the scene: it was huge, with stuccoed walls and ornate cornice work, all painted yellow. The baroque detailing clashed with the clay tile roof and Latin American architectural influence.

Dan chuckled under his breath. "This guy is a master of understatement."

Peterson gave a slight shake of his head, grimaced.

The cart stopped in front of a hand-carved mahogany door. A man in a tuxedo greeted them with a flourish. "Good afternoon, gentlemen, I'm Señor Delgado, *patrón* of the estate. I hope you had a pleasant journey. Please follow me."

Dan and the colonel looked at each other tentatively, and followed.

The opulence of the compound was both amusing and disgusting. They strolled past several rooms of elaborately detailed antiques of ancient Mediterranean and European origin. Dan had only seen such decadence in the pages of *Architectural Digest* magazine: rows of black Vienna chinoiserie porcelain jugs, a medieval oak chest with scrolling strap-work and huge escutcheon, a carved walnut dining table with lyre-shaped legs and wrought-iron stretchers, a wall of centuries-old antique tapestries. It was like walking through a Liberace museum.

Delgado led them to an elevator. After a brief trip, it opened onto a large tiled veranda. He motioned them forward, then quickly disappeared. The veranda was flanked on both sides by long rows of flowerpots cast in the shape of Mayan figureheads, each one spilling over with rosebushes of every imaginable color.

As they walked forward, a breeze caught the scent from a large trash bin filled with half-rotted cuttings from hundreds of rosebushes. Dan faltered. "That's it . . . the smell from Rachel's lab."

"Are you sure?"

"Believe me, I will never forget that smell."

Straight ahead at the end of the gauntlet stood a man in a gardening apron, humming to himself as he trimmed leaves from a rosebush. He beckoned them forward. Their footsteps echoed across the tile floor.

"Ah, Colonel Peterson," Orcus said, stepping away from the pot with a red rose in hand. "And *you* must be Mr. Clifford. I'm surprised you have the gall to show your face here. You've cost my company *billions*."

Dan stood quietly for a moment, studying the man. Orcus was surprisingly tall, with broad shoulders and wide, square cheekbones. But it was the calm gaze of his intense blue eyes that triggered a silent rage within him. "You accuse me?" he snapped, his face tightening. "You've cost *lives*."

Orcus seemed amused. "Mr. Clifford, the world is filled with petty little men like yourself, drowning in envy of those who achieve greatness." He swung his hand across the horizon. "Look around you. *I* create; *you* destroy. I have conquered unimaginable adversity to build a thriving community here. What have you done? Created a computer virus? Impugned my reputation?"

"Save your bullshit for some other gullible fool," Dan hissed. A ball of anger knotted in his chest and he stepped forward brazenly. "Your captain tried to kill me!"

Orcus was a good foot taller, but Dan's sudden aggressiveness surprised him. Orcus backed away, smiling thinly. "Ahh, my ship captain. I can understand your frustration, but even an organization such as mine has its rogues. I apologize for my misguided employee. He was hired to ship wastes to an official dumping site, but I'm afraid he chose a shortcut. It's regrettable, but we have fired him and launched a full investigation—"

"Regrettable? Is that what you call the murder of Carl Jameson?"

Peterson stepped in between them. "Just what kind of wastes were you shipping?"

Orcus smiled at the intervention and relaxed somewhat. "Oh, tailings from our gold mining operations and miscellaneous garbage. We also have disposal contracts with several companies, including this estate, in fact."

"We believe your so-called wastes have caused the deaths of two American senators and scores of people in La Ceiba."

"Really?" Orcus seemed resigned to Peterson's accusations. "You're not the first person to try and pin blame for Becker's death on me. And what possible connection could there be between an epidemic and my mining operations? It's preposterous!"

Peterson counted on his fingers. "Deaths in Washington from seafood *you* provided, deaths in La Ceiba near *your* dumping site, then a new illness right here in *your* mining camp. Should I go on?"

"I resent your accusations," Orcus said, his eyes narrowing. "I'm aware of the illnesses. So what? The natives here have terrible hygiene, constantly coming down with one illness or another. They're still better off than a decade ago. I transformed them from a bunch of illiterate savages into productive workers."

"Productive for you maybe," Dan growled. "You talk about them like they're cattle."

"Enough of this." Peterson edged forward. "I'm not here to discuss philosophy. I've been sent by the president of the United States to determine the cause of these outbreaks, and that's what I intend to do. You have an investment in NeuroSys, do you not?"

Orcus drew the rose to his nostrils, closed his eyes, and inhaled slowly. He looked up, eyes glistening. "Colonel Peterson, I'm a very rich man. I have investments in hundreds of companies. What possible motivation would I have for developing diseases? As Mr. Clifford seems so eager to point out, my interest lies in making money. I cannot do that if I kill my own workers, or senators who support my cause."

"So you're not experimenting with bioleaching?" Dan said.

Orcus seemed shocked by the question, a hint of concern rippling his brow for the first time. "What does that have to do with the current situation? Yes, we have a pilot program at our gold refinery, using bacteria to precipitate gold from our tailings. Perfectly harmless and proprietary, I might add. We are very environmentally aware."

"Is that why you engineered your precious roses into the Becker Bug?" Dan stepped forward again until his face was only inches away from Orcus. "In hopes of covering over the stench of your character?"

Orcus just stared, slack-jawed. "I haven't the faintest idea what you're talking about."

Peterson grabbed Dan's belt and forcibly pulled him back. "We'd like samples from your bioleaching operations, if you don't mind," Peterson said with a smile.

Orcus's demeanor changed dramatically. "Do you think me a fool? You are looking to assign blame. I'm afraid this conversation is over." He placed a cell phone call and turned back. "When you are done treating my workers, I expect you to leave Soluteca immediately."

"We'll leave when we're damn good and ready," Peterson said.

Delgado arrived to lead them away. As they left, Dan turned and studied Orcus over his shoulder. The man's expression was calm, defiant, his lip curled in satisfaction. Peterson's fact-finding mission had lasted but a moment, and it felt like Orcus had won the exchange. Orcus had admitted nothing, revealed little about his operations. Dan wanted Orcus to know that *he* knew. He turned and strode back until he was close enough to see the veins in Orcus's eyes. "With all the *billions* you've lost, thanks to me, I imagine you're eager to expand your mining operations into new areas."

Orcus's pupils dilated. "Your point? I'm always expanding."

"Why ship your tailings all the way through the Panama Canal, and pay those expensive fees? Why invest in a billion-dollar chip factory? That is, unless you needed something they manufacture . . . something like, say . . . huge robots the size of a car? With all these industrious workers, why would you need robots?"

Orcus glared at him intensely, a look of concern unmistakable in his expression. Unwilling to unlock his gaze, Orcus pointed back toward the elevator. "Señor Delgado will see you back to your plane."

DURING THE YACHT ride back to shore, Peterson sat stiffly, not uttering a word. When they reached the dock and stepped off the boat, he turned to Dan with a stern look. "Mr. Clifford, as I feared, you are incapable of keeping your emotions in check. Did I not tell you to let me take the lead? Now, I fear we know little more than we did before!"

This time, Dan didn't feel a hint of regret. "On the contrary, Colonel, we know a lot. We now have a direct link between Orcus and the Becker Bug. Those roses are the smoking gun. We've also confirmed his bioleaching operation, which provides a link between his mining operation and genetic engineering. We also know he's extremely concerned about his new mining toys, judging from the expression he gave me. And most importantly," Dan continued, gently pulling Peterson aside, away from their transportation back to the plane, "we now know that Orcus doesn't have a clue what the hell he's doing."

57

Eyes closed, Rachel turned to face the sun, reveling in its warmth against her skin. After her ordeal, she always welcomed the sunlight and fresh air. Directly behind the Solá Mining jeep, she could hear the throaty growl of the CBIRFs' Mobile Medic Mentoring Vehicle. Esrom was chattering about the wealth of Soluteca, but Rachel's thoughts were focused elsewhere—on Dan Clifford and the hollowness she felt. *Where's the old Ironsides Sullivan?* Carl had understood her need for emotional distance. Now, surrounded by her peers, Rachel felt totally and desperately alone.

She hungered for Dan's companionship, his ability to both comfort and amuse her. But she knew Dan would not be equipped to deal with the future that lay before her. A wave of grief swept over her. She sat up, rubbed her eyes, and tried to push her emotions back under the surface.

The jeep turned onto a narrow road that hugged the coastal plain and headed north. Skyscrapers gave way to grassy suburbs, then to clusters of industrial buildings. The road turned to gravel; soon, they were enveloped in a cloud of fine dust.

The verdant wall of vegetation near the city's edge thinned, leaving the road's left bank barren down to the shoreline. Clusters of shacks crowded the trail. Children playing in hardscrabble yards stopped to stare as the jeep passed.

"Look, over there!" Esrom pointed excitedly toward a cloud of steam. "Stop!" He jabbed the driver repeatedly in the back, to no avail.

Rachel leaned forward and barked at him in Spanish. Reluctantly, the driver pulled over. Esrom jumped out, slipped on tall wading boots, and grabbed his sampling equipment. He looked across a field of steaming mud that extended for miles along the shore. The skeletons of dead trees bleached white by steam draped their craggy limbs over the edge of the hot spring.

"My God," said Rachel. "It's huge. We could take samples here for a month and not get everything."

"This area should be teeming with thermophilic bacteria. Rachel, would you hand me that gas mask?" Esrom pulled it on and headed off toward the muck.

Rachel jumped out, intent on following him, but stopped short. Her legs felt heavy, anchored to the ground. A wave of nausea and panic passed through her. *What's wrong with me?* Try as she might, she couldn't shake the feeling of paralyzing fear.

Esrom glanced back expectantly.

She looked past him toward the endless pools of bubbling mud, perhaps the home of her nemesis, the Becker Bug. "I, uh, can you do this without me?"

Esrom shrugged. "Certainly, I've had lots of practice." He moved to the edge, poked his sampling pole into a mound of reddish bacteria, and transferred it to a sample bottle. Then he worked his way down the line of springs until every bottle was full.

She watched from the jeep, her face burning with embarrassment.

Fifteen minutes later, Esrom returned and dropped his gear into a bucket of bleach. Rachel sprayed the samples and Esrom with a fine mist of chlorinated disinfectant.

Back in the jeep, he turned to her: "You okay?"

"I don't know what happened."

"For heaven's sake, Rachel, after your recent ordeal, you should take it easy."

But Rachel vowed silently not to let it happen again.

A mile later, the jeep passed through a security checkpoint and twisted along a serpentine road for another thirty minutes, finally stopping at a large canyon. Relieved to be away from the mud pits, Rachel joined Esrom at its precipitous edge. They stared over the rim, unprepared for the vastness below.

A ragged strip mine stretched for miles toward the horizon, pushing its tendrils farther and farther into the surrounding jungle. Like a scene from the apocalypse, the raw soil had been stripped of every tree and blade of grass. Columns of sulfurous fumes rose from widely spaced cracks along the canyon's length: gases escaping from the fault line that paralleled the entire coast of South America. Huge bulldozers scooped shovel loads of ore from the canyon floor and dumped them into a line of earthmovers. Higher up the canyon wall, clay-smeared workers hacked at the soil with shovels and pickaxes. They toiled feverishly, their only relief a drink of water from a bucket strapped to the back of a stoop-shouldered man. Suddenly, two house-sized earthmovers roared down the canyon, throwing up a wall of dust that obscured their view of the activity below.

Rachel coughed, swiped in vain at the fine red clay that settled on her clothes, skin, and lips. She could literally taste the mine, its sour flavor an echo of the destruction that lay before them. Shielding her eyes from the sun, she searched each piece of machinery. "I don't see any robotics, do you?"

"No," Esrom said and swiped at his pants with the straw hat. "Come on, let's go find our patients."

A few paces farther down the canyon rim, the driver directed them toward a ramshackle building with a red cross painted on the wall. The M3V had already parked there. Inside, they found thirty workers on straw cots, all exhibiting signs of the fungal infection. Some were in advanced stages, with weeping sores where their dry skin had ruptured. The CBIRFs worked down each row, spraying the tortured patients with the clotrimazole solution and applying antiseptic cream to their wounds.

Esrom and Rachel moved outside, eager to avoid donning the sweltering MOPP gear. While Rachel stopped to talk with the field nurse, Esrom took a seat at a nearby picnic table and fanned himself furiously with his straw hat.

When Rachel joined him, he gasped: "I can't believe the temperature here! If those victims don't die from the fungus, they'll expire from heat prostration."

"The nurse told me something interesting," Rachel said. "All the victims were working in the gold extraction plant just before they got sick." She pointed toward a large building near the water's edge. A long pier jutted out from its backside into the bay. The building was heavily fortified with barbed wire and several guards patrolled the perimeter with security dogs.

Esrom's gaze fell on a line of cylindrical tanks lining a square holding pond. "See over there? That looks like a bacterial reclamation plant."

Rachel shielded her eyes. "That would be a perfect breeding ground for mutant microbes."

"All right then." Esrom stood up. "Tell our friend we want to go down there."

The driver refused at first, insisting that the area was strictly off limits. After several thinly veiled threats, Rachel managed to bargain for samples from the tailing pond, since it was outside the secure area. The jeep stopped alongside the road and Esrom scrambled down the hill, collecting another round of samples from the pond. When he returned, they decided to head back, leaving the CBIRFs to finish up treatment.

On their return trip, Rachel studied the scenery more closely. It was like traveling forward in a time machine—moving from the squalor of the mining town to the modern extravagance of the city.

Just as the jeep turned in to the airport entrance, the engine began to vibrate. It traveled another hundred yards or so, shuddered, and stalled. An acrid cloud of blue smoke billowed from the engine compartment.

"Now what?" Esrom grumbled. "It's hot as hell and no breeze."

The driver hopped out and lifted the hood. He was hidden from view, but Rachel could hear an endless string of obscenities as he fumbled with the engine. Abruptly, the cursing stopped. After a long pause, the man uttered one final phrase in frenetic Spanish, crossed himself, and bolted off toward the woods.

"What the—" Esrom watched helplessly as the man crossed the asphalt drive, leapt over a chain-link fence, and disappeared into the vegetation. "What did he say?"

Rachel shook her head. "I think he said something like 'blood of the lamb.'"

They clambered out and moved toward the front of the vehicle. Rounding the front bumper, Rachel felt a cold shiver run up her spine. Smoke still curled up from the engine, its pops and cracks the only sound in the thickening air.

Esrom edged closer, beads of sweat popping out on his pale brow. He stopped abruptly. "You smell that?"

"Yeah, rotten eggs."

He pushed Rachel away. "Get me some gloves and a sample bottle, will you?"

Rachel gladly retreated, her heart hammering against her rib cage. She returned with the bottle and handed it to Esrom. He donned gloves and lifted the oil dipstick. Holding it at an angle, Esrom stared at the thin metal with rapt fascination.

A single droplet of viscous, crimson fluid swelled at its tip and dropped into the sample bottle.

58

HIDDEN IN THE shadows of the La Ceiba pier, Duff McAlister leaned back and watched the activities on the garbage scow with bitter curiosity. Sunlight glinted off the surface of his diving knife as he twirled the cold steel between his fingers with practiced dexterity. The pier was hauntingly quiet, as quiet as he could remember. The local fishermen had abandoned their boats, leaving them to bob and creak against their riggings. No one knew how long the edict against fishing would last. But it was already too late. The epidemic had brought death to the town and to the local economy.

Eventually, the pestilence would spread to his resort.

The only sounds of significance came from the garbage scow. Despite Berto Enrique's best efforts, Hadan Orcus had managed to negotiate the release of his vessel from impound. His army of lawyers obviously had distributed the requisite bribes. Now, a fresh crew of workers hurried to load the last of several large crates onto the foredeck. There would be no drums of toxic material on this voyage. The vessel was empty except for the crates and a contingent of armed guards. If Dan Clifford was right about the crates containing robotic machinery, then they were critical to some operation.

And Duff planned to find out why.

The call from Dan had been a welcome surprise. They had shared news, guessed at possible motives. He'd eagerly agreed to offer his services to the cause, just like the old military days, before life got complicated. If he had anything to do with it, this devil ship would never drop another drum of waste near his resort.

Once the last crate was secured, the crew released the hawsers and put out to sea. Duff sat up and waited a few minutes before starting up *Little Diver*'s engines. He kept his running lights off and followed from a safe distance, steeling himself for a long trip, determined to see it through, no matter where it took him.

"WHAT THE HELL'S happening now?" Peterson's fist slammed against the conference table, sending coffee mugs skittering across the lacquered surface. "How can we have *another* new microbe?" Peterson stared at the new image. "How could this organism attack an automobile?"

Esrom scanned the latest GeneScan report. "Well, it's got a similar genetic structure to the other two, so it had to come from the same source. But this one's a *hyper*thermophile, highly resistant to heat, which explains its ability to survive inside a car engine. And it's got an appetite for oil, like the skin fungus. It *consumed* the oil, creating hydrogen sulfide as a waste product, which explains the terrible rotting odor."

"Here's something interesting." Rachel spread all three GeneScan reports on the table. "These microbes are similar to one another, *relatives*. And they're chimeras, with a mixture of genes from many different species. But get this: all three contain the same *exact* percentage of *human* genes. What do you make of that?"

Peterson took a long draw of coffee and grimaced. "Hell if I know. There doesn't seem to be any rhyme or reason to these creatures."

"Maybe there is," Rachel replied. "*Pfiesteria* is an ocean algae picked up and dumped in bilge water. The athlete's foot fungus, the human genes—they're common to the human workers. The thermophiles live in nearby hot springs. The oil-eating bacteria could come from the oil tankers we saw anchored in the bay."

"And don't forget the rose genes," Dan added. "I saw cuttings at the Orcus compound. He mentioned that his garbage gets dumped along with all the other waste."

"Exactly," Rachel said. "These creatures didn't have to come from a laboratory; they're all right here, right around the processing plant."

"Your point?" said Peterson.

"Dan was right. This looks like classic gene sharing. All these microbes mixing in this one area, stressed, their natural habitats destroyed. Then their doomsday genes get triggered somehow."

"That still doesn't explain how the chimeras were created in the

first place," Esrom said. "There would have to be some major new genetic splicer to cause such rampant promiscuity among species."

Rachel thought for a moment. "Esrom, what about the gene-
splicing bacteria you collected in Yellowstone? We have hot springs
here. Maybe Orcus uncovered some super gene splicer while breeding
his bioleaching microbes. And you know he'd be trying them out on
his own ore. What better mixing pot than a gold extraction plant?"

Peterson drummed his fingers on the table, a worried look etched
on his face. "Let's hope you're wrong, or we're in deep trouble. A
supersplicer would mean new diseases evolving at an exponential rate.
Eventually, we'll encounter a disease we can't cure."

"It sounds crazy," Rachel said. "But we have to check it out, don't
we?"

Esrom fanned through an inventory report. "If a supersplicer exists, it should be easy to find—in the water from the tailing pond, the
hot springs, and in your samples from Orcus's garbage scow. And we
have all of them on board MOBIDIC."

Peterson listened attentively. "You've convinced me. Check it out,
quickly."

Rachel grinned, gathered her papers, and rushed out, along with
Marilynn Archer and Dr. Nessen.

That left Dan, the colonel, and Rudi Plimpton at the table.

Peterson turned to Dan. "Looks like you're gathering converts to
your doomsday cult, Mr. Clifford."

"It's not a cult if it's true." Dan offered a thin smile. "Sometimes
our familiarity with the normal blinds us to the *abnormal*. Our expertise works against us. I just wanted to look at things with fresh eyes.
Try to imagine the unimaginable."

"Well, I'm having a hard time seeing how this puzzle fits together.
Whatever happened to your robots? Esrom says he saw no robotics
at the gold fields."

"They're around somewhere. When I confronted Orcus, I saw
stark fear in his eyes when I mentioned them. We're close."

"Perhaps." Peterson's attention wandered for a moment. "We have
another problem brewing. The driver has been spreading panic over
the jeep incident. We've been monitoring the local news and the mine
workers believe this is some biblical curse. They're flooding the
churches, preparing for Armageddon."

"Most Hondurans are Catholics," Dan said. "Religion is just another way to explain the unknown. Moses took advantage of that. He demanded the King of Egypt release the Jews from slavery or the rivers would run red with blood, which was an excellent bluff on his part. The Egyptian rivers were polluted sewers. It was probably the first recorded description of a red tide."

"Debunking the Bible now?" Peterson managed a chuckle. "I can't wait to hear your explanation for the parting of the Red Sea. . . ."

Dan wasn't listening. The theological discussion had triggered a thought that had been nagging him. It fluttered in his brain like a butterfly, faded, and vanished before he could grasp its essence. He let out a sigh of frustration.

It was followed by a loud burp from Rudi Plimpton, who was wolfing down a plate of microwave pasta with quirky efficiency.

"How can you have an appetite after all this doom and gloom?"

"Hey, if I'm gonna die, let it be on a full stomach. Besides, I've been digesting the genetic data for an hour." Rudi laughed at his own joke.

Quirky or not, Rudi had a way of stripping life to its essence. The ethereal thought fluttered back through Dan's mind. "The GeneScan software," he said. "You never told me how you fixed it."

"Elementary, my dear Clifford. The boneheads at NeuroSys were too literal with their programming. They tried to find *exact* matches to DNA sequences, but that's bogus. DNA mutates constantly, so the program was missing critical hits."

"And?" Dan squirmed in his seat, his sense of déjà vu intensifying.

"I looked for gene patterns with *similar* meanings, instead of exact matches. Voila! A genetic thesaurus."

Dan jumped up. "That's it! Thanks, Rudi!"

"Thanks for what?" Rudi looked up, but Dan had already vanished.

As RACHEL WORKED the controls of the BSL4 telepresence equipment, she began to feel useful again. She was eager to contribute, to finally study her original samples from *SeaZee*. Fortunately, Dr. Goodson had taken them onboard MOBIDIC, having brought them all the way from the *Sea Berth*.

Her panic attack still haunted her. In fact, everything seemed out of kilter. The events prior to her coma were a distant past life.

Is this how it starts? Losing self-control? Today, standing near that field of steaming springs, she'd lost it. She knew what would come next, but her thoughts returned to Dan Clifford. She wanted his support and intimacy, but reminded herself to stay strong . . . for him. Perhaps one day she would be able to explain.

But not right now.

She maneuvered the robotic arms to a thawing chamber and removed a defrosted sample, still sealed in its original stainless steel flask. She unscrewed the lid, sucked up a column of brown sludge with a pipette, and squirted it into two vials: one for her and one for Marilynn Archer. Marilynn's robot graciously accepted the gift and moved down the aisle to inoculate culture trays. Rachel's job was to separate different strains of microbes, like herding sheep and cows into different pens.

Rachel placed a droplet from her vial on a wet slide and loaded the video microscope. Hundreds of transparent shapes jerked and bobbed across the screen. This image confirmed her original hypothesis. On the dive to the toxic dumping field, she had spotted mats of flocculent bacteria thriving in the sludge from hundreds of barrels of toxic waste. Now she was seeing the proof up close and personal.

There was no doubt—these microbes were extremophiles.

The tiny creatures' transparent bodies made them nearly invisible, so Rachel added a drop of fluorochrome dye, designed to stain the microbe's internal parts. An ultraviolet light would cause the stain to glow, immensely increasing the contrast of the image. The result was essentially a poor man's electron microscope, only faster and easier to use.

She moved the sample back and forth, a micrometer at a time, searching for a familiar shape in the ooze. After several minutes of intense examination, she spotted her quarry and flipped on the ultraviolet light. The organelles inside its circular body glowed like Christmas lights.

It was a perfect match to the Becker Bug.

"Bingo!" she shouted. "I've got it—straight from a drum labeled with Solá Mining's logo! That places the Becker Bug directly inside Hadan Orcus's extraction plant."

"Good work!" Marilynn exclaimed from the adjacent cubicle. "Now we need to find the mechanism of change—"

A sudden movement caught Rachel's eye. "Did you see that?"

"See what?"

"*That*," Rachel said, pointing toward the video monitor.

The Becker Bug had vanished, leaving a ragged sliver of glowing endoplasm behind.

Marilynn shrugged.

"Can you rewind the video?"

"Sure." Marilynn went back about sixty seconds.

An incredible scene unfolded. They rewound it and watched again . . . and again.

An electric surge of emotion—a mix of wonder and terror—gripped her. Rachel suddenly understood the full nuance of Carl's clue, plucked from the center of his T-shirt.

The trickster had pulled the ultimate con on them all.

Tears welling in her eyes, she focused on the distant reaches of the BSL4 chamber, at the incredibly tiny thing on the slide, a discovery as grand as Earth itself. She thought of Carl's epiphany, and how he would have felt.

Finally, Rachel broke free of her trance and whispered: "Did you see what I saw?"

"I think so," said Marilynn breathlessly.

"Get Peterson and Nessen down here, *now*."

59

BURSTING WITH ANTICIPATION, Dan collapsed on his bed with a copy of *Neuvo Testamento.*

It was a bilingual edition of the New Testament, a softback he had found in his nightstand. It had English and Spanish translations side by side, and it was Catholic, the critical detail he had overlooked during his earlier Internet search back at Duff's cabin.

He flipped through the pages, scanning for a familiar cluster of words. After an hour, his eyes began to glaze over. At this rate, it would take days to find anything. On a hunch, he jumped to the end, to Revelations, and worked backward.

In a few minutes, his eyes fell on a phrase that seemed to leap from the page. He pressed a trembling finger against the onionskin and forced his eyes to focus. The room began to fade and he realized he was hyperventilating. Dropping back against the headboard, he forced long slow breaths, and counted back slowly . . . from ten to one.

THE AIR, SOUR from the sharing of breaths, hung around the huddled research team like a fog. They had formed a semicircle around Rachel, leaning in eagerly to view the action. No one spoke as she worked the video controls. They just watched, breathing collectively.

The first video clip ended and Rachel queued up the second one. "The first time this happened so suddenly," she said, "that we couldn't follow the action. This time we tracked it."

She pushed Play.

A single cell—another Becker Bug microbe—filled the screen. The muddy details soon brightened as the microscope's ultraviolet lamp bathed the cell in a purple glow. After a minute, the microbe stirred and began undulating like a termite queen. The darkened nucleus at its center migrated to one end and exploded through the cell wall like a shot from a cannon. Without its core, the empty cell imploded into a heap of cytoplasm.

The inexplicable event drew a startled gasp from the onlookers. To their amazement, the naked nucleus sprouted a spinning appendage that pushed it along with surprising speed. The video jerked along, as Rachel followed the action with the microscope's controls. After several minutes, the nucleus slowed and bumped into a large, oblong bacterium.

"This is where it gets *really* interesting," Rachel said, her voice trembling.

The naked nucleus slid alongside the bacterium. After a few seconds, the much larger bacterium seemed to recognize the intruder's presence and extended a proboscis. It touched the dark blob and spread outward, engulfing it. But, instead of digesting its meal, the bacterium became docile and passive.

A low murmur rippled through the onlookers.

"Now watch." Rachel fast-forwarded the tape. "The bacterium never kills its prey," she said. "Instead, it's been transformed, see? The two microbes are working together, as one, a new creature altogether—a chimera. And look, it's reproducing."

"I'll be damned," Esrom Nessen muttered. "No wonder we couldn't find it. The microbe was hiding *inside* the cells, like a virus."

"Yes, but *not* a virus. It doesn't kill its host, it *merges* with it."

"So we don't have three diseases after all, just one—a cell parasite."

"No, not a parasite either . . . a *symbiont*," Rachel continued excitedly, "merging with other microbes, *shape-shifting*, creating entirely new hybrid organisms."

She paused for a moment, deep in thought. Then she continued, talking to herself in an excited frenzy. "*That's* what Carl was trying to tell us when he removed the center of the medicine wheel! We were thinking too abstractly about the trickster, but Carl was thinking *literally*. The truth was *right there*, before our eyes. This creature *is* the trickster, the nucleus of a cell, sitting at the center of everything."

Colonel Peterson, his face flushed, straightened up. "Rachel, I didn't understand a word you just said, but one thing is frighteningly clear. We have a creature here that is an evolution machine run wild—a disease maker. It could create *millions* of new diseases!"

"There's a bright side, Colonel," Marilynn Archer interjected. "This thing has an Achilles' heel."

"Oh?" Peterson perked up. "*Please* . . . give me some good news!"

"The microscope's ultraviolet light triggered the symbiont's behavior," Marilynn explained. "UV destroys cell membranes, so it's a survival response. The creature searches for a new and better home, shelter from the storm, so to speak. It's like a panhandler, collecting genes and trading them to new hosts in exchange for a new home. The symbiont gets protection—the host gets new genetic capabilities."

"That's not making me feel any better, Marilynn. What's the *good* news?"

"We couldn't reproduce this effect with the other cultures," Marilynn said. "Only the sample from Rachel's dive to the abyssal plain."

"I don't understand."

"After several reproductive cycles, the symbiont becomes *permanently* dependent on its host. It's trapped. Rachel's sample must have contained virgin symbionts only a few generations removed from their original environment. That environment must have been someplace hidden from sunlight, like the dump site. When the men from Solá dumped the material overboard, some of it mingled with *Pfiesteria* at the surface, probably from their own bilge water. The next morning, the sun came up, and *bam*—instant evolution. The shrimp ate the new organism and passed it up the food chain."

"So it peters out after a few generations?"

"Exactly." Marilynn grinned triumphantly. "That's why we haven't seen a thousand new life forms. We just need to find the microbe's original home, and *contain* it."

"I still don't understand one thing," Esrom interjected. "If this isn't man-made, then why the human genes in all three samples?"

"Because we had it *backward*," Rachel explained. "They're not *our* genes. They're *its* genes. The genes we inherited from this symbiont three billion years ago! This naked nucleus is our ancestor—*the mother of the first nucleated cell*—the first eukaryote."

Her excitement increased as she continued. "Early in Earth's history, most life was made up of simple bacteria, prokaryotes, right? So, they reproduced by bifurcation and didn't change much. With no nucleus to protect the genes, they were too primitive to evolve into higher life forms. When the symbiont combined with another bacterium, it created a hybrid cell, greater than the sum of its parts, capable of evolving into multicellular creatures. It was the world's first sex act. Without it, we would have *never existed*."

Her words drew an eerie, stunned silence from the group.

As scientists, they had all dreamed of the eureka moment, the sudden discovery or invention of thought when the world gives up an ancient secret. And at that very moment, every person in the room felt it.

"This is our *matriarch*," Rachel said. "We're glimpsing the moment when everything on Earth changed: the birth of our own existence and that of all other animals! All the other organelles of our cells—the ribosomes, mitochondria, golgi apparatus—were primitive bacteria the Matriarch swallowed up and repurposed to drive the machinery of our cells." Her eyes glistened with emotion. "*That* was Carl's medicine wheel, the circle of life."

"And somewhere, Orcus stumbled onto this matriarch's ancient sanctuary," Esrom Nessen said in a hoarse whisper. "Where she must have survived, hidden for three billion years."

The room grew quiet for what seemed an interminable length of time.

"Rachel, we *must* find the Matriarch's home and plug it forever!" Peterson said. "This creature may be our creator, but she has remained isolated over the eons for a reason. She could be the destroyer of our world."

"The hot springs near the mine," Rachel exclaimed. "The Matriarch had to come from near there—maybe a cave somewhere, sheltered from light."

"I think you're right," Peterson said, his voice trembling. "We'll have to find it, concrete it over or something. We'll need a presidential directive, a United Nations quarantine order—"

"To hell with *that*," Esrom interrupted.

Unlike the others, his eyes were wide with boyish exuberance. "We could be looking at the most astonishing genetic discovery of all time! Think of it. The engine of evolution—the *ultimate* gene-splicing machine. This could revolutionize medicine!"

". . . or lead to our extinction."

Heads turned toward the new voice at the back of the room. Dan

Clifford had slipped in unnoticed. He was standing solemnly, grasping a sheet of paper.

"Everyone just calm down," Peterson grumbled.

"I've deciphered Carl Jameson's other clue," Dan said. "It was hidden right under my nose in biblical verse."

Rachel grew rigid, her eyes welling up again. "I thought you searched the Bible already."

"I searched a King James translation. Carl's message came from a Catholic Bible. The translations are different. The word 'abyss' never appears in the King James version. A stupid mistake on my part, Rachel. I'm sorry."

To Dan's relief, Rachel stared back expectantly. "So, what does it say?"

"You won't find the Matriarch near Soluteca." Dan handed her the paper. "See for yourself. Chapter nine, verses one through three."

:1 The fifth angel sounded his trumpet, and I saw a star that had fallen from the sky to the earth. The star was given the key to the shaft of the Abyss.

:2 When he opened the Abyss, smoke rose from it like the smoke from a giant furnace. The sun and sky were darkened by the smoke from the Abyss.

:3 And out of the smoke locusts came down upon the earth and were given power like that of scorpions.

Rachel's eyes darted across the page with a flash of recognition. "Oh my God, the *smokers*! It's so obvious now!" Rachel buried her face in her hands. "How could I be so blind? The *deep smokers*, the hydrothermal vents, pockets of superheated water that spew out mineralized water like smoke. They're twelve thousand feet underwater, in total darkness. The Matriarch is an *archaebacteria*, more ancient even than bacteria."

"I did some research," Dan interjected. "Hydrothermal vents are rich in precious metals, but far too deep for cost-effective mining. Unless you have an AUV."

"A what?" Peterson asked.

"An autonomous underwater vehicle," Dan replied. "NeuroSys

makes them for weather sensing. Cross them with our manipulators, and you have underwater mining robots. The manipulators were all I could feel in the crates. They were *big*. Big enough for underwater mining." He turned to Rudi, who had been watching the action from the corner of the room. "Do you still have the data you collected on Orcus last week?"

"Sure," Rudi replied. "I collected even more after you left for Washington."

"Check it for evidence of recent ocean drilling by Solá Mining," Dan said.

"I know the answer already," Rudi said. "Orcus owns a small fleet of mining ships, including a deepwater drilling rig called the *GPH Resolution*. It's mondo cool."

"Then look for the ship's registration, or manifest . . . anything that might tell us where it's been in the last month."

"No problem, I know right where to look." Rudi moved to one of the workstations and started typing.

Dan returned his gaze to Rachel. "One thing I don't understand. If the Matriarch lives in the ocean, why hasn't it surfaced before?"

"The bottom of the ocean might as well be the surface of Mars," she said. "Microbes fall to the ocean floor, but nothing comes up, unless something disturbs the water column."

"Something like a submersible," Dan said, and then thought for a minute. "Or a meteor."

"What?"

"The Chicxulub meteor. It hit a hundred miles from here sixty-five million years ago. Wouldn't that disturb the water column for hundreds of miles?"

"Yeah, sure."

"Wouldn't that drive the Matriarch to the surface? If she is indeed the engine of evolution, then she is also the purveyor of mass extinctions. New pathogens would pop up like wildfire. Other species would never be able to adapt quickly enough to protect themselves."

"I don't know—I can't process all of this." Rachel leaned back in the chair, rubbed her eyes. "How can you fathom the concept of the entire world changing overnight?"

"It's happened before," Dan said. "History repeats itself."

Rudi, keyboarding furiously, let out a yelp. "Orcus tried to disguise it." He pointed at the screen proudly. "I searched ship manifests from the Central American port authority. The *GPH Resolution* has been jogging back and forth between Soluteca and the Panama Canal for months. It stops for a day or two in port, turns around and heads back to the canal, but it never goes *through* the canal. That seemed odd, so I analyzed satellite images of the area. I found this." Rudi brought up a satellite photo of a blank patch of ocean. "Note the time and date."

Peterson leaned over. "I don't see anything."

"Precisely. That was taken three days ago. Now try this one." Rudi brought up a second image. The shadow of a ship sat dead center in the image. "This is the *GPH Resolution* a day later. It stops here for a few hours, then moves on. Looks like it repeats the same pattern every four or five days." Rudi zoomed in. A large drilling tower dominated the center of the ship. At the stern lay an octagonal landing pad. Crew members dotted the area around the tower.

"This is a ship like no other," Rudi gushed. "A deepwater drilling rig that can punch a hole twenty-seven-thousand feet deep into the ocean floor. It's got a dynamic positioning system that can hold it in place. . . ."

"Where is this?" Rachel said.

"Um, ten degrees north latitude, about a hundred miles west of Costa Rica."

"Isn't that near the Galapagos?"

"Pretty close."

"That's a prime hydrothermal vent area, over ten thousand feet deep." She glanced toward Colonel Peterson expectantly.

He caught her gaze and turned to Rudi. "Mr. Plimpton, where is the *GPH Resolution* right now?"

Rudi continued typing furiously for a few minutes. "About fifty miles from the anchor site, heading that way."

Peterson straightened, his jaw set. "Learn everything you can about this . . . *Matriarch*. We haven't a moment to lose."

60

SANDWICHED IN WITH eight CBIRFs, Dan could barely hear himself think. The beat of helicopter blades made conversation impossible. The Marines sat solemnly, staring straight ahead, their medical gear swapped out for weapons, the lethal variety this time. Rachel was sitting in the front seat, chatting breezily with the pilot over a pair of headphones. Colonel Peterson sat across from Dan, lost in thought.

Dan couldn't shake the notion of the Matriarch lurking inside each human cell, having infected us all so long ago, hoarding DNA and controlling everything. She was the ultimate trickster, a shape-shifter, perfectly designed to assume any role.

A creature void of form.

He thought of the medicine wheel and its eternal center, where life begins and ends; of old Ben Proudfoot and his world of riddles. The Matriarch needed us, and we needed her—to guard our precious DNA. What other surprises did the Matriarch have hidden in her bag of tricks?

He shrugged off the thought with a shiver.

The ship was exactly where Rudi had predicted. The drilling tower was taller than it looked in the satellite photo and dominated the ship's silhouette. It looked a little like the Eiffel Tower on floats. Workers scattered as the Huey touched down on the small landing pad near the stern. The Marines scrambled out, brandishing their weapons.

The confused crewmen on the ship moved back a respectful distance. Dan counted only eleven men, too small a crew for a ship this size. Four Marines lingered at the helicopter while Peterson, Rachel, Dan, and the others marched toward the pilothouse. As they passed the drilling tower, Dan stared down into the moon pool, a paradoxical hole in the center of the ship that allowed open access to the ocean.

Only there was no drilling equipment.

Instead, an electric winch dangled from the tower, its cable swaying with the action of the waves. His eyes followed the cable down to a large steel cage resting at the edge of the waterline. Inside sat a gleaming orb as big as a car. He could only guess at its purpose. Not so with the machinery in the surrounding equipment bays. These were built for heavy work, their titanium framework bristling with pipes, hoses, and battery banks.

And two hulking manipulator arms.

Rachel stopped dead in her tracks, changed direction, and scurried down a nearby ramp. "You were right!" she shouted. "Automated underwater vehicles—mining robots, a fleet of them!"

Dan followed her, staring at the familiar robotic arms sprouting from the sides of each submersible. When he had felt their shape in the darkness of the truck, he could never have imagined their true size and complexity. These submersible robots made the *SeaZee* look like a toy.

Rachel quickly moved to another bay, which contained an unfamiliar vehicle, its futuristic shape more like a plane than a submersible. Unlike the mining robots, this machine was long and sleek, aerodynamic, with short stubby wings projecting from the fuselage. Below its transparent nose cone were two more robotic manipulators folded like the arms of a praying mantis.

"Do you know what this is?" Rachel slid her hand down its smooth white surface, past a set of stenciled letters that spelled AQUA GLIDER. "It's a benthic submersible. I've seen drawings, but I've never seen one up close." She poked around the stubby wings. "It's a lighter-than-water sub that literally flies upside down. Ultra-high-pressure ceramic body, ported thrusters, aerodynamic design. *Jeez!* Orcus spent some serious money on this."

Crew members eyed them suspiciously from the upper rails. "Come on," Dan said. "We can look later. Let's stay with the group." He pushed her up the ramp and past two burly sailors, and they caught up with the Marines at the pilothouse. Peterson was arguing with the ship's captain.

The sight of the towering figure that confronted him sent Dan reeling against the wall. "You!" he shouted, pointing an accusing finger. "That's him! Captain of the garbage scow."

The captain glowered and took a step toward Dan, but three Marines prodded him back with their weapons.

Peterson stepped boldly into the giant's line of vision, oblivious to his stature. "I see your retirement was rather brief, Captain. Never mind Mr. Clifford. You're talking with me, remember?"

"You have no business on my boat!" he roared.

"We're making it our business, by the authority of the United States. Your operation is in violation of international law. Are you mining ore from the ocean floor?"

"I have nothing to say."

"We believe your ship is harvesting ore contaminated with virulent microbes that pose a grave danger."

"You are lying."

"I wish I were. Are you aware of the epidemics in La Ceiba and Soluteca? Some of your own crewmen have died."

The captain balked. "I demand to speak to my employer."

"Certainly," said Peterson, nodding to a Marine. "Allow the captain access to ship-to-shore radio in his quarters."

As the captain turned to leave, he exposed another man cowering in the corner. Dan's heart sank at the sight of the bald head and handlebar mustache. "Harry Adler. What the hell are you doing here?"

Harry stepped forward and smiled sheepishly. "Dan, this is a surprise. What's going on?"

"You two know each other?" Peterson said.

"Yes, of course," Dan said. "Harry works for NeuroSys in their robotics division. How *could* you?"

"How could I what?"

The captain turned around and gave Harry a fierce stare. "Señor Adler, do not speak."

The Marine poked the captain with his rifle.

"Señor Adler should come with me."

"Maybe a little later, *Capitán*," Peterson said, smiling.

The captain stared at a nearby wall clock. "You are interfering with our operations."

"You bet," Peterson said. "Perhaps if you'd tell us exactly what you're doing, we can expedite things for you."

The captain's eyes darted back and forth. He searched for the right words, but came up empty. "I will speak with my employer."

"Yes, you do that," Peterson said and turned to another Marine. "Keep the ship's crew together on the foredeck. I don't want any surprises."

Dan gawked at Harry. "How could you *do* this? I always thought of you as one of the good guys."

Harry's expression vacillated between dismay and confusion. "I don't understand. This is just a business deal. Harmless, really."

"Are you mining ore from hydrothermal vents?"

Harry glanced nervously at the entourage. "I, uh—"

"Just answer the question, damn it!" Dan paused, hoping their former friendship would move Harry's moral compass a bit. He started again, speaking slowly. "Harry, this ore is contaminated with a deadly microbe. It killed Senator Becker, and could kill *millions*."

"What?" Harry's jaw sagged. He licked his lips. "Look, I don't know anything about that, I swear! I would never . . . it's just a business deal, for God's sake! Orcus supplied us with precious metals— *gave* them to us, Dan. Financed the chip factory too. It was the deal of the century. All he wanted in return were some robots and some bioleaching research or something. I was never privy to that stuff, but it was so easy to adapt our autonomous systems for mining—you know how good our technology is." Harry's voice quivered. "They can navigate, map terrain, locate the ore visually, learn on the job. We made undersea mining feasible. It was just good business."

"*Illegal* business, Harry."

"Well sort of . . . you've got to understand these mining treaties. They're ridiculous. You sign over practically everything to undeserving governments, just because the area lies within a hundred miles of their coastline. Why bother? So, I guess they decided to keep it a secret. Tomás finally clued me in, 'cause they needed me to fix some issues. The ship drops off the robots and ore carts, then leaves. The robots are programmed to harvest the ore and return to the surface a few days later. We come back and haul it in, that's it. We're never here more than a couple of hours." Harry's eyes flickered with excitement. "You've got to see this ore, Dan. It's virtually pure, crystallized gold!"

"Well, that ore contains a nasty little surprise," Dan said. "A mutation engine that can spit out diseases faster than we can cure them. We could be looking at global pandemics, collapse of the food supply, who knows what else."

"Oh, God." Harry's knees crumpled. "Oh God, oh God."

Dan tried to help him up. "Come on, Harry. You can redeem yourself."

"*Nooo,* you don't understand!" He banged his head against the wall.

"Understand what?"

"Orcus knew we'd be discovered soon. The AUVs weren't mining ore fast enough . . . oh God. The ore's all attached, don't you see? Cemented to the bottom! We harvested all the loose pieces."

"So?"

"So, we've planted explosives, to break the ore up."

Dan, Rachel, and Peterson looked at each other, then back to Harry. "You *what?*"

"The robots are placing explosives, *right now.* That's why we gotta leave, in under an hour."

"Then call them off!" Peterson sputtered. "Call the damn things back!"

"I can't! They're autonomous, remember?"

"Send them a stop order or something!"

"We've tried that. The hydrothermal vents are too noisy for sonic commands—plus the thermals—they reflect the sound. And radio waves won't travel that far underwater."

"You have no fail-safe abort system?"

"I . . . don't know, we didn't have time to plan for this . . ."

Rachel pushed past Dan and grabbed Harry by the arm. "Let me see a map of the bottom."

"Shouldn't we be getting the hell out of here?" Harry muttered.

Rachel ignored him, focusing on the exquisitely detailed map he unrolled on the table. "Where are we positioned?"

"Here"—Harry pointed to a deep purple gorge—"at Abaddon's Gate. It's a tripolar juncture, where three tectonic plates meet. The Pacific, the Nazca, and the Caribbean spread out from here in all directions. This volcanic upwelling is millions, maybe *billions* of years old. We think it's one of several permanent relief valves in the Earth's mantle."

"And where are the explosive charges?" Rachel asked.

"Here." Harry pointed to a cluster of steep columns at the end of a shallow valley. "In Sherwood Forest, near the Rose Garden—there are two charges at the base of a gigantic vent tower called Long John Silver. It's over fifty meters tall."

"Long John Silver?" Dan said.

Harry managed a crooked grin. "You gotta understand. It's surreal down there. This vent is packed with gold and silver ore."

"That submersible outside, *Aqua Glider*," Rachel asked. "Is it operational?"

"Yeah, but it's never been used. We haven't had time."

Dan suddenly understood Rachel's keen interest in the map. His heart faltered. "Wait, you're not—"

She was already out the door, yelling back at Harry. "Bring the map!"

61

RACHEL STOPPED AT the large orb at the bottom of the moon pool. "This is one of the explosive devices?"

"Correct," Harry replied. "Well, it's not really an explosive. Nothing explodes at twelve thousand feet underwater. It's more of an implosion bomb, a special design. When it's triggered, the water pressure creates a shock wave that shatters everything into millions of pieces."

"And spreads organic material in all directions," Rachel said, groaning.

Harry stared down at his feet.

"Can you disarm it?"

"Sure." Harry pointed to a large illuminated display above a numbered keypad. "It takes a code to activate, but turning it off is easy." He grabbed the large square handle and twisted it clockwise ninety degrees, freezing the display at 50:05:33. "There, it's dead. The kill handle is designed to fit the manipulator arms."

"Is that the time left?"

"Yes. This was the last charge. You interrupted us before we could deploy it."

"So that leaves the other two on the bottom?"

"Right."

Dan's mind raced ahead. "You can't be thinking of trying to disarm those?"

"Do you have a better idea?" Rachel swung open the *Aqua Glider*'s nose cone. She slid out a horizontal bench inside that looked like the body tray at a morgue. "Help me get this in the water."

Dan turned to Peterson. "You can't allow this . . . it's crazy!"

Peterson's gaze wandered from Rachel to the orb, and then back to Dan. He shrugged. "What alternative do we have? We don't exactly have time to debate it."

It was insanity. Dan knew he couldn't talk her out of it. He could wrestle her to the ground, but then what about the bombs? The Matriarch? All the while, Rachel continued prepping the submersible. He racked his brain for an alternative. *Less than an hour. Impossible.*

There was only one option. "Then I'm coming with you."

"No!" Rachel turned around, her eyes blazing. "You're not!" She seemed to falter, then stepped forward, cupped his cheek in her hand and stared fondly into his eyes. "Don't think for a second I don't appreciate everything you've done, everything you *are,* but . . . this is *my* mission, alone."

He gripped both her arms and squeezed. "To hell with that! I'm coming with you, or stopping you, take your pick. Besides, someone has to operate the manipulators."

Rachel pulled away. "Please don't do this. I don't have time to argue!"

"Then don't."

Harry and the colonel helped slide Rachel into the cramped interior of the sub. Ignoring her protests, Dan followed and crawled onto the horizontal bench facedown. It curved up at the end, so that his head was elevated and extended into the clear portion of the acrylic dome. His arms fell naturally on the manipulator controls.

"What's the depth at the bottom?" Rachel snapped.

"Twelve thousand feet," Harry replied, showing her the route on the map. "When you reach eleven-five, level off, follow the canyon wall due north, past Abaddon's Gate. Don't stray out of the canyon. Sherwood Forest is another three hundred yards. You can't miss Long John Silver."

"God, I feel like Alice entering Wonderland," she said. "How much time?"

Harry checked his watch. "Forty-six minutes."

"Descent rate?"

"Five hundred feet per minute."

"So, twenty-four minutes to the bottom." She whistled. "That doesn't leave much time."

Harry started to close the nose cone, then stopped. "Oh, I almost forgot. Give the AUVs a wide berth, at least thirty feet. They're programmed for aggressive defense. They'll attack anything except another AUV."

Dan's eyes shot up from the map. "What . . . why?"

"Well, uh, something's been disabling the AUVs. We've lost three machines already."

"What do you mean, some *thing*?"

"We don't know, exactly. That's why we ordered the *Aqua Glider*, to see for ourselves."

"That's just great!" Dan snapped. "Marvelous!"

Rachel checked her watch. "Let's go, *now!*"

Harry slammed the nose cone shut and Dan could feel his heart thumping against the sled's padding as he watched crewmen attach a winch cable, lift the sub from the bay, and lower it into the water face-first. The winch hook jerked loose, dropping them into the ocean with a great splash of foam. They hovered in the water like a zeppelin, the boundaries of the dome dissolving away, betrayed by a thin stream of bubbles trickling along its curvature. Rachel pointed the sub downward and pushed the throttles to the stops. Dan felt a rush of vertigo as he sensed the miles of ocean beneath them.

It was like stepping off the end of the Earth.

As the sub picked up speed, his initial surge of adrenaline ebbed, leaving behind a film of dread. The water darkened quickly and he braced himself for the familiar tightness that would coil around his chest. He fought a sudden urge to make her stop, to turn the sub around and head back to the surface.

But it was already too late. He knew they had passed a tipping point. With an almost serene dispassion, he stood outside himself and saw their future in the abyss.

The odds of finding the two orbs in the blackness, threatened by hostile submersibles, with so little time—it was impossible. He looked at Rachel. She was staring straight ahead, her features ghostly in the fading light, the same fatalism etched across her face.

"You never intended to come back, did you?"

She squeezed her eyes shut. "I didn't want you to come!"

He shook his head and reached for her hand. "How could I not?"

She drew away defensively. "Please, don't. I was trying to protect you."

"I can take care of myself."

"You have no idea—" She bit her lower lip.

"That's right, I don't. Why don't you enlighten me?"

"Yes, I care for you! Is that what you want to hear?" Rachel grew silent for a moment, then appeared to make a decision. "We're both going to die down here in the dark, so I suppose I owe you the truth. I've known since that first dive on the *SeaZee,* when you pushed your fears away to be with me. Every time I needed support, you were there." She laughed. "With your quirky theories and quiet strength. That night in the cabin, I *knew.* No man has ever supported me the way you have, and I will never forget it."

"So you treat me like I shot your dog? What's up with that?"

"It was my turn to protect you, but you're so damn stubborn!" She wiped tears from her face. "You deserve so much more than I can offer."

"Why not let me decide that?" He looked into her eyes and saw a well of sorrow. "What are you running from?"

"I'm not—" She struggled for words. "I never told you how my father died."

"What does that have to do—"

"Huntington's disease, Dan," she blurted. "Do you know what that is?"

"I'm not sure—"

"It attacks the brain, usually in middle age, sometimes sooner. It starts as involuntary, rapid, ceaseless movement. Abrupt mood swings. Over time you lose balance, your speech becomes slurred, you can't eat or swallow. Your mind sinks into depression, irrational behavior, and finally dementia. You become a hunk of meat." She sobbed, tears flowing freely down her face and onto the dome's floor. "My father was such a dynamic man, so full of life! I watched him waste away before my eyes. . . ."

Dan felt as if someone had hit him in the chest with a baseball bat. He should have seen it in her, but he was so preoccupied with his own feelings. His cycle of loss seemed to be turning back on itself. . . .

"Was Carl—is it genetic?"

She laughed bitterly. "Carl? Perfectly healthy, the worst irony of all. That bastard Orcus stole him from me! That's why I can't allow you into my world—"

Dan put a finger to her lips. "What about you?"

"I have a fifty-fifty chance, yes."

"You don't *know*?"

"Never been tested."

"Why not?"

"Because, sometimes it's not good to know your future. I have no intention of wasting away in some hospital bed. I don't want to put myself, or *anyone,* through that."

Dan shook his head. "But by not knowing, you're living as if you already *have* the disease, isolating yourself from those who care about you."

Rachel's face twisted into a crooked smile. "Well, that's balance of opposition, isn't it?"

"Not funny! You might be perfectly healthy. When I saw my parents die—I remember begging God for just five more minutes with them. You and I—we could still have a life together."

"Our time together wouldn't be worth the suffering. Besides, it's moot now."

"Not if I can help it."

CAPTAIN BITTOR VINCENTO slipped his huge frame into the chair, turned on the ship-to-shore radio, and stole a glance toward the Marine outside. He quietly pulled the door shut and placed a call through a secure channel, slipping on a pair of headphones for privacy.

Hadan Orcus answered gruffly. "Yeah, what is it?"

Vincento recounted the sudden appearance of U.S. Marines, and their accusations.

"That's absurd! They have no right to board my vessel in Central American waters."

"I told them," Bittor insisted. "But they say the American president ordered it."

"Impossible! That's tantamount to foreign invasion."

"They say we are the cause of the sickness. Is this true?"

The line went silent for a moment. "Would it matter? You've been paid handsomely enough. Have the charges been planted?"

"*Sí.*"

"Then it can't be stopped."

"*Sí,* but the Marines, they are talking to Señor Adler."

"Listen, I don't care what you have to do, get those men off my ship! This operation must be completed at all costs, do you understand? Move away from the site long enough for the detonation, then return immediately and deploy the mining drones. I want that ore collected. All of it! Keep mining until your ship is bursting at the seams. I'll send reinforcements. We'll be done before the Honduran government or the Americans can stop us."

"The Marines have automatic weapons."

"Find a way!"

"How? We can't fight armed American soldiers! We'll be killed."

"Tell them of the bombs; threaten them with annihilation. You have plenty of muscle on that crew. It should be worth another million for you to get them off my ship, agreed?"

Vincento paused, letting the offer sink in. "Aye, sir." He tore the headphones off and held his hands before him, studying the large fingers that trembled with nervous energy. After another long pause, he cracked open the door and signaled the Marine. They returned to the foredeck and he was shocked to find the fancy diving machine gone. Only one of the AUVs had returned to the surface. Worse still, the atmosphere topside had changed, charged with a queer tension. Vincento began to wonder if the Americans could stop the operation after all.

Yet, something else troubled him more.

62

AT 11,400 FEET, three times deeper than *SeaZee*'s structural limit, Rachel leveled the *Aqua Glider* out alongside an escarpment of pillow lava, globular rock that littered the seafloor like monstrous droppings. The last time she had visited a hydrothermal vent was years ago at the site of Nine North, near the Galapagos, not far from their present location. Back then, she had squinted through a four-inch portal to see a surreal world flourishing without the benefit of natural light. Now, that world lay just inches beyond the clear barrier of *Aqua Glider*'s acrylic dome.

She hugged the eastern edge of a large canyon that had to be Abaddon's Gate. Its cavernous floor lay far beyond the reach of their halogen lamps, but she could see the faint glow of molten lava pulsating hundreds of feet below. The features matched the landmarks on the map. They were gliding along the edge of a fractured volcanic range, taller than the Himalayas and forty thousand kilometers long, that circled the Earth like a necklace of fire.

She took care to avoid the overhanging ledges that surrounded the canyon walls like bathtub rings, remnants of past eruptions. Sound assailed them from all sides, a combination of cracking rock and subterranean gases bubbling to the surface of the lava.

On the terrestrial surface, the ground seemed an immutable and ancient presence, but down here, the energy of the mantle's tectonic engine was dynamic and full of life, rumbling and screeching like a factory, disgorging a steady stream of lava onto the canyon floor. It was the sound of new earth in creation, the birth pangs of Gaia herself.

Rachel felt as if she had torn the covers from a sacred act. Everything began and ended here, a portal to the netherworld. It seemed the perfect place to meet her destiny. She glanced in Dan's direction and felt a stab of remorse. Beads of sweat were forming on his brow, dropping like rain on the topographic map he studied with frantic intensity.

"Where are we?" she asked.

"Here, I think," Dan pointed, struggling to keep his finger steady. "Follow the crater wall until we reach an intersection of the two canyons, then go left along the ridge." There was nothing about this landscape that Dan found fascinating. All he could think about was the five thousand pounds of frigid seawater pressing against every square inch of their fragile container.

The escarpments narrowed at a sharp angle, forcing them up toward the crater's rim. According to the map, the northern ridge of the tripolar juncture lay directly in front of them. "Head due north," he mumbled.

Rachel slid the *Aqua Glider* up and over into a narrow rift valley that had been ripped from the ridge's apex by the gradual spreading of the mantle. The topography of the sea floor at this location differed markedly from the muddy sediments they had encountered on the abyssal plain. Here, the rocks were mere infants—sharp, naked, as barren as the moon's surface.

"Over there," Rachel said, pointing toward a mass of silky strands draped haphazardly over the rocks. "Spaghetti worms. We're close."

The landscape began to come alive. A snow of bacterial flocculent drifted past in misty waves.

Dan checked his watch. "Can you speed it up?"

They swerved around a large boulder. The valley opened up and blossomed into a forest of brilliant red and white tubular creatures. Scattered among them were cones of rock like termite mounds, each one spewing a plume of dense black liquid.

"Rose Garden!" Dan gasped, pointing at the map. "It's got to be."

"*Riftia*—tube worms—my God, they're huge."

The *Riftia*'s segmented white columns were eight feet long. An oblong gill of scarlet tissue wafted in the currents at the end of each tube.

"This *has* to be the Matriarch's home," Rachel exclaimed. "This is one huge symbiotic community. The tube worms depend on bacteria in their guts to digest the vent chemicals. The Matriarch must have shared genes with every creature down here."

The abundance of life was incredible: ghostlike crabs scurrying among the tubes, primitive crinoid worms with hydra heads and rat-tailed fish loitering along the edge of the worm field.

"Over there," Rachel said, pointing to a yellow gelatinous mass the size of a softball. "Ocean dandelion, a symbiotic colony of creatures."

"Come on, come on!" Dan jabbed at his watch. "Seventeen minutes . . ."

"Okay already." She aimed the *Aqua Glider* down the valley, staying a few feet above the *Riftia* forest. A shimmer of light drew her toward the valley wall, ablaze with thousands of coordinated lumines-cent pulses. She aimed the lights at the mass, scattering thousands of foot-long creatures, half lobster, half squid. "Whoa! Octopods, only these are a lot larger than the ones we saw at the dump site—"

"Keep moving. Big vents should be straight ahead."

The worm garden gave way to a field of shattered carcasses. The rock underneath the debris had been scraped smooth by the robots. The grade began to ascend gently. Rachel swept the lights back and forth in broad swaths, searching for signs of the larger vent towers. A glint of metal caught her eye and she pulled back on the throttles. Wedged sideways in a jagged crevasse lay the twisted remains of an AUV, its large scooping arms bent and mangled.

"What the hell could have done *that*?" Dan said.

"Looks like it fell in, then tried to pry itself out with the manipula-tors."

"And the ripped hydraulic lines?"

"I don't know, but we're not hanging around to find out." Rachel gunned the submersible and arced over the wreckage with the speed and grace of a dolphin.

"Straight ahead!" Dan pointed with the manipulator. "I see blue light."

A silver orb materialized in the haze. The control panel was visible, its large blue numerals ticking backward toward zero. Rachel reversed the thrusters and *Aqua Glider* bumped gently into its side, kicking up a small cloud of silt.

"Perfect!" Dan grasped the ground with one manipulator to steady the sub and slipped the other gripper into the orb's kill switch. With a fluid motion, he twisted the handle clockwise. The LED display froze at 12:43:17.

Rachel backed the sub away. "One down, one to go."

Dan began to feel a hint of optimism about their chances. They might make it after all.

Rachel eased forward. Beyond the orb and its silt cloud, the water began to clear. A gargantuan chimney came into view, its apex disappearing into the darkness fifty feet above them. Plumes of black liquid poured from side vents. Around the opening of each vent, grape-sized crystals of gold and silver shimmered in the three-hundred-degree water.

"That's got to be Long John Silver," Rachel said. "Harry wasn't kidding about its size." She slowed the sub, mesmerized by the sight.

"Hurry!" Dan cried. "Go around—the second orb must be on the other side."

Rachel whipped *Aqua Glider* into a steep banking turn that hugged the curvature of the smoker's base. After one hundred eighty degrees of heading change, she leveled out and panned the lights across the empty valley.

"Where is it?" Dan's heart rose into his throat.

Rachel circled a bit longer, then stopped. "It's not here. If we keep going, we'll be back where we started."

"It's *got* to be here!" Dan could feel the heat from Long John Silver warming the small enclosure. Trickles of sweat merged into streams that ran down his arms and onto the controls. "It must be farther down the ridge."

Rachel edged back out into the narrow corridor and aimed toward a second, smaller hydrothermal vent fifty yards away. A faint white light behind the column began to intensify, outlining the vent's profile like a halo. As they grew closer, the light sharpened into the long, thin beam of a halogen lamp tracking its way across the valley wall.

"It's the second AUV," Dan said. "Why is it still here? It should have followed the other one to the surface by now."

"I don't know, but—" Suddenly, the beam tracked out of the shadows and swept over them, flooding the sub's interior with blinding light.

"Damn it!" Rachel covered her eyes in a futile attempt to preserve her night vision. Held in the focus of the beam, she hesitated for a split second.

The AUV closed quickly, slamming into *Aqua Glider* with incredible force. The sound of crunching metal echoed through the cockpit.

The collision threw the sub backward, slamming their faces against the dome. Dan watched helplessly as the right manipulator arm tore away from the fuselage. He instinctively swung the left arm around defensively, but the sleek sub was no match for the huge mass of the mining submersible. Its momentum drove them backward and they collided with the base of Long John Silver.

Dan's feet slammed into the rear of the fuselage. A cloud of black silt boiled up as pieces of broken lava clattered down around them. Somehow, he managed to keep the lone manipulator moving in blind arcs, knowing that the AUV was blind now too. "Go left!" he yelled.

"Can't! We're pinned!"

Through the black haze, he could see the flare of the AUV's lights amid the shadows of its robotic arms as they flailed wildly like tentacles. Dan parried their attack like a one-armed boxer, but he knew eventually the AUV would strike a lucky blow. The roar of jetting water resonated through the small hull. The soles of his shoes heated up and he jerked them away from the rear of the sub, horrified at the thought of being cooked alive or crushed.

"Get us out of here," he pleaded.

"I'm trying."

Inexplicably, the AUV slowed its attack and receded. The haze took on a new and bizarre appearance as its halogen lamps dimmed suddenly, overwhelmed by bursts of pulsating light. Then, in a final explosion of light, the robot went dark. The light show ended as suddenly as it began.

"Go, go, go!"

"I can't," Rachel said. "We're trapped."

With his single manipulator, Dan groped ahead and grabbed a nearby boulder. Rubble fell away from the sub and they inched forward bit by bit. Rachel already had the thrusters on full, and when the sub broke free it shot forward like a missile into clear water. When Rachel turned to see what had happened, she saw the AUV disappearing into darkness. Only a ragged hole remained, spewing torrents of black smoke from the side of the vent.

Dan searched the valley. "The other bomb's *got* to be here somewhere."

Rachel banked left and shot down the corridor. The area surrounding the second hydrothermal vent was a jumble of rocks and fissures. Iridescent plumes of superheated water poured from innumerable cracks around the vent's base. She ascended slightly to avoid the hottest jets.

"Over there, I see it!" Dan pointed toward a faint glint of metal. The second orb had apparently rolled away from the smoker and wedged itself like a marble into a crack. "The AUV must have been trying to retrieve it, to complete its programmed task."

They lurched forward, covering the distance quickly. The bomb's LED display was turned facedown in the fissure. Dan watched in horror as the reflection of the blue numerals flickered off the surrounding rocks. He checked his watch. Seconds remained.

He exhaled slowly. "Get into that fissure . . . *now*."

"We'll get stuck."

"We're dead if we don't."

She backed up the sub and positioned it high and parallel to the opening, hesitated for a second, then gunned the thrusters. The *Aqua Glider* squirted downward into the chasm, the sound of the ceramic fuselage grinding past pumice like fingernails on a blackboard. They stopped a few feet short of the orb.

Dan slipped the remaining robotic arm around the curvature of the orb. He was too close to see the display, but he could feel the shape through the manipulator's force feedback system. Closing his eyes, he tried to visualize his arm reaching out along the uneven surface. He felt a distinct bump, opened the gripper fingers, and grasped the Off switch.

With sudden surety, he twisted the control and felt a crisp response. The flickering reflections steadied. A shudder of relief coursed through him as he released his death grip on the controls and slumped onto the bench, his heart throbbing. "We stopped it."

A hoarse whisper fell from Rachel's lips. "Are you sure?"

"We're still alive, aren't we?" Dan couldn't believe it himself. He felt numb with relief. They hung motionless for several minutes, drinking in the calmness and the roar of the vents above.

Rachel finally broke the silence. "Now what?"

"Now we get out of here."

"Easier said than done, I'm afraid." She switched the thrusters into reverse, but the *Aqua Glider* was firmly wedged in the crevice.

After everything they had endured, Dan had no intention of suffocating at the bottom of the sea. "Try this," he said. "Wiggle the thrusters up and down."

Rachel shrugged, unsure of the purpose, but she'd learned to respect his instincts. The oscillating thrusters put the sub into an inchworm-like motion. At the same time, Dan pressed the lone manipulator arm against a nearby rock. Gradually, the submersible began backing its way out of the hole.

Finally, the *Aqua Glider* popped out of the crevice, eliciting a burst of grins and laughter.

"Let's go home," Dan said.

Rachel smiled back at him and swiveled *Aqua Glider* around toward the valley. They were about to move forward when she stopped short.

"I don't like the looks of this."

Following her gaze, Dan twisted around. Above them to the left, the walls of the rift valley were ablaze with a luminescent light show. A shimmering swarm of octopods spilled out across the rocks in a grand wave, hesitating whenever Rachel aimed the sub's lights at them. Dan studied the foot-long octopods as they moved in a graceful, choreographed fashion, like a school of fish or a swarm of army ants. Small light bursts played across the swarm. Something in their cooperative behavior—an ancient fierce intensity and purpose—filled him with terror.

"Go . . . now!" he cried.

Rachel needed no prompting. She angled the sub toward the surface, and they shot forward.

The swarm reacted instantly, coalescing into a fountain of light. A great glowing stalk shot up from the swarm's base, engulfing them in a cloud of writhing octopods. Rachel shrieked in disgust as tentacles slithered across the transparent dome just inches from her face. Dan swung the lone manipulator arm wildly as tentacles wrapped around every bend and corner. The octopods' parrot-like beaks clamped onto the hydraulic hoses, tearing out chunks of rubber. The manipulator felt like it was moving through peanut butter.

Rachel gunned the thrusters, but the blades clogged with gelatinous corpses. The mass of octopods had become a great writhing metacreature pulling them downward toward the hydrothermal column. Dan slashed the manipulator through the creatures, trying to sever the stalk, but they simply dispersed and rejoined in a flurry of luminous activity.

The *Aqua Glider* slammed into the vent and sheared off the top half of its column. A roar of superheated water poured over the sub.

Dan thought of the choreographed light show. He shook Rachel's arm. "Turn the lights off!"

"What . . . again?"

"Just do it!"

She did as instructed. Blackness engulfed them, leaving only the pulsating outline of the stalk.

Dan squirmed away from the searing walls. "Just be still," he shouted, sweat streaming from his body. The superheated water roared around the fuselage, bouncing it around like a cork in the sea. "They're using the light to communicate," he said. "Like a giant nervous system. Our artificial lights must seem like an invader to them."

The octopods paused, confused. Then the tendril softened and began to collapse in on itself, as a few light pulses rippled through the swarm. It soon dissolved into a random profusion of light.

Rachel seized the opportunity and blindly shot forward, steering away from the swarm's faint illumination and into the black void. She waited a few minutes before flipping the power back on. When she did, they both gasped at the sight.

A thick coating of slime covered the craft. The left manipulator had been reduced to a ragged stump. A dull beam of light shone from a single intact halogen. It was just enough to see by, and Rachel used the depth meter to gauge their progress toward the surface.

NOT UNTIL THE first hint of surface light appeared did they allow themselves to relax. Rachel reached over and lovingly wiped a clump of coagulated blood from underneath Dan's nose.

"We just saved the world, kiddo," she said, and smiled. "How many people can say that?" Then she did something that caught Dan completely by surprise.

She reached over and kissed him long and hard on the mouth.

63

AT SIX HUNDRED feet, Rachel transmitted their position to the *Resolution*.

"That's odd," she said.

"What?"

"No response."

She made two more unsuccessful attempts. "Something's wrong."

"Maybe the hydrophone is broken along with everything else."

"No, that's not it. Can't you hear the echo? We're transmitting—no one's answering."

Perhaps he should be more concerned, but all Dan could feel at the moment was relief. "Patience. We'll be there soon enough." With each passing moment Dan's spirits rose as the water grew brighter. He studied Rachel's expression. If she had any regrets about surviving, she wasn't showing it. She busied herself with the controls and tried to eke out every last bit of energy from the damaged thrusters. The sea light cast a glow across her face and Dan drifted into a daydream of a possible future.

Fifty-fifty.

After everything he'd been through, those odds seemed good enough. Once things wound down, they'd have a chance to discuss the situation.

A sudden gasp brought his attention back to the present. Rachel was staring at the surface a few meters away, a look of confused horror etched across her face. Dan followed her gaze.

A rain of death descended from above. Sea creatures of all shapes and sizes drifted past the sub. Their eyes were dull and lifeless, their bodies covered in black sores. A flaccid seagull bounced lazily off the acrylic dome.

"What's happening?" she gasped, and craned her neck, searching for the familiar reflections of sunlight glistening at the surface, but she found only shadow. The waters around them swelled with more dead matter. The *Aqua Glider* burst through a layer of muck at the surface. Harsh sunlight accosted their eyes.

Squinting, Dan searched the horizon. A hundred yards away to their left the mining ship bobbed gently, its waterline caked with a reddish sludge that seemed to extend in all directions. The same viscous material sloshed up the sides of the sub's dome. A floating mass bumped into the sub and rolled over, revealing the bloated face of a Marine, pockmarked with lesions.

Rachel drew back in disgust. "Oh God, no! We're too late!" She slammed the sub in reverse. "Got to get away . . ."

Dan grabbed her hands and pulled back on the throttles. "To where?"

"It's toxic algae . . . the *Matriarch* again . . . it must have traveled to the surface on the other AUV, recombined, started reproducing . . . I can't believe how far it's spread already! We can't stay—"

"Whoa, take it easy." He reached for her, struggled to keep the tremor from his own voice. "We need to get aboard, see if anyone's alive."

"No!" Rachel fought back. "If we touch it, breathe it, we'll go crazy! I can't! Not again!"

"Yes you *can*." Dan grabbed her arm, forced her to look him squarely in the eyes. "We'll figure something out, I promise." He'd never seen her so upset, and knew he had to keep her focused. "You've got to promise me something in return," he said.

"What?"

"When we get out of here safely, you've got to promise me you'll give our relationship a go. Deal?"

"But how are we—"

"Deal or not?"

A hint of the old Rachel seemed to resurface. She looked at him with forlorn eyes and nodded.

"Good, now help me look around." They started searching the sub's interior, groping underneath the benches to see what they could find. Rachel discovered a red storage box and pulled it out. Inside were two orange neoprene bundles and a medicine pouch.

"What are those?"

"Ocean survival suits."

Dan unfolded one and examined it. "A full-body wet suit?"

"Yeah, designed to protect against hypothermia."

"Great!" He checked the medical kit and found additional items he would need. He pointed toward the helicopter still resting at the stern of the ship. "Can you fly that thing?"

"The Huey? I guess. I had training a long time ago but—"

"Good enough."

By the time *Aqua Glider* had resurfaced inside the moon pool, they were ready. Both of them had wriggled into the survival suits. Dan lashed one of the emergency air cylinders to Rachel's back with duct tape, then carefully tightened the straps of her full-face mask, checking to make sure the seal was perfect. He then taped the front zippers and seams.

She did the same for him.

"Okay, we're hermetically sealed," he shouted through the mask. "When I open the hatch, gather a water sample." He held up a water bottle. "Then run to the helicopter. Don't stop for anything. Start the engines."

"What about you?"

"Pilothouse. To look for survivors." He tapped her cylinder. "How much air in these?"

"On the surface? I'd guess thirty minutes, tops."

Dan gripped the dome latch and paused. "You ready?"

Rachel closed her eyes, took a deep breath, and exhaled. "I guess."

"If I'm not back in ten minutes, leave."

"Just get there."

As soon as he jerked the latch open, a flood of seawater and sludge poured into the craft. They swam out, scrambled up the side of the pool, and watched the sleek submersible slip backward and disappear beneath the foam.

Rachel went one direction and Dan the other.

He raced past the surviving orb and struggled up the ladder toward the foredeck. Even the simplest movement was exhausting in the stiff suit. He paused at the top of the ladder and noticed an eerie silence— no gulls, voices, engines, waves—only the muted sound of red foam lapping against the hull. In spite of the suit, a chill crept down his

spine. He felt detached from reality, with only the squeal of his regulator and the pounding of his heart to anchor him to the present. He
shook the mask to clear the condensation and took a halting step.
Then another.

A noise stopped him, but he couldn't keep from breathing long
enough to localize the sound. He continued toward the pilothouse,
turning from side to side in the hope of spotting the source of the
sound. At the doorway, he took a step inside and stopped dead.

He turned away an instant too late. The grisly scene had seared
itself into his brain. The walls and floor were splattered with blood,
bodies piled in heaps, faces frozen in agony. He knelt by the railing
and gasped for breath. Air wheezed through the regulator as a stream
of shattered memories played across his mind's eye: darkness, screams,
the howl of ambulances, the stench of death.

Dan forced himself to scan the carnage, hoping against hope. They
were all there—the colonel, Harry, Marines, crewmen—dead to the
last man. He recalled his own hallucinations on the deck of the *Sea
Berth*. It would have been a horrific firefight, fueled by each person's
private terror. Seeing the gory images triggered a desperate urge to rip
away the mask, to feel a fresh breeze on his face, but he willed himself
out the door and forward toward the beating blades of the helicopter.
As he passed the drilling tower, a movement caught his eye. Shaking
the mask again, he focused through the haze. Below, at the edge of the
moon pool, a dark shape hunched over the curved side of the third
implosion bomb, the one they disarmed prior to the dive. The huge
form was wearing a scuba mask and tank and was punching numbers
into the bomb's keypad. Vincento was rearming the bomb. With an
instinctive rage, Dan hurled himself over the railing.

In an instant, he was on Vincento's back, pounding and screaming,
but he had forgotten the immense strength of the man. Suddenly he
was sailing through the air. An explosion of light and pain ripped
through his skull as he collided with the bulkhead.

He struggled up to see Vincento repositioning his diving mask.
Grabbing a large pipe wrench from the deck, Dan swung wildly, but
the blow glanced harmlessly off an arm. The captain turned and
grabbed the end of the wrench. Grunting incoherently, he jerked several times against Dan's grip, tossing him back and forth like a stick
puppet.

This was a battle Dan had no chance of winning. A few more jerks would put the weapon in the captain's hands. He tried to let his martial arts training take over and relaxed, anticipating the next pull. At the precise moment, he reversed his resistance and pushed, adding his force to the captain's momentum, causing him to stagger backward. That gave Dan time to reach a flash of red at the edge of his peripheral vision. He unlatched it and aimed. The shiny new fire extinguisher disgorged a cloud of frozen CO_2 in the captain's direction.

Vincento tore at his mask in an attempt to clear away the frozen particles. Seizing the opportunity, Dan swung the extinguisher in a wide arc. The tank bounced off the captain's right cheekbone, sending the mask and regulator flying. A blade of crimson erupted at the impact point.

Using the energy of the recoil, Dan twisted around 360 degrees and caught the captain on the left temple, snapping his head sideways and sending him slamming into the orb. It rolled out of the cage, dropped into the moon pool, and vanished.

"Nooooo!" Dan grasped at air.

Vincento teetered at the edge for an instant longer, his arms swinging, desperation contorting his features. Then he followed the orb into the water. His head bobbed up several times as he thrashed about, taking in huge gulps of red sludge. A second later he convulsed, his back arching halfway out of the water, the front third of his tongue sheared off at the teeth.

And he went under for the last time.

DAN FLUNG HIMSELF into the helicopter. "Let's go!"

"The others?"

"Gone." He gasped for air, his body sweltering inside the storm suit.

Tentatively, Rachel lifted a strut from the deck. The helicopter yawed dangerously to one side, but she corrected and they shot skyward. Waiting as long as he could, Dan finally tore the mask from his face and sucked in a lungful of air, hoping they were beyond the effects of toxic gas.

Rachel followed his cue. "Oh . . . my . . . God." She stared out the cockpit.

A bloom of red algae had spread far beyond the *Resolution,* reaching in all directions like an octopus, its tentacles smothering every-thing in its path. Suddenly, a column of water shot up through the moon pool, ripping the vessel in half. A loud *thwummmph* rocked the helicopter and Rachel struggled to maintain control.

Waves of red foam and spray surged outward from the ship like ripples on a pond.

64

DAN RUBBED HIS eyes and tried to focus. Emotionally and physically drained, he could barely remember the last sixteen hours. The deaths of the colonel and the CBIRFs had hit him particularly hard and had thrown a morbid pall over the rest of the MOBIDIC team. They may have dealt with death on a daily basis, but seldom this close to home.

There had barely been time to hold a hastily arranged memorial service in the cargo bay of MOBIDIC, amid the machines and paraphernalia of the fallen Marines. It seemed the fitting location for a memorial, one that proceeded in absentia. The bodies of the fallen would lie deep beneath the sea, at Abaddon's Gate, for all eternity. Dan felt devastated, having failed to contain the Matriarch. After all their efforts, the CBIRF team may have died for nothing.

Once the services ended, the remaining MOBIDIC team had forced themselves back to the job at hand: analyzing the Matriarch's new creation from the samples Rachel had collected at the dive site. Exhausted and stunned by events, everyone pushed themselves to the limit.

Goodson and Odom decided to identify the chimera's toxic profile, while Rachel teamed up with Marilynn to analyze its DNA signature. Dan wanted to contribute, so he suggested to Rudi that they build a data analysis set into the GAPS software in the hope of predicting the red tide's progression.

Now, after an exhausting night, they had all reconvened in the conference room to compare notes. Dan scanned the faces of the team, hoping to see evidence of determined progress, but all he saw were expressions of stunned resignation. Everyone seemed lost in their own thoughts while they waited for Esrom Nessen to arrive.

Esrom, who had been appointed interim commander, finally entered the room, his pale face showing all the strain of responsibility.

He wasted no time. "I've received the latest updates from the president and the joint chiefs. This is the latest reconnaissance from drones sent to the area," he said, bringing a video up on the conference room monitor.

The video began at a distance, showing the bright-red stain that had been growing throughout the night. It stretched beyond the horizon, its fingers of death spiraling out in all directions like demented pinwheels.

Dan gaped at the video. He could almost see the red tide growing as he watched, reaching out in pulses as ocean waves pushed and pulled the flotsam in and out like the lungs of a beast.

Gaia's bleeding, he thought.

The drone descended, bringing more of the details into focus. What at first seemed like black specks among the swirling red colors resolved into the shapes of dead and rotting sea animals. Swooping down to a few hundred feet off the surface, the drone passed over a scene of carnage: a school of tuna floating in a silvery mass that undulated with the waves, and the carcass of a blue whale, its white stomach gleaming in the morning sun. The carnage went on and on, in a grisly parade of death, until the team finally had enough and began turning away in disgust.

Sensing the group's dismay, Esrom stopped the video and scanned the faces of the group. "As you can see, things are about as bad as can be imagined."

Rudi, who had continued working throughout the video, finally looked up from the GAPS program. "So, exactly how big is this thing?"

Instead of answering, Esrom silently turned back to the monitor and brought up a satellite photo. "This was taken less than an hour ago," he said.

A chorus of gasps met the image. It showed the west coast of Central America flanked by a red stain hundreds of miles in length, positioned only several miles off the coasts of Nicaragua and Honduras.

"Estimated size is over fifteen hundred square miles," said Esrom, his expression turning to grim fatalism. "It's growing at a phenomenal rate. Obviously, we've been keeping the scope of this disaster under wraps to avoid panic. We can't tell *anyone* else about this . . . understood?"

Rachel snorted. "So, the public's not going to notice a red tide the size of Rhode Island growing off the coast of Central America?"

"We can hide its lethality for a while," Esrom said. "The Honduran and U.S. Coast Guards have cordoned the area off. It's being billed as a classic red tide, one that is so often observed in conjunction with coastal pollution. Since existing tides are often lethal to sea life, the Coast Guard's been able to justify the embargo on those grounds. That buys us some time. Rudi, can you give me an estimate as to when it will reach landfall?"

"One minute." Rudi typed into his terminal and waited for the results to display. "Based on the size you just reported and the growth rate in the last sixteen hours, I'd say another twenty-four hours . . . at least that's what GAPS says. Only that doesn't make sense," Rudi grumbled and kept typing.

Esrom swore under his breath. "It doesn't appear to be burning itself out. Once this red tide reaches shore, the real chaos begins."

"So what are we doing about it?" Dan asked.

"Not much, I'm afraid. The military is trying everything they can think of, but nothing's working. The Air Force has flown a few test sorties. They napalmed one area, to no effect, since apparently, this latest chimera is an extremophile. Then they tried spraying an area with the herbicide Guthion, but with marginal results. The Matriarch evolved around hydrothermal vents, one of the most toxic environments on the planet. Guthion must seem like candy to it. We even considered a nuclear option for a short while . . . but thankfully, the president ruled that out. A tactical nuclear explosion would likely just disperse the microbes farther and create an international uproar."

Dan thought back to the perilous dive to Abaddon's Gate and just how close he and Rachel had come to defeating the threat, only to watch victory slip through their fingers. His frustration finally boiled over. "All the technology in the world and they can't find a way to defeat a red tide?"

An air of resignation settled over Esrom's face. "We're simply not prepared for an unexpected event like this. Who could have imagined a creature that could create new life forms almost at will?"

The sound of Rudi's typing grew louder, his frown intensifying into grim determination. He banged furiously on the keyboard. "I don't understand this!" he sputtered. "This stuff shouldn't be growing so fast. I've already run several simulations on GAPS, and the tide should be a fraction of this size." He dropped his hands from the keyboard. "What am I missing? I thought red tides grew along coastal areas with plenty of nutrients. Why is this thing growing so fast in the middle of nowhere?"

Rachel finally stirred from her trance and sighed. "I can probably shed some light on that."

"Please do," Rudi pleaded.

"Marilynn and I have been examining this creature's life cycle. First of all, it's an omnivore like *Pfiesteria,* so it's feeding on the dying sea life, but it's also creating energy through photosynthesis." She squirmed in her seat. "It has traits of both *Karenia brevis,* a common red tide algae, and the Becker Bug. We think the Becker Bug hitched a ride in the drilling ship's bilge water. They probably dumped a load of bilge in anticipation of their grand haul of ore. One good dose of UV, and the Matriarch created this new chimera, with the toxic potency and abilities of the combined organisms."

"I understand that," Rudi said. "But that still doesn't explain the phenomenal growth rate."

Rachel frowned. "Yes it does. It appears the Matriarch, being a hydrothermal vent creature, has endowed her latest host with a new trick." She rubbed her face with both hands. "This chimera has the ability to metabolize sulfur compounds."

Rudi canted his head. "Yeah, so?"

"Well, algae normally excretes dimethyl sulfide as a waste product of photosynthesis, but this new chimera recycles its own waste into energy—energy it uses for reproduction. Its metabolic efficiency is phenomenal, producing almost as much energy as it consumes."

Rudi's face flushed. "Did you say, *dimethyl sulfide?*" He inputted this new piece of information into the GAPS simulation and ran another pass. "Holy shit! This is bad . . . really, really bad."

Dan had worked with Rudi for years, and he'd never seen his lighthearted friend this upset before. He slid next to Rudi's chair so he could check out the results for himself.

Rudi pointed a trembling finger at a graph that curled like a hockey stick at one end. "You know what dimethyl sulfide is good for? It's the seed for cloud formation. That's a friggin' game changer. If the red tide keeps growing at this rate, it won't stop until everything in the ocean is *dead*. The rotting flesh will release CO_2 and methane into the atmosphere, warming the planet. Normally, clouds would grow, canceling out some of the warming by reflecting sunlight. But without dimethyl sulfide—*no clouds*." Rudi stared at Dan, his eyes searching for another explanation. "It'll be a chain reaction. Combine this with existing climate change . . . you know where I'm heading, right?"

"Yes." Dan realized the horrible irony. He'd spent his career trying to prevent black swans, and now, his GAPS software had just confirmed the biggest black swan event in human history. He looked around the room at expectant faces. "Rudi's right," he said. "This is an amplified feedback loop. It will continue to spiral out of control until nothing's left. If we don't find a way to counteract this tide, and *quickly*, it will trigger other tipping points, like dominos falling. Rapid temperature rise, collapse of all fisheries, droughts from reduced cloud cover, mass starvation, political turmoil. It's runaway climate change, unstoppable and rapid."

Rachel stared at him, horrified. "So Carl was right. We're seeing a new age, one without man, just as he predicted. *A seventh sun*."

"Perhaps," Dan said and turned toward Esrom Nessen. "There must be something else we can do, right?"

Esrom remained mute, his gaze blank and distant. Everyone else in the room exchanged worried glances, looking for answers.

But no answers came.

Dan stared at the satellite photo, trying to wrap his mind around such a horrifying future. It seemed impossible, yet, mass extinctions had happened before.

Just not with humans present.

The stress was more than he could bear. He had no idea what to do. His thoughts began to wander, to simpler pleasures: childhood innocence, a breeze on his face, the beauty of nature, friendship, the joy of Rachel's touch. He suddenly felt terribly insignificant.

It's all in the hands of Gaia now. The Earth would carry on just fine without humans. It had before and would again . . .

The germ of an idea suddenly occurred to him. He turned toward Rachel and spoke in a whisper. "How do you fight a wildfire?"

Rachel looked up. "What?"

"You know, a wildfire. You fight it with a backfire, right?"

Rachel shook her head, confused.

The idea germinated, took full form in his mind. "The Matriarch is the ultimate invasive species. She can create new organisms in the blink of an eye. The Earth's ecosystem can't adjust fast enough to defend itself."

Rachel wrinkled her brow. "Yeah, we know that already. So?"

"So, these new organisms, these chimeras, rule a virgin land, with no natural predators, no defenses to overcome, no parasites. But what if we could level the playing field, let Gaia's other creatures do what they do best—*conspire and adapt?*"

Rachel's expression turned from confusion to shock. "You're not suggesting what I think—"

"Why not? Let the Matriarch create the seeds of her own destruction." He became more animated. "We have the active cultures of the Matriarch on board, the ones from the dumping field. Let's mix the active Matriarch with other predatory microbes, as many as we have on board. Then, we give them a target—the red tide chimera—and expose the whole mix to UV light. We'll let the Matriarch evolve new predators to target the red tide."

"Are you crazy?" Esrom stirred from his trancelike state. "The Matriarch got us into this mess, and you want to risk her creating more chimeras?"

"Have you got a better idea?" Dan shrugged. "Because, if we do nothing, the threat we already know will spell our doom. I'd rather risk the off chance of a threat we *don't* know."

"We could make things worse," Esrom sputtered. "What right do we have to play God—"

"Orcus already played God by invading the Matriarch's lair, remember? Besides, the Earth's ecosystem has survived for three billion years by evolving ways to stay in balance. The Matriarch ruined that balance."

Esrom stared at him, his mouth agape, processing the thought. "That would be the biggest gamble in history."

In for a penny, in for a pound. Dan managed a smile for the first time in days. "The Earth has always returned to balance, even after five previous mass extinctions. We're just going to speed things up a bit, maybe stop a sixth extinction. After all, we humans are part of Gaia too."

"THIS IS HOPELESS," Rachel said.

"No. It *has* to work." Dan stared at the fermentation tank filled with red sludge.

Inside the BSL4 lab, a mind-boggling array of microbial predators were fighting for dominance, bathed in the purple glow of the UV: zooplankton, phytoplankton, toxic algae, fungal spores, flagellates, protozoans, metazoans—all demons of the deep—all mixing with the Matriarch and its bastard child, the red tide chimera.

But so far, the sludge just sat there, teeming in silence.

"This scares me to death," Rachel murmured. "Even if this works, what kind of chimera are we creating? It could be even worse than the red tide."

"What other choice do we have?"

"There's another thing that worries me too," she continued. "We can't release the Matriarch while it's still viable. It will just create new chimeras."

Dan had forgotten that the Matriarch needed several generations before it became permanently merged with its host. "Then we release it tonight, when there's no UV to reactivate it. Hopefully by morning, it will have reproduced enough times to become benign."

"Hopefully? How will we know?" Rachel searched his eyes for some reassurance.

Dan had none to give. No one had tried anything like this before. "Wait! Did you see that?" He pointed at the tank.

A tiny pinprick of contrast appeared in the center of the tank and began to grow. Its complex tendrils pushed farther and farther into the red sludge like the rays of the sun. Dan and Rachel watched, mesmerized, as the new predator ate its way through the red tide.

"Would you look at that," Dan exclaimed. "This new predator is fluorescing."

65

"**WHAT DO YOU** mean, maritime law applies?" Hadan Orcus slammed his fist on the yacht's conference table, startling the five lawyers seated across from him. "They blew up my ship! I want to sue them for every penny in their government coffers, do you understand?"

Señor Juan Lopez had been Solá's lead attorney for twenty years, but today he wore a decidedly uncomfortable expression. "I'm afraid that's not possible. The explosion originated from your own bomb. What witnesses do we have, other than the two Americans—"

"Find a way!" Orcus shouted. "We've got the recorded phone call from the ship's captain. We have control clearances for the helicopter. What more do you need?"

Señor Lopez assumed his most calming and conciliatory manner. "Suing the United States of America is not an easy thing, sir. It's more important to resume mining operations, is it not?"

That was the first intelligent thing Lopez had said all day. "You're right, Juan. That's why I leave the lawsuit in your hands. Just get it done." Orcus turned away, irritated by the incompetence of these minions. Which was why he had decided to oversee this operation personally from his yacht. As soon as the new mining AUVs were loaded, he could have new cargo ships out to the mining site in hours.

The *patrón,* Delgado, poked his head through the door. "Sir, there's someone here to see you."

"Can't you see I'm busy?"

Delgado wore an uncharacteristic look of concern that caught Orcus's eye. "I believe you'll want to speak with this man."

Orcus waved his hands. "Very well." He stepped into his private stateroom, the walls of which were elaborately detailed with the finest teaks and mahogany, and poured himself a cognac.

The man who appeared at the door hardly seemed worthy of his time. Dressed in a pair of Bermuda shorts, a Hawaiian shirt, and sandals, the man looked like a hack straight from the tourist bus.

"Who the hell are you?" Orcus demanded.

"Duff McAlister." The man stepped forward and looked Orcus straight in the eye. Few men possessed the stature to do so.

"What do you want?" Orcus said gruffly. "Can't you see I'm busy here?"

"Why yes, I guess you are. I've been around enough drilling rigs to recognize an undersea mining operation when I see one." The man spoke without the least bit of intimidation. "That's why I'm here—to put a stop to your plans."

"What?" Orcus was momentarily stunned by the man's brashness.

"I own the resort where your devil ship dumped her wastes. In the tradition of my Irish ancestors, I'll give you an opportunity to stop your operation voluntarily, although frankly, I'd love to see your entire empire razed to the ground."

Orcus burst out laughing. "Oh really? You and what army? This is my city! Get out of here before I call—"

Duff took another step forward. "Should I take that as a no?"

"You can take that as a HELL no! Leave before I have my guards work you over."

Duff stood his ground, his gaze drifting off into the distance. "Did you know that the Conquistadors defeated this land with a mere six hundred men? You know *why*?"

"I don't need a history lesson," Orcus growled.

"The Conquistadors carried with them two frightful weapons, gonorrhea and smallpox. Their gleaming suits of armor and four-legged companions were strange and wondrous sights to the natives. True to the prophecies of their ancestors, the natives treated the Spaniards like gods, at least at first. Eight *million* deaths later, they realized how those filthy thieves had betrayed their faith. Your deeds are no better than Cortez himself."

Orcus's rage erupted. "I saved these people from their own misery!"

"Really?" The sardonic smile on this man's face fueled Orcus's anger. "These people are wise to gods bearing gifts," Duff continued. "I told them everything. How you've poisoned their waters, killed their fish, brought disease and pestilence upon them."

"Get out!"

"Fine, I leave you to them." Duff bowed and left.

Still shaking with rage, Orcus sipped his drink for a few minutes to calm himself, and then stepped out to the yacht's foredeck. An inexplicable scene stopped him cold. The loading of the fleet had come to a halt. One AUV dangled from a crane over the bow of *La Cosecha Abundante*.

A crowd of mine workers pressed against the security fence around the docks, brandishing picks and shovels. Huddled inside, the dockworkers talked excitedly to their neighbors through the fence links. Orcus recognized the local priest near the head of the crowd, standing with the strange Irishman.

Delgado rushed up and tugged at his arm. "We must flee, Señor Orcus. Now!"

Orcus stared at the crowd, uncomprehending.

Delgado didn't wait for a response. He rushed down the gangplank and disappeared into a utility building. The lawyers gathered at the door and followed Delgado's example.

Orcus stood resolute, whipped out his cell phone, and dialed for reinforcements. Before he could complete the call, the crowd pressed forward, yelling and screaming. The chain-link fence was no match for the kinetic energy of the crowd. The gates collapsed inward, releasing a mass of humanity, tripping and falling over one another in a mad rush toward the yacht.

His will crumbled, and Orcus scurried around the corner toward the pilothouse. He took one breathless look behind, aghast at the bravado of these ungrateful vandals.

"Get us out of here!" Orcus screamed to the captain.

With a nod, the captain revved the engines to full power.

Orcus turned back and shook his fist vengefully as they began to pull away from the pier. Suddenly, the yacht's engines shuddered and died. A plume of blue smoke drifted up from the engine room and hovered over the yacht like a cloud.

"What the hell is wrong with you? Let's go!"

The captain's eyes grew wide. "The engines have seized, *señor*."

"What are you talking about?" Orcus pushed past him toward the engine room and saw two crewmen struggling with large tools. The men's uniforms were soaked with red stains. "Get those engines going, *now*!"

They did not speak, and only looked past him toward the stern. Orcus followed their gaze in time to see miners swarming across the deck like ants. They encircled him, hesitating a few feet away, their eyes hot with rage.

"Why?" Orcus pleaded. "After all I've done for you."

The mob inched forward, their resolve building. Orcus suddenly realized the gravity of his situation. These hooligans meant to kill him. He turned and flung himself over the gunwale. The flight to the water seemed to take forever, and then a hard slap left his face stinging.

He was alive!

Orcus swam toward the garbage scow. In his younger days he'd been a powerful swimmer. He could feel the old engrams kicking in. At the stern of the ship, he chanced a glance behind him.

Not a single one of the cowards had followed him into the water. He'd assemble his security detail and make them pay for their insubordination. Orcus continued to tread water for a moment, looking for the best way out. The stern of *La Cosecha Abundante* loomed over him. Twin streams of bilge water poured from overhead. Some of his men were leaning over the gunwales, but none moved to throw a life preserver over the side. Orcus swallowed a mouthful of bilge, cursed, and swam around the stern.

There, he saw his salvation.

A barge transporting trash from his compound was docked alongside, rope ladders leading up to the garbage scow at the far end. Orcus headed toward it, choking and coughing on the strange bilge. In times of stress, he had always looked to his prize roses for solace, and miraculously, he found their sweet aroma lingering in the water around him.

He reached the ladder and climbed up, pausing long enough for another shake of his fist. His leg hung on the top rung and he fell ten feet into a pile of rubbish. Orcus struggled to regain his footing among the black plastic bags. The barge was at least a hundred feet long and filled with refuse. Did all this waste come from his compound? It was a mere two weeks' worth. He struggled toward the bow. It was like walking on lily pads. He tripped and fell headfirst into a pile of rotten turkey and caviar, a meal from last week. He got up, covered in stinking, rotten food and bilge. A wave of nausea swept over him and he paused, hands on his knees.

A gurgling belch rumbled up from his stomach and he felt strangely light-headed, disconnected from the moment. He became aware of a terrible pain gnawing at the base of his skull and felt the back of his neck, only to come away with a smear of gravy.

Orcus continued, his heart pounding against his chest. The pain in his head became white hot and the world twisted in a grand loop. A bundle of rose cuttings from his garden tripped him up, tearing at his flesh. He suddenly became aware of a terrible vision that defied reason.

His beloved roses were *alive*.

Writhing like serpents, they wrapped their tentacles around his arms and legs. Mayan ghosts stared down at him from the walls of the barge, laughing, their chests ripped open and disgorged. The rose tentacles tightened their grasp, ripping and tearing and pulling him down into a steaming mass of putrefaction. He tried to scream, but a gurgle of bloody phlegm drooled out of his mouth instead. He tried to wipe it away, even as a convulsion bent his body in half.

His last fleeting vision was of his skin turning itself inside out.

DAN GRIPPED THE console of the copilot seat and stared down at the stygian waters. Beside him, Rachel focused on the controls of the unfamiliar Huey, her eyes scanning its ruby-lit instruments. He was terrified by the prospect of what they were about to do. Esrom had balked at the plan, but finally acquiesced when it became clear there was no viable alternative.

They reached the eastern edge of the algae bloom sooner than expected. He'd never seen the sea so silent and imperceptible, the toxic film having snatched the surface light from a waning moon. It was like staring into oblivion.

Rachel turned from the instrument panel and met his eyes, her face ghost-like. "Are we really going to do this?"

Dan ran his finger lightly across her cheek and glanced back toward the distant coast. The dull hump of Mt. Cosigüina loomed behind the lights of Soluteca. "We have to trust the process."

She smiled at him. "Then do it, before I chicken out."

Dan turned to face the mechanical monstrosity in the rear cab of the helicopter. A large carboy of fluorescent zooplankton, purified from their culture, sloshed to and fro alongside a second one filled with detergent. Two hoses snaked from the containers to an aerosol gun taken from the minifox, its nozzle dangling from the rear bay door. He placed his hand on a red trigger release and glanced back one last time.

"Here's to a new sun," he said and pulled the trigger.

A trail of glistening foam fanned out behind them like fireflies in the wind.

66

WHEN HE STEPPED from the shower, Dan could smell the aroma of fried eggs. He toweled off and slipped into a pair of Duff's old sweats. He checked himself in the mirror. His face and body bore the marks of the past week—bruises and scratches—and yet he felt more alive than he could ever remember.

Duff's cabin looked the same, but he felt like an eternity had passed. Rachel was leaning over the kitchen stove, preparing huevos rancheros. It seemed as if every pot and pan in the cupboard had been stacked on the counter.

"Good morning," she said. "Sleep well?"

"Short, but sweet." He pecked her cheek and eyed the huevos expectantly. "You're up early too," he said, glancing toward the window. It was still dark, but a hint of green was growing in the east.

"Couldn't sleep any longer." She licked her fingers. "There's a fresh pot of coffee. Help yourself, and turn on the TV, will you?"

He prepared a cup of coffee and settled into the overstuffed couch. Rachel joined him, carrying two plates. It may have been his imagination, but she seemed more open and affectionate than usual.

"How are the eggs?"

"Mmmm, fantastic." He turned the channel to CNN.

"This is Ike Winter with the CNN Early Morning News. In an update to our top story: More disasters in Honduras. This tiny Central American country has been the focal point of a series of tragedies. First, the mysterious death of Senator Nolan Becker, traced to contaminated shrimp shipped from that country. Then, an outbreak of disease in the coastal town of La Ceiba. As we reported yesterday, this small fishing village has slowly returned to normal after containment of the recent epidemic by a crack team of American doctors. Here with breaking news is our environmental correspondent, Jenifer Coleman, live from Soluteca on the west coast of Honduras. Jenifer?"

"Thank you Ike. Behind me, silhouetted against the morning sky"—she waved across the scene with a flourish—"is Mt. Cosigüina, once the home of Hadan Orcus, one of the wealthiest men in Central America. But in a strange turn of events, Mr. Orcus died of a mysterious illness during a riot that swept through this port city yesterday. The violence was fueled by fears of an epidemic in the mines, and by the deaths of several crewmen and Marines on a mining vessel off the coast."

"Jenifer, have they found any survivors?"

"I'm afraid not. Authorities say search efforts have been hampered by an unusual, glowing red tide in the area. The latest satellite photos appear to show the tide receding, but the Coast Guard has allowed no one into the area to confirm this."

"Jenifer, CNN has recently learned that Colonel Clarence Peterson, the commander of the MOBIDIC operation, was among the dead aboard the mining ship. What have you heard?"

"So far, authorities have refused to comment."

"That was Jenifer Coleman reporting for CNN, in Soluteca, Honduras. We'll have more on the red tide after these messages."

Rachel flipped off the television and slid closer to him. "Is it really over?"

"Looks that way." Dan shrugged. "Our predators seem to be leveling the playing field. We'll have to wait and see if the red tide and the Becker Bug continue to die away or if they adapt somehow, but at least there seems to be a stalemate of sorts."

"That was a gutsy plan of yours," she said, her eyes glimmering. "What if the Matriarch shifts again?"

"No use trying to predict the future." He laughed. "Sometimes you have to go with your gut."

"That doesn't sound like the Dan Clifford I know." Her expression grew solemn again. "Esrom has his new genetic toy, but I doubt he'll be able to keep it secret for long."

"I hope he can, because the public doesn't need to know how close we came to extinction."

She squeezed his hand and smiled again. "Looks like the seventh sun has dawned."

A knowing look drifted across Dan's face. "Let's hope this new dawn ushers in a smarter age of man, instead of another extinction." He stood up. "Come on, let's go out and watch the sunrise."

From the deck, he could see the forest shimmering with a light patina of dew. The local wildlife had begun its early-morning revelry of chirps, clicks, and squeaks. Dan knew instinctively that life would continue as it always had. And he wanted to feel—*had* to feel—that humanity would continue to have a part in Gaia's grand scheme.

Rachel went to the railing and looked eastward. Dan slid in behind her, wrapping his arms around her waist. He pulled her close and she leaned back confidently. Together, they stood and watched the dawn light creep upward, spilling its emerald glow across the mountain ridge, as it had done unceasingly for the past four billion years.

EPILOGUE

THE CRIES OF children filled the balcony of Bradley Gruber's palatial estate as he sipped a Kona Nigari water. From his lofty perch, he watched their movements in the pool below, so random and innocent.

It was a simple pleasure, one that would not last.

As time passed, they would become more aware, worthy of the responsibility that would be placed upon their shoulders. Gruber hoped he would be there to watch their ascendance. It was the desire of any parent.

Thoughts of the future faded as Gruber refocused on the task at hand. The recent news from Honduras had been less than optimal, but not devastating. Considering the mess that had been made, he felt reasonably satisfied with the result.

But he'd put things off long enough. Bradley pulled out his cell phone and called the one person whose opinion truly mattered.

A familiar voice answered almost immediately.

"Good morning *Pater*," Bradley said. "I hope to find you well."

"As well as can be expected," the voice answered. "I wondered when you would call. It seems you have limited the damage somewhat."

"Thank you," Gruber said in a most deferential tone. "Considering the betrayal by Dan Clifford and all the other missteps, it was the best I could achieve. We've had some losses, surely, and Orcus's death could not have been anticipated."

"Yes, that's true," the voice replied. "But as you pointed out, Orcus's legacy was at a dead end, literally. Perhaps we're better off."

"I agree. With the transfer-on-death clause in his contract, Orcus's assets in the chip factory have reverted to the firm's ownership," Bradley eagerly pointed out. "That limits our losses somewhat. We have what we need to move forward."

Bradley waited anxiously for a reply, the minutes seeming like hours. Finally, the voice responded.

"Bradley, you've avoided a major loss this time, but this is not the kind of performance that will assure your induction. During this next phase, we simply cannot afford any more surprises. Are we clear?"

"Yes sir. I assure you—no more surprises." With that, Bradley Gruber hung up, feeling shaky but somewhat relieved. He took a long drink of water and checked his watch. There would be a few days to enjoy the family, but soon, he would have scant free time to himself.

AFTERWORD

Where did we come from, and how did we get here? It is an age-old question that *The Seventh Sun* attempts to answer in part. The explanation for the origin of nucleated cells presented in this story is based on scientific research by the late Professor Lynn Margulis, who promoted the theory of *endosymbiosis,* or the creation of new life through the merging of two existing life forms. Rachel Sullivan calls it "microbial sex."

Scientists have theorized that this process evolved over several million years as bacteria constantly fed on one another. One day, a lucky accident resulted in predator and prey both surviving in a symbiotic state. The ancestral evidence for this process has long since vanished.

But the demands of dramatic fiction require a more rapid and purposeful pace for such a process. So I created the Matriarch, a fictional creature that could fulfill the dramatic needs of the story. The Matriarch is purposeful and active, almost a thinking creature, and dramatizes the process of endosymbiosis fairly accurately.

I was shocked to learn that the Matriarch exists.

Recently in Japan, two scientists at the University of Tsukuba discovered a creature they now call Hatena for "mysterious." It is a flagellate—a small organism with a tail that it uses to propel itself. Like the Matriarch, Hatena actively seeks out and captures its prey, a green, photosynthesizing alga. The captured cell becomes a symbiont and retains its nucleus, as well as other key cell components such as mitochondria and chloroplasts. It then enlarges and nourishes the predator half, which loses its complex feeding apparatus, and becomes dependent on the symbiont.

It is a bizarre feeling when a figment of one's imagination seems to walk off the page and step into the real world. It is one of the great joys and enigmas of writing fiction.